The Serpent Pool

Books by Martin Edwards

Lake District Mysteries
The Coffin Trail
The Cipher Garden
The Arsenic Labyrinth
The Serpent Pool

Harry Devlin Novels
All the Lonely People
Suspicious Minds
I Remember You
Yesterday's Papers
Eve of Destruction
The Devil in Disguise
First Cut Is the Deepest
Waterloo Sunset

Suspense
Take My Breath Away

With Bill Knox
The Lazarus Widow

Collected Short Stories
Where Do You Find Your Ideas? and other stories

The Serpent Pool

Martin Edwards

Poisoned Pen Press

*Poisoned
Pen
Press*

Copyright © 2010 by Martin Edwards

First Edition 2010

10 9 8 7 6 5 4 3 2 1

Library of Congress Catalog Card Number: 2009931404

ISBN: 9781590585931 Hardcover
      9781590587126 Trade Paperback

Poisoned Pen Press
6962 E. First Ave., Ste. 103
Scottsdale, AZ 85251
www.poisonedpenpress.com
info@poisonedpenpress.com

Printed in the United States of America

Dedicated to Eileen Dewhurst

Acknowledgments

As usual, I would like to acknowledge some of the very extensive help and support that I have received while writing this book. Rupert Holmes, a songwriter (and crime novelist) of distinction, generously agreed to my reprinting a portion of the lyric of his song 'Him'. I've admired Rupert's work for thirty years, and I'm glad that *The Serpent Pool* has finally brought us into direct contact. Information about the police and contemporary police work has come from Roger Forsdyke and various magazines. Rare book dealers Mark Sutcliffe and James M. Pickard have given me insight into the world of Marc Amos. Paul Flint, Bursar of Windermere St Anne's School, and fellow writer Diane Janes supplied background about the Lake District generally (a night spent staying at Paul's home near Windermere enabled me to picture Undercrag in my mind) and Arthur Ransome in particular. Ann Cleeves and Rosa Plant provided comments on aspects of the manuscript, and my agent Mandy Little was, as ever, a great source of moral support. My thanks also go to everyone at my various publishers who has helped to bring this project to fruition, as well as to my family and all those others who have contributed support and helpful information in countless ways. As usual, I emphasize that all the characters and incidents are imaginary, as are the named organizations, except for the Cumbria Constabulary

Chapter One

The books were burning.

Pages crackled and bindings split. The fire snarled and spat like a wild creature, freed from captivity to feast on calfskin, linen and cloth. Paper blackened and curled, the words disappeared. Poetry and prose, devoured by the flames.

Smoke stung George Saffell's eyes. Salt tears filled them, blurring his vision, dribbling down his cheeks. His head throbbed where the club had smashed into it; he'd drifted in and out of consciousness, barely aware of the serrated blade of the knife gliding along his throat, nicking the skin as a warning, before gloved hands tied him up and pushed him on to the floor.

His assailant had said nothing. Even the soft murmur of satisfaction might have been Saffell's mind playing tricks. Now he was alone, but bound so tightly that he was as helpless as a babe. He couldn't move his arms or legs, couldn't even wipe his face. Couldn't do anything but watch the beast gorge on its prey.

Shelves stretched along both sides of this room, and rose from the floor to the sloping roof. He called this the library, with tongue in cheek, since whoever heard of a boathouse with a library? Saffell always liked to be different. Prided himself on it, liked to say that Sinatra's *My Way* might have been written for him. It was his little joke. People said he lacked humour, but that was unfair.

He was never lonely, not with his books for company. Books never complained, never asked awkward questions. Here he was free to savour the sweetness of possession.

Words of reproach echoed in his head.

You care about your books more than you care about me.

He'd protested, but even to his ears the denial sounded hollow. She was right, they both understood the truth.

De Quincey, Coleridge, Martineau, for twenty years he'd hunted down their books and thousands more. Twenty years spent searching and haggling, sorting and hoarding. He loved to touch a dusty volume, run his finger down its spines and test the boards for bumps. How intoxicating to hold a warm book to his nose and inhale that musty perfume, hear the soft rustle of pages fanning. His skin tingled at the scratchy texture of brittle paper when he brushed it with his palms or fingertips.

He thrilled to the chase, and gloried in victory, and yet the prize was never quite enough. The shape of the words laid out on the page had a sensual charm that meant more to him than what they said. He'd read a mere fraction of his purchases. One in ten, perhaps one in twenty?

So little time, and soon it would run out forever. Somehow, he'd become the hunted, not the hunter. Someone meant him to die along with his treasures.

He felt blood matting his thin hair, leaking on to his scalp. The stench of petrol burned his sinuses, filled his throat with bile. He tasted the fumes, felt himself sucking their poison deep into his gut. Yet he couldn't bring himself to shut his eyes and surrender to the dark. The fire cast a spell upon him, he was hypnotised by the horror, impossible to wrench his gaze from his books as they shrivelled and died.

Rope chewed into his thin wrists, gnawed at the bone of his ankles. He hadn't been gagged; there was no need. If he shouted himself hoarse, nobody would hear. Outside the waves lapped against the jetty; on so many nights their murmuring soothed him to sleep. He kept the window ajar even on the coldest days, and if he jerked awake, he might hear the hoot of owls, the flap of bats' wings, the scurrying of water rats. But not this evening, with all sound lost in the fire's roar. On the lake were no boats, on the shore no lights. This stretch of Ullswater was deserted in winter.

He'd chosen this spot for tranquillity; a haven where he got away from it all. Now he and the fire were alone with the night.

Wood cracked and snapped like rifle shots. Glass window-panes shattered. The shelves started to give way. A timber beam crashed on to the floor. The beast had conquered his boathouse. Soon the roof would be gone.

The shelves were crumbling, and his books were blackened beyond recognition. He felt moisture between his legs, a warm and wet trickling down his thighs. The smoke made him cough, his throat filled with phlegm, he began to choke. Flames lunged towards him, devouring the Turkish kilim stretched between the leather chairs. The beast was deranged, and bent on destruction.

Heat scorched his lips. Within moments, it would singe his hair and dry those tears. And then the fire would become him, he would become the fire.

He dreaded pain, he must keep his gaze glued to the books, empty his mind of everything but the destruction of his life's work.

No good. His brain betrayed him, and he succumbed to dread. Dread like a knife that drove between his ribs, through his flesh and ripped into soft tissue beneath. Opening him, eviscerating him.

Dread of agony to come. He was, after all, a bookish man, a self-proclaimed coward with a terror of pain. The only certainty was that he was about to die. No last minute rescue. He had no hope of salvation, no faith that it might be an easy death.

A flame licked the bare soles of his feet, then bit into his flesh. Saffell shrieked and begged for a quick end. But it was too late to pray to a God in whom he had never believed. Even though now he understood that the Devil was real, and knew that the beast took the form, not of man, but of fire.

Cruel, sadistic fire.

It took its time and, cruellest of all, he never knew who had done this to him, and his books.

Or why.

Chapter Two

'New Year's Eve.' Marc Amos swivelled on the kitchen stool, a dreamy look in his eyes. 'New house, new start.'

New start?

Hannah Scarlett gave him a cagey smile as she spooned coffee into a paper filter. She wouldn't pour cold water anywhere other than into the glass jug. Things were looking up; they'd survived Christmas without a single row. Seven claustrophobic days cheek-by-jowl with Marc's family was perfect relationship therapy for the two of them, if for nobody else. Thank God she didn't have to live with his garrulous sister, let alone his humbug-guzzling mother, or his rugby-mad brother-in-law and his rowdy nephews and nieces. Much more of their taste in holiday television, and she'd no longer be investigating murders, but committing them.

The tears and fist-fights of four unruly children aged from nine to nineteen had stifled her maternal instincts for the foreseeable future. Perhaps that was Marc's plan when he'd persuaded her to agree to a family get-together. The constant din in Gayle and Billy's overcrowded semi in Manchester made this rambling old house on the outskirts of Ambleside seem like a sanctuary. They'd moved in three months ago and, with so much work to be done on renovations, she'd rather have stayed at home for the holiday. Families fascinated her, but Marc's was the exception that proved the rule. She didn't dislike Gayle and Billy, or old

Mrs. Amos, let alone the kids; she just had nothing in common with them, except for Marc. Now they'd escaped, she didn't intend to breach the peace.

Say something bland, Hannah.

'Let's hope it's a good one.'

He dropped a colour magazine on to the breakfast bar, as if in surprise. Meek acquiescence never came naturally to her. The magazine fell open at a double page spread of horoscopes for the year ahead. She never bothered checking her stars, although her best friend Terri swore by them, and yet her eye was seduced against its will to the forecasts for Cancer.

Marc jumped off the stool and peered over her shoulder.

'"Your relationships are everything—as will become clear shortly, when planetary activity brings important issues to the surface. How you deal with them will affect not just your life, but other people's too. Make sure you get it right."' He chortled. 'Better watch your step!'

Hannah winced. Astarte the Astrologer was in sententious mood. 'It is possible to be too possessive. It is possible to care too much. You must learn to let go.'

'The woman knows what she's talking about,' Marc grinned. 'Look at mine. "You are not afraid of hard work, but you don't always receive the rewards you deserve." Spot on, I couldn't put it better myself. It can't be an accident. There must be something in this stuff after all.'

'You reckon?'

His sign was Virgo. Expansive Jupiter was urging him to devote more time to romance, while obsessive Pluto would bring greater intensity to his love affairs. But it was up to him to decide how far he wanted to go, and how deeply he wanted to commit.

Terri had once chastised him for his failure to propose to Hannah. She'd pointed out in her imitable fashion that cohabiting allowed a man to drink the milk without buying the cow. But as he retorted, who wants to marry a cow? Besides, Terri had no room to talk after divorcing three husbands. Although Gayle and Billy had stuck together, they weren't the best advertisement for the joys of married life. They'd tied the knot at nineteen, and jogged along in the same old rut ever since. Gayle talked non-stop, Billy never pretended to listen. Perhaps he found it relaxing to have the endless tide of words wash over him. For Hannah, the nadir came during the sales, when Gayle nagged her into joining the plague of locusts that descended on the Trafford Centre, and stripped the bargain counters clean. The shopping mall was only half an hour away, but the car journey there and back lasted a lifetime. Billy was right: there was no need to answer. An occasional murmur, an amiable throat-clearing were all the encouragement Gayle asked for when in full flow. She and Billy were twelve years older than Hannah and Marc. Was this how couples ended up after so long together? Was that what children did to you? Hannah wondered if she would ever find out.

'Go on, break it to me gently. What are your New Year resolutions?'

He asked the same question every year; a ritual as predictable as the chimes of Big Ben. Yet the shifting of the calendar from December to January meant nothing to her. It was simply an excuse for people to obey a civic duty to get pissed and pretend they were having a good time. In her early days as a police constable, she'd too often seen boisterous high spirits turn into something crude and ugly ever to be misty-eyed about New Year revelries. But she'd hate to sound churlish, or give him an excuse for moodiness. So she switched on the coffee machine and feigned deep thought.

'I need to lose a few pounds.'

An hour ago, she'd tried on a pair of figure-hugging velvet trousers that might be suitable for this wretched New Year party they'd been invited to. They came from a pricey boutique in Kendal, an impulse buy tinged with the guilty pleasure of self-indulgence. Six months on, the boutique had gone out of business and the trousers felt too tight for comfort. As she battled to zip them up, she had a nightmare vision of their splitting apart the moment she bent to pick up a drink. The year ahead promised more guilt, less pleasure.

'You look slinky enough to me.' He screwed his features into a comical leer and made a grab for her. 'Come here. The stargazer's right, it's time for me to receive the rewards I deserve.'

She skipped out of reach. Any moment now, he'd ask whether she was wearing the lingerie he'd bought for a special Christmas treat. The outfit was a man's idea of sexy, black and minimalist, and not designed to suit anyone who wasn't borderline anorexic. The label said it was made in Macau and the garments felt stiff and scratchy against her bare skin. She tried not to shudder when he asked her to model for him, and vowed silently never to wear it again, unless and until she owed him big time.

'Tonight. Provided we make a quick escape from Stuart Wagg's party before you're drunk and incapable. Deal?'

'You bet.'

Until she'd met Marc, she'd assumed that second hand booksellers had straggly grey hair and smelled of mildew. But he was slim and fair and gorgeous, for all the hints of below-the-surface discontent. He'd asked her to drive them to the party, so he could have a few drinks. Their host, a rich lawyer famed for conspicuous consumption, was sure to be generous with champagne and mulled wine. Ten to one, Marc would over-indulge, snore all the way home, and need to be put to bed as soon as they were back.

'We've got to stay to see the New Year in,' he protested. 'I already compromised and told Stuart we won't arrive until half ten. He's spent a fortune on fireworks, it would be rude not to watch his money go up in smoke.'

'You should have persuaded him to buy a first edition from you instead. After the quotes from the builders, we need all the cash we can lay our hands on.'

The breakfast kitchen of Undercrag looked out to the heather-splashed lower slopes of the fells. The view was worthy of a picture postcard, with an acre of grassland cropped by deer on the roam and spreading oaks whose leaves would shade the grounds in summer. But the window frames were rotten. The first priority had been to fix the roof; they'd spent their early weeks here skipping around strategically positioned buckets. Like the rest of the house, the kitchen cried out for a makeover. The wall tiles were a bilious shade of orange, the units drab and beige. The water pipes rattled and clanked, the floor was uneven and the dishwasher had sprung a leak. At least they kept warm, thanks to the Aga, but whenever they ventured into another room, it felt like walking inside an igloo. They'd need to stretch their overdraft beyond the limit before the place truly became a home.

'Stuart is an important customer. Especially since George Saffell died.'

George Saffell, yes. She'd met him once, a couple of years ago. A tall man in his fifties, he had the reserved courtesy she associated with a bygone age. Yet a streak of selfishness lay beneath the superficial charm. He'd made his money as an estate agent, flogging second homes and time-shares, and pricing properties at a level that drove away kids born and bred in Cumbria, who didn't have a prayer of raising a hefty deposit. After selling his business to take early retirement, he'd devoted much of the proceeds to expanding his collection of rare books. He'd come round to their home to pick up a copy of *A Guide through the District of the Lakes in the North of England,* by William Wordsworth. Marc had picked it up for a song from a junk shop in Penrith; he had a dealer's eye for something special, a diamond glinting in a pile of dross. And this was all the more special since Wordsworth had inscribed the flyleaf in his neat hand and presented the book to the Earl of Lonsdale. Saffell hadn't haggled over the price and the profit paid for their holiday in Tuscany that summer. She supposed the book had perished in the fire that killed Saffell. To imagine his lonely and terrible end made her guts churn.

Years ago, her former boss Ben Kind had teased her that she had too much imagination to be a detective, but for once he was wrong. Imagination was an asset, maybe even essential. If you could not picture what people endured, how could you figure out what drove them to crime?

As for Saffell, the civilised small talk hadn't masked his greed. She recalled the naked hunger for possession, the moment he took the little muslin book in his hand. His eyes gorged on it, he was salivating. He ran his fingers down the spine with the delicacy of a lover caressing tender flesh.

While her thoughts wandered, Marc was fretting about Stuart Wagg.

'The bad news is, I heard a rumour he has a new woman in his life.'

'That's bad news?'

'Think about it. Someone to squander his cash on when he ought to be investing in rare books as a hedge against a downturn in his pension fund.'

'Does anybody really do that? Treat books simply as an investment?'

'Not as often as I'd like. Though given that the economy is a train wreck, they could do a lot worse. Did I ever tell you that a signed first of *Casino Royale* would have been a better investment over the past twenty-five years than a five-bedroom house in the poshest part of Kendal?'

'Only half a dozen times.'

'Sorry to bore you.' His mock-sheepish grin still charmed her, though now she realised that he deployed it too often. 'Never mind, we'll have a great time tonight.'

'If you're still sober by the time we get back.'

The coffee was ready, and as she filled their mugs, her mind drifted back to the wardrobe challenge. Leather trousers were a safe bet. They were the colour of chocolate fudge cake—if she daren't eat it, at least she could wear something that reminded her of it. That halter neck top with copper sequins, maybe, plus the brown boots for tramping outside to watch the firework display.

'What is it with you and New Year's Eve?' He couldn't let it go. 'I mean, it's an occasion to celebrate. Turn of the year. A time of hope and expectation.'

She stifled a yawn. Mustn't sour his mood with her scepticism. Come to think of it, perhaps that should be her New Year resolution. Whether she could keep it was a different matter.

'Yeah, you're right.' Make an effort.

'Tell you what, the forecast is dry for the afternoon.'

'Mmmm.' She had as much confidence in weather forecasters as in Astarte the Astrologer.

'C'mon. Why don't we go out for a walk before it gets dark?'

'Up towards the Serpent Pool?'

His face lit up, reminding her why she fancied him.

'Perfect.'

◇◇◇

The sky was bruised. Livid patches of yellow, with deep purple streaks. Hannah stood on the back door step outside Undercrag, staring up to the heavens as Marc strode off. The colours reminded her of the cheeks of a victim of domestic violence.

That was one of the downsides of being a police officer. No escaping the brutality that human beings meted out to each other. It was so easy for a deep pessimism to seep into your mind, staining your most innocent thoughts.

Marc turned and waved to her. It wouldn't take long for good humour to segue into impatience. 'Are you coming?'

'Sorry,' she mouthed. 'I'll catch you up.'

Undercrag was the last of five houses—two of them converted into holiday cottages—scattered along a long and winding single-track road called Lowbarrow Lane. Until the 1930s, the buildings had housed the wards, offices and laundry of a cottage hospital set in five acres of level grounds at the foot of the fell, ideal for recuperating invalids to take the air. After the war, someone had run a school here, and when that failed, the estate was split up and turned into private homes. Hannah and Marc lived barely two miles from Ambleside, but the village was invisible, and the stony turning space at the end of Lowbarrow Lane seemed like the back of beyond.

He waited for her by a cattle grid, keeping a wary eye on a woman coming in the other direction, accompanied by an exuberant Labrador; dogs always brought him out in a cold sweat. When she caught up, she took his gloved hand in hers. Further on, the lane became a muddy track that ran past a solitary farm-house, a barn and a stone sheepfold. Past a super-fluous sign which said UNFIT FOR CARS, the track forked at a bridge over the beck. After several rainstorms, the stream was in a hurry to get downhill and the water level was the highest she'd seen. A bridleway ran beside the bank, while the route over the bridge led to the lower reaches of the fell. The climb to the Serpent Pool wasn't strenuous; just as well after a surfeit of Gayle's home-made mince pies.

The path wound up through gorse and a small copse of mountain ash, alder, silver birch, and wild cherries, past a ruined hut and a small stone cairn. It had been too mild for any chance of a white Christmas, except up on the tops, but all the rain had left the ground sleek and slippery. Their boots slithered through the mud and Hannah edged forward with a septuagenarian's caution. On a damp day in the Lakes, even a short walk could be dangerous.

◇◇◇

'Better not go any further,' she gasped, ten minutes later.

As she heaved herself over the iron ladder stile, her joints creaked. Time to renew her membership of that bloody gym. How did Marc manage to look so lean, after wolfing down his sister's cooking? She could only put it down to nervous energy. He was seldom still for ten seconds at a time; his litheness of movement had attracted her from the day they first met. Though sometimes she puzzled over what made him so restless.

Nudging his woolly hat out of his eyes, he grinned.

'Maybe we ought to go too far one day, you and me.'

She got her breath back.

'In your dreams.'

His playful manner harked back to their early years together. They needed more time alone, just the two of them, with no distractions. Too often she came home late, and when she wasn't at work, Marc would be checking stock or exhibiting at a fair in some distant market town. Once upon a time, she'd thought a child would bind them together, but since her accidental pregnancy and subsequent miscarriage, he'd made it clear that fatherhood wasn't on his agenda in the near future. *No rush, we have plenty of time.* But she wasn't sure that the time would ever be right for him.

As for New Year resolutions, she'd been less than frank. At last she'd reached a decision about Daniel Kind. He was the son of Ben, her former boss. Daniel was an Oxford historian who had moved up to the Lakes after the glittering prizes lost their sheen. She liked him a lot, too much for comfort. In rare flights of fancy, it seemed that, whenever she talked with him, it was as if, through a door left ajar, she caught a glimpse of an unfamiliar room, flooded with dazzling light. Tempting to explore, but she was too cautious to venture through the door, lest it slam shut behind her, trapping in the unknown.

She needed to brush Daniel Kind out of her mind, sweep away the daydreams like so much discarded Christmas wrapping paper. The historian must become history.

It shouldn't be such a wrench; they hadn't seen each other since the spring. He'd set off from Liverpool for America, supposedly on a short-term assignment giving talks on a cruise ship. She'd wondered if he would ever come back, even though he assured her he'd fallen in love with the Lakes and didn't want to leave. He'd split up from Miranda, the journalist he shared a cottage with in Brackdale. While he'd been away, they'd exchanged a couple of emails, nothing more. It was her fault. She hadn't replied to his last message, because she'd been working round the clock on a case.

She must stop wasting her time. Daniel had probably found someone to take Miranda's place. Anyway, it would never work between the two of them. How could she ever cope with the guilt of dumping Marc? Enough wishful thinking. She ought to cherish what she had.

The scenery became wild. Rock, dead bracken, and leafless trees formed a winter tapestry. As they climbed, the wind grew stronger. She'd wrapped up well, with plenty of layers, but even with her jacket hood up and fastened, the cold stung every inch of exposed flesh. Wisps of mist shrouded the upper slopes of the fells. In the distance, she heard a plaintive mewing. A melancholy sound, as if an unseen buzzard mourned the passage of the old year.

Hannah shivered as they reached a low, spiky juniper with yellow-green needles. Hanging a juniper bush outside your door was supposed to ward off evil spirits, but if she didn't believe in horoscopes, why heed old wives' tales? Their new home would be a lucky place. Marc was right; moving into Undercrag was their chance for a fresh start.

'Shall we turn back?' she asked.

He lengthened his stride. Pushing hard to keep up, she saw him shake his head.

'Five minutes and we'll be there.'

He never changed direction before reaching his destination, it wasn't in his nature. Years ago, in a hire car in Malta, they'd spent two hours driving in ever-decreasing circles because he refused to consult a passer-by about the best route to Mdina. By the time they arrived, it was so late that they had five minutes in the Silent City before they needed to race back to the hotel for dinner. Better not remind him if she didn't want to spoil the afternoon.

'Let's keep an eye on the mist.'

'We're not high enough to run into trouble. This isn't exactly Blencathra, is it?'

Sure, but each year people strayed into difficulty without realising they were at risk. You had to treat the fells with respect. No point in saying that to Marc, though. Born and bred at Skelwith Bridge, he had the innate sense of superiority of someone whose family had lived there since Wordsworth was in short trousers. Hannah had grown up in Lancaster and Morecambe—almost the opposite end of the country as far as a native of the Lakes was concerned. She couldn't claim deep familiarity with the local peaks; he liked to say she scarcely knew her Ill Bell from her Great Gable.

'The moment we reach the Serpent Pool, we go straight back, all right?'

'It's a deal.'

As they strode on, she looked up and spotted the outline of an eccentric grey building perched a hundred feet above them. Twenty feet high, it resembled a narrow ship's funnel, but made out of stone and topped with battlements. In the middle of nowhere, it had no purpose other than as a place to gaze up at and down from.

The Serpent Tower dated back to Victorian times, a folly constructed by a wealthy landowner. Now the plateau was owned by the Cumbria Culture Company, who allowed poets to read their work and folk singers to perform there, although there wasn't enough space for an audience of any size. According to the guide books, the Serpent Tower didn't have any connection with serpents, apart from having the outlines of two intertwined snakes carved above the door. The name came from its vantage point overlooking the Serpent Pool, but for the moment they couldn't see the water.

They'd once walked up to the Tower together, and the views of the Langdale Pikes snatched your breath away. But it required a scramble up a steep gradient to reach the folly, and this was no afternoon for sight-seeing. They'd not seen another soul since passing the last farm buildings. If they became stranded as the mist descended, and had to call out the mountain rescue so close to home, she'd never live it down at Divisional HQ.

Quickening her pace, she followed him along the edge of a shallow gully strewn with loose, lichen-covered stones the size of tennis balls. Lakeland guides scorned this walk as suitable for grandmothers, but her calf muscles were already aching.

'Almost there,' Marc said.

She caught him up and put her arm around his, thrusting her head down as they passed through a cluster of bare oak trees, breathing hard as she matched his rhythmic stride. Soon they were in the open.

In front of them lay a grassy platform above the farmland that reached as far as the rocky passageway leading to the ridge and the Serpent Tower. The area was featureless but for a small, irregularly shaped stretch of water. It took a fanciful turn of mind to compare it to the sinuous contours of a serpent, but the people who gave names to places in the Lakes never lacked imagination.

They halted close to the water's edge.

This was their destination. This was the Serpent Pool.

And here, six years ago, Bethany Friend's body had been found.

◇◇◇

According to the file back in Hannah's office, the Serpent Pool was never more than two feet deep. She'd read that file from cover to cover and committed the salient points to memory. There had only been eighteen inches of water on the day Bethany Friend's bound body was discovered by a group of fell-walkers. She was lying face down in the water.

She and Marc stood together on the soft ground, lost in thought.

'You'd never think a woman could drown in something so shallow,' Marc muttered.

Hannah swung round and stared at him.

'You know about Bethany Friend?'

The dark patch of water seemed to hypnotise him, as though if he stared at it for long enough, the solution to some eternal mystery would sneak into his brain.

'Uh-huh. '

'How did you hear about her?'

His gaze didn't waver. 'How did you?'

'It's my job to know these things.'

'You never mentioned Bethany when we were buying the house.'

'I read the file before I finished for the holiday.'

He breathed out. 'Please don't tell me you're treating it as a cold case?'

'It's an unexplained death.'

'She committed suicide, didn't she?'

'The coroner recorded an open verdict.'

'That isn't so unusual.'

'No, but since we moved here...'

'You took an interest just because we live close to where she died?'

'Uh-huh.' Not the whole truth, but she wasn't ready to tell him the whole truth. 'It's a strange case, so much was left unexplained. That's why it caught my interest.'

He stared at her. They'd known each other long enough for him to guess she was holding back on him. But he was holding back too, she was certain of it. That was why he didn't push his luck.

Her feet were freezing and she stamped them. 'Come on, we'd best get back before the mist closes in.'

He followed as she moved towards the trees, but they walked in silence. She wanted him to tell her how he knew about Bethany Friend. But he wasn't in the mood for talking, and she couldn't bring herself to ask him again.

Chapter Three

Back in the kitchen of Undercrag, they were shedding their outdoor gear when the phone rang. Marc grabbed the receiver, saying it might be a customer from Japan chasing a signed Edgar Wallace, but after a brief exchange of words, he thrust it at Hannah.

'Fern Larter, for you.'

Hannah took the phone into her study. It was as draughty as a barn, but she loved its solitude and stillness. Or, at least, the absence of people. Even in winter, the countryside teemed with life. Squirrels fought on the grass beneath her window, occasionally a roe deer came up to press a baffled face to the panes. Easy to persuade herself that the nearest village was twenty miles distant, instead of a stroll away.

Once, Undercrag had accommodated hospital offices at ground level, while live-in staff slept upstairs. Hannah and Marc had only afforded the mortgage thanks to a downward blip in the market, coupled with a legacy from Marc's aunt, who succumbed to a stroke a fortnight short of her eightieth birthday. Although there were only the two of them, the habitable space seemed to have vanished within weeks of their moving in. Marc annexed the reception room next to the lounge as his office. Three bedrooms were crammed floor-to-ceiling with books. Stock, he called it. She blamed bibliomania, not the business.

'Happy New Year, Fern.'

'And to you. Hey, I resolved to treat myself after Christmas. My in-laws are all bloody vegans, it's been a nightmare. I hate dieting, most of all when it's a moral obligation. Fancy getting together for a bacon butty before work one morning?'

'Love to.'

'Excellent, who cares about blood pressure? I'm pig-sick of the ACC's healthy eating initiative. I refuse to spend the rest of my life worrying about clogged arteries.'

Fern, a fellow DCI, had lent a solid shoulder to cry on when Hannah's career hit a rocky patch. Lauren Self, the Assistant Chief Constable, had shunted her into cold case work, but Hannah preferred to investigate the crimes of today. Fern argued that a cold case cop had more latitude to involve herself directly in proper detective work than anyone of similar rank in the whole Cumbria Constabulary. Especially in an age when management was all about form-filling, targets, and league tables. The higher you climbed up the greasy pole, the further you were from what made you love the job in the first place.

'Where and when?'

'That snack bar on Beast Banks? Seven thirty on Thursday?'

'You can bring me up to date with the Saffell case.'

A fractional pause.

'Actually, I'll come clean. I do have a teeny ulterior motive.'

'This isn't just about boosting your cholesterol levels?'

'We're getting nowhere fast. Thought I might pick your brains.'

'Told you last time we spoke. I only met Saffell the once.'

'Even so.' Fern coughed. 'Anyway, the business stuff will only take five minutes. Then we can catch up properly.'

Hannah hung up and wandered back into the kitchen. She smelled burning as Marc lifted two crumpets out of the toaster.

'What did Fern want?'

When police work intruded on their private time, he treated it as a personal affront. Similar principles didn't apply with books and his customers.

'To fix up a meeting, that's all.'

He tossed a crumpet for each of them onto a plate and took a clean knife out of the dishwasher. 'When are you seeing her?'

'Thursday, once I've settled in my new sidekick.'

He cut his crumpet in half with a neat stroke of the blade. He had a surgeon's dexterity, she thought. His hands were slim; she'd always liked them, and what he did with them, when he was in the right frame of mind.

'You'll miss Nick Lowther.'

Even Inspector Lestrade would have detected the note of satisfaction. Hannah gritted her teeth. Nick had been her Detective Sergeant on the Cold Case Review Team and they'd worked together for years. Marc had long been wary of their friendship, and his unvoiced, but unmistakeable, suspicion that they were more than friends had infuriated her. She'd never given him cause to doubt her fidelity.

None of that mattered now. Six months ago, Nick had met someone, and a fortnight before Christmas they had emigrated to Canada together. Marc was right. Nick's departure had left a gap in Hannah's life and she wasn't sure how to fill it.

'Uh-huh.' She took the margarine out of the fridge and spread it over the crumpet.

'Your new sergeant, what's he like?'

'Time will tell,' she muttered. Unfair to make her mind up too soon, but one thing was for sure. Greg Wharf was no Nick Lowther.

'It will work out fine.'

It should have been a kind remark, but he'd seldom been kind about Nick in the past and she couldn't resist the urge to retaliate.

'Will Cassie be at the party?'

He chewed hard for half a minute before speaking. 'Cassie?'

'You know.' Of course he knew, he'd mentioned her a dozen times since she'd started work at the shop last autumn. Hannah had called in once, during the run-up to Christmas, to soothe the itch of curiosity. The girl was in her mid-twenties, fair and slim. During their short exchange of seasonal pleasantries, she gave the impression she wouldn't say boo to a goose. But her figure was gorgeous and her eyes big and blue. She'd given Marc a jokey Christmas card, signed in an extravagant hand and adorned with half a dozen kisses. At least he'd made no secret of it, displaying it on the mantelpiece in the sitting room. Hannah hoped he wouldn't be tempted to make a fool of himself. 'Cassie Weston. Your own personal sidekick.'

'Stuart Wagg asked me to pass on an invitation to her, as it happens. I didn't even realise they'd met. She must have sold him some books. But she said she couldn't make it. Came up with some excuse about spending the evening with her boyfriend in Grasmere.'

'An excuse? Doesn't she have a boyfriend?'

'I'd be amazed if she didn't. Very pretty girl.'

As you keep telling me, Hannah thought.

'You think she was fibbing?'

'Dunno, it just didn't ring true. My guess is, she didn't fancy a night out in a big crowd. She doesn't strike me as a party animal.'

'So Cassie is like me?'

He considered the question as he gulped down the last of his crumpet, and opted for vagueness. Or tact.

'Um. Sort of.'

◇◇◇

'So what's the latest on George Saffell?' Marc asked.

They were in Hannah's Lexus, driving through the darkness. Their destination was south of the Hawkshead ferry, a modern mansion hidden among the trees on the slopes above Windermere. Marc drove half as many miles in a year as she did, but he wasn't a good passenger, and she never enjoyed chauffeuring him. When she'd owned a car with a manual gearbox, he twitched with every change of gear. Now she drove an automatic, he twitched all the time. She might have passed her advanced test, he might have picked up a couple of speeding tickets, but if

she rounded a bend at speed, his intake of breath sounded like a
pistol-shot. If she took too long to set off when the lights turned
green, his heel drummed on the floor mat in reproach.

'Still dead, last I heard.'

'You know what I mean.' The habitual impatience flared,
quick as the strike of a match. Hannah blamed his mother for
spoiling him. Even this Christmas, the old lady hadn't been able
to resist the urge to straighten his collar and brush imaginary
bits of fluff from his coat at every opportunity. She'd been in her
forties when he was born, and she couldn't stop treating him like
a precious gift. 'Has Fern Larter figured out if it was murder?'

An old Beach Boys hit played on the in-car CD player.
Smooth harmonies, a song about heroes and villains.

'It's for the coroner to decide, and the inquest was adjourned.'
She felt a flash of irritation. Why didn't he show the same interest
in her own investigations? But perhaps her reaction was unfair.
After selling books to the man for years, he was bound to be
intrigued by George Saffell's bizarre demise. It wasn't every day
that one of his most valued customers was roasted alive. 'Last
time we spoke, Fern had pretty much ruled out an accident.'

'Not surprised. Strange accident, huh? To incinerate yourself
and your prized possessions. You think he killed himself?'

'Funny way to do it,' she said. 'Burning yourself to a crisp, with
no chance of second thoughts once the flames take hold?'

Saffell's boathouse had been built of wood. Luxurious enough
to feature in glossy lifestyle magazines, but never meant for
round-the-year occupancy. Why would Saffell want to spend
dark winter evenings there when he had a lovely place out at
Troutbeck?

'Books obsessed him,' Marc said. 'Perhaps he thought it was
a fitting way to go.'

'You'd have to be very unhappy to choose that ahead of an
overdose of pain killers.'

'Yeah, he hated pain. According to his wife, even a twinge of
toothache made him whimper.'

'You know her?'

They hadn't spoken much about Saffell when they first leaned of his death. After initial expressions of shock and dismay, Marc lamented the loss of business. Not so much callous selfishness, as naked human nature. The two men were acquaintances, not friends. When a customer died, there was usually the prospect of buying his collection from the widow at a knock-down price, once a probate valuation at a pittance had been agreed. But even that consolation was denied. Four thousand books worth a small fortune, reduced to ash. For Marc, the destruction of rare books was a crime worse even than murder.

'Wanda Saffell?' Was it her imagination, or was he weighing up how much to say? 'I've met her a few times, haven't I mentioned it?'

'Doesn't ring a bell.'

'You probably weren't listening after a long day at Divisional HQ,' he muttered.

'I'm all ears now.'

'Wanda was his second wife, the first died young of breast cancer. They married four or five years ago. She was a divorcee who shared his love of books.'

'Another collector?'

'No, she runs a small printing press as a hobby, publishes an occasional limited edition. Funded by George, but I get the impression they led separate lives.'

'How do you mean?'

'Oh, I don't know,' he said vaguely.

'They hadn't split up?'

'Don't think so. I kept my nose out.'

Having aroused her curiosity, he'd failed to satisfy it. Typical man.

'The boathouse was gutted long before they brought the fire under control. It stood at the end of a track through woodland, and the alarm wasn't raised until someone on the other side of Ullswater saw the place engulfed in flames. So Forensics didn't have a lot to go on. There wasn't much left of your customer, let alone all those books you sold him.'

Marc flinched in the passenger seat, and for once she thought it wasn't on account of her driving. He didn't lack imagination— how could he, a man who loved books so much?—and it didn't do to dwell on the agonies that Saffell must have suffered. Even a few seconds before the final loss of consciousness must seem like an eternity while you burned to death.

'But they found traces of accelerant. Petrol.'

Marc groaned. 'He may have kept fuel for a boat.'

'Yeah, but there are signs that his wrists and ankles were tied.'

This was confidential, but Marc wouldn't shoot his mouth off. He knew when to be discreet.

'Jesus.' He shivered. 'Murder, then.'

'Looks like it.'

'Who would want to kill someone as harmless as George Saffell?'

'Is anyone truly harmless?'

'That's a bit profound, Hannah, don't you think? He was a quiet sort, nothing like the stereotype of a brash estate agent. Old George wouldn't hurt a fly.'

'Even so. He must have had an enemy.'

'I can't believe it.'

Hannah swore as a car raced up behind them, its full beam dazzling in her rear view mirror. It overtook them before a bend, cutting back in so sharply that she had to jam her foot down on the brake. She had the impression of a sports car, low and sleek. Tyres squealing, it disappeared into the darkness.

'Stupid bastard.'

Marc clicked his tongue.

'Someone's worried about arriving late for the party.'

'For God's sake. For all he cared, we could have crashed.'

'What makes you think the driver's a man?' He seemed about to add something, but changed his mind. 'Anyway, we survived. And here we are.'

Hannah pulled up in front of a long, narrow driveway that reached through an avenue of dark trees. The gates were open and the lights on top of the brick pillars shone bright. She peered at the house name, carved on sign made of slate.

'Crag Gill.'

'Named after Miss Thornton's house in *The Picts and the Martyrs*,' Marc said, as if that explained everything.

The title of the book stirred a memory.

'Arthur Ransome? The *Swallows and Amazons* man?'

'Spot on. Stuart has Catholic tastes, but he's especially fond of children's classics. He has every Ransome in first edition. Mind you, the stuff Ransome wrote for adults is even rarer.'

'I didn't realise he wrote for adults.'

'Believe me, his study of Oscar Wilde is fabulously rare in dust wrapper. Lord Alfred Douglas sued him for libel, and even though Ransome won the case, the controversial bits were censored from the later editions. Then there was his book on Russian folklore. You know he married Trotsky's secretary?'

It sounded wildly improbable, but Marc loved showing off the extraordinary range of trivia he'd accumulated about books and bookmen. She decided to give the answer he hoped for.

'You're kidding.'

'It's true, I swear it.' He enjoyed the idea of startling her; perhaps because she was a sceptical police officer. 'A dealer I know reckons that Ransome personally inscribed his collection of Russian folk tales to his chum Lenin. If it ever shows up, Stuart will be desperate to lay his hands on it, and he's a man who likes to get what he wants. He'd trade his granny if he could get that book.'

'So he's a true lawyer,' Hannah murmured. 'Caring and unselfish.'

'You're not going to be sarky with Stuart, are you? Chill out. Don't forget he's not just our host, he helps pay our mortgage.'

'Trust me.' She pressed her foot down and the car moved forward. 'I'll be on my best behaviour.'

◇◇◇

Marc was right, she needed to chill out. Another New Year resolution. But an upmarket party wasn't the best place to turn over a new leaf. From the moment a flunkey whisked away her coat as she stepped through the door into the vast living room of Crag Gill, Hannah realised she was out of her depth. She wasn't accustomed to how the other half live.

A singer who had reached the final of *Britain's Got Talent* was crooning 'This Guy's in Love with You', accompanied by a pianist who bore a spooky resemblance to the late Liberace. Hannah overheard a perma-tanned presenter moaning about the demise of regional television to a quiz show hostess who was even more scantily clad off the screen than on. A pair of muscular foreign blokes dripping gold and jewellery were presumably Premier League footballers. As Marc vanished into the crowd, she was plied with champagne by a handsome waiter who gave her a casual appraising glance before his eye roved past her, in the direction of a group of pretty girls in very short skirts, no doubt invited to keep the footballers onside.

Well, half a glass wouldn't do any harm.

As she took a sip, a hand squeezed her wrist. It hurt a little.

'Hannah, we meet again! And if I may say so, you're looking lovelier than ever.'

Stuart Wagg was a lawyer, so Hannah supposed he was well versed in the art of embellishing the truth. He had the knack of blending flattery with a self-mocking smile, and as she withdrew from his grasp, she felt a surge of amused satisfaction at the compliment, rather than annoyance at slick and superficial charm. The halter neck top had been a good idea, and she was glad she'd chosen the dangly ear-rings and charm bracelet. Marc had bought them as extra Christmas presents; along with a bottle of unexpectedly subtle perfume; they compensated for the tarty underwear.

'How are you?'

He treated her to an ironic smile. 'Keeping the wolf from the door.'

The entertaining room had a double-height glass wall overlooking the lake, but even with the curtains drawn apart and the terraced garden illuminated by complicated electronic gimmickry, the water was lost in the darkness. Despite its nostalgic name, Stuart Wagg's home was defiantly twenty-first century, a triumph of modernist design. It was like a bunker cut into the hillside, boasting a seeded grass roof and constructed of timber and traditional stone. Stuart was six feet four and he'd made sure his home suited tall people. The armchairs were vast, even the sink in the cloakroom was set high. Instead of doors, archways separated the rooms, so the living space seemed almost endless. Six months ago, the place had featured in *The Independent's* property supplement. Hannah recalled the journalist drooling over the white walls, plain elm floorboards, and luxurious fabrics, positively swooning over the green silk and suede throw that adorned two L-shaped sofas. After weeks spent mining interior décor magazines for cheap solutions to design challenges, she recognised no-expense-spared when she saw it.

'I see the economic downturn hasn't touched the legal profession.'

His dark eyebrows jigged. 'It's all about keeping up appearances.'

Stuart Wagg was lean and fit; she'd heard that, when he wasn't chasing rare books to add to his collection, he spent his spare time tramping on his own across the fells. Black, open-neck shirt, white trousers, big bare feet. A legal eagle without socks or shoes? No mistaking him for your average Lake District lawyer, toiling away over house conveyances or a neighbour's boundary dispute in the county court. Stuart acted for millionaires, drafting wills and trusts so as to keep their fortunes out of the taxman's clutches. His clients included sports agents and pop music impresarios and he was more at home lunching with media moguls at the Ivy in London than snacking in the cafeteria opposite his firm's main office in Bowness. He avoided the hoi-polloi in the criminal courts unless, as a rare favour, he agreed to represent a celebrity faced with a driving ban for racing his Ferrari along the A591 as though competing in the Monaco Grand Prix.

'Is that so?'

'Of course. We all take care about the picture we present of ourselves to the outside world. What lies beneath is much more fascinating, don't you agree?'

He held her gaze, as if daring her to guess what was in his mind. Better not to know. All around were people talking at the top of their voices. Stuart was a famously generous host and the Veuve Clicquot loosened tongues. With the heating on full blast, the crush of bodies made even this airy room seem stuffy and oppressive. Her head ached with the din and the lack of oxygen. Marc seemed captivated by a young redhead who was offering drink, canapés, and a generous display of tanned flesh.

Stuart's eyes rested on a dark-haired woman in the throng. She was chatting to a tall, gaunt man in a white linen suit. Hannah recognised them both. The man's mug shot had appeared in the local media following his arrival at the Cumbria Culture Company. Stuart Wagg's firm had sponsored his recruitment, to run a literary festival in aid of cancer charities. Stuart fancied himself as a patron of the arts and worthy causes. With shaven head, tanned features, and coal-coloured eyes, the man's looks were striking, but it was the woman who seized Hannah's attention.

As she watched, a woman in a black dress joined the couple. Her blonde bob and glacial elegance would have set Alfred Hitchcock panting, but the champagne had brought a flush to her cheeks. Something about her was familiar, but Hannah couldn't place it. Her arrival prompted the dark-haired woman to edge away through the crowd towards Stuart and Hannah.

'There you are!'

Stuart Wagg took her arm, lazily proprietorial. As if she were a book in his collection that he might trade in for a finer copy.

'I was starting to worry that you might have had a better offer,' he said, with the smug self-deprecating smile of a man confident that such a thing could never happen.

The woman squeezed his hand and said in a disbelieving tone, 'From Arlo Denstone?'

'Good-looking feller,' he teased.

'Not my type.'

'Phew, that's a relief. Now, let me introduce you to Detective Chief Inspector Hannah Scarlett, one of Cumbria Constabulary's finest. Hannah, please meet a dear friend of mine. Louise Kind.'

◇◇◇

Louise looked her straight in the eye, but Hannah didn't want to be the first to blink. This was the sister of Daniel, and daughter of Ben. Two men who meant a good deal to her, though she'd always been reluctant to ask herself why. Louise wore a belted, Grecian-style dress with a plunging neckline and a discreet diamond necklace that must have cost a fortune. The last time Hannah had seen her, Louise had been encased in a shapeless jacket and corduroy jeans. Admittedly, that had been out of doors at a skydiving display, but even so, the graceless duckling had transformed into a glamorous swan.

'We've met before.'

'Really, darling?' Stuart Wagg's bushy eyebrows skipped again in their quizzical dance. 'You never told me you were in cahoots with the local constabulary.'

'My brother introduced us. It's a small world. Hannah used to work with our father. Isn't that so, DCI Scarlett?'

'Small world is right.' Hannah nodded. 'Good to see you again, Louise.'

She was conscious of her host's scrutiny. It made her feel like a courtroom exhibit, or an ill-drafted codicil to a miser's last will and testament. Her cheeks burned, though surely it was ludicrous to be embarrassed by meeting the sister of Daniel Kind.

'Must circulate,' Stuart Wagg gave Louise a nod of dismissal. 'See you later.'

'So you and Stuart are together?' Hannah asked when he was out of earshot.

'Sort of.' Louise fingered the necklace in an abstracted manner. A Christmas present from Stuart, no doubt. He'd probably just walked into the jewellers' and asked for the priciest necklace in the shop. 'It's a very recent thing. We met at a legal conference. You might remember, I used to lecture in Manchester. I've only just arrived up here.'

'You've moved in?'

'Mmmm….' An evasive smile. 'Let's say, it's too far to commute with comfort and I didn't want to be a week-end visitor. We just spent our first Christmas together, and I dropped extra lucky. I start a brand new job at the University of South Lakeland next term.'

'Congratulations.'

'Well…let's see how things turn out.' Louise fiddled with her bracelet. 'How come you know Stuart?'

'My partner Marc owns a second-hand bookshop.' Hannah caught sight of him on the other side of the room, accepting the waitress' offer to replenish his glass of champagne with a broad grin. 'Stuart's one of his best customers.'

Louise tapped the side of her head. 'Doh! I should have made the connection. See, I never inherited those detective skills.'

It was on the tip of Hannah's tongue to say: *not like Daniel.* But she didn't want to be the first to speak his name.

'Your father taught me all I know about detective work.'

'He'd have been proud of your success. Head of the Cold Case Review Team? A top job.'

'It's a backwater,' Hannah said. 'I was steered into it after I messed up on a case, and I haven't managed to worm my way out of it.'

'But you enjoy being a detective.' A statement, not a question. 'Daniel was sure you did.'

Hannah clenched her fist, as if she'd scored a goal. Louise had mentioned him first.

'He was right. I was always ambitious. Driven, your father said.'

'Like Daniel,' Louise said. 'Or at least like Daniel used to be.'

'Has he changed?'

'You know his partner Aimee died?'

Hannah nodded. Aimee was the journalist Miranda's predecessor; she and Daniel had been together when he worked in Oxford and built a lucrative career writing history books and adapting them for television. By the sound of things, Aimee had been a flake, and in the end she committed suicide. After that, Daniel wanted a complete break, and as soon as he met Miranda, he'd abandoned the dreaming spires for the Lake District. The cottage in Brackdale became his bolt-hole, until Miranda went back home to London, and left him with fresh wounds to lick.

'It must have been very hard for him.'

'Aimee's death put his career into perspective. But you can't mourn forever. I want to see that old hunger in him again.'

'People don't really change.' As she spoke, Hannah realised she believed this, with a passion. 'Not in fundamentals.'

'If you're right, those cold cases should fire your own enthusiasm.'

'At least they give me the chance to be a detective again. Your father warned me, the higher I climbed, the further away from real police work I'd find myself. The upper echelons are for political movers and shakers. Not people who simply want to solve crimes.'

'I remember Dad saying that,' Louise murmured. 'Before he left us for his fancy woman.'

'It must have been tough for you when Ben left home.'

'For all of us. Daniel, me, our mother.' Louise sighed. 'It's history now. As much in the past as the stuff Daniel studies.'

Hannah could resist temptation no longer.

'So what is he up to these days?'

'You don't keep in touch?'

Hannah shook her head. 'He went to America.'

'There's always email.' Louise pursed her lips, like a schoolmarm disappointed by a feeble answer from an otherwise diligent pupil. 'He didn't intend to be away for long, but one thing led to another and he finished up on a lecture tour. He only arrived back in England yesterday.'

'He's back in the Lakes again?'

'At Tarn Cottage, yes. Brackdale is his home, don't forget.'

'I heard,' Hannah said carefully, 'that Miranda wanted them to move to London.'

'Miranda?' Louise didn't bother to hide her scorn. 'That's over and done with, surely you heard? If you ask me, it was never going to last. Chalk and cheese. She wasn't right for Daniel.'

Louise must already have had two or three drinks. The first time they'd met, she'd seemed buttoned-up, someone who never gave anything away. Her candour was as unexpected as the low-cut Grecian gown.

Hannah took a sip of lemonade. Thank God the need to drive Marc home had kept her sober. She mustn't give too much away.

'Please pass on my regards.'

'You can always lift up the phone yourself.'

That was more like the Louise of old. Awkward and blunt as a Coniston crag.

'Perhaps, one of these days.'

'I expect he'll give you a call. He may even want to pick your brains.'

'Unlikely, I think. An Oxford don…'

'You're an expert in murder, aren't you?'

Hannah stared. 'Murder?'

'Didn't you know? It's his latest obsession, it's the reason Arlo Denstone persuaded him to be keynote speaker at his Thomas De Quincey Festival. Murder considered as one of the fine arts.'

'You mean..?'

A woman cried out, a sound of anger mixed with pain. Hannah spun round, in time to see the Hitchcock blonde lift her full glass of red wine and throw its contents at her companion.

Arlo Denstone's white teeth maintained their sardonic gleam even as the wine dripped from his cheek and chin, and down his white jacket.

The woman made a choking noise, as though she'd been strangled, and ran for the door.

For a couple of seconds, nobody moved, nobody made a sound. Stuart Wagg was first to react. As the door banged shut behind the woman, he moved after her, followed by a handsome Asian man in a well-cut suit. Their swift, silent strides reminded Hannah of two panthers in pursuit of their prey.

◇◇◇

The night blazed. Shell after shell cracked like gunfire, now bursting into stars of red and white and gold, now splitting into shoals of fish swimming through the darkness, now fanning out as silver snakes that slid across the sky.

Stuart Wagg stood in front of his guests as they watched the fireworks. Feet planted on a low brick wall that fringed a circular paved area, he was bathed in light cast by lamps set above the glazed doors, holding a microphone in his hand like a singer on a stage. That little drama indoors half an hour earlier might never have happened. Arlo Denstone had changed into a striped blazer borrowed from his host and stood admiring the display as if he didn't have a care in the world. Stuart puffed his chest out like a benevolent Victorian squire, presiding over an assembly of tenant farmers.

Crag Gill basked in ever-changing coloured lights. To Hannah, it looked more like a spaceship than a home. She glanced over her shoulder. Away from the crowd, and in the shadows, Louise Kind shifted from one foot to another. Her expression was impossible to read. She didn't like the limelight, unlike her lover.

Stuart lifted his champagne glass with a flourish and bellowed into the microphone.

'Happy New Year everybody!'

As people drank and marvelled at the cascades of fire above them, Hannah spotted Marc. His gait was unsteady and he kept spilling his champagne as he traced a zig-zag route over the grass towards her.

'Darling!' Christ, he was slurring already. Just as well they'd arrived later than most of the other guests. He'd never been a hardened boozer, and it didn't take much to get him pissed. 'Happy New Year!'

She tilted her glass and turned her cheek to allow him to kiss it. Instead he fumbled for her backside.

'Come on, Marc. You've had enough.'

'Why must you always be such a spoilsport?' His breath felt hot on her neck. 'I mean, we can't leave yet. It would look rude.'

She had to raise her voice to make herself heard above the din of the fireworks. 'I don't want you falling flat on your face. We've had one scene here already tonight.'

He chortled. 'Excellent, wasn't it?'

A barrage of coloured cornets shot into the sky, transforming into graceful palms, followed by candles that soared and roared and became golden branches, seeming to reach almost to the people gathered on the ground. They gazed up to the heavens and held their breath, wondering what might come next.

Hannah feigned covering her ears as another explosion echoed in them. How many thousands of pounds going up in smoke, right in front of their eyes? Stuart Wagg never knew when to stop. He had no restraint.

'So you know the woman who had the hissy fit?'

He smirked. 'You'll never guess her name.'

'No need to guess, though I should have recognised her from the press pictures. Louise Kind told me she is Wanda Saffell.'

Yes, the recently widowed Wanda. Out on the razzle with her husband barely cold in the grave? A bit naughty, on the face of it, but Hannah knew better than to jump to conclusions. The fact the woman had chucked her drink at her companion and then run weeping from the room showed that her nerves were in bad shape.

'You always know everything,' he mumbled.

'If only.'

'All right, then. What was all the fuss about?'

'Good question.' Hannah found herself itching to know the answer.

'Tell you one thing.' He leaned towards her. 'You were wrong about the driver who nearly ran into us out in the lane. That wasn't some boy racer, it was Wanda.'

'You think so?'

'A waitress told me she'd only arrived five minutes before us. Marched in and grabbed a glass of champagne, then knocked it back in a couple of gulps and demanded a refill.'

Hannah looked round. 'Is she still here?'

'Raj Doshi, one of Stuart's partners, gave her a lift home. Said she wasn't fit to drive in her sports car.'

'We'll make a detective of you yet.'

'If you ask me, that woman has anger management issues.'

'Pscyhologist as well as detective, eh? Come on, time to go.'

As she took Marc's arm and headed back for the warm indoors, she recalled the sight of Arlo Denstone, fishing a handkerchief out of his pocket. Still with the hint of a smile on his face, he'd begun to mop his cheeks as a dull crimson stain spread across the front of his jacket.

Anyone would think Wanda Saffell had stabbed him in the heart.

Chapter Four

New Year's Day at Tarn Fold. The perfect moment, Daniel Kind told himself, to turn his mind to murder.

Yawning, he pulled apart the living room curtains. He'd landed at Manchester Airport forty eight hours earlier, and though he'd slept until mid-day and stood for the past five minutes under a hot and unforgiving shower, jet lag smothered his senses like chloroform.

Wind roared down from the fells and smashed against the windows. Spiky trees swayed like worshippers performing a sinister ritual. The sky was sulky, and a damp mist loitered over the cottage's strange grounds, with their twisting paths, enigmatic planting, and unexpected dead ends. Beyond a reed-fringed tarn, the rocky face of Tarn Fell was dour and cheerless. He ought to brave the gusts and go for a walk to pump some air into his lungs. But Louise had said she'd call round, the perfect excuse to make himself a cup of coffee instead. The kick of caffeine might do for him what sleep could not.

January the first, a perfect day to start writing his new book. His subject was Thomas De Quincey and how he changed the way we think about murder.

Flipping on the television, he found the regional news programme he'd set to record the previous day, before collapsing into bed. A pretty presenter was interviewing a man he'd chatted with on the phone, and corresponded with by email, but never met. Shaven-headed and tanned, stylish in black shirt and loafers. The screen caption said *Arlo Denstone, De Quincey Festival Director*.

'Not enough people know about De Quincey,' Arlo said. 'If pushed, some might recall the wild hallucinations of *Confessions of an English Opium-Eater*, and the savage satire of *On Murder, Considered as One of the Fine Arts*.'

'He was a friend of Wordsworth, wasn't he?'

'You've certainly done your homework, Grizelda.' The girl simpered. 'De Quincey idolised Wordsworth, and became his friend. He even moved into Dove Cottage after the poet left for Rydal Mount.'

'And he worked in newspapers while he lived in the Lakes?'

'Absolutely, Grizelda. He edited *The Westmorland Gazette*, and filled its pages with lurid accounts of trials for rape and murder.' Arlo shook his head, like a parent tutting over the escapades of a loveable child. 'Chesterton said he was "the first of the decadents".'

'Tell us about the Festival,' Grizelda said hastily.

'We mean to remind the world that De Quincey is one of the Lake District's iconic figures. The Festival will celebrate his life and work with exhibitions and readings, and the historian, Daniel Kind, will open the Festival with a lecture about the way murder fired De Quincey's imagination. We plan to publish the text, and Mr. Kind has generously waived his fee, since all the profits from the Festival are going to cancer charities.'

'And you are a cancer survivor yourself, of course.'

'One of the lucky ones, yes.' Arlo lowered his eyes. 'When the chairman of the Culture Company offered me the chance to honour a legendary man of letters, and raise funds for such a good cause, needless to say, I bit his hand off.'

A skilled self-publicist, Daniel thought, as the interview wound to an end. Arlo seemed as charismatic and persuasive in the flesh as he had been on the phone. He had a flair for picking the right buttons to press; if flattery didn't work, he exploited your better nature. Asked to lend your support to charitable fund-raising, how could you refuse? Arlo's accent hinted at years spent in Australia, first as an academic and later organising literary festivals, but he'd been a De Quincey fan since student days in Cumbria, and his passion struck a chord with Daniel; De Quincey's essays were works of genius, Arlo said, there was something unEnglish about their utter lack of restraint. Depressive, impecunious, and brimming with malicious wit, De Quincey was a reckless fantasist whose ill-health fed his addiction to drugs and voyeuristic love of violent crime. If he were alive today, he'd never be out of the tabloid headlines.

De Quincey fascinated Daniel. Common threads ran through their lives. De Quincey too came from Manchester and studied at Oxford before the Lakes seduced him. But he took his fascination with murder to the point of obsession. He argued that savage crimes might yet have aesthetic appeal, and he was the first to transform murder into literary entertainment. After De Quincey, murder was never the same again.

A book about murder, and history, with De Quincey's debaucheries thrown in? The publishers lapped up Daniel's pitch, and even his agent had stayed off his back for the last six months. He'd trawled countless digital archives, mapping out his themes. All he had to do was to write the bloody thing.

America proved the perfect place to escape from memories of Miranda, but now he must get down to work—and where better than back in the Lakes? He'd already spent a large chunk of the publishers' advance, and time was running out. No excuse for putting off the moment when he sat down and typed those two little words. Sometimes Daniel thought they were the two most terrifying words in the world.

Chapter One.

He yawned again. His limbs felt heavy, his eyelids drooped, yet he couldn't blame a night of Saturnalian excess for his fatigue. Was there any point in sitting down at the computer until Louise had come and gone? Having her live a few miles away at Stuart Wagg's lakeside mansion would seem strange. When he'd set off for the States, she'd been teaching corporate law in Manchester. He'd never imagined that, by the time of his return, she would have jacked in her job for a post at the University of South Lakeland, let alone that she'd have struck up a relationship with a local celebrity.

The coffee burned his throat. How long would this infatuation with Stuart Wagg last? Daniel had spent ten minutes in Wagg's company, on the way back from the airport, when Louise stopped off at Crag Gill to introduce them. Wagg switched on the charm for his benefit, but what else did strait-laced Louise see in a slick and fashionable lawyer? Wagg seemed to take her devotion for granted, and Daniel had seen Louise hurt too many times to be confident of a happy ending to the fairy tale.

The doorbell squealed, and he jumped to his feet. Lovers come and go, but family is forever. Or so it should be. He flung the door open.

'Happy New Year, Daniel.'

Louise kissed him on the cheek. No sign of her ancient anorak. The crisp new Barbour jacket was unzipped, revealing a clingy silk and cashmere dress that, despite the cold, showed plenty of pale skin. Her perfume was a velvety, sensual fragrance. The Stuart Wagg effect. How much had she really changed?

'Happy New Year.' He waved her inside and shut the door on the icy blast. 'Good party?'

'Um…' Louise pursed her lips. 'Memorable.'

She hung her jacket in the cloakroom. Her hair was windswept and her cheeks pink, as if she'd just been caught doing something she shouldn't. In that instant he saw what men like Wagg, men who could pick and choose, saw in her. For all her reserve, she'd never had any trouble attracting admirers. Finding a partner who stuck around proved more of a challenge.

'Tell me more.'

'Soon.' She considered him 'You look bleary. Only just got up?'

'It is New Year's Day.'

She clicked her tongue. A habit inherited from their late mother, a long-suffering woman whose default instinct was to reproach.

'I bet you haven't started writing that book. Or even decided on a title.'

'Grossly unfair. Not to mention untrue.'

'Tell me, then.'

'*The Hell Within.*'

'Charming.'

'No need to be sarky. It's taken from De Quincey, his essay on *Macbeth.*'

'What's the quote?'

'The murderer has hell within him,' Daniel said softly, 'and we must look into this hell.'

◇◇◇

'You'll never guess who I met at the party last night,' Louise said as she wiped toast crumbs from the corner of her mouth.

'Elton John?'

'Stone cold.'

'Madonna?'

'Dream on.'

'Disappointing.' Daniel glanced through the misty window as rain slanted down on the winter heathers. 'I thought Stuart Wagg knows everyone who is anyone.'

'You're so mean about Stuart.'

'I've not breathed a word.'

'You don't have to. The way you rolled your eyes when we called at Crag Gill said it all. Just because he's a rich solicitor. Behave, will you?'

'Like you did with Miranda?'

'She deserved it.'

Was that true? He cast his mind back to the first time he'd brought Miranda here, to Brackdale. A tranquil valley in the south east corner of the Lake District, shoe-horned in between Kentmere and Longsleddale. As soon as she saw the cottage in Tarn Fold, she'd set her heart on buying it and living the dream. By the time they'd renovated the building and made it what they wanted, she was ready to pursue a different dream. Yet he had no regrets. She'd steered him through a hard time, and he owed her for that.

'She rang last night, while you were at your party. She'd had a bit to drink.'

Louise's eyes narrowed. 'Wouldn't be the first time.'

'You never liked her, did you?'

'She was wrong for you.'

People could say the same about you and Stuart Wagg, he thought, but he kept his mouth clamped shut.

'I mean,' Louise said in a softer tone, 'she might have been pretty, but she was never a long term bet.'

'Too much the drama queen, you once told me.'

'Someone had to say it, Daniel. So—was she all maudlin and hankering after old times?'

'She's split up with Ethan and he's dropped her from the magazine. She's working freelance for a couple of glossies at the moment, but she sounded at a loose end. Said she might come back up here some time for a break.'

'For God's sake. I hope you didn't encourage her.' Louise uttered a theatrical groan. 'Remember, she fell in love with the Lakes for all of five minutes before the bright lights of the big city dragged her back down south. She's so bloody unpredictable.'

'When she left, we agreed to stay friends. I'm glad she's kept in touch.'

'She used you before. She'll use you again, if you don't watch out. And you'll be the one left picking up the pieces. Not her ladyship.'

Daniel perched on the arm of a leather chair. 'That's what people do, isn't it? We all use each other, in one way or another. Does no harm, between consenting adults.'

'And I thought I was the family cynic.'

'You never told me who you met last night.'

'Do you really want to know?'

Her gaze settled on him, cool and probing, as if he were a criminal in the dock about to be quizzed by counsel for the prosecution. How come she'd never practised as a courtroom lawyer? Her cross-examination technique would have wowed them down at the Bailey.

'Sure.' A smile pulled at the corners of her mouth, she was amusing herself at his expense. Okay, he'd hazard a guess, even if it smacked of wish fulfilment. 'It wasn't Hannah Scarlett, by any chance?'

'The one and only.' She inspected her fingernails. A vivid turquoise. He couldn't remember her painting them in the past. 'Father's fancy woman.'

'Don't be absurd.' He couldn't help snapping back. 'There was nothing between them.'

'How can you be so sure?'

'For God's sake. Dad was so much older. He ran off with Cheryl, don't forget. Not Hannah.'

'No, I don't forget.' Her eyes glinted with satisfaction. 'Actually, Hannah seems like a nice woman.'

'High praise, huh?'

'I don't mean to sound patronising. She told me Dad taught her all she knows about detective work. She admired him.'

'So did I.'

A sigh. 'Suppose I was too hard on him.'

Daniel had waited half a lifetime for that admission. She'd shared her mother's fury at Ben Kind's desertion. He'd walked out on all three of them and moved up to the Lake District to make a new life with a young woman. For years Louise refused to refer to her by name; she was never Cheryl, only the Blonde Bitch.

'So you and Hannah had a chat?'

'Until we were interrupted by a contretemps. She was looking good, actually. Very svelte.' Louise paused before asking, 'She asked after you.'

'Yeah?' He wanted to sound casual, but knew he'd failed.

'She hadn't heard you were back in Britain. It seemed to come as a shock. Pleasant one, though.'

Better make it clear that he remembered Hannah wasn't available.

'I must visit Marc Amos' bookshop. See if he has any local stuff about De Quincey.'

'He was there too. When I spotted him, he was ogling one of the waitresses.'

'Marc is a decent guy.'

Daniel had never broken up anyone else's relationship, and he didn't mean to start now. He was attracted to Hannah Scarlett, for reasons he couldn't fully explain, even to himself. But she was out of bounds.

'Stuart spends a lot of money with Amos Books. He must be one of Marc's best customers. Especially since that man Saffell died.'

'Saffell?'

'The book collector, the man who died in the fire at Ullswater. I mentioned it on the way up the M6, weren't you listening? It all sounds very mysterious, and I know how you love a mystery.'

He scarcely remembered. After flight delays on the way back from Seattle, he'd been pretty much out of it. Happy to let her conversation wash over him.

'Reading between the lines of the newspaper coverage, the fire didn't start by accident. If an arsonist killed Saffell, his wife must be a suspect. She certainly has a temper.'

Daniel frowned. 'How do you know?'

'She showed up at the party. Stuart invited her as a matter of courtesy, he's known her for years. He didn't seriously expect her to come. Let alone cause a scene.'

'What happened?'

'She and I were talking to Arlo Denstone.'

'You met Arlo?'

'Stuart introduced us. He's dying to meet you, now you're back in England.'

'I just watched a recording of him on TV. Not only an evangelist for De Quincey, but quite a charmer as well.'

'He's an intense guy. Intelligent, a bit hyper. Might dabble in the odd bit of opium-eating himself, for all I know.'

'Not your type?'

'No, but I can see why some women might be smitten. Not that he and I had a long conversation. Wanda Saffell joined us and the look in her eyes said she wanted to speak to him on her own. I caught sight of Hannah chatting to Stuart and made my excuses. A few minutes later, Wanda chucked a glass of red wine all over Arlo's jacket and then flounced out of the room.'

'Party-pooper, huh?'

'Stuart discovered her sitting cross-legged at the foot of the stairs, sobbing her heart out. He had her taken home by one of his partners. Her nerves are in tatters, he said.'

'Why did she attack Arlo?'

'No idea. Stuart brushed it off, said she'd had a rough time lately.'

'How could Arlo have upset her? A woman recently widowed in horrific circumstances?'

'What are you getting at?'

'He strikes me as a man who likes to provoke a reaction. Murder fascinates him. Maybe he suggested she knew something about her husband's death?'

Louise shook her head. 'You still believe historians make good detectives?'

'Why not? I got a book and a television series out of it.'

'Before you threw everything away.'

'I needed to escape.'

'I don't…,' she broke off as her brother's attention strayed. 'What's the matter?'

Daniel peered through the window. The rain was pounding harder. A dark figure in a hooded waterproof coat and hiker's boots splashed through puddles towards the cottage from the tarn.

'Someone has wandered into the garden.'

'That will be Stuart. I told him about this place and he said it sounded fascinating. I dropped him off by the old mill, so he could stroll along the beck. He could do with a breath of air, he didn't sleep last night.'

Daniel stared at the figure outside. The face was masked by the hood, but the man must have seen that he was being watched. He raised a hand encased in a black leather gauntlet.

If Daniel hadn't recognised Stuart Wagg, he'd have interpreted the gesture not as a greeting, but as a threat.

◇◇◇

'Louise tells me there was a bust-up at the party last night.'

Sprawled over the sofa, Stuart Wagg drained his tumbler of whisky. He hadn't bothered to wipe his feet properly and he'd left a trail of muddy footprints on the carpet.

'Something and nothing.'

'How did Arlo provoke her?' Daniel asked.

Wagg gave a shrug. 'Christ knows. I invited him over because we're sponsors of this Festival. Wanda's as thin-skinned as a skeleton's silhouette. They'd both had a few drinks. Maybe Arlo tried it on when she wasn't in the mood, who knows?'

'Wouldn't that be pretty insensitive, given that she was so recently widowed?'

'Tell you what, Daniel. My motto is: ask no questions, and you won't be told any lies. These things happen. Tomorrow it will all be forgotten. Nobody died.'

'George Saffell died.' Louise shivered. 'Someone turned his lakeside retreat into a ball of fire.'

'Nothing to do with what happened last night.' Wagg's jaw tightened. 'Except that Wanda is grieving. She deserves to be cut some slack.'

'You've known her a long time?' Louise asked.

'We were at school together. She was a few years younger than me, but even then, she stood out from the crowd. I remember taking her out to the cinema a few times when we were teenagers. All very innocent, of course.'

'I bet.'

'Believe me.' He feigned injured innocence. 'I never got further than a quick fumble on the back seats at the Royalty in Bowness. Very well-behaved young lady was Wanda. Single-minded, too. Obsessed with her hobby, nothing else mattered to her half as much.'

'Her hobby?'

'Vocation, business, whatever. She loves printmaking. As a kid, I promise you, she was much more interested in that than me. Still is, to this day.'

'You knew her husband?' Daniel asked.

'Old George? Sure, we moved in the same business circles. And he loved books as much as I do.'

Louise arched her eyebrows. 'Do you really love books, darling?'

'What do you mean?' Wagg sounded like a bishop accused of blasphemy.

'I wondered…if what you really love is the thrill of the chase. Tracking down a rare first edition, then squirreling it away, so nobody else can have the pleasure of owning it.'

For a moment, there was silence.

He shook his head. 'You're wrong.'

'How many of your precious tomes have you actually read?' She turned to Daniel. 'You should see his library. It's a miniature Bodleian. But I doubt if he's read a tenth of his collection.'

'One of these days,' Wagg muttered. 'When I have more time.'

'Meanwhile, you still have to keep Marc Amos in business, I suppose?'

'You know Marc's partner.' Daniel wanted to change the subject, stop Louise from needling Wagg. It was her habit to be provocative, but he sensed the man had a temper to match Wanda Saffell's. 'DCI Scarlett.'

'The lovely Hannah?' Wagg grinned. 'Your sister tells me that you managed to get yourself involved in one of Hannah's cases.'

More than one, actually, but Daniel kept his mouth shut. He wished Louise hadn't talked about him with Stuart Wagg. Even more, he wished she hadn't fallen for the man. He didn't like the way the whisky had loosened Wagg's tongue.

'Her career ran into the buffers, did you know? After she messed up over a major trial, they side-lined her.'

Louise frowned. 'Seriously?'

'It was all presented in a positive light, needless to say. Young woman detective on the fast track? They could hardly throw her overboard. Not with all those politically correct diversity targets to meet.'

'She's in charge of the cold case team,' Daniel said. 'A high profile job.'

'Not exactly at the cutting edge, though. Zero pressure. No need to race against the clock when a victim's spent years moulding in the grave.' Wagg gave a theatrical sigh. 'But Hannah will be fine. If she keeps her nose clean until she's got her years in, she'll have a nice fat pension. No need to rely on the money Marc makes from sad bibliomaniacs like me.'

Daniel felt his cheeks reddening as he counted to ten. Hannah didn't need him to defend her, but he couldn't help it.

'She doesn't strike me as a time-server.'

Wagg yawned and stretched his arms. 'Well, who cares? I'd better be getting home. Thanks for the booze.'

As Louise stood up, he turned to her and said, 'Are you staying over, or coming back here after you've dropped me off, darling?'

'Staying over, of course. Why do you ask?'

'No reason.'

'You've taken the week off work.'

'Yeah, I was thinking of getting up among the fells.'

'Term doesn't start for another week, we can explore the fells together.'

'It's not what I had in mind. For me, fell-walking is a solitary vice.' Wagg got to his feet. 'I assumed, now your brother's back in England, you'd want to spend some time with him.'

'Daniel and I can see each other any time.'

She sounded as though Wagg had smacked her face. Daniel clenched his fist behind his back.

'Fine, fine. Let's go, then.'

Daniel saw them to the door, and watched them climb into Louise's sports car without a word. Her face was as bleak as

Scafell. She crashed the gears, the ugly noise breaching the peace of the wooded valley.

The car sped off, Louise driving too fast for the little lane through the wood. Daniel stared after them.

He found himself loathing Stuart Wagg.

Chapter Five

'Bethany Friend's body was found by a group of half a dozen fell-walkers,' Hannah said. 'A damp winter morning almost six years ago. 15 February, to be precise. She'd been dead for less than twenty four hours.'

Greg Wharf swung back and forth on the plastic chair. Not quite insubordination, not far from it. Her new detective sergeant was testing her patience, but Hannah was determined not to let him win the game. They were alone in the briefing room. It was newly refurbished, with lots of greenery in posh stone pots, and a couple of abstract daubs on the wall. The money came from a budget surplus at the end of the last financial year; though the Police Federation would have preferred cash in their members' pay packets.

Hannah hardly knew Greg Wharf. He was a Geordie with bleached hair and an incipient beer gut. Dark rings under his eyes testified to intensive New Year partying. He'd spent most of his career in Newcastle, where he'd married a high-flying colleague. Once his wife discovered him *in flagrante* with a Community Support Officer, a messy divorce followed, and he transferred to Cumbria's northern division. Most of Hannah's female colleagues fancied him, and one had even dubbed him Gorgeous Greg. No accounting for tastes. Some poor soul was probably responsible for ironing that white shirt to crisp perfection. He was the sort of bloke who regarded doing the laundry as women's work.

Hannah had called him in early for a briefing on the Friend case before the rest of the team arrived. Ten minutes in, she suspected the less she got to know about Detective Sergeant Gregory Wharf, the better. That mocking light in the blue eyes made him look like a beach bum humouring a parish priest.

He wasn't overjoyed to be here. Lauren Self, the Assistant Chief Constable, had moved him from Vice after he procured a confession to the rape of a prostitute from a recidivist sex offender. It seemed like a neat piece of detective work, until the man hanged himself and it turned out that the woman had made up the complaint to take revenge on an ex-boyfriend. Greg wriggled out of it without a disciplinary hearing, but he'd taken one chance too many. Exile to Cold Cases was the price he had to pay.

'So Bethany died on February 14.' A laddish snigger. 'Valentine's Day.'

'Uh-huh.'

'Is the date supposed to be significant?'

'That's for us to find out, isn't it?'

'Sure.' His eyes narrowed, like a chess player figuring out the next move. Trouble was, she'd never had the patience for chess, and he wouldn't bother to follow the rules of the game anyway. 'Do we have any theories? Any leads?'

'Nothing to suggest that her death was linked to a romantic entanglement. Of course, she may have killed herself because her love life went wrong.'

'Flaky, was she?'

His grimace implied that, with women, flakiness was an occupational hazard.

'Bethany was quiet, bookish. A very private person, everyone agreed on that.'

'We could spend months re-interviewing reluctant witnesses and finish up back where we started.'

'Suicide is possible, but it seems unlikely.'

He nodded at a close-up shot of the corpse pinned on the whiteboard. 'Because she was gagged?'

The face of the woman in the photo was bruised and swollen. Eyes shut, mouth open, as if she were biting the woollen scarf. Hannah looked away. Nobody should finish up like that. Not only dead, but degraded.

'The gag was the tightest knot, but physically, she could have done it herself. Same with the tying-up.'

'Mmmm. Sounds kinky.'

'Her hands were bound behind her back.' Hannah wouldn't rise to the bait. 'Spark plug cables wrapped around her wrists. They were quite loose.'

'Not easy to truss someone up efficiently with jump leads.' He grinned, as if to hint that he'd tried it himself.

'Her ankles were tied together with a tow rope. It was never established whether the rope and the cables belonged to her or someone else brought them. There was bruising on the neck, from some sort of ligature. Probably the scarf. Perhaps she tied it around her throat, then thought better of it.'

'So she could have done all that and then chucked herself into the water?'

'All eighteen inches of it, yes. Or so the investigating team was told by one of the country's leading experts on knotting techniques.'

Greg Wharf's face made clear what he thought of anyone who devoted a career to studying the methodology of tying knots.

'No sign of rape?'

'No evidence whatsoever that she'd had sex lately. She was dressed, but not fully equipped for a long hike over the fells. Blue jeans, shirt and body warmer. Marks and Spencer bra and pants. Boots. No injuries or signs of a struggle—if you don't count the neck bruises.'

'Bondage game gone wrong?'

'Out in the open air?'

'All the more fun.'

'The weather was lousy. A rain storm would dampen anyone's ardour.'

'Takes all sorts.'

He made a performance of stifling a yawn. She decided to allow him the benefit of the doubt and assume he was recovering from the festivities. Better not kill their relationship on the very first morning. Though right now she didn't give it more than forty eight hours before she'd have to slap him down hard, and no doubt earn his enmity for good. Bloody Lauren. This was a decent team, why did the ACC have to sabotage it by parachuting in a misogynistic egoist?

'Can you reach the scene by car?'

'An off-road vehicle could get close, but it's not as if she was killed somewhere else and then brought to the water to be dumped. Bethany's VW was parked at the end of a lane which peters out three quarters of a mile away from the pool. She'd driven there herself, either with suicide in mind or to meet someone else. The forensic evidence was conclusive about cause of death. Drowning.'

'Did she have suicidal tendencies? Any family precedents?'

'None. Her father was long dead, and an elder brother was run over by a lorry a year before Bethany was born. She was studious, didn't have many relationships. A long-term crush on a woman who taught her English in the sixth form ended when the teacher died of meningitis during Bethany's first year at Lancaster Uni.'

'Unlucky lady. A lot of people she was close to kicked the bucket.'

'Not her mother, she's alive to this day. She was forty when Bethany was born. I don't think she ever understood her daughter, but she idolised her.'

'Was there a history of depression?'

'Nothing known. Bethany had few friends, but the people she knew found it hard to believe she'd want to end it all.'

'Friends and family are often the last to know.'

'According to the mother, Bethany couldn't swim. She hated putting her face under water, so why would she choose to drown herself?'

'Another way of tormenting herself?'

'Your guess is as good as mine.'

He shrugged. 'So why are we bothered?'

Good question. Hannah was ready with an answer. Though, as when she'd talked with Marc up at the Serpent Pool, it wasn't a complete answer.

'The SIO who led the inquiry wasn't satisfied. He mentioned the case to me before he retired. He always believed she was murdered.'

'Yeah?'

She remembered Ben Kind telling her about the investigation into Bethany's death, after he was told to run it down. She'd been embroiled on another inquiry at the time. Even now, she could hear Ben's voice.

I can't get her last moments out of my mind. A woman who hated water, drowning herself like that? She must have been terrified. Why would anyone do that to themselves?

'Bethany had a lover called Nathan Clare. The SIO wondered if Clare knew more about Bethany's death than he was prepared to admit. But there was no proof, and plenty more pressing cases where there was no doubt a crime had been committed. He had to give up. But letting go rankled with him. Unfinished business.'

'This SIO.' His white teeth gleamed. 'Not Ben Kind, by any chance?'

Shit. If this was chess, he'd placed her in check. She gave a quick nod, praying that she wasn't blushing.

'I used to work with him.'

'Yeah, I heard.'

His knowing smile grew broader. The bastard. What had people said about her and Ben?

'What he told me about the case convinced me that Bethany's death was worth looking into, once we had the capacity.'

'Yeah?'

'Yeah, your arrival is the lucky break I've been waiting for.'

Take that, you cheeky bugger.

Greg Wharf frowned.

'What do we know about her, then?'

So he was interested, after all? Better not let point-scoring wreck things between them from the start. For an ambitious guy with a high opinion of himself, Cold Cases must seem like a dead end. In the absence of material yielding fresh evidence thanks to the advances of DNA technology—the sort of stuff that had the Press Office salivating at the prospect of sexy headlines—only a minority of investigations made progress.

Leaning against the whiteboard, she closed her eyes. No need to consult her notes. After hours poring over witness statements and a transcript of the inquest, she knew the key points off by heart.

'Bethany was twenty-five. She had countless short-term jobs after she graduated. Writing was her passion, but she needed to earn enough to pay the rent while she spent every spare moment scribbling. She often worked as a temp, and she spent a whole term as a secretary in the offices at the University of South Lakeland. Until shortly before her death, she was seeing a man who gave lectures in English from time to time.'

'This Nathan Clare, her shag buddy?'

She ignored his leer. 'Clare's phrase was "lovers without commitment."'

'Don't tell me, he was married?'

She shook her head. 'Commitment wasn't his cup of tea. He never tied the knot.'

'Unless it was around Bethany's neck?'

'The sort of man who enjoys his freedom, by the sound of it.'

'My sort of bloke, then.'

'Yeah, he's keen on Samuel Taylor Coleridge and all that. You could chat about Xanadu over a pint of real ale.'

He pushed a lock of hair off his forehead and looked round, as if in search of a mirror to preen before. 'Xanadu? That's a nightclub in Whitehaven, isn't it?'

Hannah followed his gaze. It lingered on a second photograph of the victim, this time a head and shoulders snap taken by her mother twelve months before her death. Bethany was quietly pretty, with shoulder-length brown hair. Her skin was clear, her teeth strong and even. A Mona Lisa smile suggested she was enjoying a private joke at the photographer's expense. No question, Hannah thought, something about her compelled interest. There was more to Bethany Friend than met the eye.

But she wasn't Greg Wharf's type. 'One thing's for sure,' he said. 'Nathan Clare must like a challenge.'

◇◇◇

Back in the sanctuary of her own office, Hannah closed her eyes and imagined herself on the brink of the Serpent Pool. Pictured a woman in despair, unable to escape her troubles. A woman who saw only one way out.

So on a wet winter's day, had Bethany driven from Grasmere to Ambleside and walked up the fell on her own? Tightened her scarf around her neck before having second thoughts and stuffing it into her mouth? Brought the rope and jump leads from the boot of her car and tied them around her ankles and wrists? Conquered her fear and thrown herself into the water? Thrashed around for a few moments, or remained still, content to wait for the end?

Imagine the coldness of the water. Swilling over her face, filling her nose and mouth, choking her lungs.

No, no, no.

Something was wrong with the picture. Why the Serpent Pool? It wasn't as if the Lake District was short of places to drown yourself. Ben Kind thought it had been chosen because of its secluded setting. He'd never believed she'd killed herself and his failure to prove she was a victim of murder, let alone find the culprit, troubled him to the end of his days. He had a detective's nose for the truth, sensed it in the way a seasoned experience walker knew the right way down a mountainside, even when the mist descended.

Hannah opened her eyes again. Bethany Friend wasn't a quitter. She'd kept writing, despite years of nothing but rejection slips. Suicide made no sense at all.

Ben was right. Someone had murdered her.

◇◇◇

'Sorted the new lad out?' Les Bryant asked.

Hannah stood next to him in the cafeteria queue as he asked the girl at the counter for an all-day breakfast, only to be told it was no longer on the menu ('ACC's orders, Les. All part of the new healthy eating culture.') She pointed to a glossy wall poster showed a smiling group of models posing as police officers, as glamorous as they were ethnically diverse, beside a caption that proclaimed EAT YOUR WAY TO FITNESS and extolled the virtues of parsnips and pomegranates. The message was likely to induce a coronary in Les, if his crimson cheeks were any guide. With a muttered curse, he settled for a double helping of Shredded Wheat and a filter coffee into which he deposited two heaped spoonfuls of sugar.

'He isn't a happy bunny. Neither am I, come to that.' Hannah bought a bowl of muesli, a slice of melon and an organic cran-berry juice, more to provoke Les than because she was addicted to fruit. 'Bloody Lauren sent him to Cold Cases as though it's the naughty corner.'

They didn't have any trouble finding a table. A virus was sweeping the county and a lot of people had called in sick. Les slurped some coffee and wiped his mouth with the back of his hand.

'It will be all right as long as you show him who's boss. If you don't, he'll trample all over you.'

'Thanks for those words of encouragement.'

'Listen, I had a belly-full of management before I retired. I know it's a pile of shit. But you're in charge, not me. Better get on with it.'

Les was a veteran of countless major inquiries in his native Yorkshire, he'd been persuaded out of retirement to lend his experience to the newly formed Cold Case Review Team. After his wife left him, he had no incentive to go back home. Six months ago, he'd bought a bungalow in Staveley and even though a thirty-year pension meant he didn't need the money, he'd signed an extended contract. Given Nick Lowther's emigration, Bob Swindell's move to Lancashire, and Gul Khan's decision to leave and join the family retail business, Les' presence in the team gave Hannah much-needed continuity. Cold cases were never solved overnight, and staff turnover coupled with budget cutbacks made the task even tougher.

Les muttered, 'Watch out, there's an ACPO about.'

Hannah glanced across the cafeteria and spotted Lauren Self. The ACC was working the room like a politician, moving from table to table, and wishing everyone a happy new year. She didn't need to seek votes, so she must be ticking off her list of resolutions. Their eyes met, and Lauren sashayed over to join them.

'Hannah! And Les!' Lauren made a show of shaking their hands. Her grip was cool and firm, her skin lightly tanned. 'All the very best for the next twelve months. Did you both have a good break? Hope you avoided this wretched bug that's going round. We were in the Caribbean, and we only flew back into Manchester yesterday morning. I'm still adjusting to the thirty degree drop in temperature.'

You'd never have guessed it from the brightness of her eyes and the spring in her step. Hannah couldn't help wondering if Lauren wasn't quite human. If she were a visitor from a distant galaxy, it might explain her lack of empathy with traditional police work. She sought to cover it up with a ceaseless flow of jargon culled from the Ministry of Justice's guide to doublespeak, but the robotic zeal defied any disguise. Hannah fantasized about shooting at her and watching her evaporate, or turn back into an alien life form. But Lauren was so thick-skinned that a bullet was sure to bounce off her impenetrable hide.

'You'll remember this is Greg Wharf's first day with us, ma'am.' Hannah noticed the rictus of disdain. Further proof that she saw Cold Cases as a dumping ground for people she wasn't allowed to sack. Maybe they should be re-christened Hopeless Cases. 'I've briefed him about Bethany Friend.'

A frown disrupted Lauren's efficiently organised features.

'You still think there is mileage in looking into her death?'

'There's more to be found out, I'm sure of it.'

'Even though we don't have DNA?'

Lauren worshipped DNA evidence. To hear her talk, you'd never believe any crime could have been solved before the discovery of that magical double helix.

'Time has passed,' Hannah said. 'People who were reluctant to talk at the time of the original enquiry may have changed allegiances and be more willing to open up. I've briefed Maggie Eyre to trace people who gave statements to the original inquiry team. Some of them are still around, but others have moved on. Les here has his hands full with our existing caseload, but Greg and I will talk to some of the key witnesses'

Lauren tutted. 'You'll recall our chat before Christmas? We need a few more outcomes if I'm to persuade the Police Authority to maintain your team's funding at its present level. No guarantees, Hannah.'

Les Bryant feigned to choke on his Shredded Wheat. The ACC gave him a pitying glance before turning her attention back to Hannah.

'Pressure on resources is growing all the time. Money is tight and next year's allocations will come up for review soon. I need positive news to report. Otherwise…'

She shook her head, as if mourning a lost cause. So much for the cheery optimism of the start-of-year rallying call that her spin doctors had put out on the staff intranet.

'Bethany's mother is dying, she never understood what happened to her daughter and she deserves closure.'

'We're not a charity.' Uh-oh. The public-spending card. 'This is taxpayers' money we are spending. At a time when government revenues have fallen off a cliff.'

Time for Hannah to play her ace. 'I had a word with a freelance journalist who writes occasional features for the Sunday broadsheets. If we could get a result in the case, he'd run it as a major story.'

Lauren leaned forward. Had she been a bitch, Hannah thought, she would have wagged her tail. Come to think of it…

'Seriously?'

Not really. Hannah had bumped into the man at Stuart Wagg's party. He was drunk and talkative and was keen to show off. Their conversation had lasted less than three minutes and she doubted he'd remember it if and when he sobered up.

'Of course,' Hannah murmured, 'I appreciate that favourable publicity isn't the be-all and end-all.'

'Absolutely not,' Lauren said. 'However, I'll be absolutely honest with you...'

Les shot Hannah a glance which said *there's a first time for everything.*

'Ma'am?'

'A few columns of positive coverage in the media wouldn't harm. The Chair of the Police Authority is up for re-election in May. He'd welcome a few supportive headlines.'

'Reviving the inquiry might be money well spent, then?' Hannah kept her face straight.

'I think so.' Lauren was judicious. Weighing the pros and cons with care and objectivity before coming down on the side of self-interest. 'We need to reach out to the wider community in a very public manner. Good media relations are integral to what we do.'

'Of course.'

'That's settled, then. Keep me informed, Hannah. And bear in mind that solving a cold case doesn't equate to admitting the force got anything wrong in the past.'

◇◇◇

'I printed off the attachment to my email,' DC Maggie Eyre thrust a couple of sheets of paper into Hannah's hand. 'The witness details you asked for.'

'Thanks.' Hannah waved Maggie into a chair as her gaze travelled down the list. 'You've been busy.'

'Six years is a long time. So far I've traced half the people who were interviewed after Bethany's body was discovered. Most of them still live in the area.'

'And the people we haven't found?'

'Include two of her closest friends from her school days, Phyllida Lathwell and Jean Pipe. They've probably married and changed their names. The main evidence they contributed concerned Bethany's crush on a teacher, the woman who died. There was a fellow student, Gillian Langeveldt, who came from South Africa, and presumably went back there. A couple of work colleagues, with the depressingly common surnames of Smith and Brown. Plus some of the people who came forward, saying they'd seen her on or around the day she died.'

Hannah considered the names. 'Graeme Redfern?'

'Worked for an undertakers' in Ambleside. Reckoned he saw Bethany having sex in a shop doorway the night before Valentine's Day. Turns out that Redfern was sacked twelve months after Bethany died, and his old boss thinks he may have gone back home to Leeds. Not a nice man, Mr. Redfern. He took a ring from a corpse's finger and tried to sell it on the internet.'

Hannah remembered now. Ben had mentioned Redfern to her. He'd dismissed the man as a sad fantasist. People like that always cropped up on the edges of a police investigation. There were other names on Maggie's list. A pizza delivery man, Mickey Cumbes, whose criminal record included a prison sentence for indecent assault of a teenage girl, swore he'd seen Bethany kissing another woman outside the Salutation Hotel on the morning of Valentine's Day. A dropped-out student who claimed to have seen Bethany being manhandled into an unmarked white transit van by a burly bloke who looked like an off-duty soldier. Once again, Ben didn't believe a word of it. Roland Seeton was a long-haired layabout with two convictions for possession of illegal drugs, who probably nourished some sort of grudge against the Army. Any investigation attracted time-wasters, and tracking them down years after the event was a pain. But they had to give it a go. One lucky break was all they needed.

'Good, you've noted Nathan Clare's phone number. I want to talk to him as soon as I can. And to call on Bethany's mum.'

'I spoke to the care home.' Maggie's face wrinkled with dismay. 'She had flu over Christmas and they said she's fading fast.'

Hannah sprang to her feet. 'Better get a move on, then. For Mrs. Friend's sake.'

Chapter Six

Sleet slanted down outside the converted mill that was home to Amos Books. From his office on the first floor, Marc gazed out at the swollen beck as it rushed over the weir. The wooden decking beneath the window had disappeared under the water. On a fine day, customers of the cafeteria downstairs sat out and admired the scenery whilst they tucked into cappuccino and cake, but no book-buyers had ventured out there for months. Half two in the afternoon, and the sky was the colour of Coniston slate. He switched on the radio to check the forecast, and was greeted by an avalanche warning for Helvellyn.

'Snow and ice are unstable at all levels of the mountain.' The Park Authority spokeswoman raised her voice to make herself heard above the storm. 'Together with the gales, they make any ascent dangerous. High winds are moving the snow around, so it isn't bonding. Surfaces underfoot are treacherous—all the time, edges are breaking away. With the sudden deterioration in the weather, there is added danger from a cornice of snow. We think it may collapse at any time.'

Someone coughed behind him.

Marc swung round. He hadn't heard the door open. He didn't like people invading his private space or taking him by surprise. For years he'd been accustomed to a warning creak whenever someone came in, even if they didn't knock. It had been a mistake to oil those hinges;

In the doorway wasn't some nosey customer in search of a Wainwright first edition, but a woman in a thick fisherman's jersey and jeans, with shoulder-length fair hair tied into a pony-tail. Steam rose from the mug of coffee in her hand. He wasn't sure how long she had stood there. Why would she wait and watch him, without a word? His skin prickled. Her silent scrutiny was curiously exciting, as if she could see right through him.

'Our fell top assessor says he has rarely seen conditions as bad as this in the Lake District,' shouted the woman on the radio. 'The wind chill factor is severe. We urge people, however experienced they might be as mountaineers, not to venture out until the situation improves.'

Marc shook his head. 'What kind of fool would climb a mountain in this weather?'

A dreamy look came into Cassie Weston's eyes. Her lips parted, revealing front teeth that slightly overlapped. Somehow the imperfection made her all the more attractive.

'Someone who likes living dangerously?'

'Living dangerously is one thing. Killing yourself is quite another.'

'I brought you a hot drink.'

'You're very good to me.'

Her expression was unreadable. 'You were miles away.'

He waved at the chaotic mess of paperwork on his desk. 'You caught me out.'

'It's not as if you were doing something wicked.'

Most people would have said *something wrong*. But Cassie wasn't most people.

'I should be checking the unpaid invoices. Cash flow is king, and all that.'

She handed him the mug. 'What were you thinking of?'

He might have asked her much the same question. Cassie had worked for him since the autumn, but he still couldn't make her out. One minute distant, the next, almost intimate, as if she were on the verge of confiding a secret. Whenever he tried to find out more about her, she pulled up the drawbridge, but this elusive contrariness was part of her appeal. What made her tick, what turned her on? Once upon a time, he'd wondered the same about Hannah. Cassie was a fresh challenge, a conundrum he yearned to solve.

More than once, when the shop was shut and the staff had gone home, he'd pulled her file from the cabinet and pored over her CV like a detective in search of clues. But he found so few. She came from Carlisle and after a year spent studying for a degree in English Literature, she'd given up on university in favour of the real world. Over the years she'd drifted from job to job. Typing here, waiting on table there. Her job application mentioned that she wrote short stories in her spare time, but the one occasion he'd asked about them, she'd shaken her head in embarrassment and changed the subject.

'I'm a book man,' he said. 'Living dangerously isn't for me.'

'You never know till you try.'

'A place like this can't be too exciting for a young woman like you.'

'That isn't what I meant,' she said softly. 'I enjoy it here. I find it fascinating…to learn from you.'

He'd tried to explain how much he loved it here, surrounded by thousands of second hand books. Each had a story to tell, and not just in words written on the page. Every volume on every shelf had a past life. Sometimes all was revealed by an inscription in a flowing hand—'To Daisy, Merry Christmas, 25 December 1937', 'Given to Hubert Withers for one year of unbroken attendance at Cark Sunday School',—sometimes the books came with no provenance and you had to play detective to find out how a rare book printed in Gibraltar when Victoria was on the throne finished up in a junk shop at Gateshead one hundred and twenty years later.

He relished teaching her how to buy and sell rare books, couldn't help feeling flattered by the way she hung on his words as he described the tricks of the trade. How to spot books that weren't what they seemed, like alleged signed firsts of *The Man with the Golden Gun* and *Octopussy*.- neither of which was published until Ian Fleming was dead and buried. Book values flipped up and down like the stock market. Pricing had little to do with literary merit, let alone critical acclaim when the books were new. *Winnie the Pooh* wasn't worth quite as much this year, while a set of early whodunits by Miles Burton in pristine jackets would set the rich collectors aquiver with desire.

'I'd hate to bore you,' he said.

'You don't bore me at all.' She considered him. 'But has anyone ever dared to suggest you care more about books than people?'

From someone else, the question would be offensive. He wondered if she was referring to Hannah. He leaned against the desk and smelled the coffee. Pungent Arabic, spiced with cardamom. Still too hot to drink.

'Depends on which people.'

She pointed at the clutter of documents, paper clips and ring binders. 'But you hate being a businessman.'

'Running the shop and having to worry about cash flow and stuff is the price I pay for being my own boss.' She was trying to find out about him, she must be interested. 'There are plenty of other things I dread more.'

A light shone in her eyes. 'Such as?'

'The taxman, for a start,' he said lightly.

She frowned, as if the answer disappointed her. 'Sorry. I didn't mean to interrupt.'

As she moved away, he felt a stab of disappointment.

'Any time,' he said.

◇◇◇

When he took the empty mug downstairs to the cafeteria, Cassie was behind the counter, talking to a customer on the phone. Some long and complicated enquiry about a search for a book whose title and author the caller couldn't remember. A frustratingly common form of amnesia. She didn't spare Marc a glance as he walked past.

A coal fire burned in an inglenook on the ground floor, in between the bookshop and the café. The wind whistled in the chimney and from cracks in the window seals, but the crackling blaze kept the winter at bay. Marc warmed his hands before helping himself to a fat slab of chocolate gateau. As a penance, he sacrificed a couple of minutes to an exchange of pleasantries with Mrs. Beveridge, who had taken over the running of the café from Leigh Moffat. A slice of the legacy from Aunt Imelda had enabled Marc to take a lease on premises in Sedbergh, now designated as a book town. For the moment, the store was little more than a handful of shelves annexed to Leigh's café. He missed her, and wondered if she missed him as much.

Mrs. Beveridge was efficient but voluble and he was already bored with her jokes about the suitability of her surname for someone who spent her working life serving tea, coffee, and soft drinks. She was large and jolly and smelled of banana cake. Every now and then, she told him that he ought to make an honest woman of Hannah. Once, in frustration, he'd trotted out the old joke about what you feed a woman to put her off sex. When he said the answer was wedding cake, she'd uttered such a groan of dismay that the floorboards rattled. You couldn't beat marriage for companionship, she maintained, although he gathered her recipe for connubial bliss involved keeping her husband well and truly under her thumb. Mr. Beveridge was a retired chauffeur ('and he still drives me to distraction!') who spent every daylight hour on an allotment in Kendal, no doubt to keep a safe distance from his wife's relentless chatter.

The kitchen staff had left early to get home before the weather worsened, and there wasn't a customer in the shop. The mill was one of half a dozen buildings grouped around a yard; the others housed an assortment of craft shops, and visitors often drifted from one store to another. But not today.

He fled from Mrs. Beveridge's clutches to the detective fiction shelves, and blew dust off a set of squat reprints lacking dust jackets. Hack work produced by long-forgotten practitioners with names like Bellairs, Morland, and Straker. Titles as hard to shift as aged relatives who have long outstayed their welcome. It was increasingly difficult to sell anything that wasn't out of the ordinary. He blamed the internet; as most booksellers blamed the internet for whatever went wrong with their business. An Agatha Christie reprint from the sixties, a Ruth Rendell from the eighties? No, thanks. You could get them online for a handful of pennies.

Rarities. He must keep finding them, if his business was to survive. He didn't need Hannah to remind him that he couldn't live off the legacy forever. He had a few scouts, people with the know-how to search out scarce books, who were ready to sell at a hefty discount in order to make a quick profit. Charity shops and car boot sales were a waste of time, but he haunted book fairs, although the good buys were to be had from fellow dealers early on the first morning, long before the doors opened to admit Joe Public. Even the punters were savvier than ten years ago. Internet comparison sites and online auctions made everyone an expert.

The doorbell jangled, and he looked over his shoulder in surprise.

A woman wearing a hooded raincoat stepped into the shop. She dropped a zipped shopping bag on to the floor, pushed back the sleet-spattered hood, and gave him an Arctic smile.

'If you buy me a coffee, I promise not to throw it all over you.'

Marc exhaled.

'Afternoon, Wanda.'

◇◇◇

When Mrs. Beveridge brought their drinks and a plate of scones, she hung around, trying to engage Wanda Saffell in conversation. But Wanda didn't do small talk, and eventually, the cafeteria manager admitted defeat and retired to the kitchen.

Wanda watched her retreating back. 'You must miss Leigh.'

Marc frowned, but said nothing. Wanda was so bloody provocative. His fling with Leigh was long in the past, long before they'd worked together. He didn't like people getting the wrong idea about their relationship. It was purely professional.

'Thought you might like to see my latest production.' She unzipped the bag and produced a thin red slipcase. 'Of course, I'm hoping that you would be prepared to stock it.'

She slid a little book out of the slipcase. It was bound in papyrus and stitched with raffia.

'*Voila!*'

Marc had seldom seen Wanda Saffell show pleasure—her natural expression was chilly disapproval. She must be proud of what she had done. Picking up the book between forefinger and thumb, he considered the title page.

'*Pulses of Light?*'

'You don't recognise the quotation?'

He shook his head.

'Thomas De Quincey, talking about Dorothy Wordsworth. He was talking about her energy, the way she illuminated the scene. He had the hots for her, all right. Poor woman, not pretty, but full of pent-up passion. After William married, she lost her mind. Anyway, in these verses, the poet imagines himself as De Quincey, setting about the seduction of Dorothy.'

'And does he succeed?'

She smiled. 'You bet. It's a pure lust thing. No hearts and flowers. Not a daffodil in sight. Read the poems, and you'll find an explanation for Dorothy's mental breakdown that has nothing to do with her brother. It's very dark and disturbing. No prizes for guessing why he couldn't find a London publisher. But I adore his work.'

Marc stared at the author's name.

'Nathan Clare?'

'I wondered if you'd put a few copies on the counter.'

'Well…'

'Sale or return, of course, I expect nothing else. Trade terms. I have a poster, too, if you wouldn't mind?'

Marc flicked through the pages. The poems were interspersed with woodcuts. The images fell just short of pornographic.

Splayed limbs, convoluted couplings. He read a stanza of 'Taking You Beyond'.

'Strong stuff.'

'Like I said. But Nathan has a fierce talent.'

He touched the binding. 'Never mind what's inside the book. You've created something beautiful.'

'Would you judge a book by its cover?'

'A lot of people do precisely that.'

'I wanted to create a binding that was...counter-intuitive.'

Marc opened the book again and stared at a picture of a reinvented Dorothy, pleasuring her devilish lover with ferocious energy.

'I'll take half a dozen.'

'You're a star.' Wanda hesitated. 'As a matter of fact, I owe you an apology. I almost crashed into your car on New Year's Eve.'

'High risk,' he murmured. 'Hannah was driving.'

'The Detective Chief Inspector.' Wanda sipped her drink. 'I should have been more careful, but I wasn't in the best frame of mind.'

'So I gathered.'

'God knows why I showed up. Stuart Wagg said he didn't like to think of my being alone at the turn of the year. Told me I couldn't hide away forever. I should never have listened. He only wanted me there as a prize exhibit. The widow of his dead rival.'

'Rival?'

'In book collecting.' She considered him. 'What did you think I meant?'

'Of course.'

'He and George competed for years, you must have made a pretty penny out of them both.'

'George was a wonderful customer. I miss him.'

'I bet you do.' She didn't say she missed her husband too. 'At least I got something out of that fucking party. I enjoyed drenching Arlo Denstone.'

'What was all that about?'

She waved the question away. 'Never mind, it's history.'

'But...'

'I'm not sure it was worth the buzz it gave me. Denstone offered to let Nathan give a poetry reading during the De Quincey Festival. Maybe he'll change his mind now, though I hope he won't bear a grudge. It would help to sell a few more copies.' Her expression was rueful. 'Thanks for taking the books.'

'I'll put them in my next catalogue.' Marc savoured the raspberry jam he'd smeared on the scone. 'My turn to apologise. I meant to attend George's funeral, but at the last minute, something cropped up.'

This wasn't true. He hated funerals. Any form of unhappiness depressed him, and the thought of standing by a graveside on a dank and dismal day had been too much to bear. So he'd decided not to go and salved his conscience by sending a handsome cheque in favour of the charity Wanda had chosen for donations in George's memory. From her raised eyebrows, he could tell that she'd seen through his lie, but it didn't matter a jot. She had other things on her mind.

'I'm no good at playing the grieving widow. It's no secret that George and I had...drifted apart. So of course, the tongues are wagging.'

'I don't understand.'

'People wonder if I started that fire. Or hired someone to do it for me.'

'Nobody could imagine...'

'Of course they can. Sometimes I feel as though I'm the talk of the Lakes. And making a fool of myself at the party didn't help.'

'Perhaps the fire was an accident.'

'It was no accident, and suicide doesn't make sense. George would never kill himself, trust me. Let alone in that horrible way. He was a baby, like most men. Terrified of pain, he must have suffered agony. It doesn't bear thinking about. Besides, he'd never destroy his precious collection. He loved books more than anything. Includng me.'

Mrs. Beveridge emerged from the kitchen. 'All right if I close up in five minutes?'

It felt like a reprieve. Marc sprang up. 'We'll get out of your way.'

Wanda Saffell rose to her feet. 'I'd better go. Thank you for listening.'

Good manners almost prompted him to murmur: *any time.* But Mrs. Beveridge started putting chairs upside down on top of the tables around them and before he could say a word, Wanda strode out of the shop and into the shower of sleet.

◇◇◇

Back in his office, he fiddled with entries for his next catalogue, checking prices on the net, tinkering with images of dust jackets on his computer screen to make sure all the detail was visible. Digital photography made it easier to describe books accurately to prospective purchasers, and keep complaints down to a minimum. Not that he ever had many complaints. He loved books too much to want to lie about them.

The door opened. Cassie had got out of the habit of knocking. 'Shall I leave it to you to lock up?'

He logged off and said, 'I'll be ready in five minutes. We can leave together.'

'Would you mind dropping me off at the bus stop? My poor little car is in for repair. It started making unhappy noises over the holiday, so I took it in this morning and it won't be ready until tomorrow.'

'I'll give you a lift home, if you like.'

'I don't want to take you out of your way.'

He was sure she'd hoped he would make the offer. Though unsure whether that was because she liked his company, or because she didn't want to hang around in the dark, waiting for a bus. If one ever came—services had been slashed up and down the county. No wonder the roads choked with cars and lorries.

'No problem. Kendal isn't much of a detour.'

'Okay, thanks. Five minutes?'

As the door closed behind him, his spine tingled. Not that he meant to misbehave, of course. Nothing was further from his mind.

◇◇◇

'Fancy a quick drink?'

He felt Cassie's gaze, warm on his cheeks, but kept his eyes locked on the dark road ahead. A small, stone-built pub stood a couple of hundred yards further on. An isolated place, in the middle of fields and woodland, catering for the local farm workers. Litter always seemed to blow across the tiny car park, and he'd never been tempted to stop there for a drink. It was long odds against his bumping into anyone he knew. Besides, neither he nor Cassie had anything to hide; it wasn't as if they were up to no good.

'Don't you have to be getting home?'

'Half an hour won't hurt.'

'I suppose your partner works long hours.'

A reminder that he was spoken for. Cassie knew about Hannah, and that she was a cop. It was no secret.

'Too right.' They rounded another bend and he could see the pub ahead. 'But if you're in a hurry…'

'No hurry at all.'

He swung off the road and into the deserted car park. There was a *For Lease* board on the outside wall of the pub, the upstairs windows were shuttered. The sleet had stopped, but this was an evening to stay indoors.

'What would you like?'

'Whisky, please.' She gave a theatrical shiver. 'I need warming up.'

◇◇◇

The landlord was a walking cadaver in a frayed cardigan; his false teeth clicked as he pulled on the pump. Scores of hostelries in the Lakes had reinvented themselves as gourmet restaurants, but all The Old Soldier had to offer was a dusty glass cabinet containing a couple of grey sausage rolls and a Cornish pasty. Marc supposed that any customers who hadn't been driven away by the smoking ban and the smell of disinfectant from behind the bar counter would have been discouraged by the man's monosyllabic dead-batting of conversation as he poured the drinks. A handwritten sign on the wall proclaimed this as a happy hour. The landlord might not be hot on customer-focus, but he had a flair for irony. Beer and cheese and onion crisps were on sale at half price, yet there wasn't another soul to be seen.

'Slow night?'

The landlord shrugged. 'About the usual. I'm getting out at the end of the month. The brewery's selling up.'

Once upon a time, this would have been a sweaty, smoky drinking den, one of thousands across the land, a place where locals met up after a long day at work for a game of dominoes or darts. The younger generation would hate the lack of karaoke machines and football on satellite television. Kids today bought their booze from supermarkets and went bingeing on cheap Stella Artois before throwing up and fighting each other in the nearest village square or shopping parade.

At least he and Cassie had the lounge bar to themselves, and thirty minutes sped by. Marc spent most of them talking and Cassie's eyes gleamed in the murky light; maybe it was his sparkling conversations, maybe the tumbler of neat Glenfiddich had something to do with it.

She interrogated him about the new house in Ambleside, and he made her laugh with an account of his incompetent efforts at do-it-yourself. He hadn't even attempted to make the bookshelves himself; that was a job for a skilled tradesman, given the number and weight of books to be borne. He'd even had to check out whether there was a need to reinforce the first floor. But it would be worth it. The house was so close to the fells. You could walk up to the Serpent Tower without breaking sweat.

'That's an old folly, isn't it?'

'You know it?'

She shook her head. 'Only read about it. I can't claim to be much of a walker.'

'It's an easy climb, you'll have to let me show it to you, one of these days.' He hesitated, not wanting to make it sound like a chat-up line. 'Come round for lunch one Saturday, perhaps, and then we could head up the fell.'

'That would be nice.' She smiled. 'You never appreciate what's on your own doorstep.'

'Hannah and I made it as far as the Serpent Pool on New Year's Eve, but we had to beat a retreat before the mist came down.'

'The Serpent Pool.' She frowned and emptied the tumbler in a single gulp. 'The name rings a bell.'

'It's a narrow stretch of water, some people say it's shaped like a snake.' He grimaced. 'The folly is further up the fell, a much better vantage point. The pool isn't even big enough to count as a tarn.'

She didn't say anything, seemed to want him to go on.

'A woman drowned there, years ago.'

'What happened?'

'Oh, I don't know the story.' Not true, but he didn't want to talk about Bethany Friend. 'You'd best ask Hannah.'

'We hardly ever see her in the shop.'

'She calls in occasionally. Of course, she's working most of the time.'

'The hours must be tough if you're a senior police officer.'

'Yeah, it…can be difficult.'

Their eyes met for a moment, then Cassie checked her watch. 'Time to go, I think.'

◇◇◇

They didn't talk much on the rest of the journey. Cassie's flat was in a quiet back street, above a boarded-up sub-post office that had fallen victim to government cutbacks. It was happening all over Cumbria, this whittling-away of the bonds that had tied communities together. Pubs, libraries, post offices, primary schools, all closing down. Traditional village life was fading like the worn inscriptions on the stones in country graveyards. In darker moments, he wondered if the day might come when people only talked to each other on social networking sites and internet chat rooms.

He pulled up outside the building. It was behind Kirkland, a three-storey house, divided into bed-sits. Would she invite him in for a coffee? If she did, would he accept?

'Thanks,' she said. 'It would have been so miserable, waiting for the bus and then bumping along all the way into town.'

'Any time.'

'Careful. You wouldn't want me to take advantage of your good nature.'

He returned her smile. 'I'm sure you'd never do that.'

'You don't know that much about me.'

When he'd tried to find out more about her personal life, she'd parried his oblique questions. He knew nothing about her boyfriend, except that he lived in Grasmere. Maybe he was imaginary, a convenient excuse to avoid unwanted entanglements, like Stuart Wagg's party, or the attentions of a boss who was stuck in a long-term relationship.

'It's early days.'

She gripped the door handle. He wondered if she might be about to kiss him on the cheek, but if that was in her mind, she had second thoughts. She opened the door and jumped out on to the pavement, before thrusting her head back into the car.

'Goodnight, Marc.'

He nodded towards the building. 'Convenient. Close to the town centre.'

'It's all right. A bit cramped, but space enough for one.' She pointed to a window on the first floor. 'That's my room.'

The door to her flat was down an alleyway at the side of the building. As she fumbled in her bag for her key, she turned to give him a quick wave. He waved back as she disappeared inside.

He didn't start up the car at once, but sat there in darkness and asked himself again whether he would have followed her in, if she'd invited him.

A light went on in the window above the shuttered post office. He saw her shadow, stretching out long slender arms. Impossible to tell whether she was yawning—or exulting.

He was sure she was taking off her clothes. Sure she knew that he was watching from his car. Why else point out her room?

He pictured her stripping naked. Pictured her beckoning to him, to come upstairs and join her in bed.

But her face did not appear at the window.

He wasn't sure why he waited there. Ridiculous, really. Perhaps, somewhere deep in his sub-conscious, he hoped she would change her mind and call him in. Stupid, stupid fantasy. It must be the intoxicating combination of drink and her company.

The shadow disappeared, but he didn't switch on the ignition for another ten minutes. He couldn't squeeze her lovely face out of his mind.

Chapter Seven

'Bethany Friend is dead.' Nathan Clare's deep, almost musical voice made harsh words seem all the more cruel. 'They burned her body, one wet morning at the crematorium. Why rake over old ashes?'

The house was a mid-terrace in the heart of Ambleside. You stepped in through the front door, straight off the pavement. There was a pub opposite and an off-licence round the corner. During the ten years he'd lived here, he'd probably kept them both busy. In a bedroom upstairs, he'd slept with Bethany, but there was no trace of her in this living room. No fading photograph on the mantelpiece. No photographs at all, come to that. Hannah supposed he wasn't into remembering other people. She guessed that Nathan Clare had fallen in love with himself at an early age, and remained ever faithful. On a small table, books were piled high. Fanned out next to a flyer advertising the De Quincey Festival were half a dozen red warning letters about unpaid phone, gas, and electric bills.

Hannah shifted on the sofa. It was absurdly low, and as lumpy as a bad milk pudding. He'd waved her to take a seat, but wasn't foolish enough to join her. Instead he roamed up and down the narrow living room, pausing every now and then to warm his backside against a log fire. Each time he made a point, he waved his beefy arms. Every syllable of his body language said: *I am in control.*

'We never closed the file.'

Bad choice of words. She sounded like a pen-pusher, ticking off a checklist.

'So this is an exercise in bureaucracy? Presumably you have targets to meet? Bonuses to be earned?'

'This isn't about meeting targets, Mr. Clare. Bethany's mother is ill, she doesn't have long to live. She's never understood why her only child died. She needs closure.'

'Closure.' Nathan Clare lifted dark, brooding eyebrows. 'A fashionable nostrum, DCI Scarlett. Of course, it's an illusion. Life isn't neat and tidy. There are no elegant solutions to its mysteries.'

She groaned inwardly. *Spare me the philosophy.*

'Even so, I'd be grateful for your help.'

'I went through this six years ago. I can't tell you any more.'

'You and she were lovers.'

A shift of his shoulders implied: *so what?* Even in tee shirt, chinos and moccasins, he struck her as formidable. His features were simian, with prominent cheekbones and flared nostrils. As he stalked around in front of her, he reminded her of a caged animal. Untamed even after a lifetime of captivity, forever on the prowl. Strong, feral, dangerous.

'The details are hazy now.'

'Six years isn't so long. The two of you were close, and her death was very sudden.'

'I needed to move on.' A grand sweep of a huge paw. 'I made a conscious effort to scrub Bethany out of my mind.'

Hannah knew the trick he was pulling. He wanted to cover his back in case he made some mistake and contradicted his original statement. She'd fixed the appointment by phone and, caught by surprise, he'd agreed before he had the chance to fob her off. She'd half-expected when she rang the doorbell five minutes ago that he wouldn't answer. But he'd decided to indulge in a little unsubtle psychological warfare. On the wall facing her hung a sub-Modigliani daub of an angular, naked girl with legs splayed open. He wanted her to feel uncomfortable. The lumpy sofa, at least, was doing the job.

She scrambled to her feet and stood close to him. He smelled of stale beer.

'When did you meet Bethany?'

'As you well know, I held a series of evening classes at the University, and she came along. She worked in the offices as a secretary at the time. Temping, to pay the rent. But literature was her passion.'

'What was the subject of your classes?'

'Ostensibly, the Lakes poets other than Wordsworth. Coleridge, Southey, you know?' His tone implied that a detective wouldn't have heard of any poet other than Wordsworth. 'I like the discussion to range far and wide. I could never become a full-time academic. Examinations and grades only matter to second-rate minds. One night, Bethany and I talked. We went to the pub for a drink and took it from there.'

'You began a relationship?'

'It wasn't against the rules, if that's what you're suggesting.'

'She was on the university's payroll.'

'But she wasn't a student. The evening classes were just a way of filling the time when she ran out of ideas for her writing. She'd had a series of dead-end jobs. Serving in restaurants, typing in offices, earning a pittance behind the counter of a bookshop. One summer, she cleaned bedrooms at a hotel at Bowness. Her ambition was to write the Great English novel. Not that it was ever going to happen.'

'Did you and Bethany discuss her moving in here?'

'She knew I wanted to keep my independence.'

'You didn't view it as a long-term relationship?'

He laughed. 'Nowadays people spend a fortune on weddings and five minutes later they're consulting their lawyers about divorce. I'm not sure relationships actually work long-term, Chief Inspector. A few last because the parties are too lazy or frightened to make a break.'

'Did Bethany feel the same?'

'She'd had bad experiences in the past.'

'What do you mean?'

He frowned, as if he'd been lured into saying too much. 'She was an innocent. Prey to wild infatuations, followed by deep despair.'

'Is that so?' Hannah was curious. 'I heard she was a very private woman.'

'Are private people forbidden to fall in love?'

'Was she infatuated with you?'

He grinned, showing teeth as large as any she had ever seen. 'Do you find that so difficult to understand, Hannah?'

'The last time you saw her was a couple of days before she died. You admitted that you argued.'

'I told her I'd met someone else.'

'Who was that someone else?'

'I said it was a girl who'd come to one of my poetry readings, but that wasn't the truth.'

'You invented a new girlfriend because you'd tired of Bethany?'

'That wasn't...' He paused. "Please don't sound shocked, it's unbecoming in a senior police officer.'

'I'm not shocked, Mr. Clare. It just seems rather heartless.'

'As a matter of fact, I was doing the poor girl a kindness.'

'Really?'

'It would have been cruel simply to say that I found her wearisome. Her physical demands, I had no trouble accommodating, I can assure you. But she stuck to me like clingfilm. She was terrified of rejection. Utterly terrified.'

'Why was that, do you think?'

'I'm not a psychiatrist.'

Hannah waited.

'If there's one thing I can't stomach, it's a clingy woman. Freedom is very precious to me.'

Through a door opening into the kitchen, Hannah saw dirty plates and mugs piled high on the draining board. The floor hadn't seen a mop for weeks, and she caught a whiff of sour milk.

'You never married.'

He shook his head. 'Not for the want of opportuniitiess, I promise you.'

Slimeball though he was, Hannah feared he was telling the truth. There were probably a good many women who thought they could change him. Depressing thought.

'Is that right?'

'Smugness doesn't suit you, my dear Hannah. In case you're wondering, I'm not interested in my own sex. Bethany could never persuade me there was any sense in that sort of thing. But I like to do as I please, and marriage makes that difficult. Paying off the mortgage is commitment enough for anyone.'

The urge to slap his face was almost impossible to resist. No doubt, over the years, plenty of women had succumbed to the temptation. But Hannah wanted information.

'How did the argument between you end?'

'I promised to call her in a few days, once I'd given her time to calm down. There was no reason why we couldn't continue to be friends.'

'If she was terrified of rejection, she must have been upset with you. Angry?'

'These things are never pleasant. I'm no monster, Hannah, whatever feminist prejudices you may harbour. But our relationship had run its course. She was bound to get over me, sooner or later. Probably the moment she met someone else.'

'Did she seem irrational, did she make threats?'

'I don't know what you mean.'

Hannah gave him a do-me-a-favour look.

'She was distressed, naturally. I arranged to take her out for a meal, at a decent little trattoria. It closed down last year, a real loss. Bethany thought we were about to discuss a romantic holiday in Umbria when I broke the news. She wasn't irrational. Just…unhappy.'

The original investigating team had spoken to the staff on duty at the trattoria that night. Voices had been raised, and Bethany was in floods of tears. Wailing like a child, according to one of the waiters. But there was no evidence that she'd threatened any form of revenge, far less that her behaviour had driven Nathan Clare to murder.

'You told my colleagues that she must have committed suicide.'

'I thought she would get over the break-up, but...'

'You think she was so depressed that she saw no reason to keep on living?'

'What other explanation could there be for her death? Whatever her shortcomings, Bethany was an utterly inoffensive woman. How could any sane person wish to do her harm?'

Ben Kind had asked himself the same question. Perhaps, against all odds, it was a case of accidental death. One of his working theories was that Clare had invited Bethany to the Serpent Pool to indulge in some kind of sex game as a means of reviving his flagging interest. On a lousy February day, he might have been confident they would not be disturbed. Had the experiment gone terribly wrong?

'So she killed herself because she was heartbroken that you ended the affair?'

'I never said that.'

'What, then?'

'She was too intense for happiness. This wasn't the first time that a relationship had come to an end against her wishes.'

'Tell me about her previous relationships.'

'We never discussed them. Why would I be interested?.'

He'd said the same during the original investigation. At least he was consistent. Or simply careful.

'Seriously?'

'Seriously. I believe in living for the moment. All that matters is the here and now, that's what I said to her. And I meant it.'

Something he'd said earlier stirred in her memory. At once, anxiety chilled her.

'You mentioned that she worked in a bookshop.'

'Correct.'

'Waterstones?'

'No, they sold second hand books.'

◇◇◇

Bethany Friend's death haunted Ben Kind. Yet he couldn't even prove it was murder, let alone get close to making an arrest. Nathan Clare was the obvious suspect. Ben disliked him, and now Hannah understood why. There was no trace of the supposed lover who dumped Bethany before she took up with Nathan. None of Bethany's friends or work colleagues knew of anyone. Ben had wondered if the lover really existed, or was an invention of Clare's.

Next stop was a care home near Watersedge. Time for a word with Bethany's mother. Hannah wanted her to know she'd had the go-ahead to re-open the case. And now she needed to find out whether Bethany had ever worked for Marc.

As she stomped through the rain to her car, she thought back to those conversations with Ben. He shared with others of his generation an innate distrust of the Bramshill Flyers, those younger graduate officers who came fresh to policing with degrees in archaeology or classics and were fast-tracked for promotion. But he wasn't a bigot, and he'd done everything in his power to aid her progress. Despite the age gap, there was an attraction between them. Never acknowledged in words, but palpable. Neither of them ever did anything about it. He stuck with Cheryl, for whom he'd abandoned his wife and children, and she found herself living with Marc.

One wet night, over a drink after work, Ben told her why Bethany Friend's death meant so much to him. He'd interviewed Bethany's mother, and been struck by the depth of her despair. She was only in her sixties, but the combination of a weak heart and a series of personal calamities had aged her. He said she might have passed for fifteen years older, and no wonder. Her husband had died long ago, followed by her son, and finally she'd lost her remaining child.

'Sounds stupid,' he said as they sat in the corner of a dingy pub, 'but she made me think of my mother. When I left home, my wife wouldn't have anything to do with me or my family, ever again. My mum never saw her grandchildren after that, even though Daniel used to write to her in secret. It made me realise…'

His voice trailed away. Hannah had wanted to take his hand and offer comfort, but she'd been afraid of where it might lead.

'What?'

'It made me realise what a selfish bastard I was. Mum died within a couple of years and whatever they put on the death certificate, the truth is that her heart was broken and she lost the will to carry on.'

'So you want to make it up to Daphne Friend?'

'Yes.' He stared into his cloudy pint, embarrassed to meet her eyes. 'Yes.'

Now Ben was gone, and a cold case investigation was the last chance to discover the truth before Daphne died. This was why she'd been so determined to persuade Lauren Self to back the investment of time and resource in a seemingly hopeless cause. She owed it to Ben and Daphne to do her best.

And yet.

What if Marc had employed Bethany?

Or, even worse, if he knew what had happened to her and had kept his mouth shut because he had something to hide?

◇◇◇

The care assistant's name was Kasia. Like most of the staff in the home, she was Polish. Young, cheerful, and obviously over-worked. The home was a double-fronted nineteenth century house which had been much extended. A conservatory had been tacked on, affording residents a view of the fells. But nobody paid attention to the slopes beyond the rain-streaked glazing. Half a dozen elderly women and a couple of men sat around in a semi-circle, but most were fast asleep. One couple were glued to a quiz programme on the television screen facing the windows. Some of the wizened faces had changed since Hannah's last visit before Christmas, but gentle snoring that greeted her as they walked in sounded exactly the same.

'She is awake,' Kasia whispered, as if they had entered a church. 'She was unwell over the holiday, but she seems brighter today.'

Daphne Friend sat in a wheelchair, hands folded in her lap. A copy of *Take a Break* had slipped from her grasp and lay on the carpet in front of her, but she paid it no heed. She was barely seventy, no age at all these days, but illness and unhappiness had worn her down. Her skin was papery and she smelled of talcum powder. Her gaze rested on a framed watercolour of Buttermere on the opposite wall, but Hannah was sure she wasn't studying the picture of the lake. Her mind was wandering back down the years, in search of those memories she managed to retain.

'Daphne,' the care assistant said. 'You have a visitor.'

Hannah held out her hand. 'Hello, Daphne. My name's Hannah Scarlett. Do you remember me?'

Daphne Friend lifted a withered hand and brushed it against Hannah's fingers. The smile on her lips was tentative. Was that a faint spark of recognition in the watery blue eyes? When Hannah was last here, a nurse had told her that Bethany's mother showed signs of memory loss and problems with concentration. The symptoms had worsened since a minor stroke in November. Yet Hannah had caught her on a good day, and Daphne had spoken wistfully about her lost daughter. After talking to her, Hannah was all the more determined to discover the truth about Bethany's death.

'You were in Bethany's class at school.'

It could have been worse; she might have forgotten their conversation altogether. Or was she simply guessing, like a deaf person trying to keep up when they haven't heard properly what was said. The care assistant wheeled Daphne back to her room, a tiny box with barely enough space for a bed, two chairs, a wardrobe, chest of drawers and a small bookcase in which battered Catherine Cooksons stood side-by-side with novels by Pat Barker and A.S. Byatt.

'I will leave you together,' Kasia said. 'Many things to do. Ring if you need me, okay?'

Hannah sat on a chair next to the old lady.

'I'm a police officer, and we're trying to find out what happened to Bethany. When I came before, I promised I'd do my best to help and now my boss has agreed, we can get down to work.'

Daphne's eyes began to fill with tears. 'She was such a lovely girl.'

Hannah touched the age-spotted hand. The wedding ring was loose, her fingers were skin and bone. Ben Kind had been struck by a resemblance between this woman and his own mother. Another old lady whose life was ruined by loss and loneliness.

'Yes, I'm sure.'

'She deserved better, she never had much luck.'

'I wanted to ask you about her friends.'

'She worked hard at school. There was a girl called Phyllida in her class. She went to America and married a doctor. Or was it an architect?'

'What about later on? The people she was close to in those last few years.'

A tear trickled down Daphne Friend's cheek. 'Oh, I'm not sure. It's so long ago. Sometimes, I get muddled.'

'About Bethany's boyfriends, did you meet many of them?'

Daphne frowned. 'She was secretive. You know what young people are like. It wasn't that I wanted to pry.'

'You were just interested,' Hannah suggested.

'Yes, it's only natural. When she was a little girl, she used to tell me everything.' Daphne strayed into reminiscence until Hannah gently brought her back to Bethany's later years. 'She didn't settle with anyone. Such a shame. I always thought it would be so nice to be a grandma.'

'Was there anyone special at all?'

Daphne shook her head. Her white hair was sparse, the pink scalp showing through.

'She never said.'

It wasn't surprising that Bethany kept her private life away from her mother. Daphne Friend was a conventional woman, no doubt disapproving of sex before marriage. Bethany probably told her as much as she needed to know, and nothing more.

'Tell me about her jobs, Daphne. She loved writing, didn't she?'

Daphne's eyes widened suddenly as she smiled. Even though she hadn't put her false teeth in, Hannah had a momentary glimpse of what had attracted the late Mr. Friend half a century ago.

'She did that. The teachers always gave her top marks for English, you know. She studied it at university. Even as a tot, she always said she wanted to be a writer when she grew up. Though I told her she needed to have a proper job as well.'

Good advice, Hannah supposed, if Nathan Clare was anything to go by.

'What sort of proper job?'

'I wanted her to teach.' Daphne drifted into a reverie about the attractions of working in a school. 'A respectable job, with long holidays, and a decent pension at the end of it all. But she said she wasn't patient enough.'

'So what did she do?'

Daphne frowned. 'Something and nothing jobs. At least it was better than the dole, but she could have made more of herself. Working behind bars, or shop counters, that's no life for a girl with an English degree.'

'She had a job in a bookshop, didn't she?'

'She worked in several shops,' Daphne said. 'When she was at Lakeland, she bought a lot of lovely jerseys at a discount.'

Questioning people with erratic memories demanded endless patience. Police work was something else that wouldn't have suited Bethany Friend.

'And the bookshop?'

'Yes, I remember. A nice place.'

'Did you ever go to see her there?'

'Once, dear. The shop was in an old mill. They opened a cafeteria. You could sit outside on a nice day with a cup of tea and a bun, and look at the stream as it went over the whatsit.'

'The weir,' Hannah said automatically. Her heart was pounding.

'That's right, the weir.' Daphne's pallid cheeks coloured as something occurred to her. 'I'm so sorry, dear, your name's just slipped my mind.'

◇◇◇

After leaving the care home, Hannah wandered around the village, not yet ready to return to Divisional HQ. With a certain amount of well-concealed malicious glee, she had given Greg Wharf the task of checking into current wisdom on knotting techniques, to see if more light could be cast on the manner of Bethany's death. Maggie was phoning round, in search of the people on her list who remained untraced.

Pausing by the edge of the lake, she gazed at the grey expanse of water while swans flapped their wings, as if trying to dry themselves in the drizzle. She'd quizzed Daphne without success about Bethany's spell in the bookshop. It must have been during the early days of Hannah's relationship with Marc. They'd both been working long hours; she was building her career, while Marc devoted himself to getting the business off the ground. They had so little time to spare for each other. Her job meant so much to her; disappointment had yet to set in. As for Marc, books were his obsession, his life. He'd dreamed of owning a bookshop the way other kids dreamed of running a sweetshop. She'd been content to let him get on with it.

Hannah remembered the photograph that had caught Greg Wharf's attention. A young woman who was quietly intriguing. A challenge. Like Hannah herself, perhaps. There was a type of woman who appealed to Marc. Bethany fitted the profile.

As she followed a circuit around Ambleside, anorak capital of the western world, shop windows proclaimed unbeatable reductions on walking boots, and outdoor gear for sale at not-to-be-repeated prices. But she was in no mood for bargain-hunting.

When she arrived home that evening, the lights were on, and Marc emerged from the kitchen with a spring in his step.

He planted a kiss on her cheek and patted her bum. He was in such a good mood, she supposed he'd sold a first edition. Or bought one on the cheap.

'Busy day?' she asked.

'Flogged a signed copy of *Leave it to Psmith* half an hour ago over the internet. As for the shop, barely a customer. It's the weather, of course. Never mind, the Wodehouse sale more than makes up for it.' He put his arm around her waist and pulled her to him. 'I've put the oven on and dug a bottle of that nice red wine out of the cellar to celebrate.'

As his lips brushed hers, she told herself this wasn't the time to interrogate him about Bethany Friend. Moments of harmony were precious. He would hate questions, would demand to be told whether she was checking up on him. In her head, she heard his outraged innocence.

'For God's sake, Hannah, what's got into you? Don't you trust me any more? I mean—you're not jealous of a dead woman, are you?'

So she squeezed his hand and said, 'That's fine.'

Chapter Eight

Hannah didn't mention Bethany Friend's name that night. Marc did the cooking, a very good boeuf bourguignon, washed down with a bottle of Merlot. Over the meal, they watched a DVD, a sentimental romantic comedy she forgot as soon as the final credits rolled. When he suggested they go to bed early, she said yes at once. As she undressed, she tried to remember the last time they'd made love on a weekday night, when they both had to get up for work the next morning. How stupid it would be to ruin the moment by cross-examining him about the woman who had died in the Serpent Pool.

Marc was patient and tender. This was how it used to be between them. When they first met, she'd liked the fact that books meant so much more to him than soccer or rugby. As a junior police officer, she'd dated men who were keener on sport than on sex. Marc's sensitivity turned her on, made him seem different. When he asked her to move in with him, she said yes before he had a chance to change his mind. Even now, she didn't regret it. Sometimes you had to trust to instinct. Take a chance.

As she allowed him to take control, she found her body responding. Forget everything else, exist for the moment. His touch was gentle, his breath warm. Time to banish the image of drowned Bethany's swollen face. Afterwards, she settled into deep and dreamless sleep.

Marc was out of bed by the time the alarm roused Hannah. She yawned, reluctant to drag herself from under the duvet and get on with her own job. But when it came to duty or duvet, the work ethic won every time. Sad, really.

Over cornflakes and coffee, she didn't mention Bethany. Marc took a call from a customer in Denmark with a couple of titles to add to his wants list and then padded off to his study. He was wearing his boxer shorts and his body looked as trim as she could remember. Desire stirred again inside her. How did he manage to keep himself in shape when he seldom went to the gym and spent most of his time reading?

Hannah switched on the radio. The early show presenters, Nerys and Erik, were talking to Arlo Denstone about the De Quincey Festival.

'...and Daniel Kind, the historian, will be talking about Thomas De Quincey...'

'*Confessions of an English Opium Eater,*' Nerys interrupted, determined to prove she wasn't just a pretty voice.

'Yes, De Quincey was one of the most fascinating Englishmen of the nineteenth century. He had a brilliant mind, yet he admitted to "a chronic passion of anxiety", and "a perpetual sense of desperation". These were the qualities that...'

Marc reappeared. 'Seen my black jersey?'

She turned down the volume. 'I washed it over the week-end. Look in your wardrobe.'

'It wasn't in its usual place.'

'Look again.'

'You might have told me.'

He gave a theatrical sigh and banged the door shut as he left the room. Was this the inevitable fate of all long-lasting relationships? Those early days of excitement and passion slowly transformed into squabbles about laundry and loading the dishwasher? It wasn't only Thomas De Quincey who had a perpetual sense of desperation. Perhaps she ought to be thankful that the magic was still there at bed-time. Some nights, at any rate.

When she turned up the sound on the radio, the conversation had moved away from Daniel Kind and Thomas De Quincey.

She swallowed the last of her coffee and slid off the kitchen stool. Time to face the day.

◇◇◇

As soon as the briefing session was over, Hannah returned to her room and shut the door. Greg Wharf's patience with knotting specialists was wearing as thin as frayed string. Like experts the world over, they were happiest when perched upon the fence. Nobody was prepared to go on the record and rule out the possibility that Bethany had tied herself up before lying down in the Serpent Pool and submitting to her fate. Hannah guessed that Greg's scepticism had deterred the experts from inching outside their professional comfort zones. They'd worry about the blame game if fresh evidence came to light to prove that Bethany had killed herself.

Hannah shuffled circulars from the ACC as her thoughts roamed. Ben Kind hadn't been afraid to take risks when circumstances demanded it. He'd once told her there were only two types of senior cop; those with tidy desks and those whose desks looked like a bomb had struck. Ben never tolerated clutter. When his paperwork began to accumulate, it finished up in the wastepaper basket. He was a bulky man, but astonishingly neat, in his physical movements as well as in the way he marshalled his office. He'd never sympathised with Hannah's hoarding of ancient memoranda and she wasn't sure she could explain it herself. Maybe she liked the comfort of the familiar. For her, a clear desk was like a zero crime rate. A worthy aspiration, no more. In this, she resembled Marc, even though she lacked his obsessive collector's zeal. She understood why he hated to let things go.

Was that why they stuck together, because it wasn't in their nature to make the break? Even after last night in bed, she could not swear to the answer.

Her personal address book lurked at one corner of the desk, hidden by a sheaf of last month's crime statistics. On impulse, she fished it out. She'd noted the numbers of Daniel Kind's mobile and the cottage in Brackdale. Never got round to crossing them out.

Why not give him a ring, where was the harm?

As she picked up the phone, the door swung open.

'Ma'am. Something's just cropped up. I thought you'd like to know.'

Maggie Eyre, breathless and sweaty after running down the corridor. She'd put on a bit of weight, Hannah noticed. She succumbed to unworthy selfishness. *Hope to God she hasn't got pregnant yet. We're short-staffed as it is.*

She put down the receiver and waved Maggie into the chair on the other side of the messy desk. 'Be my guest.'

'Sorry to interrupt, I should have waited.'

'It wasn't important.'

Maggie tossed a sheet of paper on to the desk. It covered up the address book. 'Of course, this probably means nothing at all. But it's an intriguing coincidence, I wanted you to know straight away.'

Hannah glanced at the sheet. It was a short witness statement. The witness' name was Wanda Smith, and she had worked at a PR consultancy where Bethany temped prior to moving to a post at the university.

A yellow post-it note was stuck on to the paper. Maggie had written on it a telephone number and four words.

Married name—Wanda Saffell.

◇◇◇

Daniel Kind stared at his laptop, thinking about murder.

Thomas De Quincey had a lot to answer for. Daniel had just finished re-reading 'On Murder Considered as one of the Fine Arts', and the old essay retained its bite. De Quincey was intrigued by 'the philosophy of cleansing the heart by means of pity and terror…Something more goes into the composition of a fine murder than two blockheads to kill and be killed, a knife, a purse, and a dark lane. Design, gentlemen, grouping, light and shade, poetry, sentiment, are now deemed indispensable to attempts of this nature.' The true murderer was a romantic, who played to the gallery. The crimes that appealed to De Quincey possessed a touch of the bizarre.

Daniel thought it best not to dwell upon what his Dad would have said about making murder the subject of satire. No scope for relishing the aesthetics of murder when your job was to detect it. One of Daniel's infant memories was of staying up late one Friday night when his father was working on a case. The old man had promised to read him a story at bed-time—a rare treat, and Daniel chose a chapter about the Five Find-Outers, who were forever investigating mysteries. When at last Ben arrived home, he was haggard and weary, and he hugged his son with a strange ferocity before saying that he needed a shower before story-time. Louise was already fast asleep, but as Daniel waited in his bedroom, he overheard his parents whispering.

'What did he do to her?'

'Strangled her with his bare hands.'

'Oh God.'

'And that wasn't the worst of it.' Ben's voice was choking and, for a terrible moment, Daniel thought his father was about to burst into tears. 'A kid, that's all she was. A kid.'

At that point, Ben noticed his son's door was ajar and shut it so as to prevent any more eavesdropping. But Daniel had heard enough. He'd learned that in his father's world, real people who did things to real children, things too sickening for words. *And that wasn't the worst of it.* Those words troubled him for years.

His mother always wanted Ben to let the job drop, to shut the door on the harsh and terrifying world of crime behind when he came home to his family. She dreaded the thought that murder might taint all their lives. But Ben never managed to chill out for long. The urge to see justice done drove him; the irony was that sometimes he failed to do justice to the people who meant most to him.

Daniel had wanted to talk to Hannah Scarlett about his father. The old man must have admired her passion about what she did. It wasn't simply about ticking the boxes on the forms and building up your pension pot so you could retire after thirty years and advise businesses on security in between golf trips to the Algarve. Hannah was someone else who wanted to give to the innocent the justice they deserved.

Since meeting Hannah, he'd encountered murder at close quarters and seen the havoc it caused. Murder changed lives forever, tore families apart. Yet there was no point in trying to pretend that his interest was purely academic. Murder didn't simply intrigue him, it obsessed him. As it had De Quincey, as it had when as a small boy, he'd waited hour after hour for his father to come home and imagined that, single-handed and unarmed, he was busy slapping handcuffs on homicidal maniacs.

Might as well face up to something else. It wasn't only the fascination of detective work, and the chance to learn more about the father who had left home for another life, that drew him to Hannah. Even before Miranda's decision to leave, he'd felt a strong attraction to her, and that sense of passion burning beneath the surface of cool professionalism. But Hannah was with Marc, and that was that.

The phone trilled. He snatched up the receiver, glad of the distraction. His mind was wandering into dangerous territory.

'Daniel Kind.'

'This is Arlo.' Denstone was speaking on a mobile and the reception was poor. A common problem in the Lakes. 'I'm in the neighbourhood, wondered if you're free.'

'Sure, it would be good to meet. I heard you on the radio this morning.'

'Really?' Arlo sounded pleased.

'You pricked my conscience. The deadline for delivering my Festival paper to the printers isn't far away.'

'End of this week. I can't wait to see it.'

'Um…I'm working on it now.'

'Hope you don't mind my inviting myself round? Please don't think I'm checking up on your progress.'

Through gritted teeth, Daniel made appropriately good-natured noises.

'I promise not to disturb you for long, but I've been dying to meet up ever since you agreed to be our keynote speaker. No need to move from your desk until the doorbell rings. I can be with you in fifteen minutes.'

'I'll put on the coffee.'

Daniel put down the phone and ambled barefoot into the kitchen. Any excuse to stop work was welcome when the words stopped flowing. He felt like a quarryman, hacking at an unforgiving rock face. Yet the call had shattered his concentration, a cause for resentment. At least until he reminded himself that when the phone rang, his thoughts had already drifted away from murder, to DCI Hannah Scarlett.

◇◇◇

Cassie Weston was due for a morning off, but a couple of part-timers had called in sick, victims of the virus sweeping the county, and she'd offered to cover for them up to half-day closing. Marc hated paying overtime, but with Cassie he was happy to make an exception. He even allowed himself to wonder if her willingness to help him out was due to something more than the fact that she was at a loose end on a damp January day.

He joined her at the cash till after she finished serving a woman who ran one of the craft shops in the courtyard and was invariably accompanied by an aggressive little terrier called Whisky. The customer had driven a hard bargain over a first edition about traditional quilting, and Marc could have squeezed a couple of pounds more out of her, but who cared? Even in a shapeless blue sweater and jeans, Cassie looked good. He cast his mind back to the night before last, and her shadow in the window as she stripped.

'Thanks again for filling in.'

'No problem.' She smiled. 'I enjoy it here. And I'm happy to serve the customers with dogs. I don't mind animals, but don't I remember you told me you can't bear them?'

He felt his cheeks redden. Somehow it didn't seem politically correct to admit that he'd had a lifelong dread of man's best friend, but at least Cassie wasn't offended. 'It's only dogs that I can't bear to be near. When I was seven years old, I was bitten by a German Shepherd. The pain was appalling, I thought I was going to die. Of course, it was all right in the end, but these childhood traumas leave a mark, long after the actual scars have healed.'

'You're so right.' Her eyes widened. 'What a terrible experience.'

Thank God she didn't think him a coward. It was as if he'd tested her loyalty, and she'd passed with flying colours. All the same, he didn't feel comfortable admitting a weakness, and he was quick to change the subject.

'So what are you getting up to this afternoon?'

'Why do you ask?'

'Sorry.' He wasn't sure how to play it. 'I didn't mean to pry.'

'No, no, I wasn't suggesting…'

'It's just that…'

'Yes?'

'I'm meeting a dealer in Carnforth this afternoon. He's disposing of a collection of Wainwright firsts and he's offered me first refusal. If you were interested, you could come along, get an idea of pricing stock.'

'I sold that quilting book too cheap, didn't I?'

'No, I didn't mean…'

'You're being kind. I saw the look of triumph on her face. She knew she'd got it cheap. I'm so naïve!' Crestfallen yet gorgeous was nearer to it, Marc thought. 'I bet she waited till you were out of the way before asking how much I'd take for it. I should have…'

'Listen, don't worry. But if you come to Carnforth, you'll haves a chance to see the bigger picture. There's more to selling books than standing behind a counter.'

'I'd love to….oh, shit.'

'What's the matter?'

She shook her head. 'I just remembered. I have a dental appointment this afternoon.'

He felt as though his own teeth had suddenly started to hurt. 'Toothache?'

'No, just a check-up, but I'd better not cancel. National Health dentists are as rare as signed Wordsworths, and I don't want to be kicked off his list. Hope I don't need any treatment, my boyfriend is supposed to be taking me out for a meal afterwards.'

'Some other time.' He could scarcely contain his disappointment.

'I'd really like that.'

Her eagerness cheered him. Impossible not to feel a twinge of jealousy of her boyfriend. Though Marc still wasn't sure he really existed, or was just a convenient alibi to avoid close encounters when it suited her.

◇◇◇

'If once a man indulges himself in murder,' Arlo Denstone proclaimed, 'very soon he comes to think little of robbing; and from robbing he comes next to drinking and Sabbath-breaking, and from that to incivility and procrastination.'

He paused and checked Daniel's expression for approval. He might have been hired by the Cumbria Culture Company for his literary expertise, Daniel thought, but there was a large dollop of showmanship there too.

'Once begun upon this downward path,' Arlo continued, 'you never know where you are to stop. Many a man has dated his ruin from some murder or other that perhaps he thought little of at the time.'

Daniel mimed applause. 'Word perfect.'

Arlo stretched out his legs and lifted the coffee mug from the little table beside his armchair. His white tee shirt revealed long, bony arms. He was one of the skinniest men Daniel had met, borderline anorexic, a reminder perhaps that he was a cancer survivor. Dark, long-lashed eyes kept flicking around as he weighed up his surroundings. A log fire crackled and spat and gave off plenty of heat. Outside the cottage, the sky was morose and rain slammed against the hatchback of the Micra he'd parked next to Daniel's car.

'It's my favourite De Quincey quote. Though he wrote so many wonderful lines. Remember how he bemoans the way people will not submit to having their throats cut quietly, but will run and kick and bite? "Whilst the portrait painter often has to complain of too much torpor in his subject, the artist, in our line, is generally embarrassed by too much animation"? Masterly. Is any other writer of genius so *criminally* under-estimated?'

'Except here in the Lakes?'

'Especially here in the Lakes! We hear more than flesh and blood can bear about William Wordsworth, and plenty about Coleridge. Even Southey, and not forgetting dear old John Ruskin. Poor De Quincey scarcely gets a look in. I hope our Festival will change all that. I'd love people to realise there is so much more to De Quincey than eating opium and living in Dove Cottage. Who knows? The Festival may be the start of something big. Next stop, a De Quincey Trail across the county? He could be the Lakes' new Beatrix Potter.' The long lashes fluttered conspiratorially, encouraging Daniel to share the joke. 'In the meantime, believe me, I can't wait to read your lecture.'

'Right now, I'll be thrilled to finish the first draft.'

Arlo chortled. 'Good to hear that even Daniel Kind sometimes struggles to string a few paragraphs together. When I was an undergraduate, my ambition was to write a novel, but I never made it past the first five thousand words. Now I satisfy my creative energies through writing press releases about literary festivals. It's not quite the same.'

'Enjoying your new job?'

'The chance to return to the Lakes was a dream come true. Trust me, I didn't come for the money. But the people here have been marvellous…well, mostly.'

He paused, like a born gossip hoping to provoke curiosity.

'My sister said she met you at Stuart Wagg's party.'

'Louise, yes. Such a lovely lady. She'll have told you about the little…contretemps?'

'The woman who threw wine over you? Yeah, she did mention it.'

'I bet.' Arlo uttered a theatrical sigh, but Daniel guessed he relished his fifteen minutes of fame. 'Not back in the Lakes five minutes and already I'm making waves. Not my own choice, I can assure you.'

Years spent negotiating the minefield of Oxford college politics had taught Daniel the value of discretion. Adopting a sympathetic expression, he clamped his mouth shut. If Arlo wanted to natter about the incident with Wanda Safell, that was up to him.

'You'll have heard that her husband died before Christmas?'

'Burned to death, Louise told me.'

Arlo squirmed in his chair. 'Yes, horrible.'

'His boathouse went up in flames?'

'By all accounts, it wasn't your average boathouse. A place where he kept his rare books, by all accounts, a bolt-hole up on Ullswater. Wanda was his second wife and I dare say he found her a handful. I met them at the first event I attended, a few days after I took up my post. She'd had a few drinks and.... well, she made it clear that it wasn't just the Festival she was interested in. Very flattering, but needless to say I made my excuses and left.'

Arlo did his best to look embarrassed, but Daniel wasn't convinced. Maybe he wasn't gay, and the faintly camp manner was just a pose. Or a defence mechanism.

'Tricky.'

'Next thing I knew, she was on the phone every other day. She runs a small printing press and produces the occasional limited edition. Including a new book of poetry by a friend of hers that focuses on De Quincey, which she was keen to promote. I was happy to help, but she misread the signals.'

'And then her husband died?'

'Such a shocking tragedy. I thought Wanda would cool down, but on Christmas Eve, she called me again. I suppose I was abrupt with her. I didn't meant to be rude, but she caught me at a bad moment. When I saw her at the party, I wanted to apologise, but she wasn't in the mood for a *rapprochement*. She'd obviously got stuck into the booze at home before she set off for the party. Understandable, I suppose. Perhaps she felt guilty about her husband.'

Daniel stared. 'You're not suggesting she had anything to do with his death?'

Arlo paused before saying, 'Heavens, no. I mean, guilty about having flirted with another man when her husband didn't have long to live.'

'Was the fire an accident?'

'Rumours are flying around that it was started deliberately.'

'By Saffell himself? An insurance scam that got out of hand?'

'He didn't need the money. Wanda told me he sold his business at the top of the market. Maybe someone wanted him dead. When I met him, he seemed a decent sort, but he was an estate agent, after all, and they aren't universally popular.'

'You don't kill someone because they messed up your house move.'

Arlo gave a mischievous grin, and Daniel guessed that when it came to murder cases, he was as much of a voyeur as Thomas De Quincey. 'Who knows what people may do when driven to extremes? Anyway, I'm sorry Wanda interrupted my conversation with Louise. Such a glamorous lady.'

Daniel never thought of Louise as glamorous. She was his sister and he always pigeon-holed her as a starchy lawyer.

'She mentioned that she'd met you.'

'I hadn't realised that she and Stuart Wagg…'

'They got to know each other at a legal seminar. She teaches corporate law.'

'Whirlwind romance, by the sound of it. Stuart's a very successful lawyer, the sort of man you want on your side.'

'How do you mean?'

Arlo lowered his voice, as if afraid of eavesdroppers. 'He has a reputation for ruthlessness. A good friend, and a bad enemy, or so people say. Personally, I find him very civilised. It's wonderful that his firm is sponsoring the Festival. They've even printed a brochure, *Lawyers for Literature*. Of course, Stuart's crazy about books, he collects them with a passion.'

'Like George Saffell.'

'Funny, in other respects you couldn't find two more different characters. George was reserved, nothing like as charismatic as Stuart. Of course, Stuart is younger.'

The phone rang and Daniel reached for the receiver.

'Is that you, Daniel?'

'Louise?'

Her voice was barely recognisable. It wasn't just that she was out of breath. She sounded frightened. He squeezed the receiver tight in hand, as Arlo Denstone leaned forward in his chair, alerted by Daniel's anxious question to the fact that something was amiss.

'I'm in a lay-by near Windermere. Thank God you're at home. Can I come to the cottage right now?'

'What's wrong?'

'It's Stuart.'

'What about him?'

Daniel shot Arlo a glance. He was trying to conceal his inquisitiveness, but his ears were flapping, no mistake.

'We've had a terrible row. It's like nothing I've…'

'What sort of row?'

'Daniel.' He could hear her starting to cry. 'He's…'

'Yes?'

'It's over.' She stifled a sob. 'Dead.'

Chapter Nine

'You'd better get over here right away,' Daniel said.

Louise was gasping at the other end of the phone. She'd run out of words.

'Did you hear me? Right away.'

He was determined not to panic. Trouble was, he'd never heard Louise sound so desperate. Not cool and collected Louise. Her frosty moods and ice-axe tongue had destroyed half a dozen relationships. He disliked Stuart Wagg, and it wasn't the end of their affair that spooked him, but the fear in his sister's voice. As if something terrible had happened, something she dared neither describe nor explain.

'All…all right.'

The line went dead.

'A problem?' Arlo Denstone's dark eyes glinted with curiosity.

Daniel took a breath. 'My sister, she's….'

'Yes?'

'A little upset.'

Lame, but what else could he say? Arlo evidently relished gossip, preferably laced with scandal. Daniel didn't want Louise becoming the talk of the Lakes.

'Of course, you must look after your sister. Believe me, you're so lucky to have her.' Arlo consulted his watch. 'If she is coming here, I'd better get out of your hair. So much to do back at the office, it's all go. Our timetable is tight, let's speak again the moment you finish the Festival paper.'

'Sorry about…'

Arlo extended his hand. 'Nothing to apologise for. I hope Louise isn't in any difficulty. She's a sweet person. I'd like to help. If there's anything I can do, you will let me know?'

'Thanks, but I'm sure everything will be fine.'

As the door closed behind his visitor, Daniel hurried up to the guest bedroom and flung open the window. Rain pounded outside, but the room needed airing. What had happened between Louise and Stuart Wagg? Arlo Denstone's phrase flitted through his mind: *he has a reputation for ruthlessness.*

Not the most tactful message to give to the brother of Wagg's latest squeeze, but perhaps Arlo thought Daniel needed to know. Or did he have an ulterior motive? The faintly camp manner didn't count for much. Arlo might have taken a shine to Louise himself. He hadn't long been back in the UK, and, despite rebuffing Wanda Saffell, he might hanker after female company. Someone intelligent, attractive, self-sufficient.

Such a glamorous lady.

He slammed the cupboard door. Louise's life was difficult enough right now. She didn't need Arlo Denstone making it any more complicated.

The phone trilled.

Jesus, what now? He sped downstairs.

'Is that Daniel Kind?'

He didn't recognise the caller's voice. A slow-speaking man. Elderly, well-educated, Irish accent.

'Speaking.'

'It's about your sister.'

Daniel checked the screen. The number of the caller's phone was familiar. It was Louise's mobile.

Fear clutched his throat. When he spoke, his own voice sounded scratchy and unfamiliar.

'Who are you?'

'My name's O'Brien, but that doesn't matter. I'm calling about your sister.'

'Is she all right?'

'She's had an accident, but...'

'For God's sake!'

He had to force himself not to scream. Impossible for Louise to die. He couldn't cope without her. In that instant, he realised how much she meant to him, even though he'd never acknowledged it, even to himself. But he'd lost his father, and later his mother. Then Aimee. Even bloody Miranda had left him, but Louise was always there. Intense and prickly, yet the one person he could trust. The one person who understood him

'Keep your hair on. She's alive and kicking, thank goodness. She asked me to let you know. Car's a write-off, I'm afraid. The police are here and a couple of paramedics, but...'

'Where are you?'

'On the Brack Road, half a mile from the village.'

'I'm on my way.'

◇◇◇

'We all had a lucky escape, if you ask me. A very lucky escape.'

O'Brien was a talkative Dubliner in his early sixties. He and his wife, a tiny woman with dyed red hair who sat knitting in the passenger seat of their ancient Vauxhall and kept her thoughts to herself, probably the result of long marital experience, had been spending the New Year with their daughter and son-in-law at their bungalow in Brack. They were driving off to the Holyhead ferry when Louise's Mercedes skidded as it raced round a bend and finished up on the wrong side of the road. Steering into the skid at the last moment, she had caught the Vauxhall's front bumper a glancing blow before finishing up in a shallow ditch.

'Too right.'

It was a miracle that she was still in one piece. The front of the car was crumpled like a used tissue, but she'd clambered out with no more than a twinge in her shoulder and a bruised elbow. O'Brien had been driving at a sedate twenty five miles an hour and had kept his car on the road. The damage looked superficial and neither he nor his wife seemed to have suffered whiplash. The paramedics had checked Louise and the O'Briens, and they all briskly declined the offer of a more thorough examination at A&E in Westmorland General.

The rain had paused for breath, and patches of lightness softened the sky. In a field beyond the hedge stood a spiky, windblown oak tree, back bent by a century of gales roaring through the narrow valley. A quartet of Herdwick sheep surveyed the activity of the emergency services with bemused fatalism. In the distance, mist cloaked the corrugated ridges of the fell-tops that made up the Kentmere Horseshoe. The air was filled by the hum of the recovery wagon, as it hauled the Mercedes out of the ditch.

Louise waited on a sodden verge of grass and mud. For a woman who had made such a frightened phone call and then come within kissing distance of death minutes later, her apparent calm was surreal. Daniel's knees felt as though they might give way with sheer relief. She was charming a tubby middle-aged constable in an attempt to convince him that this sort of accident could happen to anyone in treacherous weather conditions, and that it would be absurd to contemplate a charge of driving without due care and attention. From the constable's sympathetic nods and failure to get in a word edgeways, Daniel suspected she might just get away with it.

'So your sister lives with you here in Brackdale?'

It struck Daniel that he and Louise had never lived together, just the two of them, with nobody else in the house. How would it work? Even after Ben deserted them, their mother was always around.

'Um...yes.'

'You seem more shocked than she is.' O'Brien rubbed his hands with theatrical vigour, as though an anorak and chunky sweater weren't enough to keep him warm. 'Tell me, do I know your face from somewhere?'

At least it was better than: *didn't you used to be Daniel Kind?* Daniel's instinct was to brush away questions about his years as a media tart. He'd come to the Lakes to escape from that stuff. But he didn't want to be rude. All things considered, O'Brien was a model of Christian forgiveness. Daniel guessed that he prided himself on remaining calm in a crisis.

'I've done a bit of television.'

'History!' O'Brien beamed in triumph at his feat of memory. 'Thought as much. I never forget a face. I've always been interested in the Second World War, myself. The Dunkirk spirit, we could do with more of that these days.'

Daniel made polite conversation as the car was towed away. He supposed Louise regretted that, in the first moments of shock after the crash, she'd begged O'Brien to send for him. She always liked to be in charge. But she needed a lift to Tarn Fold. That squashed Mercedes was destined for the crusher.

By the time she was ready to go, the chime of the clock in Brack village marked one o'clock. The police constable decided not to add to Cumbria's crime statistics, the paramedics departed to tend to someone less fortunate, and Louise lavished thanks upon the Irish couple and made sure they had her insurance company's details. With handshakes, waves and a cheerful toot of the horn, the O'Briens resumed their journey home.

When they were finally alone, Louise breathed out. She stared towards the horizon, as if trying to pinpoint an invisible hill, not yet trusting herself to look into her brother's eyes.

'Another fine mess I got myself into, huh?'

'Could have been worse.'

'You know something? I'm sure you must be right, but at this precise moment, I don't see how things could be any fucking worse.'

She'd kept her composure for long enough. Suddenly she was vulnerable and scared, and that cool façade crumpled like the front of her sports car. Daniel wrapped his arms around her and felt her shudder as she surrendered to loud, racking sobs.

◇◇◇

Back at Tarn Cottage, Daniel made himself a sandwich, but all Louise wanted was brandy, insisting that if she had anything to eat, she'd throw up. As she curled up in an armchair in the living room, and dozed, Daniel warmed his hands in front of the fire, waiting for her to come round so that he could find out what had gone wrong.

'How are you feeling?' he asked when she stirred and opened her eyes. 'Headache, muscle pain?'

'Stop fussing.'

'You could have broken your neck. When I saw your car in that ditch…'

'I know,' she muttered. 'I'll be all right, promise.'

He stretched out his legs. 'You want to rest, or talk?'

She gazed at a hairline crack that ran across the whitewashed ceiling, and didn't utter a word. Her eyelids were heavy. No wonder after a night without rest, never mind the brandy.

'What happened at Crag Gill, Louise?'

'You don't want to know.'

He shook his head. 'Tell me.'

In a muffled voice, she said, 'Shall I tell you what's so funny? When I fell for Stuart, I actually thought this was the real thing. Him and me. Can you believe it?'

He waited.

'I've not fallen head over heels for a man since…God knows, when. I was nineteen or something. I thought I was armour-plated against infatuation. But Stuart knocked me sideways.'

She stared at her nails. Today they were deep purple, a vivid contrast to the white of her thin, delicate fingers. Daniel kept his mouth shut. Let her take this at her own pace.

'I thought he was so amazing, you know? I so like successful men.' She was talking to herself. 'Stuart was different from your average small town lawyer. A City slicker, but his love of the Lakes persuaded me he was special. The look in his eye when he spoke about clambering over the crags and along the coffin trails. He liked to wander…'

'Lonely as a cloud?'

A feeble attempt at humour. Louise groaned.

'You hated him, didn't you?'

'I hardly know him.'

'Ever the diplomat, Daniel.'

'One of us needs to be.'

'Stuart is the most selfish man I've ever met.'

He breathed out. 'That's saying something.'

'Given my track record in choosing lousy lovers? No need to rub it in.' Her voice rose. 'I'm quite capable of flagellating myself, thanks. Besides, it's not simply his selfishness. He's cruel.'

Daniel leaned forward. 'Cruel?'

'He has no conscience. You should hear the way he talks about people, as though they were only put on Earth for his convenience. When they aren't useful to him any longer, they might as well be dead, for all he cares. Like Wanda Saffell.'

'What about her?'

'They had something going at one time.'

'While she was married to George?'

'Don't sound so shocked. Stuart couldn't care less. For him, women are like books, though he prefers books, because they don't answer back.' She was talking rapidly now, fired up by the alcohol, determined to make him understand. 'But books or women, they're trophies, to be collected and then stashed away. It's not just the thrill of the chase, for him it's about having something that looks good. Along with the private pleasure of possession. He savours it, you've no idea. I doubt he reads one in ten of the books that he buys. Spends a fortune on them, then locks them away. He told me ninety per cent of the value of a rare book is in the condition of the dust jacket. Can you imagine? Nothing to do with what's inside. They have to be kept out of the bright light. It wouldn't do for the spines of those lovely jackets to catch the sun. So he keeps them hidden away, as long as he knows they are his, that's all that matters. It turns him on to have something that someone else yearns for. Now it's a book, now it's another man's wife. Same difference, as far as Stuart Wagg is concerned.'

Tirade over, she slumped back in her chair. Daniel gave her a minute before he spoke again.

Tears welled in her eyes again as she said, 'It's my fault, nobody else's. How could I have been so daft?'

Daft. He'd not heard her use that word since they were kids together in Manchester. 'We all do daft things sometimes.'

'I chucked away a decent job and followed him up here, like a star-struck schoolgirl. I suppose I heard the biological clock ticking, but that's no excuse.'

'You want children?'

He couldn't help asking. The drink had loosened her tongue; she'd never hinted at maternal instincts before. Since her teens, she'd made a song and dance about building a career, scornful of stay-at-home mums who lived vicariously through their offspring and failed to make the most of their own abilities.

Through gritted teeth, she said, 'I may be stupid and naïve, Daniel, but I'm not quite as inhuman as you think.'

'It's just that you never said…'

'I can't bear people who wear their heart on their sleeve. I thought, if kids happen, they happen. But as I've grown older, I haven't always found myself good company. It wouldn't hurt to focus on looking after a child, instead of just myself. I might even find I was a good mother. Stuart said I would.'

'You discussed having children with him?'

He couldn't disguise his amazement. That bastard Wagg, he'd figured out which buttons to press with the skill of a lifelong manipulator.

'He murmured once or twice about wanting to settle down. The single man's equivalent of "My wife doesn't understand me." I was blind not to see through the sales pitch. He saw me as a challenge. That's what turned him on. Once he'd proved he could bend me to his will, he'd won, and it was game over. I should have known better. I blame myself.'

'Forget about blame.'

'How can I? You saw what happened.' Two pink spots appeared in her pale cheeks. 'He wanted company for Christmas, plus loads of sex. I wanted to be the perfect hostess for his fucking party and he was prepared to pay. He spent more on that necklace for me than I earn in a term at Uni. But his New Year resolution was to get rid of me. Your return to Brackdale was ideal timing. His plan was to lumber you with me while he disappeared off up the fells. When I didn't go along with his script, he made life hell for me.'

'How did he do that?'

'Let's just say, he has a nasty imagination.'

With windows and door shut tight, the living room was hot and stuffy. The only sound was the roaring of the fire. Daniel clenched his fist.

'Jesus, did he hurt you?'

'Only my pride.' She breathed hard. 'I'll spare you the gory details. Some things stay private, all right? Trust me, I recognised it was a huge risk, giving everything up to follow a man I hardly knew. But I was bored with Manchester, ready for a new challenge at work. And, frankly, gagging for excitement. Does that make any sense?'

'I came up here on a whim with Miranda. Same thing.'

She blinked. 'Look, I don't want to impose on you. I'll get out of your hair as soon as...'

'Stay as long as you like. Please.'

She reached out and squeezed his hand.

'I don't want to be nosey,' he said.

'Oh yeah?'

'Seriously, I don't. But I don't get it. How come everything fell apart so fast?'

'It dawned on me that he was treating me like one of his bloody books. He lavished a lot of money on me. Not only the necklace. Designer clothes, a new hairstyle, you name it. But once he'd showed me off to his friends at the party, he was ready to put me back on the shelf. His last two girlfriends were leggy models in their twenties. I was different, having me in tow proved he could turn even a hard-bitten old cow into a simpering groupie.'

'You're not hard-bitten, or an old cow. And I've never seen you simper.'

'I didn't simper enough to suit Stuart, for sure. He became secretive, I convinced myself he was texting another leggy admirer.'

'Might have been your imagination.'

'I've been cheated on before, Daniel. I can pick up the signs.'

He bit his tongue. She was making a supreme effort to keep herself together. He mustn't say anything to precipitate another collapse.

'At bed-time last night, we had a terrible row when I told him I wasn't a toy he could pick up and drop as he pleased. He finished up snoring in one of the guest rooms while I tossed and turned. By the time morning came, I was ready for a showdown. The affair was dead and buried, but I wanted to end it on my terms. I packed my case and put it in the boot of the Merc. I parked by the back door, ready for a quick getaway, but I refused to scuttle off like a thief in the night. I had to tell Stuart what I thought about him. He got up late, and said he was setting off for a walk, but he didn't expect me still to be there when he got back. So I let rip and told him a few home truths.'

'I don't suppose he's accustomed to people standing up to him.'

Voice breaking, she said, 'It was horrible, like nothing I've experienced before. He didn't shout. Not like me, I must admit. But he said some…vicious things. I won't repeat them. I'll never tell anyone what he said. His raw anger terrified me. I realised I didn't know him at all, I didn't have a clue what he was capable of.'

'So you walked out on him?'

She buried her head in her hands.

'I lost it, Daniel. You'd never have believed it, would you? But I was furious and frightened, half out of my mind. We were in the breakfast kitchen and Stuart came towards me. He was only wearing his shorts, but his face was crimson with rage and I thought he was going to hit me…'

Daniel knelt beside her and took her hand. It felt as cold as snow.

'I'm sorry,' she whispered.

The logs on the fire growled. For all the warmth of the room, he shivered. She was summoning up the courage to make a confession, he was sure of it.

But a confession to what?

Louise murmured something inaudible and he bent closer to her lips to hear.

'I wish I was dead.'

'You did your best to kill yourself on the way here.'

'I…I should have done.'

'You mustn't ever say that,' he snapped.

She lifted her head and a damp face brushed against his cheek.

'I picked up the kitchen scissors and lashed out, like a crazy woman. I just meant to scare him off, but the scissors caught him as he came for me and he screamed with pain. I saw blood trickling down his chest. Then I ran for the door and jumped into the car. Put my foot down and didn't stop till Crag Gill was out of sight.'

Chapter Ten

An indigo sky glowered at Daniel as he prowled the strange, haphazard grounds of Tarn Cottage. Although he'd solved some of the cipher garden's mysteries, it remained as remote and unknowable as a lover who spoke a different language. Today it seemed dank and sinister, with secluded corners, meandering paths and unexpected dead ends. The ground was greasy after so much rain, and the excess water that hadn't yet seeped into the soil formed criss-crossing puddles that resembled an exquisite calligraphy. He picked his way with care past the reed-fringed lake, towards a clearing separated from the rest of the garden by a picket fence and bounded by two monkey puzzles, a yew and a weeping willow.

The dark bulk of Tarn Fell reared up in front of him and through scraps of mist he could make out Priest Ridge, and the Sacrifice Stone. The wind chewed at his cheeks, and sliced through his clothes. His hands were numb, his feet tingling with the cold. The atmosphere was pregnant with the threat of thunder. If he didn't head back for the hot living room, he would be soaked to the skin. But he wasn't ready to go back indoors.

Louise was asleep in the guest bedroom. A torrid night and calamitous morning had drained every last scrap of her energy. His temples throbbed, his thoughts were as tangled as the undergrowth. It was hard to grasp. Louise—of all people—had stuck a knife in her lover before running off to crash her car into a ditch.

What scared him was that she had form. If asked to describe his sister, he'd say without thinking that she hadn't a violent bone in her body. But it wasn't the whole truth. Once before, she'd defended herself when afraid, a defensive act of violence that briefly threatened her future.

During the summer between finishing at school and starting her law degree course at Durham, she'd gone out on a few dates with a student who lived nearby. At midnight one drunken evening, he'd tried to seduce her on the front room sofa, while his lone parent mother was out at a hen party. Frightened by his refusal to take no for an answer, she tried to fend him off by slapping his face. The lad lost his balance and fell against the side of a wrought-iron coffee table. He smashed his cheekbone and suffered severe lacerations to his face. When his mother arrived home moments later, he tried to cover the pain and humiliation by claiming Louise had gone berserk and attacked him simply because he'd ventured a clumsy kiss. The mother, furious and over-protective, insisted on calling the police. The boy's injuries needed surgery, and it looked as though Louise's career in the law might be still-born. In the end, the police saw through the lad's story and he was lucky to avoid a charge of attempted rape.

Daniel and Louise had only ever spoken about the incident once, and he'd never forget her unrepentant ferocity.

'He got what he deserved.'

When cornered, Louise's instinct was to lash out. She would grab the nearest weapon at hand. The time before, no lasting harm had been done. But Daniel knew that history never repeats itself in precisely the same way. Just as well Stuart Wagg didn't keep a shotgun.

Was her car crash all it seemed? He refused to believe she meant to kill herself when she hurtled round that bend on the Brack Road. He knew about the impulse to self-destruct. Aimee, his lover in Oxford, had plunged to her death from the old Saxon tower in the middle of crowded Cornmarket. Yet Aimee was fragile, a polar opposite from his sister. Louise was resilient—at least until she'd succumbed to Stuart Wagg. The affair left her like a druggie on a bad trip; reckless, frantic, and out of control. Moving in with a man she hardly knew, waving a pair of scissors at him the moment he wanted rid of her. She must have been very unhappy with her old life. And he'd swanned off to the States without having a clue.

Pangs of guilt assailed him. He'd been preoccupied with his own losses, first of Aimee and then Miranda, barely giving Louise a second thought. He owed it to her to make amends. As the first drops of rain flicked his cheeks, he touched a branch of the monkey puzzle tree. The spikes were sharp and left a tiny drop of blood on the edge of his fingernail.

Had she thrust the scissors into Stuart Wagg with sufficient force to cause serious harm? She thought she'd only caught him a glancing blow, on the shoulder rather than the chest. But she hadn't hung around to check.

In the trees, an invisible owl hooted. If Wagg was badly hurt, he'd have dialled 999. The police would soon be on the scene, as well as an ambulance. Only a question of time before they came knocking on Daniel's door. Or suppose the injury was life-threatening, suppose Wagg had lost consciousness even as Louise made good her escape? Suppose he lay sprawled on the kitchen floor, helpless and alone?

Heart beating faster, he turned on his heel and raced back towards the cottage as the rain drove down. He took a short cut across a tangled patch of couch grass and brambles that divided the labyrinthine paths. Before leaving for America, he'd laid stepping stones, but now they were coated with moss and as treacherous as on the gravel and stone flags. Within moments, his feet gave way under him and he crashed to the ground.

He ended up in a heap amongst the stinging nettles. Bruised and aching, he hauled himself back on to his feet and wiped the mud off his jeans. The moment he got his breath back, he set off again. Must keep moving. No time to lose.

◇◇◇

'You can't go to Crag Gill!'

Louise was awake and aghast. She couldn't have slept for more than half an hour before he roused her, but already the spark had returned.

'No choice. We don't know what state he's in.'

'I barely touched him. I only picked up the scissors to defend myself. I'd never even have made contact if he hadn't lunged at me.'

'He might be badly hurt. Unable to call for help.'

'It was only a scratch!'

'We have to make sure.'

Her voice dropped to a whisper. 'Stuart will lie about what happened.'

'Meaning what?'

'He's brutal, vindictive, you have no idea. It will be like Jeremy, but a thousand times worse.'

Jeremy was the student with the over-protective mother.

'It's not the same…'

'Listen to me, Daniel. The things he said simply because I decided to walk out on him before he dumped me…you've no idea. His pride's hurt, he'll destroy me if he can. He did his best before I picked up those scissors. Now…'

He picked up Louise's mobile from the bedside table. Cradling it in his palm, he scrolled down the list of dialled calls. She dropped off the bed and tried to snatch the phone from him, but she lost her balance and slipped back down on to the duvet.

'You can't do this to me!' she muttered. 'It's so…'

A throaty rumble of thunder interrupted her, followed by rain hammering down on the cottage, like a wild creature demanding admission. Lightning flashed through a slit in the curtains. They were only a mile from the eye of the storm.

'You're already in the shit, Louise.' He found the number for Crag Gill and started to dial. 'Don't make things worse.'

'You've reached Stuart Wagg.' The voice sounded congratulatory. 'I'm not at home at present. You know the drill, leave your name and number after the tone and I'll get back to you soon as I can.'

Daniel ended the call and said, 'I'll try his mobile.'

'Hi, this is Stuart Wagg. Leave a message after the tone.'

Daniel took a breath and hissed at the handset. 'Stuart, this is Daniel Kind. Can you ring me at the cottage as soon as possible?'

'For fuck's sake!' Louise's voice shook. 'Why did you have to leave a message?'

'I need to find out what shape he's in. For all we know, he's in Westmorland General at this very moment. Let's hope he's not in intensive care.'

She wasn't listening. Her eyes locked on the framed print of Derwent Water that hung above the chest of drawers, she murmured, 'I'm begging you not to do this. I really don't want you to talk to him.'

'And I didn't want you to stab him with his own kitchen scissors,' he snapped 'Did you keep a key to the house? I'm on my way to make sure he's all right.'

◇◇◇

Bullets of rain bounced off the windscreen as Daniel sped out of Brackdale. The road surfaces were uneven, with deep pools everywhere. Each time he passed another vehicle, spray squirted across the windscreen, blinding him. He couldn't put his foot down for fear that he too would skid off into the hedgerow. If he crashed, he might not be as lucky as Louise.

Not that she saw herself as lucky. The words echoed in his brain.

He'll destroy me if he can.

All Daniel wanted right now was to be sure that Louise hadn't destroyed Stuart Wagg. He hadn't worked out what to say, assuming the man was still in one piece. Better make it up as he went along. He wouldn't plead, or threaten, just make sure that Wagg didn't cause his sister any more grief. If he left Louise alone, she'd get over him, given time. She'd had plenty of practice in coming to terms with relationships that didn't work out.

The storm had eased to an ill-tempered drizzle as he pulled up outside the entrance to Crag Gill. A pair of heavy oak gates barred the drive. On either side of them stretched a seven foot high hawthorn hedge. He grabbed a pencil torch and yanked the hood of his jacket over his head. A CCTV camera squatted on top of one of the gate pillars.

He gabbled into the entry phone. 'Stuart, are you there? This is Daniel Kind.'

No answer.

He yanked his mobile out of his pocket and rang his sister.

'What's the code to open the front gates?'

'2011. His birthday is 20th November. But…'

'Better get back to bed.'

'Daniel, this is crazy. It was only a flesh wound, I swear. Anything worse…it isn't possible.'

As she talked, he keyed the security numbers in sequence, but the gates did not as much as twitch. He tried again. Still no joy.

'Did you close the gates when you left?'

'Of course not. I wanted to get away as fast as possible. There's a lay-by half a mile from the house. That's where I stopped to phone you.'

'So he must have closed the gates himself?'

'I expect so. You're worrying about nothing.'

'Louise, you stuck a pair of kitchen scissors into him. Left him bleeding. I don't want you to finish up in court on a charge of GBH.'

He switched off the phone. Was he making a drama out of a crisis? Neither of them was exactly rational this afternoon. She claimed Wagg's injury wasn't serious, but she might be fooling herself. Wagg could have shut the gates and then collapsed. It wasn't unknown for stab victims to walk around for a while as if nothing was wrong before they dropped down dead.

There was the narrowest of gaps between one of the stone pillars and the hedge. Barely enough for a child to squeeze through. He took a couple of paces back, put his head down and forced his way into it. The branches fought hard and the thorns tore at his clothes, but he managed to overcome their resistance. Soon he was out on the other side.

It wasn't yet half past three, but the light was fading. Night came early in winter here. Ahead was the low bulk of Crag Gill. On his previous visit, when Louise brought him to say hello to Stuart Wagg, she'd explained that house was built on the site of a rambling mansion, for forty years home to an ancient bachelor. The man had inherited it on the day of the Coronation and hadn't so much as given it a lick of paint since. Not even the most zealous conservation officer could argue when Wagg knocked down the old ruin. To replace it, he hired a Swedish architect to indulge in a flight of fancy green enough to dazzle the planning authority. The rebuilt house was modest in size compared to some of the palaces bordering the east bank of Windermere.

Daniel splashed across ruthlessly cropped grass, between a pair of mountainous rhododendron bushes with dank and dripping leaves. But for a scattering of winter heathers, purple and white in the borders, the garden was asleep until spring. Tall lamp-stands lined the long drive, but no lights shone. The house was in darkness. His torch beam was thin, but it helped keep his bearings.

As he drew close to the front porch, his skin prickled. The torchlight picked out another surveillance camera, suspended beneath the line of the grass roof of the house. No surprise—Wagg's collection of books alone must be worth as much as the average semi-detached. But if the owner of Crag Gill was watching, he would only see a hooded figure, striding towards his door.

A security alarm was fixed to the front wall, six feet above the porch. Daniel had seen its red light winking, when Louise brought him here to introduce Stuart Wagg. Now it was dead. The electricity supply to Crag Gill must have been cut off. Chances were that the thunderstorm had brought down the power lines.

He rang the bell for the sake of it, but no sound came. There was a huge brass knocker on the door and Daniel rapped hard for thirty seconds. In the silence, the crash of iron against wood was deafening. If Wagg was inside, he must have heard.

No answer.

Daniel touched the handle of the door, not expecting it to move, but it swung open. A swift movement, unexpectedly light.

'Shit.'

People who lived in the Lake District were inclined to be trusting. Crime rates were low compared to most of England; that was one of the reasons why so many fled here, sick of crime in the city. He often left the door of Tarn Cottage on the latch when he headed off for a walk along Priest Ridge, or to shop in the village store in Brack. But he didn't have so much to lose— Crag Gill was stuffed with treasures. He couldn't believe that Wagg would forget to lock up.

He shivered, as if from a weird thrill of excitement. Was this how it felt to be a burglar, breaking into the home of people whose lives meant nothing to him? He had to enter the house, he dared not leave now. Impossible to guess what he would discover inside Crag Gill. Stuart Wagg might be unconscious, or so incapacitated that he could not call for help.

Or dead.

One stride, and Daniel was over the threshold.

In his imagination, lights blazed and sirens screamed and the place filled with people, shouting and waving their arms. He'd walked into a trap and tomorrow's headlines would gloat over the story: *Former TV historian found breaking into top lawyer's home.* Pop psychiatrists would be wheeled out to analyse how Aimee's suicide, his abandonment of Oxford and the glittering prizes, and the flight to Brackdale all played a part in his downfall.

None of it happened.

Nothing stirred.

Crag Gill's entrance hall wasn't much smaller than Carlisle Cathedral. According to Louse, Wagg suffered from claustrophobia, and he'd insisted that even the cloakrooms should be airy and spacious. Daniel's torch played on the white walls, lingered on the whirls and splodges of the trendily unpleasant paintings that hung on them. This wasn't so much a home as a showcase; the modern art looked as if it had been bought by the yard. Probably at enormous expense, even if its value might one day plummet like derivatives from a bank gone bust. Wagg was rich enough not to care. Dust jackets were the artwork he loved, and they were too precious to be flattened and framed.

A door on the left led into the entertaining room. The curtains weren't closed. No hint of the New Year revelries, not even a crumb. A massive L-shaped sofa occupied the middle of the room. Daniel marched over to it. Thank God, there wasn't a corpse hidden behind it.

Next stop, the dining kitchen. Gleaming cedar units, a glass table almost as long as the platform at Oxenholme Station, a dozen chairs in pristine black leather. This was the scene of Louise's supposed crime. What had happened to her weapon? The scissors weren't lying on any of the surfaces, and when he looked in the drawers, he found a clean pair with the cutlery. He bent down and studied the slate floor tiles, but couldn't see the faintest smear of blood. Had Wagg, a tidy man, washed the scissors and put them away? He sniffed the air. Nothing but the sterile smell of emptiness. This was the deepest point of winter, but the house wasn't cold. He brushed a wall radiator with his palm. It felt warm, so the gas supply was still working.

On the other side of the hall was the library. Wagg had brought him in here on his previous visit. The window was tiny, with blinds drawn to minimise the risk of sunlight fading the spines. Bookshelves stretched from floor to ceiling. Like the rest of Crag Gill, the library was as lifeless as a tomb.

He checked upstairs, starting with the master bedroom. Black silk sheets, and above the king-size bed was a huge mirror. The furnishings had cost a fortune, but the room looked like a set for a seedy movie. Daniel decided not to think about it.

Soon he had inspected every corner of the house. No sign of Wagg, no clue to his whereabouts. He spent a few minutes prowling around outside, but it was too dark to make a thorough search of the grounds. Wagg wasn't sprawled over the grass that stretched down to the water's edge, but the garage and the outbuildings, unlike the house, were locked.

Daniel recalled Louise taking about her lover, on their way here from the airport.

'When Stuart is in the mood, he can be so much fun. But his boredom threshold is even lower than yours. He's a mass of contradictions. A party animal who is happiest when he's walking the fells on his own. That's why he never moved from the Lakes. He has the luxury of being able to head into the hills at a moment's notice. If his partners or his clients don't like it, tough. Because he's so good at what he does, they put up with his maverick ways.'

This could explain it. After Louise had fled, Wagg must have set off for the fells. All the forecasters' warnings about bad weather wouldn't faze a man in a temper who needed solitude, He returned to the warmth of the kitchen and dialled Tarn Cottage. Louise snatched up the receiver on the second ring.

'Daniel?'

'The house is unlocked, and the power is off, but I can't find him anywhere.'

'Where are you now?'

'Unfreezing my hands on the kitchen radiator.'

'There's no trace of blood?'

'Why would there be? You only gave him a tiny scratch, remember?'

She ignored the jibe. 'It doesn't make sense.'

'Might he have stomped off and forgotten to lock up?'

'Not Stuart. He's fanatical about security. The thought that anyone might nick his beloved books…'

'Maybe he was so furious that he wasn't acting rationally. Might have headed for the Langdale Pikes.' He hesitated. 'Or A&E.'

'Why don't you believe me?' She was shouting into the phone, and he moved it away from his ear. 'I barely grazed him.'

'Whatever. The fact is, he isn't at home, and anyone could walk into Crag Gill like I just did and loot the place from top to bottom.'

He heard her swearing to herself and waited.

'There's a spare set of keys hanging up on the inside of the door of the cupboard over the microwave. I left them there this morning. No more use for them. You'd better lock up.'

'Okay. I'll call his office and see if they've heard from him. Can you give me the number?'

He found the keys and re-dialled. The receptionist put him through to Wagg's P.A. She couldn't tell him anything other than that her boss didn't like to be disturbed on holiday, unless for a real emergency. When Daniel pressed, she gave in and transferred him to another partner.

'Raj Doshi speaking.' Smooth and reassuring as music from pan pipes, a calm bedside manner conveyed in three little words. Louise had mentioned Doshi a couple of times. He specialised in divorce work. It was Doshi who had taken Wanda Saffell home after the contretemps on New Year's Eve. 'How can I help you, Mr. Kind?'

'I need to speak to Stuart Wagg.'

'Your sister doesn't have a problem, I hope?'

Doshi must know Wagg's reputation with women. Did the way he used them impact on the business, or his colleagues? Or was he so important to the firm that he was untouchable, that whatever he did, they were happy to turn a blind eye?

'Stuart and I need to talk. Soon, if you don't mind.'

'I'm sorry, Mr. Kind, but I cannot help. Stuart isn't due back until next week, and if he's not answering his home phone or his mobile...'

'Does he often blip off the radar screen like this?'

'You have met Stuart, Mr. Kind?'

'Twice.'

'Then you will realise he is his own man.'

'Look, my sister and I are worried. I'm at Crag Gill right now. The power lines seem to be down and he appears to have left his house unlocked.'

A discreet cough. Possibly the closest Doshi ever came to expressing shock-horror.

'Unlocked, you say?'

'Uh-huh.'

'How do you know?'

'I...um...I tried the front door.'

Best not to admit to a solicitor that he'd spent the past hour trespassing.

'I used my sister's keys to lock the door and secure the house.'

Or at least he would do, the minute he walked out of this empty place.

'That's good of you.'

'It doesn't explain what has happened to Stuart Wagg.'

'He loves walking, Mr. Kind, he's probably on his way home even as we speak.'

'And the fact he left his house open to any Tom, Dick or Harry in the middle of a power cut?'

'I don't always lock my own front door, Mr. Kind.'

'So you think there's no cause for concern?'

'I am sure there is a straightforward explanation. Thank you, though, for letting us know. Good afternoon.'

The phone was put down. See no evil, hear no evil, speak no evil. Doshi wasn't a lawyer for nothing. Not knowing what to do for the best, Daniel decided to trust to instinct.

Time to call Hannah Scarlett.

Chapter Eleven

Was it significant, Wanda Saffell's name cropping up in the Bethany Friend enquiry? In conversation with Maggie, Hannah played it down. The young DC's enthusiasm was one of her virtues, but no sense in jumping to conclusions. Cumbria was a small world, albeit so diverse that anyone could be forgiven for forgetting. The local population was tiny, once you stripped out seasonal workers and tourists who came from all four corners of the globe. For the wife of suspected murder victim to be interviewed in relation to the unexplained death, six years ago, of a work colleague barely registered on the Richter Scale of coincidence.

But you never knew. Wanda intrigued Hannah. The sight of Arlo Denstone, drenched with red wine at the New Year party, remained as vivid in her memory as the stain on his white jacket. Wanda had a temper, and she lacked restraint. She'd had too much to drink that night, and seemed at the end of her tether. But it didn't mean she had anything do with Bethany's death. The brutal shock of having a husband roasted alive was enough to drive anyone to distraction.

'I'll pay her a visit.'

'She has this little business in Ambleside, can't be more than a mile away from your new house.' Maggie thrust a scribbled note into her hand. 'Here's the address.'

'Thanks. I'm having breakfast with Fern Larter tomorrow. She can brief me on Wanda.'

'I don't like the sound of her.' Maggie folded her arms as she pronounced judgement. She was a sturdy young woman, from a family which had farmed in the Lakes for five generations, and were the sort of people who believed that there was no such thing as bad weather, only bad clothing. She didn't have much time for shades of grey. Or for posh women who printed obscure volumes of poetry. For all her diligence, she'd need a more flexible mindset if she wanted to shin up the greasy pole. 'Her witness statement is only a page long, but she comes over as heartless. And she must be in the frame for her husband's murder.'

'Assuming he was murdered. Let's not run ahead of ourselves before the Coroner has had his say. Let alone the CPS. Wanda is a grieving widow, we'd better not forget that.'

Maggie's jaw was set firm. Like most of the foot-soldiers in the force, she suspected the Crown Prosecution Service of devoting its time and energy to thinking up reasons not to prosecute.

'A black widow, maybe.'

'We'll see.' Hannah slapped Maggie on the shoulder, a gesture of encouragement to counter-balance her caution. 'In the meantime, well done.'

◇◇◇

Hannah asked the admin assistant to set up a meeting with Wanda while she attended a New Year sermon from Lauren. The ACC's theme was that the CID had to change with the times and she went on and on like an automated phone system. Press one for inclusive policing. Press two for a critique of gender stereotyping. Her latest big idea was a weekend conference for senior detectives at 'a top secret location' which would turn out to be some dreary hotel in the Yorkshire Dales. The ACC droned on ad nauseam about the force's ever-increasing number of 'partnerships' with assorted authorities, units, agencies and projects before introducing a shiny young woman called India Sturridge, the latest recruit to Cumbria Constabulary's team of spin doctors. India looked barely old enough to be out of university, but she was bound to be paid more than the likes of

Maggie Eyre, although she'd never be asked to put her life on the line. Having taken the precaution of wearing a very low-cut blouse, she was assured of the attention of a predominantly male audience. Hannah sensed Greg Wharf shifting in his chair, as he composed his next chat-up line.

'We wanted to make a statement,' Lauren announced, though India's tanned flesh was the only statement Greg and most of the others were interested in. 'This appointment is a tangible sign of our commitment to effective and targeted communication with local communities.'

'My aim is simple,' India trilled. 'To support the fantastic job my new colleagues do in making the Lake District an area that is not only safer, but feels safer. Our business is not just to cut crime but to manage the public's perception of crime.'

So that was all right, then.

'CID?' Les Bryant demanded when they repaired to the bar at the end of the shift for a quick drink and communal moan. 'Criminal Investigation in Decline, if you ask me. In my day, you'd fill a page of a notebook writing up a sudden death. Now you have to produce War and Bloody Peace. That's why the likes of Nick Lowther are fucking off to places like Canada and Australia. I can remember the time when detectives dreaded the thought of demotion. Now they punish you by keeping you in the CID. Loading up your unpaid overtime, taking away your plain clothes allowance.'

'Why do you think they didn't send me back to uniform?' Greg Wharf asked, wiping the froth from his pint from his mouth. 'That's where you get a decent work-life balance.'

'You'd never have dreamed…' Les began, before breaking into a violent sneeze.

'No wonder the CID is advertising so many vacancies.'

The pair had already formed a double-act, Hannah thought, as she sipped her lemonade. The Disgruntled Detectives. But she guessed Ben Kind would have agreed. Fewer cops aspired to be a chief inspector these days, simply because of the long hours. Rest days routinely cancelled, duty rotas and shifts changed at short notice. Performance targets were poisoning police work. The government had created three thousand new offences in the past decade, to prove they were dealing with crime. So stupid kids had to be 'sanctioned' for offences such as being in possession of an egg with intent to throw it. Detective work was skewed towards statistics, and away from time-consuming stuff like burglary and rape. Officers were nailed to their desks, filling out forms to satisfy the demands of an army of lawyers and social workers.

'You don't calm down a domestic nowadays.' Greg leaned back in his chair, lamenting the Good Old Days. 'You provoke someone to lash out, then arrest them. Crime, detection, clear-up, all in a couple of minutes. Easy peasy.'

'We do need to reach out more…' Hannah decided it was time to give the ACC a bit of support, but was at once drowned out by a chorus of protests.

'You wait. There are forces out there wearing sponsored base-ball caps instead of helmets. They've privatised forensics, and the computer geeks will be next. How long before we're….'

The moanfest was interrupted by the chirruping of her mobile. She glanced at the number on the screen, and recognised it at once.

Daniel Kind.

The jolt of excitement travelled through her like an electric shock. Was this how addicts felt, when after months of cold turkey, the drug entered their veins?

She muttered an excuse, vague and inarticulate, and hurried away from their table. Must make sure she was out of earshot.

'Hello?'

'Hannah? This is Daniel, Daniel Kind.'

He didn't need to introduce himself. There was only one Daniel.

'Sorry.' He sounded unaccountably nervous, as though he'd taken her silence as frostiness. 'Is it inconvenient, am I inter-rupting something?'

'Only a rant from my sidekicks about the downsides of modern policing.'

'I'll keep it brief.'

'No need to apologise.' She hesitated. 'Fact is, I could do with being distracted. Preferably until they both drink up and bugger off home.'

'You sound fed up.'

'Shouldn't be, should I? Not long back after the holiday and already I feel as though I'm on an endless treadmill, as per usual. How are things? I saw Louise…'

'I know.' Still that note of anxiety. What was wrong? 'It's because of Louise that I'm ringing. I'd like a word with you, off the record.'

'Your sister isn't in trouble?'

'Well…'

He was floundering.

'Then, what?'

'She's split up with Stuart Wagg, and now he's…'

The super-articulate Daniel Kind, lost for words? Amazing. But—admit it, Hannah—it was impossible not to feel a *frisson* of excitement. Quite a turn-on that, when he needed help, he'd called her.

Striving for her best chief-inspector tone, she said, 'I'm sorry to hear that.'

'Don't worry. She's well rid of him…sorry, he's a friend of yours, he invited you over for New Year's Eve.'

'Police officers don't make friends with lawyers. No, he's a customer of Marc's, a rare book collector. You were saying, about him?'

'Look, it's difficult to talk about over the phone. I wondered if you could spare me half an hour?'

She almost succumbed to the impulse to clench her fist and shout, 'Yes!' Sod the New Year resolution and all that crap about clean breaks and fresh starts. It would be fantastic to see him again.

'When were you thinking of?'

'As soon as?'

Keen, or what? This wasn't like Daniel.

'You mean this evening?'

'If it's too much to ask…'

'How about we meet in an hour's time?'

'Terrific! It's really good of…'

Her skin prickled, and she spotted Greg Wharf watching her with undisguised curiosity. She imagined him speculating about the call that she didn't want overheard.

'How about The Tickled Trout?'

'Perfect. And Hannah…'

'Yes?'

'Thanks.'

◇◇◇

Walking through the front door of The Tickled Trout, Hannah glanced to right and left, to see if she recognised anyone. Or, more to the point, if anyone was likely to recognise her. It was second nature for a police officer to check out any room he entered. But no-one at the tables or gathered at the slate-topped bar took a blind bit of notice of her. If anybody felt a pin-prick of conscience, it was her. This wasn't a secret get-togethers with a CHIS, (no informants in modern policing, only covert human intelligence sources.). More like a tryst; though she was still in her work clothes—there'd been no question of nipping back home to change. Fobbing Marc off with the news that he'd have to make his own meal was the easy bit; she'd given him the same message a hundred times before.

A text popped up on her mobile.

Running late. Traffic. Daniel.

So she needn't have arrived twenty minutes early, but never mind. Turning up early for meetings away from home ground was a habit learned from Daniel's father. Ben said it gave you a chance to scope out the meeting place, and to keep an eye on the door. You never knew when you might need to get out in a hurry.

Painted on a beam above the counter was a quote from *Twelfth Night*. 'Here comes the trout that must be caught with tickling'. Hannah had a hazy recollection that this was something to do with Malvolio but she hadn't paid much attention to Shakespeare since she was sixteen. On a pillar facing the bar, a notice explained that, by rubbing a trout's underbelly with your fingertips, you could send it into a trance, so it's ready to be thrown on to the nearest scrap of dry ground. It dated back to the days of the ancient Greeks, apparently, but although Hannah thought it might be rather nice to be stroked into a trance, in twenty-first century England, tickling trout was illegal. Not that Hannah had ever collared anyone for it. Before long, the Home Office was sure to embark on a media blitz, celebrating the low incidence of offences as evidence of their success in being tough on crime.

The Tickled Trout was one of the most renowned gourmet pubs in the county and had escaped the malaise affecting other rural hostelries. Two hundred years back, the place had been a coaching inn. Now run by two generations: father, mother, two daughters and their husbands, it had evolved over the years in response to the changing demands of Lakeland visitors, combining the pub with a micro-brewery and gourmet restaurant. Marc had once brought her here for a meal as a birthday treat, but the prices were pitched at American and Japanese tourists, or wealthy professionals with week-end cottages in the posher parts of the Lakes, not at second hand book dealers.

She resisted the temptation to warm her hands in front of the open fire, or linger near the restaurant door and savour the aroma of roast venison and guinea fowl. There were a couple of secluded booths at the corner of the room, suitable for guests who didn't want to be disturbed. Debussy piano music tinkled in the background as she positioned herself in a seat behind a pillar. From here she could spot people walking in, without easily being seen herself. In the Lakes, rumours spread faster than ripples on a tarn. She'd traded on hearsay often enough to know its potency. For all that Lauren waxed so lyrical about modern, technological, intelligence-led policing, what detectives really relied on was good, old-fashioned, gossip-led policing.

Daniel arrived barely five minutes late. As his gaze swivelled round the bar, she raised a hand. He moved towards her with brisk, athletic strides. Her stomach knotted as he approached. She'd thought she was anaesthetised to this. Thought that she'd rid herself that ludicrous desire for him, the desire she'd refused to acknowledge, even to herself. But the anaesthetic had worn off. She simply couldn't help it.

'Hannah.' He was breathing hard, as though he'd run from his car. 'Sorry, there was an accident, a tree blown down on the road.'

'No problem. You're pretty much on time.'

'I'm not saying I didn't break one or two speed limits once I got past the hold-up. Sorry, I shouldn't be confessing that to a police officer, should I?'

'I just went off duty.'

'I feel guilty, asking you to see me at the drop of a hat.'

'All part of the service.' Too glib a response, she chided herself even as she spoke. He had this knack of making her say the first thing that came into her head.

'What would you like to drink?'

She asked for a lemonade, and watched him at the bar. Saw the barmaid study him curiously. They exchanged a few words before Daniel returned with two soft drinks.

'The girl recognised you from your TV series,' Hannah said. 'Am I right?'

'She's a first year history student working in her vacation, and you're a good detective,' he said. 'I wrote books that sold thousands and nobody ever stopped me in the street. I never realised the reach of television until I appeared on the box.'

Another reminder that, if people saw the two of them together, Daniel's fame meant that word would soon get around. Hannah leaned back in the booth. Another reason to be paranoid.

'I suppose you're wondering why I wanted to see you.'

She resisted a flirtatious reply. 'Take your time.'

His brow furrowed and he looked down, as if mesmerised by the pattern of the wood grain in the table that separated them.

'Stuart Wagg has disappeared.'

◇◇◇

'Am I making a mountain out of a molehill?' he muttered ten minutes later.

'No,' she murmured. 'You did the right thing, telling me. But don't worry about Louise. If she did lash out at Wagg in a moment of temper, I'm sure she didn't do him much damage. You said yourself that there was no sign of blood in his kitchen and the scissors aren't stained.'

'That doesn't mean he isn't seriously injured.'

'Your theory is that he staggered off before slumping unconscious?'

'Or bleeding to death.'

'You didn't see him lying in a heap in the grounds of Crag Gill.'

'He could be sprawled in some dark corner. I wasn't equipped to carry out a fingertip search of an acre of land in the dark.'

'My guess is, he set off to walk the fells the minute Louise ran off.'

'Leaving his house unlocked?'

'Marc forgot to lock up our new house only a fortnight before Christmas. I wasn't impressed, given that Cumbria Constabulary is spending a fortune on a campaign against burglary and sneak theft. But we all make mistakes. Crag Gill has a sophisticated security system. He wasn't to know there would be a power cut.'

'He's a lawyer. Cautious by nature.'

'You should meet some of the lawyers I know. Did you check whether his car was still in the garage?'

He coloured slightly. Hannah supposed he was chastising himself for overlooking the obvious.

'He drives an Aston Martin DBS. Marc says it gives him whiplash just to look at it. If he's dead, the likeliest cause is that he took a bend too fast and wasn't as lucky as your sister when she crashed.'

'Okay, Hannah. You win. I wasn't thinking straight.'

She allowed herself a smile. 'Your secret is safe with me. You've done Wagg a favour by shutting up after him. If the worst that happens is that he's locked out because he forgot to take his keys when he stormed off, he'll have nothing to complain about.'

'I can't help wondering…'

'One thing lawyers obsess over is proof. Where's the proof that your sister harmed Stuart Wagg? There isn't a shred of evidence. If she hadn't opened her heart while she was in a state of distress about the way Wagg treated her, nobody would be any the wiser. If anything has happened to him, maybe it's because he's missed his footing on a rocky path up the Langdale Pikes.'

'Sorry to have wasted your time.'

'Hey, you haven't wasted my time.' She leaned across the table. 'I felt rotten for not keeping in touch while you were in the States. I should have answered your last email.'

'You work all hours. I wasn't surprised.'

'I meant to get back to you. When Louise told me you'd arrived home, I wondered if we could meet up.'

'And thanks to Stuart Wagg, we managed it.'

'Can I get you another drink?'

'Marc will wonder what's happened to you.'

'Trust me, the only thing he'll wonder about is which ready meal to sling in the microwave. I rang to let him know I'd be late. Comes with the territory, when you're with a police officer. He's accustomed to it.'

'You've been together a long time.'

It was on the tip of her tongue to say, 'Yeah, feels like it.'

But there must be a limit to disloyalty. Prudence—and nosiness—dictated a change of topic.

'So Miranda is back in the big city?'

'We spoke the other day. But she wasn't suited to the pace of life in the Lakes. You can take the girl out of London, but you can't take London out of the girl.'

'Pity.'

Chapter Twelve

Overnight, the temperature dived below zero. For once, no mist curtained the garden of Undercrag when Hannah opened the front door, but frost glittered on the grass and trees and there were streaks of snow on the higher ground. Not a smart move to leave the Lexus out in the open. She spent five minutes scraping the windows clear of their hard, opaque glaze so that she could see to drive into Kendal.

Twenty to seven and, apart from a few farm vehicles, the lanes around Ambleside were deserted. Muddy tracks left by the tractors had frozen over, and the dry stone walls were powdered white. Passing Waterhead, she glimpsed ice on the surface of Windermere. Since childhood, she'd adored crisp, dry winter mornings, but that didn't account for her lightness of mood. Seeing Daniel again had given her a buzz. Until yesterday, she'd refused to admit to herself how she missed him. She found herself humming along to an old Cliff Richard number on the car radio. 'Devil Woman'.

Daniel fretted too much. A bluestocking law lecturer transforming into a crazed scissors killer? Unlikely. Yet she was glad he cared enough about Louise to go on that strange expedition to Crag Gill. Just as well Stuart Wagg didn't have his premises guarded by a Rottweiler. She doubted whether any harm had befallen Wagg, though she'd promised Daniel that she'd ask someone to check things out. It was unwise to turn a blind eye to

'I'm glad she persuaded me that Tarn Cottage was a good buy. Even without her around, it suits me. Even in dead of winter, Tarn Fold seems like Paradise. The stillness, the peace. To wake up in the morning and hear—nothing.'

'Not tempted to stay in America?'

He shook his head. 'I love the States, but I'd never move there permanently. I can't scrub the Lakes out of my system. And I don't want to.'

'So we'll be seeing more of you around here from now on?'

''Fraid so.'

For a few moments neither of them spoke. She finished her drink, savouring the tang of lemon.

'I want to visit Marc's shop. I'm working on this book about the history of murder.'

'Murder?' She leaned forward. 'Tell me more.'

He explained about *The Hell Within* and the talk he was working on for Arlo Denstone. 'I'd like Marc to look out any obscure local materials from De Quincey's years in the Lakes.'

'He'll love that, he fancies himself as a book detective.' She put down her glass. 'Actually, I forgot to mention that I was seeing you this evening.'

Their eyes met. She wasn't sure if he gave a slight nod, or if her imagination were running riot.

'I still feel guilty.' He leaned back. 'Wrecking your evening after you've been slogging down the mean streets all day.'

'The mean streets of Kendal?' She grinned. 'Well, it ain't L.A, that's for sure. It's not even as gritty as Lancaster. As for this evening, it's been great to catch up. Tomorrow, I'll ask someone to check up on Stuart Wagg. Once we know for certain he's alive and kicking, we can all breathe again, eh?'

'What if he makes a complaint to the police?'

'It's a domestic, his word against hers.'

'But she told me, and I told you.'

'This isn't an official conversation. Didn't we agree it was off the record? And since you asked, I wouldn't mind another drink.'

His brow was still furrowed, but he mustered a grin.

'Lemonade, or something stronger?'

She gave him a direct look.

'Lemonade would be best, I think.'

◇◇◇

Driving back to Undercrag, Hannah asked herself if Daniel's darkest fears might be realised. No question, Louise was highly strung. Hannah recalled conversations with Ben Kind, as he fretted over the destruction of his relationship with his daughter. Louise had sided with her mother after his desertion, and he'd never seen her again. He'd gone to his grave regretting his betrayal of his little girl, but Hannah suspected there were two sides to the story. She would never have cut off all contact with her own dad, even if he'd walked out on them to share a bed with another woman.

Tomorrow, more than likely Stuart would turn up safe and sound. Even assuming Louise had cut him with the scissors, Hannah doubted that he'd bring in the police. He was good at playing the percentages. There was more risk for him in complaining that Louise had attacked him. He wouldn't want a police investigation looking into his personal life.

She owed Stuart. Without today's bizarre incidents at Crag Gill, she and Daniel would have had no excuse to meet. In her head, she could hear her friend Terri demanding to know what had *happened*, and groaning loudly when told the answer was nothing. Terri's live now, pay later philosophy had seen her through three marriages, three divorces and even a blind date with Les Bryant that had become the stuff of legend. But for Hannah, it was enough to enjoy Daniel's company. She'd even told him a little about the Bethany Friend case. But she hadn't forgotten that although Miranda was off the scene, Marc wasn't.

Turning into Lowbarrrow Lane, she mentally donned her body armour, rehearsing answers to Marc's complaints about her work taking over both their lives. She didn't waste time putting the car in the garage, but when she marched into the front room, she found him with his feet up on the sofa, watching a sitcom

on telly. He jumped up at once and kissed her on the cheek. He never lost the ability to nonplus her.

'I opened a bottle of Chablis.' There were two glasses on an occasional table, full to the brim. 'Come on, take the weight off your feet. It's just out of the cooler, I poured it the moment I heard you scrunching up the gravel when you reversed outside the front door.'

She had half a dozen questions for him about Bethany Friend. But with the first sip of the wine, she decided to leave them for one more day. It was all about timing.

'When you've finished, if you like, we can get an early night.'

He smiled. A handsome man, still. Desirable.

'Give me ten minutes.'

She needed that long. Not to knock back her wine, but to rid her mind of the picture of Daniel Kind, sitting on the other side of the pub table. And of the sudden urge—conquered, thank God, how could she be so pathetically adolescent?—to kiss each and every furrow in his brow.

any misper report, even when you couldn't care less if the misper in question never turned up again. And it provided a reason to call him again, to confirm that Wagg was back home, safe and sound. After that, she didn't have a script for the conversation.

At this hour, she had her pick of parking spots at Divisional HQ. She left the car there and set off for her meeting with Fern Larter. The shutters were down over the shop windows in Stricklandgate, and even at opening time, some of the stores would remain empty and lifeless. Local retailers faced a harsh winter; nobody knew when the economic chill would ease.

The sharp air chafed her cheeks, and turned her hands blue, but she felt a stab of virtue as she strode up the one-in-seven gradient of Beast Banks. This was one of her favourite parts of the town, reeking of history, ancient and modern. Up above, footpaths led to the earthworks of Castle Howe. The Normans chose this hill to construct Kendal's first castle, a motte and bailey burned to the ground by Scottish raiders. An obelisk loomed up from the summit. Hannah recalled it was erected to celebrate the Glorious Revolution, and bore the inscription, *Sacred to Liberty*. Only a question of time before someone decided to monitor it with surveillance cameras.

A newsagents' was open and a billboard for 'The Westmorland Gazette' screamed the breaking story in bold black lettering: *Cold Snap Helps Police Cut Crime.* Another triumph for India Sturridge's PR machine. It was simply a story about bad weather deterring rowdy rampages by drunken revellers.

She strode past the building that had once housed a sub-post office. It had inspired a local teacher to dream up the adventures of Postman Pat, before Royal Mail, ruthless as the marauding Scots, shut it as part of a 'service improvement programme.' Now there was only a red commemorative plaque to show for it.

◇ ◇ ◇

'I could murder a fry-up,' DCI Fern Larter said as they exchanged a New Year embrace outside the steamed-up windows of the Beast Banks Breakfast Bar.

Hannah detached herself and fought to get her breath back. It was like being hugged by a pink elephant. Even allowing for a bulky winter jacket in a shade even more shocking than her latest henna hair dye, Fern seemed larger than ever.

'Looks like you've been a serial offender over the holidays.'

'Don't be such a mean cow. My New Year resolution was to lose a stone in January.'

'This is no time for recidivism.'

'Sod off.' Fern mopped her brow with her leather gauntlets; the climb had made her sweat as if it were the height of summer. 'Life's too short for guilt. I deserve a greasy spoon breakfast after slogging up Beast Banks. See that patch of green over the road? They used to bait bulls there. Reckoned it improved the quality of the meat.'

'You're a mine of information.'

Fern's was the first name chalked up on the police quiz team sheet. Her magpie mind accumulated vast quantities of useless information, along with a few nuggets that made her a formidable detective. She'd once told Hannah that William Wordsworth had been Collector of Stamps for Westmorland, and cringed when Hannah said she didn't even know he was into philately.

'There's more. The butchers' shops of Kendal were originally congregated around the corner in Old Shambles, but the site was too flat for the blood and offal to drain away. That's why they built New Shambles on the slope by Finkle Street. For better drainage down to the river.'

'Lovely. Still in the mood for breakfast?'

'Lead me to it, I'm famished. God knows why we're faffing around out here in the freezing cold when there's food inside.'

◇◇◇

Already a queue had formed at the counter. Hannah recognised half a dozen colleagues, émigrés from the police canteen ten minutes away at Busher Walk. She and Fern were served by an obese woman in a ketchup-stained overall, and carried their trays to a table at the back. Not to avoid prying eyes, but to put a bit of distance between them and a battered transistor radio on a shelf near the door. Radio One blared, the brothers Gallagher yelling like angry old men, as if trying to make themselves understood through the fuzziness of the reception. The subtle charm of The Tickled Trout might have belonged to a different continent, a different century.

'How goes the Saffell case?'

Fern pushed a hand through her thick hair. If she'd combed it that morning, it wasn't apparent. Fern was a fashionista's worst nightmare, one of many reasons why she was Hannah's best mate in the Cumbria Constabulary.

'If you'd asked me a month ago, I'd have said Wanda Saffell murdered George. In fact, I'd have staked my pension on it.'

Fern squeezed a sachet of HP sauce over her breakfast. Her plate was as big as a Michelin tyre and crammed to overflowing with eggs, bacons, sausage, baked beans, fried bread and black pudding. There was something pleasingly shameless about the Bar's commitment to clogging its customers' arteries. It was good business, at least in the short term until they were wheeled into intensive care. The smell of hot fat alone was enough to send your cholesterol count zooming into the stratosphere.

'Who says you'll live long enough to collect your pension? You realise eating that meal probably invalidates your life insurance?'

Fern wiped her mouth with a paper napkin emblazoned with the logo of the Beast Banks Breakfast Bar, featuring a bull with a libidinous smirk. Presumably an ironic nod to the bull baiters of yesteryear.

'You know my motto. A short life, but a merry one.'

'Like the late lamented George?'

'He wasn't that merry. Boring old fart is the phrase that springs to mind. Really, an estate agent who threw it all up to collect smelly old books, I ask you.' A momentary pause and an uncharacteristic blush suggested that Fern had forgotten how Marc earned his living. 'Not that there's anything wrong with old books, of course. But you can have too much of a good thing, and George Saffell did own a hell of a lot of them. Give me chick-lit and trashy magazines any day.'

'So have you linked Wanda to his death?'

'Uh-uh.' Fern stirred a couple of sugars into her mug of coffee with enough pent-up aggression to spill half of it on to the formica table top. 'I swear George didn't tie himself up and the boat-house didn't set fire to itself, but...'

'You've ruled out some bizarre form of elaborate suicide?'

'Who would end it all like that? Imagine how it feels to be burned alive. More painful than a day of being force-fed Lauren's homilies.'

'A weird form of atonement?'

Fern put her elbows on the table, heedless of the fact that it was still swimming in coffee, and gazed pityingly at Hannah. 'Estate agents don't do atonement.'

'Do forensics confirm suicide is absolutely out of the question?'

'You know forensics, they won't confirm that night follows day, unless you promise not to sue if it turns out they've mucked up the chain of evidence.' Fern glared at her coffee. It had the consistency of the sludge visible in harbours at low tide. Hannah had ordered an orange juice and couple of slices of toast; her concession to living for the moment was to smear a pat of butter on to the crumbling surface of the toast. 'Everything is hedged with disclaimers. But the official *working hypothesis* is murder most foul. If you ask me, it's a racing certainty.'

'Motive?'

'Money, has to be. Otherwise, why not simply divorce him?'

'He bailed out of house-selling at a good time.'

'Yeah, he was doing fine until his luck ran out.' A forkful of baked beans disappeared into Fern's mouth. 'The conglomerate that took over his firm have closed half the offices and laid off two-thirds of the staff. Economies of scale, they call it. Asset-stripping to you and me.'

'Did anyone connected with the firm hold a grudge against him?'

'On the contrary, the people he left behind saw him as a decent old stick. All the more so, once they had a taste of their new masters. A gang of venture capitalists whose only concern is to screw the workforce into the ground.'

'So George made millions and threw everyone else to the wolves?'

'Nobody seems to have resented him enough to do him harm. His father founded the business and he expanded it over twenty-five years. Built up a decent reputation, didn't get involved in the murky tricks of the property trade. Plenty of Jack-the-Lads buy at an under-value through a shell company and then sell on at full price. It's an easy route to big bucks, but Saffell concentrated on the quality end of the market. Selling seven-bedroomed mansions on fat commission to rich Southerners. Rich pickings, and relatively ethical.'

'Relatively?'

'If I was Prime Minister, I'd pass a law to give local first-time buyers a break. I hate people treating houses as an investment when kids can't find anywhere they can afford in the place their family has always lived. But that's just me. If everyone said Saffell was a saint, I'd be truly suspicious. His social life revolved around the Rotary Club and the golf course, yawn, yawn. At least until his first wife died. She was a childhood sweetheart who rejoiced in the name of Jennifer. They married young and had one daughter called Lynsey. Lynsey trained as a doctor and now lives in New Zealand with her husband and a couple of little kids. Jennifer died shortly after her daughter emigrated, and Saffell's comfortable world was shattered.'

'Until he married glamorous Wanda.'

Fern shovelled a huge chunk of fried bread into her mouth, pausing only to belch as a sign of what she thought about glamour. 'Jennifer was as ordinary as her name, by all accounts. Second time around, he opted for someone very different.'

'He must have been quite a catch. A rich, reasonably pleasant man, left on his own through tragedy rather than divorce.'

'When you put it like that, I might have been tempted myself. The boring personality and the musty old books kind of fade into insignificance when you think of shopping without a budget.'

A bell rang as the door of the Breakfast Bar opened, and in walked Les Bryant and Greg Wharf. Les sneezed furiously in lieu of a greeting, but Greg wandered over to their table and stared at Fern's plate.

'Morning, ma'am.' He grinned at Fern. 'Glad to see you're a connoisseur of a tasty pork sausage.'

Fern gave Greg and his juvenile *doubles entendre* the withering look they deserved and bit the sausage in half before chewing very hard and very noisily.

'DCI Larter is updating me on the Saffell case,' Hannah said. 'There's a possible overlap with our inquiry. I'll brief you later this morning.'

'Look forward to it, ma'am.' Greg bestowed a cheeky smile upon her and strode off with a spring in his step to join Les in the queue.

'Naughty boy,' Fern said. 'But I like him.'

'Keep your hands off,' Hannah said. 'He should carry a health warning, everyone tells me he's bad news.'

'But a good detective, I hear. Don't worry, I'm not into cradle-snatching. He's closer to your age than mine.'

'Only by two or three years. And you must be joking if you think I'd ever take a shine to him.'

'So how is Marc?'

'Fine, we spent Christmas with his family.'

'And you're still speaking to him? The last Christmas I spent with my in-laws nearly turned me into a spree killer. Go on, then, any chance Marc will make an honest woman of you this year now you've bought that posh new house?'

'Leave it, Fern.' Hannah snapped a corner off the burnt slice of toast and chewed it furiously. "I want to hear about your prime suspect.'

'Wanda? She met George after her firm won the PR account for Saffell Properties. Her maiden name was…'

'Smith.'

Fern raised her eyebrows. 'Actually, that was the name of her first husband. Her maiden name was Hart. Someone who knew her at school told me she was known as Cold Hart. No change there, then. How come you knew she was called Smith—doing a bit of moonlighting away from Cold Cases, are you?'

'I'll fill you in after you've told me about her life with Saffell.'

'Once she spotted her chance of a lifestyle of conspicuous consumption, old George didn't have a chance. Creating positive PR for estate agents must be a challenge, but she rose to it. They hired Wray Castle for a huge wedding. The photo-shoot was all over *Lake District Life*. Big mistake. Like the celebrities who give gushing interviews to *Hello* about their undying love and then start clawing at each other's throats within the year.'

'Whatever happened to fairy-tale romance, eh?'

'Trust me, kid. Most relationships are nothing like yours and Marc's.'

Hannah fiddled with the stained gingham tablecloth.

'I missed out on the glitzy wedding, remember?'

'You wouldn't want it,' Fern assured her. 'Not your style, kid. Don't get in a huff, he's a gorgeous feller. Most women would scratch your eyes out if they thought they could get their shoes under his bed. Me included.'

Hannah couldn't help laughing. Fern was, in her way, as provocative as Greg Wharf.

'There's no room under his sodding bed because of all those musty old books. You'd hate it.'

'I'd cope.' Fern leered as she polished off her baked beans. 'Any road, George plus Wanda didn't equal a match made in Heaven. She isn't cut out for the role of dutiful little woman, small-talking her way through golf dinners and cocktail parties. Her first husband was a drummer in a band. Not a very successful band, but it must have attracted a few groupies, because he ran off with one of them years ago. No kids, she doesn't seem the maternal type.'

'Is there a maternal type?'

'You know perfectly well what I mean. Once Wanda was married, she threw up her job and started this little printing press. She turns out arty-farty stuff—poetry and something called *belles-lettres*. A lifelong ambition, she told me. Huh, takes all sorts.'

'And kindly old George helped her to realise her dream.'

'For him, the cost of setting up the business was small change. A price worth paying, to get inside her knickers. His staff were loyal and mostly discreet, but he had a reputation for a roving eye. You know the sort of thing. Patting the office juniors' bums and peering down the secretaries' tops. Middle-aged man's syndrome. One girl said that she only had to undo an extra blouse button or two to have his tongue hanging out like a roller blind.'

'Any complaints?'

'One or two girls left in a hurry, but no formal grievances were lodged, let alone any sexual harassment claims. The women who worked there seemed to feel sorry for him. I'd guess some were disappointed when Wanda snared him. I've visited their house, it's fabulous. Then there was the converted boat-house at Ullswater. Plus half a dozen refurbished terraced houses with long-term tenants. For good measure, there's a villa in Spain, but so far I haven't managed to wangle a trip out there to hunt for clues.'

'You're slipping.' Fern's ability to persuade the top brass that trips overseas were vital to her latest investigation was the stuff of legend. 'How about New Zealand, for a word with the daughter? They say it's a beautiful country.'

'Lynsey came back to England for the funeral.' Fern pouted. 'We talked, but she wasn't able to shed much light. She hadn't been back since George and Wanda tied the knot. The Saffells visited four years ago, but she and Wanda had nothing in common. She didn't even seem that heart-broken about her Dad's demise. They were never that close, and she wasn't pining for an inheritance. Her husband is loaded, he's a stock-broker in Christchurch.'

'The money motive, then. Any other sizeable legacies apart from Wanda?'

'The National Trust does very nicely, but I think it's against their rules to murder people to raise funds.'

'How much does the grieving widow inherit?'

'Not as much as you'd expect. She has the right to live in the house unless and until she re-marries. And she gets the proceeds of his insurance. The lawyers are sorting out George's estate at their usual snail's pace. They say it's complicated, with a rich deceased and properties overseas. Meanwhile, the insurers haven't paid out a penny as yet.'

'Praying they can rely on a sneaky get-out in the small print of the policy?'

'Like insurers the world over. When I talked to head office, they seemed resigned to coughing up. They'd be thrilled if we could prove that Wanda murdered George, but the way it looks today, I'll never conjure up evidence to satisfy the CPS, let alone a jury. Wanda is playing a good hand. So far she hasn't chased for payment.'

'She doesn't need the cash in a hurry, surely?'

'Sooner or later, she'll need a few bob. Her printing press loses money hand over fist—but she won't want to look like a gold-digger.'

'Bit late for that. Does she care much about appearances?'

Fern speared the last piece of black pudding, and contemplated the blood oozing out of it.

'She's a funny mix. Part Ice Maiden, part drama queen.'

'And you think she's also part murderer?'

Fern devoured the black pudding with a cannibalistic relish and then banged down her knife and fork.

'Between you and me, Hannah, doubts are creeping in. I thought I had this one figured. But if she's guilty, God knows how I'll prove it.'

'Which firm of lawyers is handling George's estate? Stuart Wagg's outfit?'

'Now what makes you ask that?' Fern said softly.

'Just wondered.'

'Yeah? Actually, the executors are two partners in a big outfit called Boycott Duff. As for Wagg's firm, he and George were book collecting rivals. They did plenty of business together over the years, but were never close. What I don't know is whether George knew that Wanda consulted Stuart's firm about a divorce.'

Hannah sat up in her chair. 'She did?'

'Three weeks before he died, she saw a partner called Raj Doshi.'

'I know the name.'

Doshi was the gallant knight who had taken Wanda home after she poured wine over Arlo Denstone. Hannah didn't know they were already acquainted.

'Good-looking feller. How good a lawyer he is, I've no idea. Wanda says she didn't find his advice encouraging. The bottom line was that she'd be worse off if she left George than if they stayed married.'

'Because they'd only been married for a few years?'

Fern nodded. 'I checked with Doshi. He hummed and hawed about client confidentiality to salve his lawyer's conscience, but Wanda had authorised him to disclose his advice. Disappointingly, he backed up everything she'd told us.'

'Had she primed him? Did he admit to anything more than a solicitor-client relationship?'

Fern's eyes widened. 'What makes you ask?'

'Just a long shot.' Hannah told her about the New Year party at Crag Gill. 'Is Doshi married?'

'He mentioned a disabled wife to the DC who conducted the interview. Turns out she's older than him and suffers from early onset Parkinson's, but everyone assures us he's a devoted husband. That's as may be, but my DC was quite taken with him. Stuart Wagg isn't the only charmer in that firm.'

Hannah wondered if Stuart Wagg had turned up yet. Which in turn reminded her talking to Daniel last night. She told herself not to become distracted.

'Maybe the guy she drenched in wine was a lover,' Fern mused. 'Or he'd turned her down. Wanda doesn't strike me as someone who'd be philosophical about rejection.'

'Not many of us are.'

Fern shot her a sharp glance. 'Bet you have less experience of rejection than most of us.'

Hannah said quickly, 'Why did Wanda admit to considering divorce?'

'It was a smart move. People knew she'd consulted him. Even if solicitors keep their traps shut, receptionists talk, and so do secretaries. Wanda probably thought it better to be upfront.'

'So what was her explanation?'

'Said she realised they weren't suited within the first twelve months of the marriage. If you ask me, it didn't take her twelve minutes. They shared an interest in books, but it wasn't enough. She's a high maintenance lady, and George was accustomed to a little woman who knew her place. Wanda got itchy feet and nagged him into flogging his business, assuming they'd spend his retirement jetting off on luxury holidays. But the villa in Spain was as exotic as it got, and even there he devoted himself to playing golf and drinking with his expat chums. She said she didn't hate him, far from it. There was nothing nasty about him.'

'Except that he liked golf?'

'Spot on,' Fern chortled. 'He used to joke that when he died, he wanted *Fairway to Heaven* inscribed on his coffin. Doesn't seem so funny now. Especially when there wasn't that much left of him to put in a coffin. Wanda's story is that she was in no hurry to split with George.'

'And how did he feel?'

'Wanda says he was happy with her. She never denied him his conjugals, and that was enough to keep him funding her printing press. She decided to give the marriage until the new year, and see how she felt then.' Fern paused in the act of swallowing the last morsel of her breakfast. 'Next thing she knew, he'd been burnt to more of a crisp than this streaky bacon.'

'What about other men?'

'She admitted to a couple of flings, but not with Doshi or Denstone.'

'Did she fling the boyfriends, or vice versa?'

'She claimed they were old pals. One was Stuart Wagg, the other Nathan Clare.'

Hannah put down her knife and fork. 'I talked to Clare yesterday.'

'A right charmer, isn't he?' Fern scowled. 'Five minutes into our conversation, I found the urge to cut his balls off almost irresistible.'

'Why did it take you so long?'

A throaty chuckle. 'How come your path keeps crossing mine? You don't think our cases are related?'

'Good question.' Hannah stood up and reached for her purse. On the other side of the room, Greg Wharf was chatting up a waitress. He treated them to a cheeky wink. 'Let's discuss it on our way back to the Centre of Excellence.'

◇◇◇

Something extraordinary had happened while they were inside the Beast Banks Breakfast Bar. The sun had come out of hiding. It hung so low over Kendal's rooftops that you'd have thought it ashamed of its long absence, but its glare was uncompromising. Hannah needed to shade her eyes as they passed the old slaughtering ground on the way to All Hallows Lane.

'So did Wanda kill George?' she asked.

'She has an alibi. At the same time the boat-house was going up in flames, she'd finished a committee meeting of the Letterpress Publishers Association in Leeds by having a shouting match with the chairman. In front of a dozen witnesses. She didn't leave until ten to eleven, and rather than drive home, she spent the night in a hotel near the main station. Alone, as far as we can tell. She called for room service at midnight and flirted drunkenly with the waiter who brought the tray.'

'Making sure she was noticed.'

'Yeah, but I bet that's how she always behaves. Quarrelling and making eyes at blokes half her age.'

'Any chance she hired a hit man?'

'We found no unexplained payments out of her bank or building society accounts.'

'Don't those guys usually insist on cash?'

'Sure, they're as bad as plumbers, but if she had any spare funds, she's kept them hidden. And there's no suggestion she knows anybody ready, willing and able to burn her husband to death. Cumbria is hardly knee-deep in contract killers. If she found someone in Manchester, Liverpool, or Leeds, she's covered her tracks to perfection.'

'Suppose it was an amateur job. Murder by someone without a criminal record. A friend.'

'Not Arlo Denstone, then?'

'If he did help her out, she behaved very ungratefully at Stuart Wagg's party.'

'Suppose she wanted to throw everybody off the scent. Make believe that she and Arlo are at daggers drawn, when really…'

Fern made a face. 'I suppose it's possible, but…'

'There are other possibilities.'

'You're thinking Nathan Clare?'

'Do you have any better ideas?'

Fern sighed. 'I had his movements checked, and physically, it was just about do-able. He spent the first part of the evening in a pub in Ambleside. After he'd finished boozing, he's supposed to have gone home to prepare for a lecture. He can't prove it, and it's just about possible that he had time to jump into a car and head up to Ullswater, burn George to death and nip back home. There's only one snag.'

'He was pissed out of his brain?'

'Not just that.'

'Break it to me gently.'

'The bad news is, Nathan can't drive.'

Hannah halted in mid-stride. 'Seriously?'

'Seriously. Nathan has never had a full licence. We've checked. He says he's never had any interest in driving. He takes taxis if and when the need arises. Other than that, he has a touching faith in Cumbria's public transport. The mark of a true eccentric.'

'Not having a licence doesn't mean you can't drive.'

'True. But if he got hold of a vehicle, and despite knocking back five pints managed the journey to Ullswater and back on a dark winter night, he doesn't just deserve to get away with it, he deserves a bloody medal. It's typical of this inquiry—wherever we turn, we end up facing a brick wall. So tell me about your cold case.'

Hannah finished running through the edited highlights of Bethany Friend's story as they reached Bushers Walk. Half eight, time for noses to the grindstone.

'I've arranged to see Wanda this afternoon,' Hannah said.

'You never did like delegating, did you?'

'There has to be some compensation for working in a backwater. Besides, half my team has succumbed to this bug going round.'

'Let me know how you get on with Wanda. Interesting that she and Nathan both knew Bethany, but two unexplained deaths, six years apart? Hard to see a connection. Bethany drowned, and George was burned to death.'

'In each case, suicide was left as an alternative to murder."

'Nothing unusual in that.'

'There's something else.'

'Go on, surprise me.'

A vague idea loomed in Hannah's mind, unrecognisable as a stranger approaching through the mist.

'Nobody really disliked them. There was no good reason for them to be murdered.'

Chapter Thirteen

Louise was asleep in bed when Daniel returned to Tarn Cottage, and he spent an hour tinkering with the first chapter of *The Hell Within*, achieving little more than replacing a few commas with semi colons and exterminating a rogue split infinitive. That night he dreamed about the bright September afternoon when Aimee died, and his heart-stopping race through the streets of Oxford after he picked up the message she'd left on his voicemail, desperate to reach her before she jumped. The nightmare was vivid enough for him to recall the slow-motion agony of failure to save Aimee. He never dreamed about Miranda, which said it all.

When he awoke, his head felt though someone had tightened an iron band around it. After a scalding hot shower, he padded down to the kitchen to find Louise seated at the old pine table, cocooned in a thick white dressing gown. In front of her stood a half-full cafetiere and a mug which proclaimed *I'm a pleasant person* after *I've had my caffeine fix*. She was munching her way through a large bowl of cornflakes as she read a moral dilemma column in *The Independent*.

'Morning! Help yourself to some coffee.'

He halted in his tracks. 'You sound cheerful.'

She stiffened, and put her spoon with a bang. A confrontational expression. all too familiar from her teens, spread over her face like a dark red stain.

'You prefer doom and gloom?'

'No, it's just…'

'Forget it.' She slumped back in her chair. 'I'm the one who should apologise. When I opened my eyes this morning, I said to myself, "today's the day when I start making changes in my life." And the moment you walk in the room, I bite your head off.'

'Old habits die hard, I guess.'

She winced. 'I suppose I deserved that.'

'Yep.' He pointed at the newspaper. 'What's the dilemma today? *Should I confess that I stabbed my boyfriend?*'

'Hey, Daniel, I'm trying to be nice.' She nodded at the slogan on her coffee mug. 'And I haven't even absorbed all the caffeine yet. Meet me half-way?'

He dropped down on to the bench and swung an arm around her. Under the fluffiness of her dressing gown, her shoulder was hard and bony. Until that moment, he hadn't realised that she was shaking slightly, or how much of an effort she was making to conquer the fear she'd felt the day before.

He poured himself coffee. 'Okay, let's start again. I had a useful conversation with Hannah last night. She seemed confident that Stuart would turn up soon, safe and sound. '

Louise's eyes widened in horror. 'You didn't tell her everything?'

'Pretty much.'

'Holy shit. She'll think I'm a neurotic sociopath.'

'She's a detective chief inspector, she should be unshockable. You don't spend years in the police without coming face to face with plenty of bad stuff.'

Louise crunched on her cornflakes. 'I suppose Dad came across a lot of it, too. How can anyone want to do that job? I couldn't bear it. Especially not in the CID, dealing with death and disaster. Imagine having to break the news to someone that a child has been murdered. The work would crucify me.'

'When I was a boy, he told me it was like an addiction. Once the drug got into his system, he could never imagine doing anything else.'

'You understood how his mind worked.' She turned her face to him. Without make-up, her flesh seemed raw. The breezy mood had evaporated. 'I never did.'

On another day, he might have resorted to a teenager's jibe. *You never tried.* Like a lot of siblings, they often brought out the worst in each other. Instead, he said, 'Hannah said she'd keep in touch, and let me know the news about Stuart.'

'She's interested in you.'

He withdrew his hand from her shoulder. 'What do you mean?'

'Touched a nerve, did I? It's obvious, there's chemistry between the two of you.'

'Don't be stupid, she's in a long-term relationship.'

'Tell you something.' She leaned towards him. 'Marc Amos didn't pay her much attention at the party.'

'Nothing odd in that. Plenty of couples make a deliberate effort to socialise with other…'

'You're making excuses for them.' A touch of Louise's habitual asperity; she couldn't help herself. 'Familiarity breeds contempt. Or at least boredom.'

'Slow down, Louise. I enjoy talking to Hannah about Dad. Filling in gaps, you know? But that's as far as it goes. I don't even want another relationship. Certainly nothing as heavy as I had with Miranda. I'm ready for a break.'

The look in her eyes said: *you're protesting too much.*

'You've had a break. That's why you pissed off to America. To lick your wounds before you came back to start again.'

He groaned. 'You sound like an agony aunt.'

'You ought to study the problem pages.' A mischievous grin. 'All human life is there.'

'No matter how many I read, I'll never figure out how women think.'

'Like I never understood Dad?' she asked softly. 'I never worked out why left us for that woman. As for Stuart, why did he treat me the way he did? Men and women, trying to read each other's minds? It's like trying to crack an unbreakable code.'

◇◇◇

Marc didn't haul himself out of bed until Hannah sang goodbye up the stairs. A sign of good humour; often she left without a word, her mind already focused on the day ahead at work. The sex had been good last night, and he wished he could be sure that was the reason for her cheeriness. But his confidence was in bits.

It was too easy to blame her job for what had gone wrong. In their early years together, it suited him that she was a police officer. He was happy to have time and space for himself, the chance to get lost in books and dreams. Hannah's anecdotes about her cases fascinated him; she was a good story-teller and long ago, he'd encouraged her to embellish the tales and put them into a book—*It Shouldn't Happen to a Policewoman* or something—but the suggestion made her laugh in appalled amazement. She preferred action to words.

In her haste to be away, she'd forgotten to put her breakfast things in the dishwasher. He lined up the dirty cups and plates in neat rows, in their early days together, he'd found her lack of domesticity endearing; now it provoked irritation. A DCI should never be slapdash, surely? Order and method pleased him; the real world was messy and unsatisfactory, this was why, at every opportunity, he escaped into a well-made Victorian triple-decker.

He forced on a pair of new trainers. They were tight and the only other time he'd worn them, they'd made his heels bleed, but today he'd wear them as a penance. An antique mirror hung in the hallway; he'd picked it up at a craft fair at the Brewery in Kendal the day after they'd moved in here, an over-priced impulse buy. His reflection glowered at him, scornful of his extravagance. After the lawyers shelled out his aunt's legacy, he'd allowed himself to become carried away. He'd bought in too much stock that he couldn't shift, while repairs and renovations to the house and the new shop in Sedbergh swallowed far more than he'd budgeted for. The new roof alone cost double the estimate. At the end of December, the quarter day's rental payments on the two shops came close to cleaning him out.

Thinking about it brought him out in a cold sweat. Hannah wasn't aware; he kept meaning to break the news, but the time never seemed right.

He stood in the cloakroom, zipping his windcheater. The washbasin taps dripped permanently and the wooden window frame was too rotten to survive another Lake District winter. So much work still needed to be done, and he wasn't sure Hannah's heart was in their new home. Had she agreed to move to Undercrag just because it was close to the Serpent Pool?

He couldn't bear to live here alone. To be comfortable with his own company was one thing, the echoing emptiness of solitary existence very different. Until early this morning, he'd presumed he and Hannah would spend the rest of their lives together. When they'd made love, there was no hint of anything amiss. But he'd woken and couldn't get back to sleep. He got up around four to make himself some hot chocolate, and noticed her mobile, lying on the chest of drawers. Something prompted him to pick it up and check her messages. Unforgivable, but he couldn't help being nosey, and she'd been annoyingly vague about the police business that had kept her out that evening. He expected it was something she could easily have ignored, if she hadn't been a workaholic.

She hadn't deleted her latest text. Carelessness, again. Reading the four words dried his throat, and made his heart hammer against the walls of his chest.

Running late. Traffic. Daniel.

◇◇◇

Traffic, bloody traffic. As he queued at a red light on the A591, Marc told himself that Daniel Kind must have sent the text. Newly returned to England, a free agent after splitting with his girlfriend. Marc had always wondered about Hannah's devotion to Ben Kind. Was she making up for missed opportunities by starting an affair with Ben's son? She was getting itchy feet, and so she had lied to him. It felt like being battered about the head with a brick.

If she had nothing to hide, she'd have been upfront and said she was seeing Daniel. He might have suggested coming along himself. Hence why she'd pretended she was up to her eyes in work. Sometimes three was a crowd.

An impatient horn blast ripped through his reverie. The light had turned to green, and he was dawdling. He raised a hand in apology to the guy in the car behind and put his foot down, rounding the next bend so fast that he veered on to the other side of the road. Lucky there was a gap in the line of vehicles heading towards Ambleside.

'Shit,' he muttered. Too close for comfort.

The low sun half-blinded him. Squinting through the windscreen, he spotted a police car lurking in a lay-by four hundred yards ahead. A burly PC stood on the verge, lifting a speed gun with the dead-eyed menace of a latter day Sundance Kid. Marc slammed on the brakes and the speedo pointer plummeted. As he crawled past, the sharp-shooter scowled at him. Marc fixed his gaze on the road. Today of all days, he was in no mood to be caught out by the Cumbria Constabulary.

He reached the courtyard in one piece, and as he unlocked the shop, he heard the clatter of footsteps on the gravel. Turning, he saw someone in a hooded duffel coat and black boots walking towards him. A gloved hand pulled down the hood. Cassie Weston, her expression stony. Surprised to see her here so soon, he fixed on a smile and gave her a wave. She gave a curt nod, said nothing.

'Bright and early, Cassie!'

'Why not?' she said, shrugging off the duffel coat.

'Everything all right?'

'Yeah, why shouldn't it be?'

'You look knackered, that's all.'

'I'm fine.'

Her eagerness of yesterday had vanished. Even her clothes looked drab. She'd put on a shapeless sweater and a grubby old pair of trousers and hadn't bothered with the dark eye-liner, either.

He lit the fire in the inglenook. The prospect of a cosy refuge from the bitter cold might tempt some passing trade. You had to stay optimistic if you earned a living from selling old books. No blazing logs in his office; he had to make do with a noisy fan heater. He booted up his PC for the customary morning trawl through emails from customers in different time zones. An American fan of the Lake Poets was planning for retirement and wanted to know if Marc would like first refusal on his collection. In the current market, it might take years to get a decent return on the investment. There was more money to be made from breaking up the set and selling the individual titles, since the likeliest buyers would have collections of their own and wouldn't be keen to spend on duplicates. But that game required patience, and deep pockets.

He'd left the office door ajar, and he heard Mrs. Beveridge greet Cassie with a jovial complaint about the weather. The reply sounded grumpy. Why she was in such a funny mood? Stupid to become intrigued by someone who worked for you. Never mix business with pleasure.

His thoughts strayed to Bethany Friend. How long before Hannah discovered that he'd known the girl? On New Year's Eve at the Serpent Pool, she'd looked at him sceptically when they spoke about Bethany.

He remembered his last conversation with Bethany. Her face, tarnished with dismay. What she said....

No, don't even go there.

◇◇◇

Daniel suspected that, if and when he finished *The Hell Within*, his royalties would be swallowed by the cost of heating Tarn Cottage. Winter's bite was sharp this morning, and Radio Cumbria reported that teenagers were cavorting on the frozen surface of Derwent Water. They interviewed an elderly woman who reminisced about skating on Windermere in the sixties. A safety expert warned against venturing on to thin ice. But people did it all the time.

He left it until mid-morning before phoning Stuart Wagg. The man was supposed to be on holiday. If he had spent the previous day traipsing over the fells, he might be having a lie-in. There was no answer on the land-line and the call to his mobile again went straight to voicemail. Daniel left a brief message, and tried Wagg's office. The receptionist said he wasn't expected in this week. Perhaps Wagg had instructed them to dead-bat all inquiries. Did he have reasons of his own for blipping off the radar?

'Where is he?' Louise demanded.

'Nobody admits to having a clue.'

She closed her eyes. 'God, I'd persuaded myself you were right, and I was worrying myself sick over nothing. But…'

'Hannah Scarlett will let us know as soon as there is any news.'

Louise's cheeks were as white as the frozen earth outside.

'We can't just sit around. We have to do something!'

'For instance?'

'Let's ring the cleaners. Stuart hired a firm in Newby Bridge to look after the housework in Crag Gill.'

Louise found the number, and he phoned the woman who owned the business. No joy. The Bug had laid low most of her staff and she said she'd left messages on the answering machine at Crag Gill, apologising for their non-arrival this week. Normal service would be resumed as soon as possible. She hadn't spoken to Stuart Wagg in person, or received any response to her calls.

'The gardener!' Louise said once she'd digested this. 'He has a key to the outbuildings.'

'I'll call him.'

◇◇◇

When Marc wandered into the café at eleven, Mrs. Beveridge made him a latte and presented him with a slice of chocolate gateau. To keep the cold out, she said. Half a dozen people were taking refuge and warming themselves up with tea or coffee, but the shop was almost deserted. Without his online business, bailiffs would be hammering at the door. He'd spent the morning preparing a new catalogue to be emailed to regular customers before he uploaded it on to the website. It was a job he enjoyed. The wonders of digital photography meant he had less need to worry about grumpy buyers complaining their books didn't live up to the catalogue description. Usually Cassie popped in at regular intervals to ask a question or pass the time of day, but so far she'd kept her distance.

He finished his elevenses and strolled to the counter. Cassie's eyes were locked on the computer screen as she checked the market to help her price the books piled in front of her. Her expression didn't flicker as he approached, though she must have heard the floorboards creak.

'Are you okay?' he asked.

'Uh-huh.'

He perched on the desk and at last she dragged her gaze from the screen. Her eyes had red rims. She fished a tissue out of her bag and blew her nose loudly.

'Doesn't look like it.' He cleared his throat. 'You haven't picked up this bug that's doing the rounds?'

'I said I'm all right.'

'Listen, if you need to take the day off...'

'Trust me, I'm better in work.'

'You want to talk about whatever is bothering you?'

To his surprise, she hesitated. Weighing something up. 'Not really.'

'I'll leave you in peace, then.'

He heaved himself off the counter. As he turned to go, he heard her whisper. 'Thanks, anyway.'

◇◇◇

A breakdown in the heating system had turned Divisional HQ into an ice-house. Today the Bug had claimed two more members of Hannah's depleted band. Linz Waller had rung in sick and so had the remaining admin assistant. Les' voice sounded raspy, and Maggie blew her nose three or four times as Hannah gave a short briefing to the walking wounded. Only Greg Wharf seemed immune, wondering whether they should ask to be re-named the Sub-Zero Case Team.

Half an hour later, Maggie stuck her head round the door. The sparkle in her eyes told Hannah that she'd discovered something new.

'Spare me a minute, ma'am?'

'Anything to take my mind off the monthly stats is very welcome. Take a seat.'

'No joy yet tracing Cumbes, Redfern, or Seeton, so I've taken a break and checked out Bethany's career history.' She produced a sheet of paper. 'Want to take a look?'

Hannah swallowed. Did a spell at Amos Books feature in the list? She couldn't put off the awkward questions forever.

She shook her head. 'You tell me.'

'You'll never guess who Bethany once worked for.' Maggie beamed, prolonging the suspense.

She wouldn't be so pleased with herself if she'd found a connection with Marc. 'Surprise me.'

'She had three months at George Saffell's estate agency, eighteen months before her death.'

'All right, let me see.'

Hannah stretched out a hand for the sheet. But the name that caught her eye first wasn't Saffell's, but that of Stuart Wagg's law firm. Bethany Friend had spent a fortnight there, the summer before her death in the Serpent Pool.

◇◇◇

When Marc was not out buying books or manning a stall at a book fair, he took his lunch in the café. Lately he'd fallen into the habit of sharing a table with Cassie, but when he emerged from his office at one o'clock, there was no sign of her. He gobbled a sandwich and after making good his escape from Mrs. Beveridge, he wandered over to the till for a word with Zoe, a student who helped out on half-days during her vacation. She was a diminutive, chatty nineteen-year old who reminded Marc of a small, inquisitive bird.

'Cassie asked me to tell you she'd gone out for a walk.'

'In this weather?'

'Yeah, exactly.' Small brown eyes peered at him through the thick lenses of her spectacles. 'Said she needed some air. If you ask me, she's upset.'

'What about?'

'Some man, is my guess.'

'Boyfriend?'

'Partner,' Zoe corrected him. 'Least, I suppose it's him.'

'I'll have a word with her.'

'Be careful.'

He stared. 'What do you mean?'

Zoe enjoyed pretending to be discreet. 'Not for me to say.'

'Come on, we've known each other a long time.' It was true; her parents lived in Staveley and had been customers since the shop opened. When he'd first met Zoe, she'd been a tongue-tied schoolgirl. 'You can be frank with me.'

'Hey, Marc, Cassie's sweet, okay? But I don't know much about her life and my guess is, we get on better that way. If you ask me, she's…um… a complicated person. Better not to get involved.'

He didn't know what to say. Zoe liked Hannah; had she worked out that he was attracted to Cassie? He'd done his best to conceal it, even from himself.

'Thanks for the advice.'

The moment he was out of her sight, he pulled his coat off the hook and opened the back door.

◇◇◇

Cassie hadn't gone far. A bridle path ran close to the beck, curving past spiky trees in the direction of the village. She'd found a bench half a mile from the shop and was looking out towards the whitened slopes on which half a dozen kids were tobogganing. Again she didn't look up until he sat down next to her.

'Zoe told me you'd set off for a walk.'

'I didn't mean you to chase after me.'

'I'm concerned, that's all. You're obviously upset. You can tell me it is none of my business…'

'It is none of your business,' she retorted. He started to get up, but she laid a gloved hand on his arm. 'Sorry, that's rude. I do appreciate your kindness, Marc. I try not to let personal stuff get in the way of work, but it isn't easy sometimes.'

'I'd be glad to help, if I can.'

She groaned. 'I might as well spill the beans. My boyfriend and I have had a huge row. I think it may be over between us.'

'I'm sorry.'

She was on the brink of tears. Anxiety welled inside him as he realised he didn't know how to play this. Zoe might be right. His life was messy enough.

But he felt her leaning into him.

Even in the cold winter air, he smelled a musky perfume on Cassie's skin. He closed his eyes, remembering the text.

Running late. Traffic. Daniel.

In his head, he heard Mrs. Beveridge's confident advice. *Might as well be hung for a sheep as a lamb.*

He turned to Cassie, but felt her body shift on the bench. As he opened his eyes, she was scrambling to her feet.

'My lunch break's over. We mustn't leave Zoe on her own too long.'

'In case there's a rush?'

'You never know.' Her smile was unnaturally bright. 'Race you back to the shop?'

Chapter Fourteen

Wanda Saffell's letterpress business occupied a squat, white-washed building in a quiet side-street. She'd called it Stock Ghyll Press after the beck that ran down to the centre of Ambleside, flowing beneath that photographer's Mecca, Bridge House, on its way to the Rothay. Once, the ghyll had powered the town's bobbin mills, but the cotton trade they served was long gone, and the mills had either fallen down or metamorphosed into holiday lets.

A signboard hung over a window display of half a dozen finely bound books, a couple opened to show off the woodcut engravings. In pride of place was a slim volume bearing the author's name in intricate lettering.

Nathan Clare.

The door creaked open. Wanda Saffell stood in the doorway and looked Hannah up and down. A minute scrutiny, as if she were checking a page proof for typographical errors.

'I saw you from upstairs, inspecting my books.'

'They are beautiful.'

Okay, it was soft soap, to get the interview off on the right foot. But it was also true.

'Your partner loves them. Oh yes, only this week, he agreed to take half a dozen copies of Nathan's book. He probably mentioned it?'

No, he bloody hadn't. Hannah choked back a groan of irritation and Wanda Saffell raised her eyebrows. Elegantly, as she seemed to do everything. She'd even drenched Arlo Denstone with a smooth movement of the hand that held the wine-filled glass. Today she wasn't dressed up for a party at a rich man's mansion, but still she managed to make a sweatshirt and jeans look chic. Yet there was a jarring note, a pungent fragrance that clung to her. Sharp and almost metallic, it seemed oddly familiar, though Hannah couldn't put a name to it.

'I have heard about you from Marc.'

'And I saw you at Stuart Wagg's party, even though we weren't introduced.'

'I can't claim it was my finest hour.'

Hannah waited.

'Needless to say, I was pissed out of my brain. Lucky for me that your chums in Traffic didn't catch me while I was driving to Crag Gill. I'd hate to think what my breath test reading might be.' Her smile showed pointed incisors. It didn't touch her cool blue eyes. 'Naturally, I would be forced to deny everything if there were witnesses to this conversation.'

'You were obviously unhappy that night.'

Wanda rested her hands on her hips. 'My husband died rather horribly a few weeks earlier, Chief Inspector. Mightn't that explain it? Now, this weather is too cold for me to stand here without a coat. I'm sure you don't usually conduct your interviews on doorsteps like a tabloid reporter. Come in, before we both catch our deaths.'

She led Hannah into a narrow passageway. This was where she'd insisted on meeting, and at first, Hannah was disappointed. Since her early days as a DC, she'd preferred to interview people in their home environment whenever possible. After the normal working day, if possible, when they might be more relaxed, perhaps off guard. While you talked, you could learn so much about someone from scanning their shelves, weighing up their tastes in décor, the books and music they liked to surround themselves with. But then, Wanda had shared the house with the late lamented George, and it probably still said more about the deceased than his widow. There might be more clues here.

'Do you know much about letterpress?' Wanda asked over her shoulder.

'Next to nothing, I'm afraid.'

'Marc's interested, as you know.'

She didn't, actually. Even after all these years.

Wanda halted outside a door and threw it open. It gave on to a large room, with three different printing presses, and a table covered in sheets of paper with engravings. The far wall was lined with cabinets. One, left open, was crammed from top to bottom with chunks of type.

'This is where most of the work is done. Take a look.'

The first thing that struck Hannah when she stepped inside was the smell. So this was Wanda's perfume—the tang of good old-fashioned ink. And mixed in with the ink was the earthy aroma of newly cut paper, and a whiff of fresh glue.

Wanda breathed in deeply. 'Intoxicating, don't you think? Since I started up here, I need a fix pretty much every day. The full-on, whole-sensory experience of a printing press in action. Even the rattle and clank of the machinery excites me. We live in a virtual world these days, but this is *real*.'

'Uh-huh.'

'Not your cup of tea, Chief Inspector? Ask Marc, he would understand.'

Why did Wanda keep dragging Marc into the conversation— to make her think that someone her partner knew couldn't possibly be a murderer?

'I'm sure he would.'

'At least I can't be arrested, not for getting high on ink and bound sheets of paper.' She gestured to a large, heavy piece of equipment in the corner. 'An Arab treadle press. A wonderful machine, a century ago you found it everywhere. I've always been fascinated by letterpress, but I never had the time or money to indulge myself. But this was going for a song at an auction, because it was all in pieces. A few days later, I met George, when his firm put their PR work out to tender. I couldn't resist mentioning that I'd just picked up a stripped-down Arab.'

'And what did he say?'

'Within twenty four hours, he'd taken me to his bed. Three months later, we were honeymooning in the Maldives. I packed in PR for the joys of running my own print shop. No need to disapprove, I'm scarcely a hardwired gold-digger. My first husband was a musician, and I kept him for years.'

She looked Hannah in the eye, as if defying her to make something of it. A combative woman, this. A bad enemy.

'We'll go into the other room.' Wanda announced, as though it was time to bite her tongue. 'You will have a cup of coffee.'

A statement, not a question. She shepherded Hannah into a smaller room on the other side of the passageway. Hannah's stomach rumbled. If Wanda offered her biscuits, or better still, buttered crumpets, she wouldn't say no.

Stock Ghyll Press titles filled the shelves which ran from floor to ceiling. There was a desk with a computer, and a small circular table surrounded by three chairs. Lying on a table was a copy of Nathan Clare's book. While Wanda busied herself in the little kitchen area at the end of the corridor, Hannah leafed through it.

Not her sort of thing.

Wanda returned and set down two steaming mugs on the table. There wasn't a biscuit in sight.

'Nathan has a marvellous talent.'

'So he told me.'

'Yes, he mentioned that you'd interviewed him. No doubt he explained to you that Fate has cheated him of fame and fortune. The curl of your lip suggests his work is not to your taste, Chief Inspector. But your partner was impressed.'

'Then I bow to his expertise.'

Wanda sat back in her chair and put her hands behind her head. The body language of negligent command.

'So you have re-opened the file on poor Bethany Friend, and you want to speak to Nathan and me, and presumably anyone else who had the slightest acquaintance with her?'

'More than slight in Mr. Clare's case,' Hannah said. 'He and Bethany were in a relationship not long before her death.'

'I wouldn't read much into that, if I were you. Nathan has had countless relationships, he's famous for it.'

'And you and he...?'

Wanda wasn't fazed. She'd prepared for this conversation, and she didn't mean to lose control.

'...are consenting adults, Chief Inspector. Which is all that I intend to say on the subject. As for Bethany, I met her through work, as I met hundreds of other people.'

'You were friends.'

'She was a pleasant girl.' Her tone was neutral. Wanda didn't do displays of emotion, except when she was pissed or angry or both. 'Pretty, and rather naive. Reserved in manner, but charming once she got to know you and started to thaw.'

'Did you know that she had temped for your husband?'

'George?' Wanda's eyes widened. 'No, she never mentioned it.'

Hannah sensed the news had come as a surprise to Wanda, but she decided to persist. 'Really? Did George not mention it either?'

'No, why should he? Bear in mind, he and I hadn't met at the time I knew Bethany. And we never discussed her.'

'Sure about that?'

'Absolutely.'

'And how about Bethany's stint working for Stuart Wagg, did that pass you by as well?'

'What on earth are you driving at, Chief Inspector? Do you interrogate everyone you meet about all their previous employments? Me neither. Bethany flitted all over the place.'

Time to change tack. 'You said she was naïve?'

'Easily led.'

'Who tried to lead her?'

'I didn't pry into her life, Chief Inspector. We were different ages, when we talked, it was mostly about the latest book we'd read.'

'What else can you tell me about her?'

'Nothing additional to the statement I gave after she died.'

'You must care about what happened to her?'

'Nobody ever proved that she was murdered. For all I know, she committed suicide.'

'Was it in her character to kill herself?'

'I was a work colleague, not her psychiatrist. We didn't even share the same employer. My firm had the contract to promote the University's image and Bethany and I met because she was typing for the Director of Communications, and sat in to take notes of our reporting sessions.'

'And you hit it off together?'

'We discovered we had similar tastes in literature. She wanted to write, while my creative urge is confined to printing. But a love of books is a bond.'

'And she never confided in you about her personal life?'

'No.'

'There were no rows between you?"

'Why would we quarrel? We weren't competing against each other.'

Time to give her a shake, even if it meant the kiss of death for any hope of co-operation

'Not even over Nathan Clare?'

Wanda frowned, but gave no sign of being rattled. Her annoyance resembled that of a long-suffering mother whose child embarrasses her in public.

'That's a ridiculous suggestion.'

'Any reason there why she would want to end it all?' Hannah persisted. 'Or why someone else would have a reason to kill her?'

'I can't imagine anyone wishing to murder Bethany. She was a sweet girl, it's inexplicable. Her death saddened me, but it's not my business to solve the mystery.'

Hannah felt like chewing the table. The woman was holding back on her. And there was an air of superiority about Wanda Saffell this afternoon, a suppressed self-satisfaction that irritated and puzzled her. Anyone would think she had an ace up her sleeve, but couldn't be bothered to play it.

'Did she talk about why she split up with Nathan Clare?'

'She didn't need to. There are people who dump and others who get dumped. Nathan fell into the former category, and Bethany into the latter. It was inevitable that he would tire of her, as he has tired of a long list of other women.'

'Nothing personal, then?'

'Sarcasm is unworthy of you, Chief Inspector. Nathan is an artist. He lives on his own terms.'

'Like so many men?'

'Don't scoff, Chief Inspector, it doesn't suit you. Believe me, I'm as much a feminist as any women.'

'You were making a feminist statement when you threw wine over Arlo Denstone at Stuart Wagg's party?'

'I was drunk and depressed, that's all.'

'What had Denstone done to deserve it?'

'He was in the wrong place at the wrong time, if you like.'

'Meaning what?'

'We'd met before George died. He's an attractive man, in a gaunt sort of way. He seemed interested in me, obviously I read too much into it. There's no point in denying that I propositioned him. He said no thanks, but it was the disgust in his eyes that seemed so cruel. As if I were ugly and desperate. That's why I was so angry with him, and at the party I wanted him to apologise. But when I sobered up on New Year's Day, I realised I should have left it. All I did was make myself look sad.'

'Your solicitor took you home from the party.'

Wanda Saffell looked wary. 'You know I consulted Raj Doshi for matrimonial advice?'

Hannah nodded.

'I didn't take it any further. Not in terms of splitting up with George, that is.'

'What, then?' An idea struck Hannah. 'Have you been seeing Doshi?'

Wanda's face darkened. 'He's married, Chief Inspector. And my private life is none of your business.'

'Must have been difficult for you, after your husband was murdered.'

'As you well know, the inquest has been adjourned. The Coroner hasn't delivered a verdict.'

'Do you doubt that he was murdered?'

'Since you ask, no.'

'Any idea why anyone would want to kill your husband in such a cruel fashion?'

'None whatsoever. But you didn't come here to discuss what happened to George, I hope. In the military jargon, that surely is mission creep.'

'Let me be the judge of that, Mrs. Saffell.'

'Another officer is in charge of the investigation into my husband's death.'

'DCI Larter knows I am speaking to you.'

'Doubling up? Not a very good use of resources, Chief Inspector.'

Stung, Hannah gave in to temptation. 'You must admit, it's a coincidence. Two people, apparently murdered in mysterious circumstances and for no obvious reason. Two people whom you knew.'

Wanda flushed, and Hannah felt like shouting in exultation. At last, she'd registered a hit.

'You can't be suggesting a connection between the deaths of Bethany and George?'

'Do you believe there is a connection?'

'Don't be absurd. I knew them both, but that's neither here nor there. You might as well...'

'What?'

A question too far, although she didn't realise.

Wanda's expression became a blend of contempt and savage triumph.

'You might as well investigate someone much closer to home. After all, George spent a fortune with Amos Books—where Bethany worked before moving to the university. She fancied Marc like crazy. Whether they slept together, I never enquired. As I said, I don't pry into other people's lives. But of course, he will have told you the full story, Chief Inspector Scarlett. Won't he?'

◇◇◇

Hannah had never been kicked in the stomach by a donkey, but it must feel like this. At least if you were coshed by some thug, it wasn't accompanied by this sickening sense of betrayal by someone you trusted not to hurt you.

In the course of a year, up to a dozen casual workers worked at the shop, helping out at busy times and in the holiday season. The Lake District was full of young people passing through, gap year students, migrants and assorted drifters, who took a job for a while, then left for something else. Marc couldn't be expected to remember every single person. But he'd remembered Bethany Friend. You wouldn't forget someone who died in such mysterious circumstances; the story had been all over the local papers for a couple of weeks. Especially if they'd been infatuated with you.

She found herself taking the track that followed Stock Ghyll. Swelled by the rain of the last few days, the ghyll squeezed through narrow channels in the cliff on its way down to Ambleside. Where the path forked, she continued right, climbing steps of rock and oak root before reaching a fence with iron arches. Beyond was a railed viewpoint, overlooking the stream, but she ploughed on, along more rough steps until she reached the footbridge at the top. The paths were thick with mud; her shoes would be ruined, but she didn't care. At last she stopped, and closed her eyes, listening to the roar of the white water below.

This was Stock Ghyll Force. The waterfall threw up clouds of spray, and Hannah felt drops of water on her skin. A rib of rock showed through the foam; it split the falls like a dorsal fin before the waters converged again, meeting in mid-air to form a raging torrent. If you shut your eyes, you might believe a dam had burst.

Or that all hell had been let loose.

During the original investigation into Bethany Friend's death, a member of Ben's team had produced a rough *curriculum vitae* summarising her work experience. She'd moved around so much, the document was bound to be incomplete. It wasn't too surprising that there was no mention of a spell at Amos Books. Probably the job amounted to nothing more than a few weekends, paid cash in hand while she worked somewhere else Monday to Friday, and served behind a bar at night.

Marc should have come clean. Wanda Saffell hinted that he and Bethany had been lovers. Mischief-making, but that didn't mean she was wrong. Even after Hannah had started seeing Marc, he'd dallied with Leigh Moffatt. If an affair with an employee turned sour, maybe she'd become difficult. Threatened a sexual harassment claim or something.

Cold and hungry, with tears pricking her eyes, Hannah leaned on the railing and glared down at the cascade. A couple in their seventies walked past, and looked at her with undisguised anxiety. But she wasn't contemplating a leap into the abyss. Just facing up to the question she could no longer dodge.

Was the man she'd loved for years capable of tying up Bethany Friend and leaving her to drown in the Serpent Pool?

◇◇◇

On her way back to the car, she called at a shop that was holding a sale and bought herself new shoes. Three pairs. Retail therapy was her best chance of de-stressing—she didn't expect to break open a bottle of wine with Marc any time soon. The old, mud-caked shoes she stuffed into a litter bin. If only you could ditch everything wrong in your life so easily.

Within two minutes of her arrival at HQ, she found herself bellowing at a temp who had messed up some photocopying. As the girl's face crumpled, she apologised, and cursed herself inwardly. Wrong to vent her ill-humour on subordinates, however lazy and incompetent: wrong, wrong, wrong.

Fern wasn't around, which was a relief. She didn't want to feed back on her conversation with Wanda until she'd had a chance to confront Marc. But she'd barely stomped into her office and slammed the door to discourage interruptions, before it swung open again. Maggie bounded in like an eager spaniel expecting to be taken out for a walk.

'Are you all right, guv?'

'Can't it wait, whatever it is? I'm busy.'

Maggie's face fell. She threw a reproachful glance at the pc screen, yet to be switched on.

'I thought you'd want to know.'

Give me strength.

'Fire away, then.'

'You'll never guess what's happened.'

Hannah was about to snap: *I'm not into guessing games, just spit it out.* But if she wasn't careful, she'd burst a blood vessel. She was too hunched up in her chair, too rigid and tense. Lean back, breathe out, strive for calm.

'Tell you what, Maggie. Why don't you pull up a chair, and then break it to me gently?'

◇◇◇

'The boss has gone AWOL, then?'

Alf Swallow's van and trailer were already outside the front porch when Daniel and Louise arrived. The gardener was a muscular man with a square jaw and features as rugged as the Langdale Pikes. He had close-cropped greying hair and Daniel was sure he'd never tugged a forelock in his life. The rolled-up sleeves of his mud-stained overall revealed brawny arms with blue tattoos. A lifetime spent out of doors in the Lake District meant bad weather didn't bother him. Probably not much did.

'He hasn't answered his phone for twenty four hours,' Louise said. 'Of course, I may be worrying unnecessarily, but...'

Swallow considered her, much as he might assess a choice bloom in a nursery. 'He'll be all right, love, don't fret.'

'Did he mention going away?'

'You'd know better than me, love. The boss and I don't see much of each other. When I'm here, he's in his office or at court. He leaves it to me to keep these grounds spick and span.'

'You neatened things up before of the New Year's Eve party, didn't you?'

'Tidied all the rubbish people left a couple of mornings later, come to that. I saw the curtains were closed, so I figured out he couldn't have gone back to work yet. But I didn't want to disturb anyone. Stuffed my bill through the letter box as usual and went on my way.'

'You can't guess where he might be?'

'Likes to go walking, doesn't he? Told me once he was a fresh air fiend.'

He spat on the ground, as if to indicate his private opinion of a soft solicitor who fancied himself as an outdoor type.

'But he's disappeared.'

'Maybe he's holed up in a B and B somewhere. Or a luxury hotel, more like.'

'He might have tumbled down a gully,' Louise said.

'Trust me, love. Stuart Wagg will always fall on his feet.' A crooked grin. 'Least, I hope so. Can't afford to lose a good customer.'

'Do you have keys to the outbuildings? If he's had an accident...'

'Can't imagine he's trapped himself in there. But you can have a look, if you like.'

It was clear he thought she was making a song and dance over nothing, but he led the way around the side of the house to the tree-fringed gardens looking out to Windermere. This stretch of the lake had not frozen over, but there wasn't a single boat on the water. As befitted a house that took its name from a Ransome novel, there was a wooden landing stage where a sleek fibreglass boat was moored. Just for show, Louise said; Stuart Wagg was too often sea sick to be much of a sailor. This was the first time Daniel had seen the view in daylight. Crag Gill's location was perfect. The house crouched on the slope, quiet as a church in prayer.

The grounds were bordered by tall hawthorn hedges; thick but not impenetrable, like the hedge Daniel had squeezed through the previous day. At the end of the drive stood a triple garage linked to a large brick store-room.

Louise murmured. 'I never went into the garage, I always parked outside. Too afraid of clipping the wing of his bloody car. The other building is full of garden equipment, but we'd better look inside, in case…'

Swallow opened the store and waved them in. There was a sit-on lawnmower and an array of hoes, spades and scythes suspended from a rack that ran the length of one wall, but no Stuart Wagg. Daniel looked through the doorway that gave on to the garage. Parked in a neat line were a rich man's toys. The Bentley to impress clients, an open-top Mercedes for casual driving and a gleaming Harley Davidson for fun.

'He takes the bike over to the Isle of Man for the TT races,' Swallow said. 'That apart, I doubt if he rides it more than once in a blue moon. Anyhow, you can see he's gone walking. Else a car or the bike would be missing, wouldn't it?'

'I suppose so.'

Louise sounded miserable, as though she guessed that Swallow was laughing to himself at her silliness. She hated making a fool of herself.

'Suppose you'll want to see the summer house?' Swallow's bushy eyebrows lifted. 'Make sure he's not keeled over while he was inside, watching the rain pour down?'

He spat on the path before striding off across the garden in the direction of a pine summer house with a verandah. He was whistling something that sounded like an approximation of 'The Dambusters March'. A son of the soil, humouring folk who ought to know better.

Daniel whispered, 'They should have called him Alf Spit, not Alf Swallow.'

Louise didn't appreciate his attempt to lighten the mood. 'Something bad has happened,' she hissed.

She was shivering beneath the heavy fleece. He grabbed her arm, and squeezed it tight. They hurried after the gardener and caught up with him as he rattled a key in the lock securing the summer house. Inside stood a table and a set of stacked garden chairs. Boxes of cutlery and crockery occupied a single shelf at the back of the building. Cobwebs criss-crossed the windows and when they stepped over the threshold, a cloud of dust blew up and made Daniel sneeze.

'Bless you,' Swallow said.

'Is there anywhere we haven't searched?' Louise demanded.

A shake of the head. 'There's the well, of course, but no way would he be down there.'

'Oh God, I'd forgotten the well,' Louise said. 'Stuart pointed it out to me, when he showed me round here.'

'It's not been used for many a long year. Dates back to when the old house was on this site. It may have been dug out before then, for all I know. Once upon a time there were wells like this all over the countryside.'

'How deep is it?' Daniel asked.

'Thirty feet, maybe less. The bottom's silted up. The boss talked about filling it in, but we haven't got round to it yet. It used to be covered with wooden boards, but they were rotting, so I put a new metal sheet over the hole this time last year. Heavy bugger to shift. You needn't worry, love. Nobody could fall down there by accident'.

'Let's have a quick look,' Daniel suggested. 'Better not leave any stone unturned.'

Swallow shrugged and led them along a grassy path, past a couple of dense mahonias and into a small clearing with a compost heap, a short distance from the boundary hedge. Daniel wrinkled his nose at the stench of the rotting vegetation. On a small platform of broken house bricks lay a round metal cover showing the first traces of rust.

'That's funny,' Swallow said.

'What?' Louise sounded hoarse.

'I could have sworn the metal sheet wasn't in that position last time I dumped a barrow load of compost. You've got me imagining things myself now.'

'Can you move the cover?' she asked in a small voice.

Alf Swallow cast a glance to the heavens. 'There's a hell of a lot of weight in that, love. Look at it. No way could anyone shift that bugger by mistake.'

'I'll give you a hand,' Daniel said, moving towards the well. 'Let's do it.'

'You're all right, mister, leave it to me.' Swallow's good humour sounded as though it was wearing thin. 'Don't want you to put your back out.'

After a preparatory spit, the gardener bent down and, with a loud grunt, like a Wimbledon star striving to serve an ace, he heaved the metal cover to one side. A small dark opening appeared.

The moment Alf Swallow glanced down into the well, his eyes widened. His face grew dark as scorn gave way to horror, and he swore with primitive savagery.

Daniel's gorge rose. He'd dreaded this. Tried to persuade himself that it was not possible.

Louise gave a strangled cry. 'What…what is it?'

Daniel stepped forward, pushing past the gardener to see for himself. The well-hole was a black abyss. When he knelt down by the edge and peered inside, the stench hit him like a blow from a knuckleduster. He recoiled, but with a frantic effort, managed not to fall down.

Wedged fifteen feet below ground level, before the hole narrowed to nothingness, was the bruised and broken body of a man in shirt and trousers, not dressed for outdoors, let alone for the cold underground . He'd curled up into a foetal ball—whether to ward off blows, or to avoid confronting the fate that awaited him, Daniel dared not guess. The face was hidden, thank God, for the insects must have been busy. No question about the corpse's identity, though. No mistaking that proud mane of dark hair, even though now it was dirty and matted with blood.

The gardener had been wrong.

For once, Stuart Wagg had not fallen on his feet.

Chapter Fifteen

'Hannah, you've heard the news?'

Daniel's voice was low and tense and disturbingly good to hear. She pressed the mobile closer to her ear. He'd rung the moment she hurried out of the well-lit entrance of Divisional HQ into the night. It had been a long and hard day and it wasn't about to improve. Tonight she had to confront Marc about Bethany Friend.

'Stuart Wagg is dead.'

'Louise and I found the body.'

'Horrible for you. I'm sorry.'

'Louise has never seen a corpse before.'

'Is she okay?'

'Shocked, as you'd expect. He was so wrong for her, but she can't understand why someone murdered him.'

'Assuming he was murdered. Until the forensic people have finished…'

'His head was badly wounded and he'd been shoved down an old well which was then covered up. There wasn't a snowball's chance in hell that he could climb out. I really don't think there's any chance of accident or suicide, do you?' He paused for breath. 'Hey, this is a bad idea. You're a chief inspector, it's more than your job's worth to discuss what has happened.'

She dug her nails into her palm. *I've blown it.*

'I didn't mean…'

'Louise is a suspect, bound to be.' He groaned. 'Stupid of me to call. As a matter of fact, I don't have an alibi myself.'

'Don't talk nonsense.'

He didn't reply. One of the senior women from Legal stepped into a pool of light cast by the security lamps. She waved as she headed at a brisk clip for her people carrier at the other end of the car park. Hannah waved back and mouthed goodnight.

She softened her tone. 'Listen, I'm glad you rang me. You want to meet?'

'Thanks, but I don't want you to feel compromised,' he muttered.

'This isn't my case, there's no question of compromising me.' She was far from certain about that, but what the hell? She was sick of trying to do the right thing. 'You and I are friends. Your dad was my boss. Nobody can stop us having a conversation.'

A pause.

'You're sure?'

'Cross my heart and hope to die.'

Despite himself, he laughed. 'All right, you've persuaded me. When?'

'When suits you?'

A pause. 'I suppose there's no chance of later tonight?'

◇◇◇

And then there were two. The last customer had long gone when Mrs. Beveridge finished cashing up and disappeared into the evening cold. Cassie put the *Closed* sign on the door and collected her coat and scarf. Marc stood at the counter, checking an internet auction sale, as she approached him.

'Goodnight, Marc.'

'Your car's fixed, I hope?'

She shook her head. 'The garage said it will be a couple more days. No problem, the bus journey gives me a chance to unwind.'

'Am I such a taskmaster that you need an hour to unwind?'

'You know what I mean.'

'What time is your bus?'

She clicked her tongue in annoyance as she checked her watch. 'Bummer. I just missed one. Never mind. I think they run every half hour.'

'In January? You'll be lucky. Don't worry, I'll give you a lift.'

'Very kind, but I don't want to take you out of your way again.'

'It's not out of my way at all.' He spun round quickly, before she could protest, then called back over his shoulder. 'Give me five minutes.'

As he busied himself, quite unnecessarily, behind the closed door of his office, he told himself this was what she wanted. No harm in it, he deserved a bit of pleasure. Especially after Hannah had concealed her encounter with Daniel Kind. But he didn't want things to get out of hand.

'Ready?' he asked, emerging from his retreat as soon as the stipulated five minutes were up.

'When you are.'

He set the alarm and followed her outside. The courtyard was deserted. As he locked up, she stamped her feet. He could hear her teeth chattering.

'God, it's freezing.'

'See, I couldn't let you hang around in the dark, waiting for a bus that might never show up.'

'I can't believe you're my boss,' she said. 'Some of the other people I've worked for simply couldn't care less about their staff. But you're so kind.'

He zipped the shop keys up in his shoulder bag. 'Perhaps I'm just not very good at being a boss.'

Her smile glittered in the night. 'You shouldn't do yourself down all the time. You're fantastic.'

'And you're very good for my morale.' For a moment, his hand touched hers. Her flesh was cold. 'You were right, you are freezing.'

She took a couple of strides towards where he was parked. 'I'll need to warm up when I get home.'

They climbed into the car. 'If you like, I'll buy you a Jameson's at the God-forsaken pub.'

She fastened her seat belt, and smoothed her coat down, demure as a nun. 'I don't think so, thanks all the same.'

'Up to you.'

The car seemed as quiet as a hearse. To break the silence, he switched on the radio. Duffy, covering a sixties heartbreaker, begging her lover: *don't go, please stay.* He squeezed the steering wheel, aware of Cassie's body, inches from him. He couldn't guess what might be in her mind. She kept blowing hot and cold. Was teasing her stock-in-trade, a means of exercising her power over men? The ballad reached a melodramatic climax as he paused at the junction with the main road. At this hour, he usually had to queue, waiting for a gap in the traffic, but tonight both lanes were deserted, as if everyone had already fled home.

Six o'clock. Time for the local headlines.

'The body of a man has been discovered in the grounds of a house near Bowness,' the announcer said. 'Police have refused to confirm reports that the deceased is prominent local solicitor Stuart Wagg. Mr. Wagg is believed to have been missing for the past twenty-four hours. Meanwhile, as weather conditions deteriorate across the county…'

'Shit!'

Marc came within inches of steering the car into a road sign at a fork. They juddered to a halt. Neither of them spoke as their breath misted the windscreen.

'It's…' He found himself lost for words.

'Unbelievable?' she murmured.

'It must be a mistake.'

'It's no mistake.'

He peered at her through the darkness. 'What makes you so certain?'

'Elementary, my dear Amos. The media wouldn't mention the name if they weren't sure of his identity. Imagine the outrage if they'd got it wrong.'

'I suppose you're right.'

'Don't take my word for it. Your partner's a detective, she's bound to be in the know. Why don't you ask her?'

He'd forgotten that Cassie had once met Hannah. At the time, he'd felt a pin-prick of irritation about her visit to the shop; she didn't take any interest in the business usually, and he suspected her of wanting to size up his latest recruit. Still, it was as well that Cassie knew he was in a relationship. That way there could be no misunderstanding. No recriminations.

'She's in charge of the Cold Cases team. Investigating crimes from the past, not in the here and now.'

'Yes, but she'll have the inside track. She knew Stuart, you told me you were taking her to his party on New Year's Eve.'

'He was in good form that night.' Marc gazed out into the night. There was no moon; they might be anywhere. Just the two of them, alone in the dark. 'What in God's name has happened to him? They said the body was discovered out of doors.'

'It must have been an accident.'

He gave a bitter laugh. 'Like George Saffell?'

'Hey there.' She might have been a mother soothing a fractious child. 'They were customers, not your best friends.'

'George Saffell was murdered, it's a stone cold certainty.' He was almost talking to himself, struggling to get his head round what had happened to his clients. 'For all we know, so was Wagg. The same person may have killed them both.'

'Or else it's a spooky coincidence.'

'The police don't believe in coincidences. That's one thing I've learned from Hannah.'

'Don't say you're worried they will treat you as a suspect?'

'Christ knows.'

'Hannah will look after you.'

He didn't answer.

'I mean, you're the last person who would have wanted them dead. Two rich book collectors?'

'Of course, it's madness. But I've learned from Hannah how the police work when they are in a jam. If they find a convenient fall guy…'

'Don't sound so anxious.' Her fingers brushed against his cheek, then scuttled away, as though embarrassed at their presumption. 'You feel like a cold case too, Marc Amos.'

His body tensed, his heart was beating faster.

'You need that whisky more than I do,' she murmured.

In for a penny…

He cleared his throat. 'Won't you change your mind about having a drink with me?'

'In that wretched pub? Are you joking? I've visited more cheerful mausoleums. Or do I mean mausolea?' She hesitated. 'Tell you what, if you have a few minutes to spare, come up to the flat and I'll make you a mug of Irish coffee. Special recipe, with double cream to soak up the alcohol.'

'Sounds tempting.' He paused, as if deliberating over pros and cons. 'Okay, it's a deal.'

'Fine.' As he turned on the ignition, she settled back in the passenger seat and shut her eyes. 'How good to have a chauffeur. Wake me up when we get home, will you?'

He listened to her soft, rhythmic breathing as he drove, unsure if she was asleep or dreaming. This felt different from the last time he'd taken her home. They were growing closer to each other, but he meant to be careful. Go so far, but no further.

When they arrived at her place, he nudged her awake and then, without a word, followed her up a narrow flight of stairs to a tiny landing on the first floor. There was a door with her name next to the bell.

'Welcome,' she said, shrugging off coat and scarf and waving him into a small sitting room. 'Sorry, it's not exactly Crag Gill.'

Stuart Wagg again. For a few minutes he'd banished the man's suspected death from his mind.

'It's incredible. Within a few weeks, my two best customers…'

The gas fire roared into life, and she lit a trio of candles before switching off the main light. In one corner stood an old-fashioned Japanese hi-fi unit; she pulled a Neil Young CD out of a rack and put it on. The room reminded him of a student house. Furnished on the cheap, but she had an eye for casual chic. Indian wall hangings, throws over the armchairs and sofa, and a warm red and brown kilim spread over the carpet tiles. On every available surface were incense burners decorated with Chinese dragons, exotically carved wooden boxes and trinket pots. Even the paperbacks in the bookcase by the window seemed chosen to fit the colour scheme; although every spine was creased with reading.

'Maybe someone has got it in for you.'

The ironic grin made him blush. It was a knack she had, of constantly pushing him on to the back foot.

'Sorry, did I sound very self-absorbed?'

'No need to look shame-faced. You run a business, and times aren't easy. The likes of Stuart and George pay the bills. And my wages, I'm not forgetting. I hope this won't cause you any grief.'

'Don' worry, I'll get by.'

'Phew, that's a relief. I've had more jobs already than some people have in a lifetime. I'd be sad if you chucked me out on the street.'

'No danger of that, Cassie.'

'Let me fix that Irish coffee while you take the weight off your feet.'

She vanished into a tiny kitchen, leaving him to sprawl across the sofa. Neil Young was singing 'Tonight's the Night'. It excited him, to be invited up here, but he was determined not to succumb to his old weakness of allowing himself to get carried away. He didn't want Cassie to misunderstand him. Not that he was confident that he entirely understood himself.

He closed his eyes. How easy to drift away. What if she invited him to smoke a joint, or share a line of cocaine? He found it impossible to predict her; there was no knowing how far she might go. Suppose the invitation to coffee was a ruse? He'd made himself vulnerable, he wasn't in control. What might she be stirring into his drink, what pills or potion might the whisky and cream disguise?

As he opened his eyes, she walked through the door, carrying a tray. She cleared a space on the bamboo table by the sofa and set the drinks down.

'Here.' She passed him one of the mugs and sat down in the chair facing him. 'Take a sip. See how you like it.'

He tried the coffee. She'd made it very strong.

Cassie's lips were parted as she waited for his reaction.

They exchanged smiles. Yes, he was taking a risk, but the weird thing was, he didn't care.

He took another taste.

◇◇◇

'What did Hannah say?'

Louise was curled up on the sofa in the living room of Tarn Cottage, dressing gown wrapped tight around her. The lights shone bright, the fire blazed, the aroma of their hot chocolate lingered in the air. It couldn't seem cosier; but appearances deceived.

She had barely stopped shivering after an hour spent answering questions from the police while her lover's body was hauled out of the well by the CSI specialists. Daniel had called in a solicitor from Preston to represent her, a cadaverous pessimist in a washable but unwashed brown suit. All the lawyers they knew in the Lakes were either colleagues of Stuart Wagg or competitors with an axe to grind. The solicitor's demeanour suggested that all his clients pleaded guilty in the fullness of time. His advice so far consisted of instructing her to say as little as possible about her relationship with the dead man, and at least this curtailed the inquisition. Perhaps he was smarter than his clothes. But the DC conducting the interview made it clear that Louise was only postponing the inevitable. He'd talk to her again, once the shock began to subside.

Daniel prodded the burning logs with a poker before warming his hands in front of the fire. Louise must feel as numb. If only he could scrub from his mind the surreal vision of Wagg's body, stuffed down that hole in the ground. Perhaps he'd imagined it, and was about to wake from a nightmare.

Except for this—how could anyone invent that foetid smell wafting up from the hole cut in the ground, that rotten stench of dirty death?

'We've agreed to meet at The Tickled Trout.'

Flames leapt in the fireplace. Louise seemed hypnotised, like an onlooker spellbound by a ritual dance.

'Who could have done this?' she whispered.

'Stuart was selfish, and ruthless. Must have made a new enemy every week.'

'It's not a motive for murder. The legal profession is full of people like that and they aren't all cramming the mortuary drawers. Trust me, I've met plenty, and most of them didn't have a fraction of Stuart's charm.'

'His mask slipped sometimes. Remember?'

She flinched, as if he'd prodded her with the poker. 'You think this is personal?'

'What else?'

'He was the most self-centred man I ever met. Which is saying something. But his ego was part of the package.'

'He hurt you,' Daniel said. 'I won't forgive that.'

'But people did forgive him, that's the whole point about Stuart, don't you see? However badly he behaved, he managed to get away with it. I lost control when he dumped me, but I'd have got over it, promise. It's not as if I really loved him.'

He stared at her, 'Are you serious?'

'Never more so.' She kept her eyes on the fire. 'I was infatuated, it's not the same as love. A temporary insanity. By the time Christmas came, the magic had worn thin.'

'You changed jobs, you moved home, you were willing to turn your life around for him.' It was as if he'd never really known her. 'Are you telling me it was all done on a whim?'

'The truth is more complicated, as usual.' She sounded as though she'd suddenly sobered up after an all-night drinking binge. 'Meeting Stuart gave me the chance to break with the past. I was bored with my job, bored with my students, bored with my bloody ordinary life. He offered me an escape route. It wasn't his money that turned me on, it was the excitement. Coupled with the ego boost, that a man who could have pretty much any woman he wanted had fallen for me. I'd dared to do something different. Something wild and life-changing. Like you did, when you left Oxford and moved up here with Miranda.'

'You told me not to be a fool.'

'My mistake, as usual.' She turned to face him. 'Here in the Lakes, I could start again. Don't forget, I haven't sold the house in Manchester yet. And I knew if it didn't work out with Stuart—at least you'd be here, and I'd have a shoulder to cry on.'

'Always,' he said, 'but then, why go off the deep end when he dumped you?'

'Pride and temper, of course, what else?' She seemed astonished that she needed to explain. 'I'd told myself that the minute I felt trapped with Stuart, I'd make the break. But I never dreamed it would come so soon. And I didn't want Stuart to be the one who finished it. I've never trusted men since Dad walked out on us, but I keep making bad choices. How humiliating to be thrown out as soon as the New Year party was over. It was as if he'd made a resolution to tidy up his life, and get rid of me along with the ripped wrapping paper and empty champagne bottles.'

'I'm sorry.'

'It was so sudden and brutal. Even now, I can't believe he changed so quickly.'

'What caused it, do you think?'

'God alone knows. I hate not being able to understand what's going on in my life. Which is why I lost control. Does that make sense?'

'Sort of.' He shook his head. 'I bet you barely touched him with that knife.'

'I suppose you're right. For a few moments, I hated him. I might even have summoned up the anger to do him real damage. But now the red mist has cleared, I feel so bad. It's as if I wished him dead.'

'Not your fault. Whoever killed him, he brought it on himself.'

'Nobody deserves to die in such a terrifying way. I can't imagine anything worse for him, to be trapped underground, cold and alone, with no means of escape. You saw the steep sides of that well, he couldn't have got enough of a grip to climb out, even if he hadn't hurt his head, even if the well hadn't been covered over. What makes it even worse is his claustrophobia. He never even took the lift in his own office block, he always ran up the stairs. I pray he wasn't conscious when he was dumped down the well. Otherwise, his suffering must have.'

'Someone must have hated him intensely.'

'Impossible. Nobody hated Stuart.'

'Are you kidding? Come on, he trod on a lot of toes.'

'Yes, but whenever he did someone a bad turn, he managed to wriggle out of the consequences. I saw it time after time. An apology, some ludicrously generous gesture to show his remorse, he was brilliant at *mea culpa*. It was his redeeming virtue. And he never bore grudges.'

A picture swam into Daniel's head. His last sight of Stuart Wagg's body. He needed to learn how to forget, or the scene might haunt his nights as Aimee's suicide did.

'But someone bore a grudge against him.'

◇◇◇

Hannah spoke with Fern Larter before leaving for the day. For the brass, the decision to ask Fern to handle the Stuart Wagg case was a no-brainer. Not only because of a possible link with George Saffell's death, but because the Bug meant nobody else of sufficient seniority was available.

The only sign of a knife wound on the corpse appeared to be a graze on the shoulder. So Louise Kind was in the clear. No surprise there, but at least Daniel had no need to worry about her.

Fern intended to quiz Wagg's partners and staff in the morning, but Hannah expected Raj Doshi and the rest would close ranks. She gave Fern a quick summary of her interview in Ambleside, without mentioning what Wanda had said about Marc. Better talk to him first, see what he had to say for himself.

'Not only did Wanda work with Bethany Friend,' Fern mused, 'she was married to one dead man, and caused a scene at a party given by another.'

'Why would she want to kill Stuart Wagg?'

'God knows.'

'The fact that Bethany worked for George and Stuart. You think it's significant?'

'Unlikely.' Fern frowned. 'I can tell from your expression that you don't agree, but think about it. Bethany was a temp, they were employers in the neighbourhood where she worked. It would be as much of a surprise if she hadn't spent time in their offices.'

'Saffell and Wagg both had an eye for a pretty girl. They may have tried their luck with Bethany.'

'Even if they did, does that take us anywhere?' Fern shook her head. 'I'm not convinced. But believe me, if there were any clandestine affairs, I'll ferret them out.'

It was so hard to keep secrets in the Lakes, Hannah thought as she drove into Lowbarrow Lane. A detective simply needed to know the right questions to ask. Cumbria comprised so many small, tightly-woven communities that someone always knew more than they should about someone else's business. Just as Wanda Saffell knew about Bethany and Marc.

As she rounded the last bend, Undercrag stood in front of her. There were no lights on, other than the security lamp that came on as the car came within range of the front door.

He hadn't warned her that he would be late. What was he up to?

◇◇◇

'Comfortable?' Cassie asked.

Marc stretched his legs and stifled a yawn. Not that he was bored, just weary. She hadn't poisoned him with the Irish coffee, though she'd gone overboard with the whisky, and he had to hope that tonight was too cold for the traffic cops to be out with their breathalysers.

'Perfect.'

'I'm glad.'

On top of the bookshelves was a clock fashioned from a seven-inch vinyl single by the Beatles. 'Please, Please Me'. Quarter to seven. She'd perched on the edge of the sofa, but he couldn't tell if she was waiting for him to go, or hoping he would stay.

'More coffee?'

'I'd love to, but no. I'd not be fit to get behind the wheel if I had any more.'

'My fault,' she said. 'I have this terrible habit of going overboard.'

'Is that so terrible?'

She leaned closer to him. 'Believe me, Marc.'

His throat was dry. He wasn't sure where this would lead, but he had a good idea.

A mobile ringtone chirruped. Another snatch of the Beatles: 'Lady Madonna'.

She stood up and moved towards the kitchen . 'Saved by the bell, huh?'

She left the door ajar and he strained to eavesdrop. But she was whispering, and he couldn't make out the words. Within a moment she was back in the sitting room, clutching the phone as tightly as though it were a grenade. Breathing hard.

'Is anything wrong?'

'No.' Her eyes were fixed on the patterns of the kilim, avoiding his scrutiny. 'Well, in truth, yes. But it doesn't matter.'

'You look unhappy all of a sudden.'

'It's nothing.'

'The boyfriend?'

'Ex-boyfriend.' She coloured. 'He's so persistent.'

'Can't blame him for that.'

She looked at the mobile screen. 'Oh God, he's just sent a text.'

He craned his neck to read the message.

Got 2 c u

'He's stalking you?'

'It's my problem, not yours.'

'Can I help?'

'I'll sort it.'

'What are you going to do?'

She thought for a moment and mustered a sardonic grin. 'Let you get back home to your chief inspector.'

'Is that what you want?'

She took a stride towards him and dropped a kiss on his cheek. Her lips were chilly, but for a moment he felt her slim, hard body press against him, before she withdrew.

'Don't worry, I'll be fine. Thanks for the lift, I'll see you tomorrow.'

◇◇◇

Showdown time.

Hannah was checking her lipstick in front of the hall mirror as Marc banged the door shut. She was due to see Daniel in half an hour, and she didn't want to keep him waiting. But she didn't mean to delay questioning Marc until she arrived back from The Tickled Trout.

'I didn't expect you to be this late.'

'Sorry, I didn't realise I needed to seek permission.'

She groaned inwardly. Sounded like he'd had a bad day at the bookshop. Maybe he'd heard about Stuart Wagg. He couldn't afford to lose too many good customers.

'There's food in the kitchen.'

'Thanks.' He eyed her suspiciously. 'Going out?'

'Sorry, I didn't realise I needed to seek permission.'

'Ouch.' For an instant, she glimpsed the grin that had attracted her so much the first time they met, all those years ago. But it faded as fast as the gold and silver cascades of fire they'd watched at Crag Gill, and was replaced by an expression both watchful and sardonic. 'Meeting a source?'

'Not exactly.' She was about to tell him she would be seeing Daniel Kind, but something stopped her. Maybe she just didn't want the conversation to digress. 'You know Stuart Wagg is dead?'

'Uh-huh.' He sighed. 'So two people I know have died in mysterious circumstances.'

He'd gifted her with an open goal. 'Three people, surely?'

'Three?'

'There's Bethany Friend as well.'

'What makes you think I know Bethany?'

'Do you deny it?

'Deny what?'

'Deny knowing Bethany?'

She recognised his expression; she'd seen it a thousand times on the faces of politicians playing for time while they groped for a form of words that avoided the lie direct.

'No, I never have denied it.'

'You never said she worked for you. Not at the time of her death, not even when we discussed her on New Year's Eve, when we walked to the Serpent Pool. Are you telling me it slipped your mind?'

'I was sad about what happened to her. It depressed me, she was a nice girl. I preferred to remember her as she was, not dwell on her death.'

'For God's sake, Marc! I'm re-investigating her death, and it was asking too much to expect you to tell me what you knew about her?'

'Nothing to tell.'

'She fancied you.'

He gritted his teeth. 'You have been doing your homework.'

'Did you shag her?'

'No!'

They stared at each other. His gaze didn't waver. She decided that probably he was telling the truth.

'Okay. So what did you make of her?'

'What else do you want to know? She was a sweet girl and I don't have a clue either why she might commit suicide or why someone might kill her. Satisfied?'

'Why weren't you straight with me?'

He wagged a forefinger at her. 'Don't push your luck. Everyone has secrets, even you.'

Her spine chilled. 'What are you talking about?'

'Where are you off to this evening? You never wear lipstick to office briefings. Anybody would think you were scuttling off for a tryst with some man?'

Hannah strangled a cry of anger and snatched her jacket from the stand near the door. The zip stuck and as she fumbled, it broke. Bloody typical. Everything was falling apart.

She took in a gulp of air. 'I'm meeting Daniel Kind, if you want to know. It's no secret. He and his sister found Stuart Wagg's body.'

'Don't try to tell me you're investigating Stuart's death.'

It felt as though he'd kneed her in her weakest part, but she fought for calm. 'There may be a connection between the deaths of Saffell and Wagg, and what happened to Bethany Friend.'

'A woman who died six years ago?' His voice rose. He was a skilled exponent at phoney outrage as a weapon whenever they had a row, but she didn't think his astonishment was feigned.

'She worked for both Saffell and Wagg. Did she sleep with them, too?'

'Don't be stupid. Bethany was confused about her own sexuality, she wasn't some sort of slapper. It's madness to think anything could link those three deaths.'

Wanda Saffel is one link, she thought. And there are bound to be others. But she buttoned her mouth. She'd already said more than she should. The snag was, he took her silence as a sign she had a chink in her armour. He was determined to seize back the initiative.

'Go on, Hannah. Admit it.'

Her gaze settled on the hall ceiling. It still needed plastering. The way she and Marc were heading, it would be a job for some other couple.

'Admit what?'

'This is your second cosy get-together with Daniel Kind inside twenty-four hours. What did he want to talk about last night? Not prophesying Stuart's death, I bet.'

Shit, shit, shit. The spasm of guilt was like stomach cramps. For a moment she wished the ground would open up beneath her. Why hadn't she come clean about last night, when there was nothing to hide? She couldn't guess how he'd found out. Maybe one of his customers had spotted Daniel and her at The Tickled Trout.

'Don't be ridiculous,' she muttered.

'Touched a nerve, have I? Of course, Daniel is Ben's son.'

She spun round. 'Meaning what?'

'You had the hots for Ben.'

'We were colleagues, it never went further than that. Now I'm going out. Not sure when I'll be back.'

'Take as long as you like.'

She knotted the scarf in silence. Resisting the temptation to wrap it around his neck.

'Oh, and Hannah?'

'What?'

'Your lipstick smudged. Better wipe up if you want to look your best for Daniel Kind.'

Chapter Sixteen

The route from Undercrag to The Tickled Trout took Hannah past a trendy bar at the end of a terrace row. Outside it were road-works and a temporary traffic control, and as she waited an age for the lights to change, a couple of people spilled out of the bar. A man and a woman, arm in arm. Their unsteadiness suggested they'd each had a skinful. As they sank into an embrace, Hannah thought they looked familiar, even though she couldn't make out their faces. The woman put her back to a brick wall as the man pressed up against her. His hands moved behind her, as if to lift her skirt. Hannah stared with shameless curiosity. Sometimes a detective must become a voyeur.

A furious tooting from the next car in the queue jerked her attention away from the lovers. The lights had changed to green. As she wavered, reluctant to move off, the light switched to red again. She imagined a cry of disgust from the driver in the car behind, and raised a hand in apology, but it was too dark for him to see.

At the sound of the horn, the couple sprang apart. Perhaps they thought the salvo was aimed at them. In a moment, they vanished into a shadowy passage that ran behind the terrace. For a split second, their faces shone in the glare of light from the street lamp. Hannah's instinct was spot on.

Nathan Clare and Wanda Saffell were back together again.

◇◇◇

She put her foot down the moment she escaped the thirty mile limit, but arrived at The Tickled Trout ten minutes later than promised. The car park was crowded, but she saw Daniel's Audi and squeezed in to the marked space next to it. As she raced across the asphalt to the pub's front entrance; raucous cheering broke out from the locals' end of the lounge bar. Nothing personal: this was quiz night, and the home team had taken the lead with two rounds to go.

Daniel leaned against the counter, scanning the crowd. Her heart lurched as their eyes met. Absurd; the last thing she needed was to start behaving like a seventeen-year-old on a date. She pushed through the mass of drinkers, envying Daniel's cool. Nobody had the right to look so laid-back, hours after discovering a tortured corpse. Like his father, he took disasters in his stride. He'd lined up two glasses of Chablis for them. His knack of reading her mind meant she must take care; she'd die of embarrassment if he could read her most private thoughts.

'Hannah, thanks for sparing the time.'

They shook hands, his grip firm. As he led her to the corner booth they'd occupied the previous evening, a bell rang and a tubby quiz master, who looked as though his specialist subject was chip suppers, bellowed the next question.

'Who was murdered by his wife at Battlecrease House in Liverpool?'

'James Maybrick,' Daniel murmured. 'Although some people doubt whether his death was murder.'

'Is that so?'

'James developed a taste for arsenic as a medicine, and it boosted his virility into the bargain. His wife served fifteen years in jail, but she may have been innocent. Unlike James. According to one school of thought, he was Jack the Ripper.'

She settled into her seat. 'You know a lot about crime.'

'Necessary research. Don't forget I'm writing a history of murder.'

'So how is *The Hell Within*?'

'Hell to write, frankly. I've not even finished my lecture for Arlo Denstone's festival. Real life keeps interrupting.'

'And now you've stumbled on a real life murder.'

'Finding Stuart's body reminded me why I chose academic life.' He gazed up at the black wooden beams, as if trying to decipher a pattern in the knots of the timber 'That's the difference between me and my father, I'd rather watch the world from a safe distance. Thomas De Quincey went into rhapsodies about murder as a fine art, but it looks pretty coarse when you come face to face with it. No way could I ever do your job.'

'I'll let you into a secret. At times, I'm not sure I can do it, either.'

He shot her a sharp glance. 'Are you all right?'

Irrationally, her hackles rose. 'Any reason I shouldn't be?'

'You look unhappy, that's all.'

She gritted her teeth. 'That obvious?'

''Fraid so.'

'Sorry, didn't mean to bite your head off.'

'Wretched day?'

'Not as grim as yours.'

'It was much harder for Louise. The first corpse she's ever seen, and it belongs to the man she spent Christmas with. Not a pretty sight. But she'll get through. This evening she said she'd already fallen out of love with Stuart Wagg before he sent her packing.'

'He was a bastard.'

'But a charming bastard, by all accounts.'

'Charm alone is not enough,' Hannah said fiercely.

'Louise reckons he used to get away with murder. Now someone has murdered him. The well wasn't covered up by accident. The sheet lying on top of it was heavy. You'd never shift it from underneath, even if you could climb up that far.'

'His legs were broken, and his knee-caps shattered.' Why shouldn't Daniel know, where was the harm? He'd already seen the body; and the precise nature of the injuries didn't need to be a state secret. 'There was a monkey wrench down underneath the body. Someone tossed it into the well after using it to cripple Stuart before they dropped him down.'

His eyes widened with horror. 'He was deliberately maimed?'

'Presumably to prevent him hauling himself up to safety. Whoever put him down there was determined he would never escape.'

Daniel winced. 'Don't tell me he was alive when he went down there?'

'Still conscious, yes.'

'Fuck,' he said quietly.

'Yes,' she said. 'Whatever his faults, he didn't deserve to die like that.'

'What was the cause of death?'

'The post mortem results weren't ready when I left work this evening. Hypothermia, possibly heart failure, I'd guess. His head was gashed, you must have seen, that may have been the blow that incapacitated him before his legs and knees were smashed. His injuries didn't kill him, but he wasn't kitted out for a night underground in these temperatures.'

Daniel swallowed hard. 'Imagine his last hours. Trapped in the dark, suffering terrible pain. Nightmarish for anyone, but for a claustrophobe…'

'Your father thought I relied too much on imagination.' The wine tasted flinty on Hannah's tongue. She should have grabbed something to eat, so there'd be no risk of the alcohol going to her head. 'He worried that I'd let it get in the way of the business of detection.'

'Dad wasn't always right.'

'It helps to try to think myself into the head of the victim. And the criminal.'

'Not easy to inhabit the mind of someone capable of torturing a man before killing him.' Daniel swallowed more wine. 'Someone must have hated Stuart very badly to do that to him.'

'Has Louise any clue about who might fit the bill? Did Stuart admit to having enemies?'

'This isn't a rational crime. Surely it's the work of a socio-path.'

'Maybe, but I don't believe it was a random crime, either. Stuart Wagg wasn't a fool. How did he allow someone to do that to him?'

'If the killer incapacitated him with a blow to the head, maybe he was dragged to the well at gunpoint or knife-point.'

'How did the murderer get so close? Crag Gill was fitted out with state of the art security.'

'The storm…'

'Had nothing to do with the fact that the power supply to the house wasn't working. I gather the lines were cut. Deliberate sabotage.'

'So the murder was premeditated?'

'Uh-huh.'

'Stuart didn't have to let anyone into his home if he was suspicious or afraid.'

'The best guess is that he knew his visitor. He or she was a friend or acquaintance.'

'Not Louise,' he said quickly.

'Of course not.' So he wasn't quite as laid-back as he looked, at least where his sister was concerned. 'There will be more questions for her, I'm afraid, but she'll be okay. I'm sure she couldn't have hurt Wagg like that. Lashing out with a knife in a moment of despair is very different. The sheer brutality of this murder isn't in her nature.'

'Let's hope your colleagues are equally open-minded,' he muttered.

'They are only doing their job, Daniel.' Why did she sound so defensive? 'Everyone who knew Stuart Wagg will come under the microscope.'

'Are we talking about a hired killer?'

'Who knows? Nine times out of ten, hit-men shoot their victims. Why dump him down the well without even making certain he was dead first? That's gratuitously vicious.'

'Maybe not so gratuitous,' he suggested. 'A sign of intense personal hatred.'

'Which is why I'm surprised Louise can't come up with any likely candidates.'

'Wagg acted for the rich and famous, people who have skeletons in their closet. If he was caught up in criminal shenanigans, money laundering, or drug deals or something…'

'Did he use drugs?'

'Not to my knowledge. Louise would never touch them, and if she'd found out that Wagg was involved with drugs, she'd have run a mile. When she was sixteen, the brother of her best friend died after taking an ecstasy tablet and the tragedy left a scar. She's never so much as ventured a quick drag on a joint.'

'Ever heard Louise or Stuart mention the name of Bethany Friend?'

From the other side of the bar came a chorus of whistles and guffaws. It sounded more like the climax of a rugby match than a general knowledge quiz.

'Never. Why would there be a connection between Stuart and a young woman who died of drowning?'

Hannah looked down and saw her glass was empty. 'Can I get you another drink?'

'Don't you need to get back home?'

'No rush.'

When she glanced up, she saw his gaze fixed upon her. She'd taken care to make sure that her expression gave nothing away, but he was his father's son. Skilled at seeing through people.

'Then I'll have a cranberry juice.'

Waiting her turn at the bar, she decided it made a change to be looked at with any sort of curiosity. Stuck in a rut, at work and at home, she was bound to feel flattered by the attention of an attractive man. Especially one who wasn't spoken for any longer. Miranda, the lovely narcissist, hadn't appreciated how lucky she was. As the barmaid dragged herself away from a chat with a colleague, Hannah ventured a quick glance back at the corner booth. The shape of Daniel's head, the jut of his chin, reminded her of Ben. If the hair had been grey instead of dark, she'd swear she was seeing a ghost.

Physical, primitive desire jolted her. Hot and shocking, as if she'd touched a live wire

'What would you like?' the barmaid asked.

Hannah's throat was dry, her knees were mushy and about to buckle. Stuttering her order, fumbling with her purse, she felt her cheeks burn, as though all her clothes had slid off, and everyone could see exactly what she was made of. The barmaid rolled her eyes, thinking she was pissed. Somewhere in the distance, the question master announced that the capital city of Senegal was Dakar.

Pull yourself together. You're not sixteen any more.

Deep breaths.

The moment she'd steadied herself, she ferried the drinks to their table, taking extravagant care not to spill a drop. Daniel stuffed a felt tip pen back in his trouser pocket. He'd been doodling on a beer mat. A picture of a hangman.

'Cheers,' he said absently. 'I was thinking…'

'Yes?'

Shit, she was almost reduced to a nervous squeak.

'They are an odd trio, aren't they? Bethany Friend, George Saffell, Stuart Wagg? But they do have at least one thing in common.'

She stiffened. 'And what's that?'

A roar of delight gusted over from the other side of the bar. The fat question master had finished reading out the answers, If only every puzzle had a ready-made solution. Daniel drummed his fingers on the surface of the table.

'All three of them loved books.'

◇◇◇

A ludicrous connection, yet the more they tossed it around, the more she was intrigued. Millions of people still loved books, even in the electronic age, but with Bethany, George, and Stuart alike, books were a consuming passion. Bethany yearned to write books, the two men simply collected them.

'So what are you suggesting?' She enjoyed playing devil's advocate with him. 'Three people murdered by someone who loathes the printed word?'

He grinned. 'Maybe the opposite. The man you're looking for might be mad about books.'

Marc? No question, her partner matched the profile. He knew each of the victims. But the idea that Marc might be responsible for three deaths made no sense. She'd lived with him, slept with him, she believed with all her heart that he was incapable of violence. No doubt he'd revelled in Bethany's admiration. As for Saffell and Wagg, how absurd to imagine that he'd bite the hands that fed him, far less cut them off forever.

'What makes you think the murderer is a man?'

'The level of cruelty, I suppose.' Daniel ticked the names off on his fingers. 'Bethany, tied up so that her head could be put beneath the water. George, bound so that he couldn't escape being roasted alive. Stuart, crippled and then dumped down a well hole so that he froze to death.'

'Women can be crueller than men, I think.'

'When provoked?'

She gave a tight smile. 'Men can be very provocative.'

'It would take muscle power to lift that metal cover over the well,' he mused. 'Though a strong woman could do it.'

'Your father always warned me against making assumptions based on stereotypes. Not a matter of political correctness, just good police work. You can't presume that Stuart was murdered by a man.'

'I stand corrected,' he said, so meekly that she had to laugh.

'That's one difference between you and Ben. He never admitted he was wrong.'

'Yeah, I remember.'

'Not that he was often wrong. He decided early on that someone had murdered Bethany. It hurt him that he never managed to give her justice.'

'Suppose the same person killed George and Stuart. Why the six years of inactivity? Hardly the pattern of a conventional serial crime.'

'You're an expert in serial crimes?'

'Everyone is nowadays. Have you not seen the television schedules?'

'No time for telly, but of course, you have a point. The time gap is a puzzle.'

'There must be an explanation.'

'The simplest being that the literature link is coincidental, and Bethany's death has nothing to do with the other two.'

'Is that what you think?'

He sounded like a crestfallen teenager. It took an effort of will not to squeeze his hand and reassure him that his theory was plausible. Even though she couldn't see where it took the investigation.

'To tell you God's honest truth, Daniel, I'm not sure what to think.'

'Doesn't sound like you, ma'am.'

Out of nowhere, DS Greg Wharf had appeared at her elbow, twinkling like a genie unwilling to wait for a lamp to be rubbed. His breath smelled of beer and his expensive teeth formed a smile bright with lascivious triumph as his gaze flicked from Hannah to Daniel and back again. Anyone would think if he'd caught them *in flagrante*.

A tidal wave of embarrassment swept through her. For a moment, she thought she was going to throw up all over his nice new lambswool jersey.

She managed a curt nod, not trusting herself to speak.

'This your local, ma'am? First time here for me. Cosy, innit?' Greg squatted on his haunches, relishing her discomfiture. 'The bloke next door found out I like a good quiz and asked me along. Our team lost, the other lot had a couple of ringers, one of them was last year's Brain of Cumbria. No worries, it's all a bit of fun.'

He beamed at Daniel and offered his hand. 'Greg Wharf. I'm lucky enough to be a member of DCI Scarlett's team. First week, and so far I'm loving every minute.'

Sarky bastard. Hannah pictured him regaling the lads back at Divisional HQ with the story of how he'd chanced upon the DCI, playing away from home. He'd probably attribute it to good bobbying. Following his nose.

'Daniel Kind.'

'I recognised the face. Seen you on television, haven't I?' A wolfish grin, 'You're the son of the detective?'

'You remember my father?'

'We never met, but I've not been in this neck of the woods for long, and even I have heard about Ben Kind. You worked for him, didn't you, ma'am?'

Hannah nodded, not wanting to guess what Greg had heard about her and Ben. She stole a glance at Daniel. His face gave nothing away.

'You've heard about the lawyer who was found dead this afternoon, Sergeant?'

'Stuart Wagg? It's…'

'My sister and I found his body,' Daniel interrupted swiftly. 'DCI Scarlett wanted to ask me a few questions, and naturally, I'm glad to help. She seems to believe there may be some tie-up with a cold case she's investigating.'

Hannah found her voice. 'We're almost done, thanks, Greg, we have a joint briefing tomorrow with DCI Larter's team. Nine o'clock.'

Wharf scrambled to his feet. She saw he was itching to ask why their inquiry was to be joined with Fern's. But in front of Daniel, he could not talk shop.

'Good to meet you, Mr. Kind.' His eyebrows lifted; he just couldn't help himself, Hannah thought. 'See you in the morning, ma'am.'

Turning on his heel, he blew a kiss towards a skinny girl with a sun-bed tan and a skirt slit to her thighs. Her name was Millie, and she was a clerk from Payroll at Divisional HQ. Say what you liked about bloody Greg Wharf, he was a fast worker.

Daniel leaned back in his seat and expelled a breath.

'Don't worry about him.'

'Who says I'm worried?' she said tightly. 'Greg's a stirrer, but you handled him perfectly. All those hours in front of lecture audiences and television cameras were well spent. Of course, a decent DCI shouldn't be fazed by a subordinate turning up out of the blue.'

'You have nothing to be fazed about.'

Something made her say, 'I'll let you into a secret.'

He leaned towards her, his expression unreadable.

'Go on, then.'

'When I worked with your Dad, there was a bit of banter about the pair of us.'

'Banter?'

'Young woman, older man, you can fill in the blanks. The canteen culture thrives on gossip, preferably salacious. Of course, it was all made up. There was never anything personal between Ben and me. No relationship, I mean.'

'He rated you as a detective. And he liked you.'

'The feeling was mutual. But he never laid a finger on me.'

He checked his watch. Reluctantly, she hoped. But the conversation was straying into dangerous territory.

'Marc will wonder what is keeping you.'

'He won't wait up.'

'No?' He frowned, but if he meant to say *more fool him*, he changed his mind. 'I'd better let you go, all the same. Writing a book is a perfect excuse for not working office hours, but I suppose you'll be up at the crack of dawn. Let me see you to your car.'

Outside, flecks of snow had begun to stick on the ground. The roads would be icy in the morning. When they reached the cars, he stopped in his tracks. The bright light of a security lamp illuminated his face; but she couldn't see what was in his mind. She murmured goodnight and grasped the door handle. For a moment, he was motionless. Then a strange look came into his eyes and, in a smooth, swift movement, he bent forward and kissed her hard, full on the lips.

'Goodnight, Hannah.'

He strode away and was starting up his car before she'd drawn breath. She sat in the driver's seat, not switching on the engine, watching his tail lights disappear down the lane.

It took her five minutes to move off. How to deal with Marc? By the time she was back at Undercrag, it would be past eleven o'clock. The best guess was that he'd be up in bed in the spare room, like a teenager in a strop, punishing her for having the temerity to challenge him. One of these days, maybe he'd grow up.

As for Daniel, she'd made her first resolution of the new year. She was determined not to feel guilty about him. Nor about the look in his eyes, something so rare and unexpected that it had taken a moment to recognise it as the gaze of a man who yearned for her, body and soul.

◇◇◇

No lights shone from Undercrag as she pulled up outside. A fox scurried away as she jumped out of the Lexus. An owl hooted as she heaved open the garage door.

Marc's car was nowhere to be seen.

She walked a hundred yards up and down the lane, to check that he had not, for some bizarre reason, parked outside the holiday cottages or under the trees. Of course, he hadn't. The front door of the house was locked, a sure sign that he wasn't inside. She checked the downstairs rooms, to see if he'd left a message for her. He might have ventured out for a night drive, to clear his thoughts.

The house was as cold as a cemetery. Bare floor boards creaked, and the wind whistled through the windows yet to be replaced by double glazing. Only two of the bedrooms were habitable, and there wasn't even a railing at the top of the stairs—the first floor was work-in-progress and the builders hadn't started work again after their New Year break. Marc said there was an argument about an overdue payment. He said he didn't owe a penny, and their accounts people had made a mistake.

Better check the first floor, just in case. But the instant she pressed the light switch by the staircase, the house plunged into darkness.

'Shit, shit, shit!'

All of a sudden, this didn't seem like home. Why had they come to Ambleside? Since moving in, they'd seen everything turn sour.

Picking her way down the steps to the cellar, she found the fuse box and the lights flicked back on. She ran back up and searched the bedrooms. Not a trace of him, but their best suitcase had vanished, along with some of his clothes. At least he'd left of his own accord, and wasn't trussed up somewhere, the latest victim of whoever killed Stuart Wagg. But this wasn't the comfort it should have been. She conducted a quick inventory and concluded that he'd taken enough to get by for several days. Maybe a week.

Bastard. He must be determined to make her sweat. They'd had rows before, plenty of them, but he'd never walked out on her. It was in his nature to fret about her friendships with other men—Ben Kind and Nick Lowther sprang to mind—but she hadn't expect him to go overboard about Daniel. It wasn't even as if anything had happened between them. Not counting the kiss.

Back in the kitchen, she filled a mug with coffee. Strong, black and scalding hot. Pinned up on the cork notice-board by the filter machine was a photo of the two of them. He'd asked a fellow diner to snap them, in a restaurant outside Keswick where he'd taken her to celebrate her last birthday but one. They were laughing for the camera. His hand snaked around her waist. She had a bad habit of frowning when her picture was taken, but in this snap, neither of them looked as if they had a care in the world. She'd wondered if he kept it to remind himself that sometimes they could make believe they were a typical happy couple. Tonight they needed more than a photograph to bind them together.

Where could he be? Her best guess was that he'd run off to his mother's in Grange-over-Sands. Mrs. Amos would welcome him back with open arms. He was her pride and joy, and no woman was ever really good enough for him. The old lady had never been a member of Hannah's fan club; as recently as their shopping expedition over Christmas, she'd mused aloud that there was something *unfeminine* about police work.

A phrase of Daniel's sneaked back into her head. For once she shivered at the sound of his voice, as it echoed in her brain.

'The man you're looking for might be mad about books.'

Not Marc, surely.

It couldn't be Marc.

Chapter Seventeen

Marc's mother had suffered from insomnia ever since the day ten years ago when she woke up next to her husband to find that he'd died while she slept. She was up at five, and Marc lay in the room adjoining hers, listening as she shuffled about downstairs. All night, he'd tossed and turned, excited yet fearful that everything might go wrong.

Pale streaks of dawn crept through the curtains, furtive as trespassers. Birds chirruped on the branches outside. He levered himself from the warmth of the bed, shivering as he peered through the window. A haze hung over Morecambe Bay, but he saw none of the snow that had slanted down the previous evening as he drove from Ambleside to Grange. Perched on the slopes of the Cartmel Peninsula; the resort was sheltered by fells, and warmed by the Gulf Stream. It liked to think of itself as Cumbria's Riviera. The climate was mild enough for a palm tree to have grown old in Mrs. Amos' small, steep front garden, although this morning, crystals of frost coated the leaves.

His mother had asked no questions when he phoned and asked for a room for the night. Give her half an hour, she'd said, and a bed would be made up and ready in his old room. She didn't approve of Hannah's job, and therefore of Hannah herself. He knew that, secretly, she would never think any woman good enough for him, but she contented herself with just an occasional snipe from the sidelines.

They breakfasted together, but he resisted her conversational gambits and, in silent reproach, she switched on the radio. He lingered over a second cup of milky tea, anxious to catch up with the local headlines. Police had confirmed that the body found in the grounds of Stuart Wagg's house belonged to the well-known solicitor. Fern Larter explained that a witness had seen a small purple hatchback parked on the verge next to the house on the day of Wagg's death, and asked the owner, or anyone who had seen the vehicle, to contact the police.

Back to the breakfast show presenter. 'And now,' he said, 'here's an oldie but goodie from Rupert Holmes.'

Marc winced as he listened to the words.

'Over by the window, there's a pack of cigarettes,
Not my brand, you understand,
Sometimes the girl forgets,
She forgets to hide them,
But I know who left those smokes behind,
She'll say, "Ah, he's just a friend,'
And I'll say, 'I'm not blind
To...
Him, him, him,
What's she gonna do about him?'

So what was Hannah going to do about Daniel Kind? He turned the radio off with such force that he almost snapped the knob.

His mother exclaimed with annoyance. 'I was listening to that! So much nicer than the news. All these murders. I suppose Hannah is up to her neck in them?'

'She investigates old, unsolved mysteries, remember? Cold cases.'

Mrs. Amos sniffed to demonstrate what she thought of cold cases.

'We're not safe in our beds these days. They should build more prisons.'

An eerily cheerful weather girl warned of dense fog blanketing northern and central parts of the county. The best advice was not to travel if your journey wasn't really necessary. Mrs. Amos clicked her tongue and said she blamed global warming.

Marc swallowed a last mouthful of tea and announced that he was setting off for a walk before he went in to the bookshop.

'Should you be driving at all if the fog…'

'Look outside, Mum,' he said. 'There's even a glimmer of sun in the sky over the Bay.'

'Well, I suppose you know best. But do wear something warm, dear.'

Once a mother, always a mother.

He kissed her leathery cheek and set off for the old promenade. Threads of mist gathered around the fells above the town, and he supposed that Undercrag would be wrapped in a cold grey shroud. Hannah's problem, not his. She should never have set up secret meetings with Daniel Kind.

He passed the causeway leading to Holme Island, nowadays separated from the mainland by yellow-brown spartina grass so rampant and powerful that some people said it was all that saved the promenade from destruction by the waves. Sheep grazed where once children built sand castles. Eventually, they'd have to rename the town Grange-over-Grass. Even the metal posts from a long-gone pier had been engulfed by the salt flats.

He leaned on the railings at the spot which marked the end of an invisible route across the Bay. A month after his first date with Hannah, he'd taken her on the eight mile walk from Arnside to Grange, led by a guide who knew the shifting sands like the back of his hand. At times, the water reached up to their thighs. One false move, and you were sunk. That summer Sunday afternoon, the hint of danger added a *frisson* as he squeezed her hand and whispered what they'd do when he got her back home.

Along the way, they'd watched oyster catchers probing for shellfish, and ducks whirring overhead, while she'd listened to his stories about books with the intense concentration of a woman newly in love. He told about chancing upon the handwritten manuscript of a famous mystery novel in a Lunedale junk shop and selling it to a Japanese collector for a small fortune. The murderer in the story constructed an ingenious alibi. It was only broken when the detective realised the suspect could have reached the victim in time if he travelled, not around the long and winding coast roads, but diagonally across the still waters of the Bay.

Murder, murder, everywhere.

Times changed, familiarity bred boredom. Hannah was weary of books, and his business. Weary of him, too; he was afraid he didn't turn her on the way he once had. Cassie was different. She was younger, not obsessed with her own career, but the clues suggested she fell for men who adored her, yet let her down in the end. She was ready for kindness. Last night, he'd sent her a text the moment Hannah slammed the door behind her on her way for a tryst with Daniel Kind.

What r u doing 2mrw?

Cassie wasn't down to work a shift at the shop; and he didn't need her to provide cover. In addition to Zoe, Judith, a long-serving part-timer, was due in today. He craved Cassie's company, the ache of emptiness like a physical hunger, chewing at his guts.

Within thirty seconds, she texted back:

Nada.

Straight away, he asked if she fancied a drink, but she said sorry, no can do.

Shit; was the boyfriend back on the scene? Feeling sick in the pit of his stomach, he punched out another message, wanting to know if they could meet in the morning.

Another instant reply.

Love to.

She even added a couple of kisses.

On a clear day, you could see Blackpool Tower from the crumbling promenade, but this morning he could barely make out the water stretching beyond Holme. The sun had fled, leaving the sky as grey and cloudy as a fortune teller's ball. But who cared? His spine tingled.

Go for it.

He fished his mobile out of his pocket.

◇◇◇

'Daniel.' Hannah's voice was soft in his ear. 'Sorry to disturb you.'

He rubbed his eyes. Seven thirty, and the phone's relentless wail had dragged him from under the duvet. Thank God he'd resisted the temptation to let it ring. He'd not climbed into bed until three that morning. Too tense to sleep, he'd switched on his laptop, determined to chisel the final paragraphs of his talk for Arlo Denstone's Festival. He hated missing deadlines, often labouring long and late into the night to meet an editor's time-scale, and he'd crafted a dozen fresh sentences to sum up Thomas De Quincey and the fine art of murder.

But his heart was no longer in his subject. It was one thing to play witty and imaginative games with the notion of murder for pleasure, quite another to stumble across its cold reality. There was nothing exhilarating about murder in the flesh. For all its brilliance, De Quincey's gleeful prose was streaked with cruelty, and Daniel saw something repellent in his morbid fantasies of vengeance. De Quincey was a voyeur, ogling murderers from a safe distance. His addiction to violent death might have been cured if he'd ever looked down into a disused well, and seen and smelled a rotting corpse.

'Hello, Hannah.'

He squeezed the phone so tight it hurt. To prove he wasn't dreaming? His brain was sluggish, he needed a cold shower and a hot coffee. But she wouldn't call at this hour unless it was urgent.

'You said something about Stuart Wagg last night. I was knackered, otherwise I'd have picked up on it at the time.'

'Sorry, I don't...'

'It hit me at half four this morning. Woke me up.'

He blinked hard. 'What's bugging you, Hannah?'

'You mentioned he suffered from claustrophobia.'

'Louise told me. It was no secret. Apparently, he never even used the lift at the office, he always took the stairs up to his room on the top floor.'

'So that's why his architect designed Crag Gill with such vast rooms, and archways instead of doors?'

'Yes, even though he made a joke of it, the fear was real. Louise said that when he was at school, another kid locked him a cupboard as a prank, and Stuart was scared witless. He never quite got over the trauma. Hard to imagine a more agonising death for him. To be trapped underground, with no hope of escape.'

While Hannah absorbed this in silence, he moved to the window and nudged the curtains apart. Fog shrouded the cipher garden. Trees and bushes were dark, shapeless forms. The tarn was invisible. He might have been anywhere.

'Perfect,' she said at last. 'Thanks for your help.'

'What is this about?'

'The link between Stuart's murder and the other two deaths.'

'I don't understand.'

'Me neither. But believe me, I will.'

Her voice hardened. Raw anger, he thought, on the behalf of the victims. He'd heard the same edge of furious determination before, in the days when his father lived at home.

'What do you think it means?' When she hesitated, he said. 'Sorry, I shouldn't ask.'

'It's all right,' she said. 'If you really want to know.'

A moment of intimacy, like the night before. He had to give her the chance to change her mind, and back away.

'I don't want you to breach confidentiality.'

'It's not against the rules to think aloud,' she said. 'Okay, here goes. Bethany Friend was afraid of water, George Saffell was terrified of pain and dreaded losing his book collection, and Stuart Wagg was claustrophobic. Their lives all ended in circumstances that they would have found truly appalling.'

◇◇◇

Hannah's heart beat faster as she dropped the phone into its cradle. Mustn't let thoughts of Daniel distract her; she had enough on her plate. It had seemed strange, to wake up alone, even though Marc often stayed away from home, when exhibiting at book fairs, or visiting collectors with books to sell. But this morning was different. The draughty, echoing house felt too big for her. She didn't know when he'd be back. Or if.

She checked her mobile to see if he'd sent a text. Nothing. The mean sod. If he was staying with his mother, he'd soon tire of the tug of her apron strings. Okay, let him sweat. No way was she going to make the first move. Not today, at any rate.

Number one priority was to report that Bethany Friend had worked for Amos Books before moving to the university. Whatever she said to Daniel in rare moments of bravado, if she screwed this case up, her career would be flushed down the pan. Lauren would have to be told that Marc knew Bethany, but first she wanted to break the news to Fern Larter. She texted Fern, asking to see her before the joint team briefing. The reply was instant. Fern was in buoyant mood, pleased with her crack-of-dawn radio interview and that the investigation into George Saffell's death, stalled for so long, was at last on the move.

The grass outside Undercrag did not look frozen, but when she stood on it to de-ice the windscreen of the Lexus, it felt as hard and crunchy as icing on a cake. The frost had preserved countless deer-slots and Hannah wondered if, while she slept, a large number of the animals had roamed outside her home in the moonlight. Or maybe a handful of them had danced round and round in ever-decreasing circles. She knew exactly what that felt like.

The fog clutched at her throat as she locked the front door, and turned the journey to Kendal into a nerve-wracking crawl. Hannah hated fog, and the way it stagnated in the valleys, transforming the Lakes into a cold and alien land. And she hated driving through it even more. You could never tell what lay round the next bend. A car without lights, a multi-vehicle pile-up.

The twists of the road demanded all her concentration. But she couldn't rid her mind of a single image: the rictus of anger on Wanda Saffell's face, on New Year's Eve, as she threw red wine over Arlo Denstone's white jacket. Wanda was drunk that night, and a woman scorned. But did the incident reveal a dangerous lack of restraint, was she capable of much worse than making a scene at a party? Or was Hannah simply hoping so because she'd hinted that Marc had slept with Bethany?

She made straight for Fern's office. Fern organised a coffee for each of them and spent five minutes putting things into perspective. Marc needed to be interviewed, for the record. If he could contribute anything more to the inquiry, fine. But Bethany had finished at the bookshop months before her death. She'd had countless previous jobs if you included all her part-time stints behind bars or waiting on table. It was no big deal.

'Marc has moved out,' Hannah said.

Fern swallowed a mouthful of coffee. The slogan on her coaster read *Well-behaved women seldom make history.*

'After you read him the riot act?'

'He ought to have been up front, and admitted that he knew her. Not leave me to find out from Wanda Saffell.'

As she spoke, she realised she sounded flinty and uncompromising. Mulish was how Marc described her in this kind of mood.

'Yeah, but we don't always do the right thing, do we? He must have worried that you'd react badly.'

'He was right to worry.'

Fern put her head on one side, as if this might help her read Hannah's mind. 'You're not seriously thinking that he might have anything to do with Bethany's death?'

'No…'

'Well, then.' Fern stood up. 'With a bit of luck, he'll come to his senses. And so will you. All right, let's marshal the troops.'

◇◇◇

The joint team briefing threw out questions like sparks from a Catherine wheel. None of the radiators were working, but for once nobody complained. The detectives working for Fern on the suspected murder of George Saffell had run into a brick wall. Discovering fresh lines of enquiry gave them an adrenaline rush.

Fern reported that CSIs continued to swarm over Stuart Wagg's home in the hope of finding forensic evidence to link his murder with the fatal fire in the Ullswater boat-house. Differences in the MO did not disguise similarities between the cases. Two wealthy professionals, who moved in the same social circles, and even shared the same expensive hobby, both killed at home. Nobody believed the choice of victims was random. The murderer must be known to both victims. Throw into the mix a possible sighting of the culprit's car, and no wonder the room buzzed with anticipation.

A farm worker had spotted a small purple car parked across the road from Crag Gill for three quarters of an hour shortly after the last known sighting of Stuart Wagg by Louise Kind. The car was tucked away among the trees, but the man had seen it from his tractor cab, as he travelled to and from a nearby field. The windows were steamed up and he'd supposed a couple of teenagers were getting it together inside. If only he'd given a more precise description; in a perfect world, he'd have noted the registration number too. But the world wasn't perfect, and he knew more about tractors than cars. Maybe it was a Nissan Micra, maybe something else. Even so, the sighting was a break.

Now Hannah had raised a possible link with the unexplained drowning of Bethany Friend in the Serpent Pool. Bethany, like the two men, had a passion for books—and she'd worked for both their firms. And then there was the connection between the psychology of the victims. Each of the three victims had died in terror.

'Should we call in a profiler?' asked a young DC called Ciaran who had the manner of an eager puppy.

Hannah ignored the mutterings from the sceptics, Greg Wharf among them, who stood at the back of the room. For some detectives, psychological profilers ranked with witchball-gazers and folk who offered racing tips, but you couldn't ignore any tool in the box.

'We've put a call in to Trudy Groenewald at Lancaster University. She's due here to look over the files this afternoon.'

'Why the six year gap between the crimes?' a DS in Fern's team asked.

'Of course, we're keeping an open mind about whether the deaths are connected. Bethany's hydrophobia might just be a coincidence. But if the same person or people are responsible for all three deaths, there may be various explanations for the years of inactivity.'

'For example, that the killer hasn't been inactive,' Hannah added. 'There may be other deaths in the meantime where a connection hasn't been identified. Think of the MO in the Bethany Friend case. Drowning didn't exclude the possibility of suicide. With Saffell, the killer didn't try so hard to disguise the murder. And Wagg couldn't have killed himself. We have a progression, a murderer becoming increasingly reckless. And we can't rule out that there were other victims, after Bethany and before Saffell.'

'Ciaran, I want you to check the records,' Fern said. 'Do any other cases fit the pattern? Remember, assumption is the mother of all cock-ups. But if we're just looking at these three deaths, we need to focus on sadists who spent the past six years out of circulation. In prison, for instance—anyone released last autumn who fits the bill? A job for you, Roz.'

Roz nodded. A dark-haired DC with a toothpick figure, she'd attracted a couple of glances from Greg Wharf. Whether she fancied him or not, she was smart enough not to give the slightest hint that she was aware of his existence.

'Nathan Clare was in Ambleside yesterday evening.' Hannah indicated his photograph on the whiteboard, a shot in which he looked more like an apeman than ever. 'Locked in an embrace with Wanda Saffell. Nathan was Bethany's lover, although he left her to start an affair with Wanda. And Wanda worked with Bethany, claimed to be her friend. All this was long before she met George.'

'And the connection with Wagg?' asked Ciaran

'She had a fling with him during her marriage to Saffell. And she was a guest at his New Year party. She was pissed out of her mind, and threw wine all over a man who was rude enough to say no when she propositioned him.'

'Donna and I broke the news that her husband was dead,' Ciaran said. 'She didn't shed a single tear.'

'She's a flake,' Donna diagnosed. 'Alcoholic too, if you ask me.'

'Stuart Wagg had a history of dumping his lovers,' Hannah said. 'He was pretty brutal about it, his policy was to go for a clean break, not to let the woman down gently.'

'He got away with it,' Fern said. 'Until the day before yesterday, when his luck ran out.'

'Suppose Wanda had a grudge against him,' Maggie Eyre said. 'What motive could she have for harming Bethany Friend? She was a gentle soul. People liked her.'

'We also believe Bethany Friend had a relationship with a woman, around the time that she and Wanda were colleagues,' Hannah said.

'You think she and Wanda slept together?' the puppy asked.

'The original investigation never picked up anything. But Wanda isn't short of charisma, and Bethany was pretty and impressionable. She'd had a crush on a teacher when she was at school, and she liked older lovers. Nathan Clare, for instance. Maybe she and Wanda fancied an experiment.'

A furrow appeared in Maggie Eyre's forehead. She wasn't the quickest thinker in the room, but she gnawed at problems as if they were chicken legs.

'If we put Wanda in the frame, doesn't the connection between the cases break down? The relationships ended in different ways. If Stuart dumped Wanda, revenge might be a motive for her to murder him. But Bethany was dumped by her lover, we were told. Not the other way around. Just like she was dumped by Nathan Clare.'

'We don't know for sure there was a relationship between Wanda and Bethany,' Fern said. 'But DCI Scarlett and I agree about the importance of close liaison. Assuming a link between the cold and current cases, we're not going to be territorial about this. Maggie and Liam will cross-check the lists of people who had a connection with Bethany against those associated with Saffell and Wagg. Meanwhile, DCI Scarlett will question both Nathan Clare and Wanda Saffell again.'

'Pissing in the dark, aren't we?'

Greg Wharf's murmur was so audible, he must have meant everyone to hear. His hands were behind his head. For the past half hour, he'd been leaning so far back in his plastic chair as to be in imminent danger of tipping over on to his backside. No such luck, but that was Greg for you. Never quite as unbalanced as he seemed. He'd kept so quiet, Hannah wondered if he was sickening for something. But he'd just been biding his time, waiting for the chance to make waves.

'All right, Greg,' Fern said. 'Let's have the benefit of your wisdom, eh?'

'So Bethany knew Wanda, George, and Stuart through work, so what? This is the Lake District. The most incestuous bloody place n Britain, if you ask me. Leave out the tourists and itinerants, and everybody knows everybody else. Sometimes seems like everybody shags everybody else, too, it's the only thing to do in this bloody place during the long cold nights of winter.'

Maggie Eyre, fiercely loyal to her home turf, turned crimson with outrage. She shot him an angry look, but it would take more than that to bother Greg Wharf.

'We need to face facts. If every dodgy relationship led to murder, the streets of Windermere would be as deserted as Wasdale.'

Fern intercepted the glance he tossed at Hannah.

'Hang on, Greg. Touch of exaggeration there, don't you think? Grasmere isn't exactly Gomorrah.'

He shrugged. 'You know what I mean.'

'Sure, but you know rejection can be painful. It breeds resentment, might even be a motive for murder. Though I guess you're lucky, and nobody's ever turned you down.'

Donna sniggered, and Roz raised her neat eyebrows, but Fern's sarcasm bounced off Greg Wharf like slingshot fire off armour-plating.

'These people live in each other's pockets. If someone knows one of the murder victims—assuming they were all murdered—chances are, they will know the others. The question isn't whether Wanda was one of Wagg's fancy women, never mind Bethany's. What we really want to know is this.' He allowed himself a rhetorical pause, a performer skilled at holding an audience in the palm of his hand. 'A woman drowned, a man burned to a cinder, another buried alive. So brutal—but why?'

Fern frowned. 'And your answer?'

'Sorry, don't have one. That's why I'm still a DS.'

He leaned back even further in his chair, testing gravity to the limit. Drawing everyone's eyes to him. A sly smile crept across his face, and Hannah saw how much he loved to be the centre of attention.

'One thing is for sure. The motive has to be powerful. Overwhelming, I'd say. Never mind profilers, we need to ask what could drive someone to such extremes? Find that out, and we'll find our murderer.'

◇◇◇

On her way out of Divisional HQ, Hannah looked in on Fern's office. Both of them were pleased with the briefing, except for the last few minutes.

'Bloody Greg Wharf,' Fern said. 'Complete pain in the arse.'

'I'll have a word with him after I've seen Clare and Saffell.' Hannah hesitated. 'There is just one thing.'

Fern gave her a curious look. 'What?'

'Has Greg worked this patch before?'

'Don't think so. Spent most of his career in Newcastle, hasn't he?'

'Can you check if he ever had a secondment on this side of the Pennines? Keep it low key, I'm just ticking a box.'

Fern was suspicious. 'So what box do you want to tick?'

'Don't get the wrong idea. I'm sure there's nothing in it.'

'Come on.'

'Well, he arrived in the county a month before Saffell was killed. If he was around six years ago…'

Fern laughed. 'You can't seriously believe he had anything to do with those three deaths?'

'No, but…'

A wicked glint came into Fern's eyes. 'Yeah, but I catch your drift. Won't do any harm to rattle his cage, will it?'

◇◇◇

'I've moved out,' Marc said.

Cassie took a long time to answer. He began to worry that she'd hang up. For the past hour, he'd kept wandering the streets; now he was perched on a low wall near the library. This was the third time he'd called her. Until now, her phone had been switched to voicemail. He'd left two messages, but she hadn't called back. Busy, or simply playing hard to get?

'You've left home?' Her voice small and wondering, like a child's at Christmas. 'I never expected…'

'Things are…difficult.'

'I'm sorry.'

'Don't be. Hannah's seeing someone else.'

'What makes you think so?'

'I know so. The man is Daniel Kind, the television historian. They've been meeting in secret. She used to have a soft spot for his father. Daniel's better looking and more successful than his old man, no wonder she's acting like a star-struck teenager.'

'She'll get over it. And come back to you.'

He took a breath. 'I'm not sure either of us want that.'

Was that true? He didn't know, he wasn't sure of anything any more.

'Really?'

He didn't answer.

'So where are you?'

'Staying with Mum in Grange. For a day or two, while I make plans.'

Another pause. What was Cassie thinking?

'And what plans do you have in mind, exactly?' she asked.

◇◇◇

'Hate to disappoint you, Hannah, my dear, but not only don't I own a car, I never even learned to drive. My contribution to saving the planet, you know. Sorry I can't be of more assistance.'

If Nathan Clare experienced even a twinge of dismay at his inability to help, he hid it with an insolent leer. Pay-back for Hannah's temerity in interrupting his day.

They were sipping allegedly hot, but actually tepid, chocolate in a draughty cafeteria on the Staveley campus of the University of South Lakeland. There wasn't a student in sight; term hadn't started yet and in any event, Hannah guessed the first thing they learned here was the inadequacy of the catering. Clare had been summoned to a meeting of external lecturers, and at first he'd insisted he didn't have time to fit her into his busy schedule. When she offered an alternative of an interview at Busher Walk, he grudgingly agreed to spare her ten minutes. No more, he was a busy man.

'How do you get around?'

'Some of us possess genuine green credentials.' He tutted in mock-rebuke. 'I'm a passionate believer in public transport. If only the people who run the trains and buses shared my faith, all would be well. As it is, I do a lot of walking.'

Hannah suppressed a groan of irritation. She'd speculated that Wanda might have borrowed his car to drive to Crag Gill. Someone could check whether he held a licence, but she didn't hold out much hope of catching him out in a lie. Nathan Clare might not be as clever as he thought he was, but he wasn't stupid.

'And Wanda Saffell?'

'She drives a sports car. A BMW, I believe, but you'll need to confirm that. Cars mean nothing to me.'

'She doesn't happen to have a second car?'

His nose twitched, as if smelling sour milk. 'Why would she bother with two cars?'

'She could afford to buy a runabout. What about her late husband's car?'

With exaggerated patience, he said, 'George's car was leased by his firm, I remember her mentioning that it went back when he died.'

'It's clear the two of you are very close.'

He took a swig from his mug, and the chocolate left a frothy moustache.

'What do you mean by that?'

'You don't deny it?'

'You know Wanda and I have been friends for years.' He wiped his mouth, rather to Hannah's regret. 'She admires my work. Why do you think she published my latest book of poetry?'

'Because you sleep with her?'

'Hannah, you have a waspish tongue in that pretty head of yours. No-one would ever realise.'

'So you admit that you and she are lovers?'

'It's no cause for shame. Wanda and I have been intimate for years.' His long tongue licked the rim of his mug. 'Off and on, as you might say.'

'You first slept together around the time of Bethany's death.'

His brows knitted together, increasing his resemblance to an ill-tempered gorilla. 'Poor Bethany's death had nothing to do with our relationship. Or with either of us.'

'Did she commit adultery during her marriage to George Saffell?'

'I would not presume to speak for Wanda.'

'Did she sleep with you before he died?'

He shook his head. 'A gentleman never tells. Suffice to say, we all deserve a little treat, now and then. Live for the moment is a good philosophy, don't you agree?'

'Did you know Saffell personally?'

'We weren't friends, we had nothing in common, except that we'd both shagged Wanda. Not that the poor old fellow did it particularly well, I gather. As for books, their appeal for him was as items for his collection. His understanding of literature itself was skin deep.'

He'd answered a question she hadn't asked. 'So you did meet him?'

'Our paths crossed a few times. His firm sponsored various University activities. Showing the acceptable face of estate agency by subsidising the work of needy academics. I bumped into him once or twice at events.'

'What form of sponsorship?'

'I struggle to recall. The Bursar can provide you with the details. He and the Vice-Chancellor will still be in mourning. Losing George Saffell's munificence must have hit the University hard. I expect they'll use it as an excuse to hike up tuition fees.'

'Wanda must be a wealthy lady. No wonder you were keen to renew the relationship.'

'I couldn't care less about Wanda's money.'

'Is that so?' At last she'd touched a nerve. 'What were you saying about deserving academics? How refreshing to meet someone who is not remotely interested in filthy lucre.'

He slurped another mouthful of hot chocolate, didn't speak.

'You'll have heard that Stuart Wagg's body was found yesterday afternoon. His business supported the university too. Did you know him?'

'You think I could afford his fee rates?'

'Are you saying the two of you never met?'

His eyes narrowed, as if he'd detected a trap she didn't know she'd set.

'When you look into his records, you will find that he represented me once. Six or seven years ago, when his reputation was a little less lustrous and he undertook work on legal aid, not just for privately paying fat cats.'

'Why did you need his services?'

'If you must know, I was charged with supplying cannabis to some of the students I taught.'

She gripped her mug handle. 'This would be about the time you were seeing Bethany Friend?'

'What of it?'

'Was she a witness in the case?'

'It was nothing to do with her, and the only time we smoked a joint together, she nearly choked. Bethany craved excitement and fresh experiences, but in truth she was an innocent. She'd led a dull life, and I'm afraid it rather suited her. Of course, the charge against me was a deplorable misunderstanding.'

Somewhere behind them, a member of the cafeteria staff broke the silence by rattling a canister of cutlery. Hannah leaned towards Nathan Clare.

'Did the case reach court?'

'Unfortunately, yes. However, Stuart Wagg managed to pick so many holes in the prosecution's version of events that the judge threw the case out. It never even reached the jury, and I walked away with my character unstained.'

'Oh yes?'

Justice denied, as per bloody usual.

'I was innocent, naturally, but the experience destroyed my remaining faith in British justice. Without Stuart Wagg's advocacy, I might have been found guilty.'

'Perish the thought,' she said through gritted teeth.

'So I had every reason to be grateful to the fellow. If you're suggesting I had a reason to murder him, my dear Hannah, you're not only barking up the wrong tree, you aren't even in the right forest.'

The self-satisfied grin was back. Even if he dabbled in drug dealing, so what? When it came to finding a motive for three murders, she'd drawn a blank, and they both knew it. He made a show of consulting his watch, and then leapt to his feet with agility startling in such a heavy man.

'Your ten minutes ran out some time ago, Hannah. Sorry, must dash. Can I leave you to find your own way out?'

Chapter Eighteen

The fog cloaking Tarn Fold didn't lift an inch as the hours drifted by. Louise said she ached to escape from the cottage, and do some shopping; besides, the cupboards of the cottage were bare. Daniel, ready to seize on any excuse to avoid being handcuffed to *The Hell Within*, proposed lunch in Ambleside. He could drop in on the De Quincey Festival office. Arlo Denstone hadn't answered his latest emails, or a voice message asking if the talk needed any revision. Once that was sorted, he could make headway with the book. Or maybe it was just a writer's displacement activity.

Neither of them spoke on the journey. Louise wrestled with her private thoughts and Daniel needed to focus on the road. Visibility was down to fifty metres.

Ambleside seemed to be brooding because normal life was on hold. Doom-mongers from the Met Office had scared off even the hardiest walkers, and Daniel was spoiled for choice when looking for a space to park. Louise hurried away to indulge in some retail therapy, while he picked up a copy of *The Westmorland Gazette*—the newspaper De Quincey edited was still going strong—before strolling past the market cross to the Festival office. Above the door, you could still see the name of a vanished photographer's studio killed off by digital technology. The unit was surrounded by charity shops on short-term lets, windows stuffed with dog-eared chick-lit, faded watercolours, and second hand climbing gear. Even affluent Ambleside wasn't spared the tide of change washing through the high streets of England.

The tiny office overflowed with glossy posters advertising the Festival, racks of tourist information leaflets, and a display of classics by the usual Lake District suspects. Behind a desk sat a large, grey-haired woman, whose yellow and red badge proclaimed her as *Sandra, Festival Volunteer*. She was engrossed in a chat magazine and Daniel found himself hypnotised by its lurid cover *'Life! Death! Prizes!' 'A vulture tried to EAT me', 'The wife who SLICED OFF her hubby's bits ('I still love him')', 'We sold our pets to pay for Mum's funeral', 'My Wilf was banged up for being psychic', 'Fab Faye's Big Day boob job'*. When he coughed, she treated him to a cheery smile.

'At last a customer!' she exclaimed. 'How wonderful to see you, Mr. Kind.'

Daniel hadn't given his name, but she was a fan of the TV series, and had just bought his latest book. They chatted for five minutes about history and when she might see him on the box again. If, rather than when, he said.

'But you're far too young to retire!' she protested.

'Too young to stay on a treadmill, you mean. I'm happy to hide away in my cottage and write.'

Try to write, you mean.

'I've been looking forward to your talk at the Festival.' The note of regret puzzled him. She sounded like a child expecting to be deprived of a long-awaited treat.

'Speaking of which, is Arlo Denstone around?' The grey head shook. 'Could he give me a ring, when he gets back?'

'Don't hold your breath.' She lowered her voice, as if about to confide a secret vice. 'To be perfectly honest, I'm not sure if he's coming back.'

'Later today, you mean?'

'No, ever.'

His stomach tightened, a spasm of selfishness tinged with outrage. Had Arlo walked out on the job, or chucked it in? And after he'd sweated blood to deliver the wretched talk by the deadline?

'I don't understand.'

Sandra became pink and indecisive, torn between discretion and the desire to unload. 'The last time we saw him was when he did an interview on television with that Grizelda Richards,' she said. 'Nobody seems to know where he is.'

'Is he poorly?'

Arlo Denstone was a cancer survivor, he recalled. Sometimes cancer came back.

'He seemed as right as rain when I last saw him.' The corners of her mouth turned down. 'To tell you the truth, he's never here. It's us who are worried sick.'

'What's wrong?'

'Nothing's happening with the Festival, not a sausage. One of the other volunteers told me yesterday that the conference centre arrangements still haven't been confirmed. The University phone us every day, chasing the deposit. They've threatened to scrub the booking if we ignore the latest reminder. The lady who does our accounts says we don't have any funds in the bank. Two of the other speakers are losing patience because he hasn't been in touch. We don't know what to say.'

'Arlo is still making plans for the Festival. He called at my cottage this week, chasing my talk before the printers' deadline.'

'I don't know about any deadline.' She twisted a skein of wool around her fingers. 'See those posters? We owe the printers for them, the bill's seriously overdue. At half past nine, they rang to say they were putting the matter in the hands of their solicitors. I know cash is tight, but we feel so embarrassed.'

'Perhaps he's lined up another firm of printers.'

'I don't know if he's bothered about the Festival any more.'

'Surely he wouldn't walk out on it?'

'He's a volunteer, like the rest of us. What if he's received a better offer?'

A volunteer? Arlo was keen on De Quincey, but Daniel hadn't realised he was that keen.

'Seriously? He isn't being paid?'

'He was full of enthusiasm at first, we were thrilled when he agreed to do the work for nothing but expenses. He's organised festivals all over Australia, you know. But…'

A movement on the other side of the window caught his eye. Someone walking past on the pavement. Hannah Scarlett, brisk and full of purpose.

'I'm sure it's a misunderstanding,' he said hastily. 'Now, if you'll excuse…'

Sandra reached into the knitting bag and pulled out his most recent book, beaming like a conjuror with a rabbit. 'I wonder, before you go, would you mind signing this to me? I must have something to write with somewhere…'

He itched to dash out and buttonhole Hannah, but good manners held him back. Sandra produced a ballpoint pen, and the chance of escape was gone. By the time he made it to the pavement outside, Hannah had disappeared into the mist.

◇◇◇

'There's something special about foggy days.' Even on the mobile, Cassie's voice sounded warm and tempting. 'I love it that everything is so blurry and mysterious.'

'Like life, really,' Marc said.

He'd been back at his mother's house for the past hour, chewing his nails up in his room while downstairs, her vacuum cleaner roared. Yearning for the phone to ring, hating himself for acting like a heart-sick adolescent. Cassie had cut their first conversation short, saying she needed time to think. Despite the weather, she was setting off for a walk to clear her head. She'd promised to call later, but he hadn't been sure she'd keep her word.

'Mmmmm.'

He waited.

'So.' She was breathing hard. 'Would you like to come over?'

◇◇◇

Wanda Saffell made Hannah wait in a cubby-hole while she chatted on the phone with someone who was mixing pigments for her next book of woodcuts. From the fragments Hannah overhead, Wanda was spinning out the conversation. The buggeration factor, Les Bryant called it. For all her fortysomething elegance, Wanda was a stroppy teenager at heart. Was that common streak of adolescence the bond between her and Nathan Clare? She'd go berserk if Hannah arrested her. It might be worth it, just to wipe the sneer from her face.

'How long will this take?' Wanda demanded when at last she hung up. 'You see how busy I am.'

The table in the little room was piled high with vast printed sheets, ready to be folded. 'Don't you have anyone to help you?' Hannah asked. 'Nathan Clare, for instance, does he lend a hand?'

'Why would I want help?' Wanda asked. 'I adore the physical act of making books. Not for one second would I go back to public relations, and all the false smiles and back-stabbing. As for Nathan, he's a creative writer. A very different craft.'

'But the two of you are very close.'

Wanda put her hands on her hips. Even in a thick Aran sweater and grubby chinos, her figure curved in provocation. Easy to understand why Nathan was smitten. Let alone old, priapic George.

'Is there a law against it?'

'Do you or he drive a small purple Micra?'

'Nathan never learned to drive. He hates following rules, the Highway Code would bore him rigid. My car is a BMW, you must remember when I carved you up on the way to Stuart's party?'

'And now Stuart is dead.'

'Don't tell me you're poking your nose into that case now. Given up on Bethany Friend?'

'Did Bethany and Stuart have a relationship?'

Wanda moved closer. Even her breath seemed to smell of ink. 'What are you driving at?'

'Can you answer the question, please?'

'Who knows? I doubt it, they swam in different pools.'

'She temped for his firm the year before her death.'

'I didn't know.'

'Did you know Nathan Clare was a client of his, then?'

'So what? Any minute now, you'll hint that Bethany rented a flat through George.'

'Did she?'

'I haven't the faintest idea. This all sounds like wild guesswork. To my knowledge, only one person links the three of them.'

'Namely?'

Wanda smiled. 'Marc Amos, of course. George and Stuart were his customers, Bethany... '

She let the sentence trail away, but Hannah was ready for her this time.

'Aren't you forgetting? You are another link.'

'I wished George no harm. But even if I did, why should I want to kill Bethany or Stuart?'

'And you're suggesting Marc has a motive?'

'That's your department, Chief Inspector. I'm not accusing anybody of anything. Though if I were you, I'd pay attention to what your man gets up to with the hired help.' A mischievous smile. 'Don't look puzzled, it might shake my faith that our police are wonderful. Haven't you met that foxy assistant of his?'

'Assistant?'

'Cassie Weston. I spotted her when I called in with copies of Nathan's book. She tried to keep out of sight, but I'd recognise that slinky figure a mile off. Tell you what, Chief Inspector, instead of hassling me, you'd be better keeping an eye on her.'

'Meaning what?'

'Meaning that when she worked for George, the two of them had an affair.'

Hannah dug her nails into her palm. Just as well that she'd steeled herself for this interview.

'Cassie Weston worked for your husband?'

'And slept with him. Not that I minded much, our relationship was fucked by the time she was. She's trouble, always has been.'

'When was this?'

'Not long before he died. He made quite a fool of himself over the girl. Every Thursday lunch-time, they'd nip off for a bit of hanky panky in a hotel. He did his best to keep it quiet, nobody knew. I only found out when he fessed up after she finished with him. He was an old goat with all the pretty girls in his office, but Cassie made a deeper impression than the rest. He was badly cut up when she said it was over. She'd teamed up again with the love of her life, and she told George what he could do with his job. To say nothing of his Thursday lunch-times.'

◇◇◇

'Am I leading you astray?' Cassie asked.

Despite the cold, and the fact that she obviously didn't spend much on heating, she was only wearing a tee shirt and jeans. Bare arms, bare feet. And there was no mistaking that she hadn't put on a bra. They were in her living room, a couple of half-empty flute glasses on the table between them. On the way over, Marc had stopped at an off-licence, and splashed out on a bottle of Bolly. The opened bottle was in an ice bucket in her kitchen. He wasn't rushing it. They had all the time in the world. This wasn't about sex. He'd been at pains not to touch her since she'd greeted him at the door with a peck on the cheek. All he wanted was to get to know her better.

'What makes you say that?'

'Well, I have an excuse, it's my day off. You're a businessman, you ought to be minding the shop. Or out bidding at auction, or exhibiting at a fair.'

He settled back in his chair. 'All work and no play, et cetera.'

'So I'm therapy for a stressed entrepreneur, is that it?'

'We can all do with a bit of therapy, now and then.'

She stretched out her legs. Toenails painted pink to match her fingernails. 'What can I do for you, then?'

'Tell me your life story. We've worked alongside each other for months, but I don't know enough about you.'

'You wouldn't be interested.'

'Wrong.' He took another sip of champagne. 'I'm fascinated.'

'Okay, you asked for it.'

◇◇◇

As Hannah departed the whitewashed home of Stock Ghyll Press, she checked her messages and saw that Maggie Eyre wanted her to ring as soon as she was free.

'Any news?' she asked.

'We've found a fresh name.' Maggie sounded as though she'd run a four-minute mile. 'Someone whose path crossed with all three victims.'

'Go on.'

'She was on the list of students at the University at the time Bethany died. It was her first year, though she dropped out at the end of her second term, a few weeks after the body was found. And she had a spell with George Saffell's firm last year. Go back eighteen months, and she temped on maternity cover for Stuart Wagg.'

'Don't tell me,' Hannah said. 'Cassie Weston, right?'

◇◇◇

'Hannah!'

She was striding past the Salutation Hotel when Daniel hailed her. He and Louise had just left the bistro where they'd had lunch and were heading back to the car. This time he was determined not to let her disappear without a word.

'I'll be in the handbag shop,' Louise said quickly, as Hannah waved and began to cross the road towards them

He gave her a crooked grin. Surely she wasn't becoming tactful in her old age? 'See you in ten minutes?'

As Louise vanished into a misty side-street, Hannah arrived at his side.

'How is she?'

'It hasn't hit her yet. Infatuation, break-up, discovery of the body. A lot to cope with. In the long run, she'll be fine, but…'

'You'll take good care of her.' She scrutinised him. 'Anything wrong?'

'Not wrong.' She saw him, he guessed, as pretty much an open book, whereas he could never read her mind. 'But...odd.'

'Want to get it off your chest?'

'You're too busy.'

She dug gloved hands into her pockets, pulled the scarf tighter around her neck to keep out the cold. 'You never waste my time.'

'I'll try not to.' He recounted his conversation with Sandra. 'So Denstone is a volunteer, not a hired hand.'

She reached back into her memory. 'I seem to recall the publicity in the local press when he took up the post. I didn't get the impression he was working for free.'

'When he got in touch, he told me he was a cancer survivor. Perhaps he wants to do good by stealth, without a thought of kudos for himself.'

'Does he strike you as selfless?'

'Not really.' He heaved a sigh. 'I shouldn't be surprised at being messed about, after years of working with television people. They love to impose crucifying deadlines, and when you kill yourself to do the work in time, it turns out they put the pressure on you to cover up their own incompetence.'

'Ouch, that came from the heart. But I agree, Arlo's behaviour is strange.'

'Louise reckons he's been spending too much time with the likes of Wanda Saffell instead of making the Festival happen.'

'Nothing happened between him and Wanda.'

'Allegedly.'

'They both tell the same story. Why else would she throw wine over him, if she didn't feel humiliated by rejection?'

'Unless that's what everyone at the party was intended to think?'

Behind them, a car hooted at a van that had stopped on double yellow lines while the driver carried a delivery into a shop. Tempers were as harsh as the weather.

'Ingenious.'

'Over-ingenious, I guess,' he admitted.

'Perhaps.'

She took her right hand out of her coat pocket and offered it to him. An oddly formal gesture. He wondered if she wanted to put their relationship on a different footing, after that kiss outside The Tickled Trout.

'Keep in touch, Daniel.'

'You bet,' he said.

◇◇◇

Hannah needed to talk to Marc about Cassie, but first, she'd better get her head straight. Watersedge wasn't far away; she'd call at the care home and see if Daphne Friend could shed any more light. Cassie Weston's name might ring a bell. The longest of long shots—but you never knew.

On arriving at reception, she was greeted by the familiar aromas of old age and disinfectant. When she gave her name to the spotty teenager at the desk, the Polish girl she'd met on her last visit was summoned.

Kasia's manner was subdued, verging on grumpy. Without looking directly at Hannah, she said, 'You have heard about Mrs. Friend?'

Hannah felt her throat constrict. Easy to guess what was coming.

'What about her?'

'She died last night.' Kasia was pale, and Hannah suspected she minded suffering too much to work in a place like this, where death often came to visit. But she hoped the young woman would not change. 'Very peaceful, she…slipped away.'

'I'm sorry.'

'This weather.' Kasia's voice hardened, as if she'd found something to blame for her melancholy. 'It is not good for the residents. Not merely cold, but damp as well. Unhealthy.'

'I'm sorry, I didn't know.'

'I liked her,' Kasia said. 'You should not have favourites, it is not good. But I cannot help it.'

'Don't be hard on yourself, it's human nature.' Hannah considered. 'What happens to her things?'

'There is a niece in Shropshire. She saw Daphne once or twice. It was a duty, I think. She said she was too busy with her family, and her job.'

'Did Daphne keep any papers, anything about her daughter?'

'The girl who died?' Kasia was sombre. 'Nothing much. Only a few books.'

Books, there was no escaping them.

'May I have a quick look?'

A tired flap of the hand. 'You are the police, you can do whatever you wish.'

'If only.' Hannah smiled. 'I'm grateful for your help, I won't keep you long.'

Kasia led her to a store room. Daphne's worldly goods had been bundled into a handful of brown paper parcels loosely tied with red string, and a large, battle-scarred suitcase. Not much to show for seventy-one years, but it would make no difference if the old lady had left a house as full of rare treasures as Crag Gill. Stuart Wagg was no less dead than Daphne Friend.

'Her clothes are in the suitcase.' Kasia started to open the parcels. 'The books and her reading glasses are in here.'

There were a couple of dozen books. Three Catherine Cooksons, and a handful of well-read Liverpool sagas. Most of the remaining novels were different, not least because their spines weren't cracking with wear. *The Shipping News*, *Captain Corelli's Mandolin*, *Midnight's Children*, *The Ghost Road*, and among the shiny paperbacks, a pristine, dust-jacketed copy of *Possession*.

Call herself a detective? After all these years of sleeping with a bookseller, she had glanced at the titles in Daphne's bookcase, and still failed to appreciate the wild variation in tastes. Of course, the same reader could love both Catherine Cookson and Pat Barker. It wasn't breaking any rules. But really, was Daphne Friend a likely fan of Salman Rushdie? Hannah picked up *Possession*. It was the only book by A.S.Byatt she'd ever read, mainly because she'd watched the film on TV with Marc, a sort of detective story that wasn't about professional detectives.

She began to flick through it, but didn't get past the title page. Under Byatt's name a gift inscription was scrawled in a round, extravagant hand that she recognised from the Christmas card the same woman had sent to Marc.

To my darling Bethany, who knows that Possession is nine points of the law.

With all my love, Cassie.

◇◇◇

Cassie was a born teller of tales. She had it all: soft, husky voice, and a gift for keeping him on tenterhooks for the next Chapter of her story. And God, she was good to look at, as she talked with her long lids half-closing her eyes. The tee shirt had ridden up, showing a flat stomach. Her skin was smooth and without a blemish, the rise and fall of her breasts hypnotic. Forget the booze, a man could get drunk on the sight of her.

'More champagne?' she asked.

'Don't stop talking. Please.'

She'd never known her father; she'd been conceived after an alcohol-fuelled kids' party. Her mum was a week past her fifteenth birthday when she was born; and her grandparents threw her out the moment they learned she was pregnant. Mum did her best to look after her; she drank and did drugs, and was a lousy judge of men, but she was intelligent, and she loved to read to her little girl at bed-time. Cassie owed her passion for stories to those precious times together. But at school, the other kids taunted her because of the rumours that her mum screwed old blokes for money.

'I never believed the gossip, until the day the police came to school and told me that Mum was dead. One of the dirty old men had buried a kitchen knife in her throat.'

'Jesus,' Marc breathed.

'I refused to believe what had happened, screamed myself sick until they let me see her body. They'd done their best to hide the wound, but...'

'It must have...'

'Every night after that,' she interrupted, 'my dreams were haunted by the sight of her. Visions of blood gushing from her jugular vein.'

'It's...;

'The man who murdered her was a neighbour, and a client too. He stank of cigarettes and sweat. Mum wanted me to call him Uncle Bob, but I never did. He pleaded guilty to man-slaughter, reckoned that Mum waved the knife at him when she was high on heroin, after he told her he was going back to his wife. He said he'd grabbed the knife from her, but somehow it finished up in her neck. He wept in the dock and said he'd loved the woman he killed. Lying bastard. They gave him nine years, but he died of a coronary within six months. He really didn't suffer enough for what he did.'

'I understand how you must feel,' Marc said.

'Do you? Do you really, Marc?' She shook her head. 'Love and pain, where does one end and the other begin? I was so mixed up, every relationship I ever had, I destroyed. I wanted to give my love, and ended up making people suffer.'

'Don't be so hard on yourself,' he muttered.

A demure smile. 'Marc, you're not drinking.'

'I'm fine.'

'Give me your glass.' She reached out towards the table. Her gentle persistence reminded him of a nurse administering medicine to a recalcitrant patient. 'Let me go to the kitchen and fix you a re-fill'

◇◇◇

Hannah's phone sang as she climbed into the Lexus. On the screen, Daniel's number flashed.

'Sorry, I don't want you to think I'm stalking you.'

I wish.

Hey, police officers were supposed to be unshockable, though sometimes she shocked herself with the stuff swirling around in her subconscious. A shrink would have a field day.

'No problem, Daniel.'

'Are you all right? You sound faraway.'

'We are in the end game.'

'You know about the car, then?'

'What car?'

'I heard the radio news soon after Louise and I arrived home. The reporter said the police are looking for a small purple car in connection with Stuart Wagg's death.'

'For elimination purposes, at least. A farm worker noticed the vehicle hidden away near Crag Gill at about the time someone was stuffing Wagg down the well.'

'Chances are, it's a coincidence, but guess who drove a small purple car this week?'

'Tell me.'

He couldn't resist a ham actor's pause. Building the suspense.

'Arlo Denstone. He parked it in the Fold when he visited Tarn Cottage, chasing after the text of my talk.'

Hannah's fingers tapped against the steering wheel as this sank in.

'On the morning that Louise walked out on Stuart Wagg?'

'Correct.'

'Why did he need your talk if he hadn't even paid the printers for their last job?'

'Good question. What answer would you give?'

'Perhaps he had another reason for calling on you.'

'Excellent.' She might have been one of his students, back at Oxford. Those lucky kids, she envied them. 'Such as?'

'Did Arlo say where he was going after he left Brackdale?'

'Back to the office. Things to do, busy, busy, busy. Which was a complete load of balls, according to my new friend, Sandra the volunteer.'

'How well do you know him?'

'Hardly at all. He contacted me whilst I was in the States. He'd picked up on the Internet that I was planning a book about Thomas De Quincey and the history of murder. He flattered me into agreeing to participate in the Festival. When it comes to De Quincey, he knows his stuff. He can quote it verbatim, he loves the man's work.'

'Is that right?'

'Yes, he can quote chunks from the essays by heart. He's a dyed-in-the-wool fan. He said in an email that in his opinion, De Quincey is one of the few English men of letters who is undoubtedly touched by genius.'

'Forgive my ignorance, I've never read him.'

'Not that many people have. If they think of him at all, it's as a man with twin addictions. Opium and murder.'

As she mulled this over, a car emblazoned with the name of a local undertaker's drew up next to hers. A tall, sombre man got out and made for the entrance to the home. Come to sort out the arrangements for Daphne's funeral, she supposed.

'Hannah, are you still there?'

'Sorry, I just remembered a detail from the Bethany Friend file. And I was chewing over what you said. Opium and murder, a deadly combination.'

'What's in your mind?'

'Still working it out.' She didn't want to be evasive, not with Daniel, but her latest idea was a tender plant, not ready to be exposed to analysis by a formidable intellect. 'Listen, thanks for the information about the purple car. I'll pass it on to the team, someone will be in touch to take a formal statement.'

'I'd better let you get back to work.'

'Uh-huh.' Before cutting him off, she remembered to add, 'Talk soon.'

Hunched up on the leather seat, she allowed her thoughts to roam. The truth had begun to loom up in front of her, dark and dangerous as a ten-ton truck, emerging from the fog. Pulling a notebook and pen from her bag, she wrote down a name.

Arlo Denstone.

She peered at the letters, checking them over and over.

Surely she was right?

She struck a line through each letter, one by one, before spelling out another name.

Roland Seeton.

The witness whose statement lurked in the file on Bethany Friend. The long-haired drop-out who claimed to have seen Bethany in Ambleside, talking to a soldier with a white transit van. Ben Kind had been sceptical, suspecting he was an attention-seeker who had invented the sighting. But maybe Seeton had some other reason for telling a lie to set the police chasing wild geese—and a non-existent white van.

The two names were anagrams of each other, and she refused to believe it was coincidence.

No wonder Maggie hadn't traced him yet.

In the space of six years, Roland Seeton had metamorphosed into Arlo Denstone.

Chapter Nineteen

'Your ex,' Marc said drowsily. 'The boyfriend. What happened to him, then?'

No longer was he sitting upright on the sofa. Too much like hard work. After following her example and kicking off his trainers, he'd slumped down, and spent the last few minutes fighting the urge to close his eyes. This was his chance, and he dared not botch it. Cassie knelt beside him on the sofa, legs tucked beneath her, breasts almost caressing his chest. Breathing hard.

'Long story.'

'We have all the time in the world.'

'You think so?'

'Sure.' He tried to order his thoughts. 'The shop is covered. I don't need to go back.'

'Listen, I have a confession to make.'

'Tell me anything.'

'My boyfriend is still around.'

He moved his head close to hers. 'You mean…?'

'I'm sorry, Marc.'

'You sound like a manager, about to make someone redundant.' He smiled, to show he was simply trying to lighten things up.

'You know something? I was once diagnosed as an addictive personality. That was after the two of us split up, and I dropped out of uni. The psychiatrist said I was stressed, impulsive, I lacked self-esteem. *A disposition towards sensation-seeking*, that was her phrase.'

'Sensation-seeking, huh?'

'You may laugh, but she didn't know the half of it. Not a tenth of it.'

'I don't believe you're addicted to him.'

'You don't understand, I'm not in control. What he and I did was so terrifying that he ran away.'

Marc made a derisive noise. 'Ran away?'

She took no notice. 'I spent years fighting against myself, desperate to get over him. And not just him, but the way he made me feel, knowing he wanted me so much, knowing the jealousy hurt him so much, that he'd do anything—yes, *anything*—to destroy the pain.'

'You're right,' he said. 'I don't understand.'

'It's the nature of addiction,' she said, as if lecturing a classroom of under-achievers. 'Progressively, you need more and more stimulation. The psychiatrist warned me about it, and she wasn't wrong. She encouraged me to write about my fantasies, but when I turned the truth into short stories, they never worked. What happened between him and me was something you couldn't make up. When he came back into my life, it started all over again. I'm ashamed to admit it, but I got such a buzz from his heartache, the way it crucified him when I explained about the other men. His imagination works overtime, always has done. Fiction can't compare to real life, that's what I discovered. We can't help ourselves. He's hooked on me, and my addiction is nothing compared to his.'

His cheeks stung, as if she'd slapped his face. 'The chap's obviously a loser. Wrong for you. You need to start again.'

'I need what he does for me.'

'Cassie, you said yourself, he causes you grief. Seriously, you don't want him to become dependent on you. It isn't healthy.'

'Too late for that,' she murmured.

Marc hauled himself up on the sofa. Knackered he might be, after a bad night in his mother's spare bed, but he must sort things out, once and for all. He couldn't abandon her to some no-mark.

'Don't worry.' He stroked her cold and lovely cheeks. 'You can break the habit.'

'You think I haven't tried? When I went into hospital, and he disappeared, I thought I'd never see him again. But the moment he turned up again, I was lost.'

'Is he stalking you? Making threats?'

'Don't be silly. He isn't like that.'

'I'll look after you.'

She wrinkled her nose. 'Like I said, you don't understand.'

'What is there to understand?'

'It's a two-way thing. Something unique and precious. He and I, we have a bond.'

'Break it. Cassie. Please, he's not good for you.'

'No.' Her expression hardened. 'Nobody can rip us apart. Not me, not you, not anyone. The two of us are shackled together. For better or worse. We've been through too much, there can be no going back.'

The champagne was talking, he told himself. She'd not kept pace with him, and had barely finished her second glass, but bubbly must go straight to her head. He must make her see sense, he couldn't sit back and let everything fall apart, after he'd given up so much, just to be with her.

◇◇◇

When Hannah stopped talking, Fern Larter chewed the cap of a ballpoint pen as if it were a snack substitute,

'East Londoner.'

The drive back to Divisional HQ had been slow and tortuous, but in Hannah's mind at least, the fog had started to clear. She wanted to share her theory that Arlo Denstone was the same man who, six years earlier, had claimed to see Bethany Friend talking to a white van man. A lead that went nowhere, because there was nowhere for it to go. Hannah was sure it was an invention, meant to steer the investigation into a cul-de-sac. An unnecessarily elaborate touch from someone who couldn't help himself.

'What?'

'It's an alternative anagram of Arlo Denstone.' Fern beamed. 'Actually, you can make countless groups of words from that set of letters.'

'Are you seriously telling me this is just a coincidence?'

'Seeton was a long-haired university drop-out. Arlo is a respected expert on literary festivals who happens to be a folli-cally challenged cancer survivor.'

'Seeton was an English student.'

'So are thousands of other people. Some of them are quite respectable.'

'Hair can be shaved. You can't...'

'All right, all right!' Fern put up her hands in surrender. 'Calm down. I just wanted to see the look on your face. You're right, Arlo has a load of explaining to do. But I'm not clear how this Cassie woman fits in.'

'I've been thinking about that.'

'Tell you what, first things first, let's ask Donna to track Arlo down. He was involved in a scene at Wagg's party, and seems to have some sort of relationship with Wanda, even if they never slept together. So we're entitled to ask him a few questions. The only snag is that if nobody's seen him since Wagg's death, he might be anywhere by now.'

'He won't have gone far.'

'What makes you so confident?'

'He won't want to be parted from the object of his affections. Not after they have been through so much together.'

'Go on.'

'It grieves me to say it, but Greg Wharf was right. We're talking about murder for an overwhelmingly powerful motive.'

'Namely?'

'Jealousy.'

'You reckon?'

Hannah nodded. 'Jealousy was the cancer that Arlo Denstone suffered from.'

◇◇◇

'How come he has such a hold on you?' Marc struggled to find the right words. The fog had sneaked inside the flat and seeped into his brain, confusing everything. But he was too stubborn to give up without a battle. 'You don't owe him.'

Cassie tightened her grip on his fingers. Through the fuzziness in his head, he was aware of her touch. It excited him, persuaded him that everything would turn out fine.

'Even if I explained, it would make no difference.'

'Try anyway.'

'Okay, you asked for it.' The faraway, story-teller's look returned to her eyes. 'To begin with, I felt sorry for him, because his sister died when he was a kid. Olivia was fifteen, and he adored her. When she died, he was heartbroken. She'd fallen off her bike on the way home from a first date and wasn't wearing a helmet. A boy had taken her out to the cinema, and he'd teased her about the colour of the helmet. Olivia insisted she was fine after the accident, and their parents didn't call an ambulance. By the time she started vomiting, and they rushed her to hospital, it was too late. The doctors said she was brain dead.'

Marc shivered. 'A sad story, for sure, but…'

'It ruined his life, the worst thing that could have happened to him.' Cassie was almost talking to herself. 'They were so close, it was unhealthy, but that doesn't make it easier to bear. He told me her death sent him mad with grief and rage. It made him hate the boyfriend, but that wasn't all. He blamed their parents, the family was in pieces. He was only thirteen, it's a tender age. Within eighteen months, his mother and father died in a car crash. The boyfriend was killed too, a climbing accident. Sometimes I've wondered if…well, it's speculation. Nothing has ever been said, not even between us. Better not go there.'

'You wondered if what?'

'Aren't you listening?' Her voice rose in fury. 'I'm baring our souls here, the least you can fucking do is pay attention.'

He felt as if she'd clubbed him over the head. This wasn't the Cassie he knew. She must be suffering such strain. The on-off boyfriend's fault, no question.

'Now do you understand why he feels the way he does?' She gritted her teeth, battling for control. Marc could not guess where this was leading. 'We're all the product of our experiences. When we first met, the forces that pulled us together were uncanny. Not so much lust as a shared sense of loss. Though there was lust too, of course.'

Too much information. He really didn't want to know about her past infatuations. The future was what mattered.

'Books were in our blood.' Her temper faded, she sounded dreamy again. 'He introduced me to De Quincey, the most famous addict in English literature. And he told me about Elizabeth. The sister who died when De Quincey was a boy. A tragedy that shaped his life, the way Olivia's death shaped Ro's.'

'Ro?' His tone implied: *for God's sake, what sort of a name is that?* His head was spinning. In Cassie's company, he never felt quite in control, but this was something else. 'Ro?'

'His nickname. His parents were teachers, it was sort of a classical allusion. They named their kids Roland and Olivia. Ro is what I always call him. The moment I set eyes on him, I wanted him. He became an obsession. Still is, I suppose.' She tightened her grip on his fingers, crushing them in her bony hand. Marc felt tears pricking his tired eyes. 'And it was mutual, that was the perfect thing. He was crazy about me. Couldn't bear to think of anyone else so much as touching me. To start with, I teased him about his jealousy, but soon he made me realise, it was no laughing matter. Even if I'd never done anything—like you and I have never done anything, it was just the same. He hated it.'

'You haven't told him about…you and me?'

'What is there to tell?' Her lips curved in a malicious smile. 'But Ro and I have no secrets. I wondered how it would make him feel.'

His throat was dry, his voice hoarse. 'You haven't told him that we're lovers?'

'Isn't that what you wanted?' Again the smile. 'Or am I wrong?'

'But…'

'I belong to Ro—and him alone.'

'You're not a chattel,' he said. 'Not a poss…possession.'

Shit, he was slurring his words, he couldn't believe it. And that hammering in his temples. How could he have drunk so much and not even noticed?

'Don't you see?' she demanded. 'It's so wonderfully terrifying, to be possessed.'

'But…'

'Have you never felt like that, with your straight-laced police inspector lady? Never yearned to indulge yourself in absolute surrender to your most powerful, most prurient instincts? Never longed to abandon yourself to the darkest desires of life and death?'

'What are you… on about?' he mumbled.

For all his pent-up excitement and fear, he was slipping away. Clinging to consciousness as a desperate man hangs by his fingertips to the top storey window ledge, not daring to look down on the city street below.

'I thought I wanted to possess someone, but I was wrong. Bethany was a failed experiment. Far better to be possessed. Oh, Marc, do you still not get it, despite surrounding yourself with all that learning, all those books?' She gave his fingers a final squeeze, then dropped his hand as if it were a scrap of litter. 'What are you like? I'm talking about murder. Considered as one of the fine arts.'

◇◇◇

While Fern briefed Donna about Denstone aka Seeton, Hannah shut herself in her office and steeled herself to speak to Marc. Of course, she'd have to tread with care, given that she was so close to the situation. Cassie must be questioned about her relationship with Bethany Friend, and that was a job for Maggie. But Hannah needed to prepare the ground. Solving the case might prove to be a Pyrrhic victory. It had the potential to destroy her life with Marc.

Judith answered the phone and after an exchange of pleasantries about the dreadful weather and the horrible nature of the Bug, she said she supposed Hannah was after Marc.

'If he's not too busy.'

'He rang to say he won't be in today. There's a collection of Olaf Stapledon manuscripts he's chasing, owned by some bloke in Keswick.'

'All right.' Hannah paused. 'Could I have a quick word with Cassie, please?'

Did Judith hesitate before replying, or was that just her imagination?

'Cassie isn't in today, either.'

Hannah digested this in silence. She didn't like the path her thoughts were taking.

'Fog-bound?'

'I suppose so.'

'Can't blame anyone for not wanting to turn out in this weather. You've done well to make it in.'

'I live on a bus route. It only took five minutes longer.'

'Does Cassie drive to work, as a matter of interest? Or does she catch a bus too?'

'No, she drives.'

'Yeah, now you mention it, I think I've seen her car parked in the courtyard.'

Not true, but who cared?

'Can't miss it, really, can you?' Judith obviously wanted to say something bitchy, but wasn't sure how far she dare go with her employer's partner. 'Between you and me, it's not a colour I care for. Rather gaudy. I certainly wouldn't fancy a purple car myself.'

◇◇◇

Momentum. Every investigation needed momentum, and at last they had it. Typical—you wait ages for one suspect to turn up, and then two arrive at the same time. The immediate challenge was to find them. Cassie Weston lived outside Kendal, and Arlo Denstone in Grasmere. While members of the joint team were despatched to track them down and invite them in to answer a few questions, Hannah texted Marc and left a voice message, asking him to call her urgently, then headed to the cafeteria to kick the case around over a coffee with Greg Wharf.

'Bethany Friend and Cassie Weston,' she said. 'Two attractive young women whose shared love of literature brought them together.'

'So they had a fling?'

For once, his tone wasn't prurient. He was getting his head round it all. Beneath the bravado and bluster, he wasn't a bad detective. Greg was very different from Nick Lowther, but maybe they could work in tandem after all

'An intense relationship, yes. Whether sex was part of it, who knows? For Cassie, in particular, it was probably a matter of curiosity. Just seeing what it was like, being with another woman. Probably she's someone who likes breaking taboos. She made Bethany a present of a novel about possession. A joke, or a sign of self-awareness, who knows? They'd been extremely discreet, that suited them both. But the inscription is a giveaway. It proves they were close, and that's all we need.'

'Yet Cassie finished with her.'

'The minute she met Arlo, is my guess. Or should I say the minute she met Roland Seeton?'

'The long-haired drop-out?'

'He's charismatic.'

His eyebrows lifted. 'Oh yeah?'

'Don't start,' she said wearily. 'But he's the sort of man who attracts women. There's something…I don't know, masterful about him. Cassie could pick and choose her men, and Wanda's no mug, but they both fancied him like mad. Takes all sorts.'

'Okay, ma'am.' He took a slurp of coffee. 'And meanwhile, Bethany teamed up with Clare on the rebound?'

'She didn't choose her lovers wisely, for sure.'

A stab of self-knowledge stopped her short. *Who am I to talk?*

'After Clare abandoned Bethany, it was plausible that she might have become depressed enough to kill herself.' He was thinking aloud, working it out for himself. Hannah approved. 'Cassie and Seeton took advantage.'

'He was jealous of Bethany.'

'Even though Cassie had already dropped her?'

'There's nothing logical about jealousy.' *Don't I know it?* 'Suppose it excited Cassie to torment Seeton, by inflaming his desire for her—how better than by making him as jealous as hell? A pair of passionate lovers, turned on by pushing the boundaries. One of them fanatical about De Quincey, the other an eager disciple.'

'Wasn't there a book, *The De Quincey Code?*'

'Very funny. De Quincey once lived in Grasmere. For all we know, Arlo moved to the same village as a sort of homage to his hero. De Quincey was famous for two things. He was a drug addict, and he was obsessed with murder.'

'I suppose your mate Daniel Kind gave you the low-down.'

She gave him a sharp glance, but this afternoon, there wasn't a hint of innuendo in his tone. Though she didn't under-estimate his capacity to make mischief, if she didn't watch her step.

'He's been helpful.' Brisk and business-like, that must be the way when Daniel's name cropped up. 'At present, it seems he was the last person to talk to Arlo Denstone.'

'Useful contact.' Greg kept his face straight.

'De Quincey had a craving for opium. In those days, it wasn't even against the law, you could buy it over the counter, dirt cheap. Seeton had a record for illegal possession, the odds are he never kicked the habit. If he and Cassie were high on something, it may explain how they came up with such a crazy idea. To kill an innocent woman, simply because of a past relationship. And not only that, to punish her and extract revenge by killing her in the way she feared most. Death by drowning.'

'Bethany died on Valentine's Day. If Cassie encouraged her to hope they'd get back together, she might have invented a pretext to persuade her to come up to the Serpent Pool.'

'Such as? It was a bit cold for outdoor sex, surely?'

'Like you said, ma'am, it takes all sorts.' He pursed his lips. 'Suppose Cassie made use of the fact that Bethany was desperate for affection to persuade her into playing some kind of bondage game. Bethany would have made herself vulnerable.'

'Yeah, that may have been what happened.'

'You think Roland Seeton was present at the scene?'

'The kind of man I think he is, it would turn him on. For all we know, they shared the work. Say Cassie hits Bethany on the head, and while she's stunned, Seeton leaps out of the undergrowth and pushes her head under the water. The details don't matter.'

Greg nodded. 'It's easier to get away with a weird crime, than something orthodox—until you come under the microscope.'

'Which Cassie never did, because Bethany kept their affair secret. She was afraid her mother would be upset if she found out her daughter was mixed up with another woman. And Seeton may never even have met her. He took a risk by coming forward as a witness.'

'But he got away with it.'

'Not completely. Cassie had a breakdown when it sank in that she was responsible for someone's death. Seeton lost the plot and abandoned her. Left the country, took a new name, forged a new career.'

Greg put down his cup. 'He couldn't keep away from her forever.'

'He'd re-invented himself successfully as Arlo Denstone. Nobody was likely to remember Roland Seeton, and in any case, his appearance had changed almost beyond recognition. When the Culture Company dreamed up a De Quincey Festival, and looked around for someone to lead it, the temptation was irresistible. He didn't even ask for payment. So long as he could get back together with Cassie. He liked to say he was a cancer survivor. A good metaphor for jealousy. Once he was back with Cassie, he found himself succumbing again.'

'Because she'd slept with Saffell and Wagg.' Greg's expression hardened. 'Even though the affairs were over and done.'

'That's the nature of jealousy. It's a disease. Left untreated, it destroys everything.'

'Spoken from the heart.'

Greg scanned her face for clues, but she was determined to give nothing away.

'Yeah, well. I'm trying to get inside Arlo's head. Not a nice place to be. He's obsessed with Cassie Weston, and with anyone who's been involved with her. Two murders in a matter of weeks? He's losing the plot all over again.'

'Saffell was a loner. Easy to target him when he was in the boat-house. Wagg must have been a trickier target.'

'My guess is that Cassie never quite got Bethany out of her system. Bethany had worked for Wagg and Saffell. They were older, successful men, perhaps she carried a torch for them.' She paused, unable to resist asking herself the question: *is that how it was with Marc, as well? She fancied him, and he was flattered, but did either of them do anything about it?* She cleared her throat. 'Cassie followed in her footsteps, she was fascinated by the woman she'd slept with and then helped to kill. But she went further than Bethany. She had brief flings with each of them, but after she teamed up with Arlo again, she re-kindled the relationship with Stuart. Possibly George too, for all I know. She's gorgeous, and they were weak.'

'Yeah, well, men are different from women.'

'Brains in their underpants, tell me about it.' She shook her head, trying not to think about Marc. 'Wagg even invited her to the New Year party, but she played hard to get. She and Arlo didn't want to bump into each other in public, and besides, Louise Kind was in the way.'

'What about the wine-throwing incident?'

'My bet is that Wanda told the truth.'

'Don't tell DCI Larter. She'd rather believe that pigs do fly.'

'Arlo provoked her as a distraction from any possible link with Cassie.'

'Over-elaborate.'

'Like everything about Arlo is over-elaborate. He's a drama queen, same as his hero, De Quincey. Once the party was over and done with, Cassie persuaded Wagg to drop Louise like a hot potato. As soon as she packed her bags and left Crag Gill, Cassie and Arlo seized their chance. The M.O. varied each time, but they were variations on a single theme. They relied on making people vulnerable. Provoking a kind of crazy desire for Cassie. Then destroying them because of it.'

'Dangerous lady.'

He was right, Cassie was bad news.

She shivered, remembering that Bethany had worked for Marc, and now Cassie did too. What if Marc were with Cassie now?

◇◇◇

The cold woke him. That, and the pain. As consciousness returned, he became aware of the throbbing of his head and arms. His wrists and ankles felt as though they were on fire, but the rest of him was freezing.

Where in God's name was he? What was happening? He didn't have a clue how much time had passed since he'd rung Cassie's doorbell. His eyes were shut, and he dared not open them. He dreaded the truth.

'Coming round?'

A man's voice, soft, yet not in the least reassuring.

Marc tried to speak, but no words came. He couldn't open his mouth. Someone had taped it shut. His hands were bound up above his head; impossible to move them an inch.

'Open your eyes.'

Marc did nothing. For as long as he did not see, he could imagine the possibility of escape. Hope, he must cling to hope.

'Open your eyes!' the man shouted.

Marc obeyed.

He was in a small, circular room. Old stone walls, rough floor hewn from rock. A single narrow window, boarded up with a couple of dirty old wooden planks. Ten feet above his head was a brick roof. He was naked, his body shrivelled and defenceless. No wonder his arms ached; they were covered in bruises, and so were his chest and legs. Someone had manhandled him on the way to this place. His wrists were fastened by thick black cord that cut into his flesh. The cord was tied to a rusting hook on the wall. His ankles were bound to each other.

The man stood in front of him. He was wearing a bright yellow fluorescent jacket, but Marc's eyes were dragged away to something lying on the floor. A nauseous fear seized him at the sight of it.

A huge creature lay sprawled on the rough ground, motionless.

Sedated, must be.

It had a fawn and white coat, red nose, tail thick and tapering to a point.

No muzzle.

An ugly, savage beast of the kind that growled and slavered through the worst of nightmares.

A pit bull terrier.

Chapter Twenty

'Marc, where are you?' Hannah hissed into the phone.

His failure to return her calls was eating into her nerves. At first she'd assumed his silence was pay-back following their row. Now her anxieties were growing like bindweed. He fancied Cassie, and she wouldn't put it past him to try his luck with her. If Cassie got a thrill out of provoking Arlo Denstone into jealous crimes of vengeance, she might encourage Marc's advances.

Why didn't he answer?

'Everything all right, ma'am?'

Greg Wharf had come up behind her. On his way to see the Chairman of the Culture Company and check out Arlo Denstone's background.

'Fine,' she muttered. 'Fine.'

Talking the case through with him had helped sort it out in her mind, but she wasn't in the mood to confide her anxieties. He'd interpret it as a sign of weakness.

A sceptical glint lit his blue eyes. 'If I can help, ma'am, let me know.'

'Thanks, Greg.' She forced a weary smile. 'And—the name's Hannah.'

◇◇◇

Phoning Mrs. Amos was a last resort. Right or wrong, the old lady always took her son's side. Hannah didn't blame her, perhaps she would understand better if ever she had a child of her own.

But did a mother have to be so blinkered? Rather like Daphne giving birth late on to Bethany, Mrs. Amos had had Marc at an age when she'd never expected another baby. It helped to explain why she spoiled him rotten.

Negotiating the conversation was a test of her powers of tact and diplomacy. At first Mrs. Amos made it plain there was nothing for them to discuss, and that she had no intention of disclosing Marc's whereabouts. She might not know the details, but she was clear that Hannah had blown the relationship apart, and it didn't come as a huge surprise. Police work wasn't a suitable job for a woman.

'There's a serious problem. It's connected with the shop,' Hannah said when she managed to get a word in.

'What sort of problem?'

'One of my colleagues needs to question someone who works for Marc. I wanted to give him advance warning, but he isn't answering his phone. I'm worried something has happened to him.'

She didn't want to be unkind, or to play on a mother's fears for her favourite child, but needs must. She was desperate to get Mrs. Amos to open up.

'I already said, he isn't here right now.'

'When is he due back?'

'He doesn't tell me everything, you know. And he wasn't even sure he'd be home tonight.'

Home? Hannah clenched her fist. Undercrag was his home.

'What did he say to you?'

'He just told me not to stay up late.'

'Where did he go?'

'He didn't say, except that he wasn't due in the shop today. Or in Sedbergh. He told me he was off to buy a collection of books. I don't pry, you may be surprised to hear. He has his own life to lead.'

What she meant was that she didn't pry successfully, but this wasn't the moment to start a row. If something happened to Marc, it would shatter Glenda Amos. Hannah's relationship with her was uneasy, but she didn't want to see her harmed.

'The fog is dreadful.'

'So they said on the radio.'

The reedy voice betrayed a note of uncertainty. Hannah hated herself for planting seeds of fear in the mind of an old woman, but it was the lesser evil.

'I'm worried he might have had an accident. You know what these country lanes are like when visibility is so poor. Every bend a potential death trap. Have you really no idea where he was heading?'

'He…he never said.'

'Are you sure he went to buy books? Not to see someone else?'

'I don't know.' Glenda Amos paused, and then the words started to come in a rush. 'He spoke to someone on the phone, I heard that, though I couldn't make out the words. I'm not as deaf as he thinks. He didn't want to me to listen in, I can say that. He went up to his room and shut the door while I cleaned downstairs. But I knew what he was up to. He's my boy, and I can read him like one of his own precious books.'

'But you never got past chapter one.'

'He's involved with someone else,' Hannah said. 'I'm aware of it, Glenda. But she's about to cause a lot of unhappiness for him, and I'd hate that.'

'You think he's driven somewhere to meet her?'

'I hope not,' Hannah said. 'If he has, he's made the biggest mistake of his life.'

◇◇◇

Ten minutes later, she was steering through the fog-wrapped Kendal streets. Fern was off to a press conference about latest developments in the Stuart Wagg case. It was too soon to give out detailed information about their interest in Arlo and Cassie, but they could give the registration number of Cassie's Micra. The priority was to trace the pair before they did any more damage.

Especially to Marc. Hannah wanted to believe she was over-reacting. With any luck, he'd be fine, hunting mouldy books in some God-forsaken attic or cellar. But in her heart, she suspected his luck had run out.

The case against their two suspects was circumstantial. Her team and Fern's faced a huge task in assembling enough evidence to persuade the CPS to bring the couple to court. But even as she'd talked through her theory with Greg Wharf, Hannah found herself believing in it more strongly with each passing minute. Arlo and Cassie were guilty, she was certain of it. Between them, they had killed Bethany Friend, George Saffell, and Stuart Wagg.

The surging sense of success reminded her of one Good Friday years ago, after she and Marc had bought a flat-pack self-assembly cupboard over the internet. When they opened the box, the components had seemed to bear no relationship to each other. The instructions were in Japanese, and the accompanying diagrams more inscrutable than the Beale Cipher. It had taken hours, but she still remembered their shared triumph when at last they figured out how to fit the pieces together to form something recognisable as furniture. Marc had carried her off to bed to celebrate their achievement, she remembered. They'd dumped the cupboard in a skip the day they moved into Undercrag.

What drove Cassie and Arlo on? She suspected *folie à deux*. Madness shared by two people, whose psychotic bond brought out their worst impulses. The key to detection was to separate the suspects, so they could be interrogated without being able to give each other mutual support. In view of her relationship with Marc, there was no way she could be involved in interviewing either Cassie or Arlo, otherwise the defence lawyers would have a field day. All she wanted to do was to find Marc, and make sure he kept away from the woman who was mad, bad, and dangerous to know.

Thanks to the fog, traffic on the A591 was bumper-to-bumper, but Hannah strove for patience. Please God, this would prove a wild goose chase. But owed it to Marc to check it out for herself.

She was on her way home to Undercrag. To make sure that her partner hadn't taken Cassie there to commit the ultimate betrayal.

◇◇◇

When Marc started choking on his own bile, the man tore the tape from his mouth. It hurt, and made his eyes fill with tears. He found himself spewing on to the rock beneath his feet.

'That isn't to allow you to talk, do you understand?' the man said. 'I'm not into dialogue. But I would hate you to choke on your own vomit, Too quick, too easy.'

This was Ro, had to be. But he was Arlo Denstone, the expert on Thomas De Quincey. Marc understood nothing, except that he was in danger. The man had brought him here to die.

His mouth formed a single word.

Why?

'I don't believe in explanations,' Ro said. 'Life and death, how can they be explained? De Quincey knew what I'm aiming for. Virginia Woolf said he was transfixed by the mysterious solemnity of certain emotions. How one moment might transcend in value fifty whole years. An impassioned man, Thomas, but he got his kicks from writing, not from the things he did. A difference between us, though I swear he'd share my taste for Grand Guignol. My destiny is to make nightmares come true, the way they came true for me.'

The dog made a dozy noise. A throaty rumble.

Ro nodded towards it.

'A wild creature. I bought him illegally, and that isn't my only crime. I didn't feed him for forty eight hours. And then I slipped something into his last supper.'

Marc forced his gaze away from the pit bull. His heart bumped inside his chest. Much more of this, and he'd have a coronary.

It might be for the best.

'I named him Thomas, what else? Trust me, when he wakes from his sleep, he'll be in a very bad mood. And he will be hungry. Ravenous.' Ro threw a scornful glance at Marc's trembling body. 'He's a carnivore. Not fussy about the quality of his meat.'

Tears ran down Marc's cheek. He couldn't help himself. Couldn't dry the tears, either.

A noise attracted his attention. Someone was moving away the boards at the narrow window. He peered round and saw a face he recognised.

It was Cassie. Standing outside, looking in.

Through the opening in the wall of the tower, Marc saw no expression in the gaze she fixed on the man who called himself Arlo Denstone, but the faintest of smiles played on her lips.

'Murder is a fine art,' the man said. 'But it evolves with time. It needs updating. This is an age when we watch the world go by, on our television screens or laptops. Cassie, and I, we have turned it into a spectator sport.'

'Wagg was good in bed,' Cassie whispered. 'But nowhere near as good as you. No-one is as good as you, my love.'

Marc wanted to scream. *It's a lie, a wicked lie. I only wanted to be her friend. I never even touched her.*

But he knew nothing he might say could save his life, and no words came.

The man grinned at the dog. 'Last week, I watched Thomas chew a rabbit that had escaped from a hutch next door. Call it a rehearsal. Took a while, but there wasn't much left by the time old Thomas was done.'

Marc shivered uncontrollably.

Jesus, was the dog stirring?

◇◇◇

Undercrag was melancholy in the fog, a sombre, hollow shell. Hannah was no longer sure she wanted to live here, but that was a decision for another day. Marc's car was nowhere to be seen. Hannah searched the ground floor and then ran upstairs to look into each of the bedrooms. Nothing.

Okay, it would have been extraordinarily crass for Marc to bring Cassie to their home for a quick shag. Hannah was ashamed of herself for having feared it possible.

But if he wasn't misbehaving here, that begged the question of where he might be, and what he might be doing.

Hunger pangs assailed her. She needed to eat. This wouldn't be a good time to fall down in a faint. She found an apple from a fruit basket in the kitchen, and was starting to peel it when her phone rang. She took a quick bite and shoved knife and fruit in her jacket pocket. Food would have to wait.

Greg Wharf's Geordie tones filled her ear. 'I'm just leaving Sir Julius Telo's mansion.'

Sir Julius was the chair of the Culture Company. 'What did he have to say about Denstone?'

'He's been fretting about the guy for weeks. He had a great CV, and he was brimming with enthusiasm as well as expertise. The clincher was that he offered to do the job for free. It sounded too good to be true.'

'Did nobody wonder how he could afford to be so altruistic?'

'He said he'd inherited money from his uncle, but the key point was that he loved the Lakes, and was crazy about De Quincey. He'd fought cancer and won, and now he wanted to make every day count, plus raise money for a good cause. This was only a six month contract, and he saw it as a dream job. A challenge combined with a chance to put something back into the community.'

'So Sir Julius bit his hand off?'

'Not the done thing to cross-examine a cancer survivor who behaved so selflessly. Especially if you have more money than brain cells. Sir Julius accepted his CV at face value, there wasn't any due diligence. At least not until the Culture Company realised that the start date of the Festival was drawing near, and there was still a vast amount of work to do. The troops were becoming restless, and there was gossip about Denstone's habit of disappearing for hours or even days at a time.'

'To shag Cassie Weston, I suppose,' Hannah said bitterly.

'Some people guessed he was conducting an affair, and that was taking his eye off the ball. Sir Julius rang up the Australian university where Denstone was supposed to have held some senior post, only to be told that the guy's track record was much less high-powered than he'd led everyone to believe. It's the old story, there are lies, damned lies, and CVs. Arlo Denstone was a foot soldier who promoted himself to field marshal.'

'Why didn't Sir Julius take action?'

'He called Denstone in straight after New Year. They met here in Rydal, but the conversation didn't go to plan. Denstone played the sympathy card. He said the cancer had come back.'

'We know what he really meant, don't we?'

'We sure do, but Sir Julius fell for it, hook, line, and sinker. In his words, he felt he was treading on eggshells. Denstone reckoned he had a wonderful new idea for the Festival. Holding a De Quincey event at a folly near Ambleside.'

'A folly?'

'Yeah, he'd dreamed up a *son et lumière* production. Said it would give the Festival an added wow factor. Load of bollocks, if you ask me. Even Sir Julius wasn't convinced it was practical, but he let Denstone go ahead with a feasibility study. The place was disused and locked up, to keep out trespassers, so he made arrangements for Denstone to be given the key.'

'The folly, Greg,' she said, trying to control her impatience. 'What is it called?'

'Didn't I say? Some place known as the Serpent Tower.'

◇◇◇

Hannah flung on a pair of heavy boots and jumped into her car. She headed down the lane that led to the fell. The last time she'd come this way was on New Year's Eve. A lifetime ago. She couldn't drive far, and had to get out and walk once she reached the end of the lane, but every second saved was precious. She couldn't be certain that Cassie Weston and Arlo Denstone had taken Marc to the Serpent Tower, but it was a decent bet. What they had in mind for him, she dared not guess.

The shape of a car loomed out of the mist. At the sight of it, Hannah felt her guts churn. She pulled up and gave it a once-over. A purple Nissan Micra hatchback. Empty, but there was some stained matting at the back, as if something had been transported in it.

Something, or someone.

She swore under her breath. Her guess had been right, but it wasn't cause for celebration. God knows what Marc might be going through if they had him. This wasn't a good time to let her imagination rip. Must keep a cool head.

Fingers trembling, she dialled Greg's number and told him what she'd seen.

'You reckon Denstone and Weston are up in the Serpent Tower?'

'Yes. And they may have Marc.'

'You're kidding.'

'I wish. She works for him. I think…she may have lured him away on a pretext.'

If he thought she was holding back on him, he was too shrewd to say so.

'Don't charge in there on your own,' he said. 'You need back-up.'

'No, in this fog, it will take too long.'

'I said, leave it.' His voice rose. No doubt he thought she was a loose cannon. Apt to panic if her man were put in jeopardy. And was he that far out? 'Don't worry. I've left Rydal, and I'm only a mile away. Stay put, ma'am, and I'll be with you before you know it.'

'I told you to call me Hannah,' she said, and ended the call.

◇◇◇

Fog snatched at her throat and sinuses as she hurried up the slope. The atmosphere was cold and moist, the dark bushes and trees seemed malevolent as they reared up in front of her out of the grey nothingness, as if intent on blocking her climb.

She couldn't wait for the cavalry to come. What if the killers were torturing Marc? She pictured them shoving Stuart Wagg down the well in his back garden, and dragging the metal sheet across the opening as he screamed for mercy. Impossible to live with herself if she hung around while they murdered the man she loved.

Or used to love.

It made things worse, that Marc had walked out on her, and run to Cassie. If she let him down now, people would suspect she'd extracted a form of revenge by letting him suffer. She'd even suspect it herself.

No, she had to move. Do everything in her power to save him.

She could scarcely keep her bearings, but she pushed herself on. The Serpent Pool couldn't be far away. The place where it all began, where the lovers lured Bethany Friend to her death.

Suddenly, she was there. The fog confused her, and she came within a couple of strides of the water's edge before stopping short. The pool was as lifeless and sombre as a grave.

On a good day, the Tower was fifteen minutes away, less if you moved fast. Today, it would take longer. For a moment, she hesitated.

In her jacket pocket, her mobile rang.

Greg said, 'I'm at the end of Lowbarrow Lane. Where are you?'

'At the Serpent Pool, below the Tower. I couldn't wait.'

'Don't go any further. Please, not on your...'

She switched off the phone. Her choice was made, though the truth was that she had no choice. She moved swiftly through the trees, locating the muddy path that led to the ledge on which the Serpent Tower squatted. She looked up and caught sight of the folly rising above her, an ill-defined shape barely visible in the greyness.

But Greg Wharf wasn't finished yet. Through the foggy blanket, she heard the police siren wail.

Oh God, what was he doing? No chance of taking Denstone and Weston by surprise after that fucking cacophony.

She held her breath. For a moment, nothing.

And then she heard a woman scream.

'No!'

For a few moments, nothing happened. Finally, she heard a noise. Footsteps pounding, a racket deadened by the fog.

Looking up, she caught a glimpse of yellow in the gloom. A hi-vis jacket, but who was wearing it?

'The police are coming!' the woman screamed. 'It's time!'

Cassie, it must be, although Hannah could not make out her figure on the narrow plateau up above.

'Two more minutes. Please, I'm begging you. It won't take long, the dog is waking.'

Arlo's voice was unmistakeable, but Hannah couldn't guess what he was ranting about.

'I can't live without you, my darkest fear is…'

'Cassie, this isn't what we planned.' the man cried. 'Don't jump yet.'

'Please…'

'Remember what we agreed. Murder is a thing of beauty…'

They were off their heads. Hannah ground her teeth. That fucking De Quincey, he should never have been born.

Hannah craned her neck and shouted. 'Cassie, don't do it! Let Marc go!'

'Too late,' the woman screamed.

A moment of silence was followed by a crash. Something had smashed into the stony ground, twenty yards away from her.

And then another cry of wild pain tore the silence.

Followed by a wild, unintelligible roar, a flash of yellow tumbling from the ledge above the Serpent Pool, and seconds later, another sickening noise.

Hannah was sure it was the sound of death.

◇◇◇

She hauled herself up the fell, driven by desperation. Every few seconds it seemed that she missed her footing, and collided with jagged rock, collecting one more gash on hand or cheek. But she was beyond pain. Only one thought in her mind. To find Marc, if he was still to be found.

As she climbed, she mumbled incoherently to herself. Praying to a God in whom she wasn't sure she believed. The fog around her was nothing compared to the fog in her brain. One day she'd clear her head, but for now, all she knew was that she had to reach the Serpent Tower.

At last it rose in front of her. A narrow structure, like a Victorian chimney. Dark stonework, the only decoration those serpents entwined above the entrance in a macabre embrace. What had possessed that long dead landowner to build such a dismal monument?

She peered at the door. The key was still in the lock. Denstone had meant to shut Marc in, she supposed, but Greg's siren had spooked him.

She threw the door open.

First she saw the dog, then Marc.

Hanging naked from the wall. A pitiful, degraded spectacle. She covered her mouth, fearing to throw up as he had done.

The pit bull lay on its side, eyes half-closed. Even as Hannah took in the sight of the creature, it twitched. A convulsive movement. The dog was coming round. Striving to get its bearings.

'Save me!' Marc hissed.

She took a step forward. He shook violently. A strip of tightly wrapped plastic cord linked his wrists to the hook on the wall. Another bound his feet.

The pit bull made a throaty rumble.

'Quick!'

A quick fumble inside her coat. Thank God, she hadn't tidied away her last hope of keeping Marc alive. The knife she'd taken to peel the apple at Undercrag was still in the pocket.

She sawed at the cord. Christ, Marc stank. He'd wet himself, but it didn't matter. All she cared about was setting him free before the dog came round.

'Faster!'

The pit bull had opened its eyes and panted hard as it tried to struggle on to its feet.

Hannah sawed harder. The cord was tough, but had begun to fray. This wouldn't take long.

'Please, please, hurry!'

Marc was dribbling, but it was too late for disgust or nausea. Numb with cold and horror, she felt herself sweating as she tried to cut the cord.

Suddenly, it snapped.

Marc would have collapsed to the ground if she hadn't caught hold of him.

She needed to sever the cord around his ankles too, but the pit bull was clambering to its feet.

The animal's gaze met hers. In its eyes, she saw only hate.

Wrapping her right arm around Marc, she bundled him to the door. He was a dead weight.

The dog found its voice and bellowed. A cruel roar, brimming with fury.

She pushed Marc through the door and threw herself out after him. The dog was moving, but it slipped on the rock, unsteady on its legs after a long drugged sleep. The stumble gave Hannah the chance to turn the key in the lock.

She stood with her back braced against the door, as the pit bull charged into it and then howled in pain as its head struck the unyielding oak.

Marc lay on the patch of mud in front of her. Eyes open wide.

Pleading for forgiveness.

Chapter Twenty-one

'A bloody good result,' Fern said as she munched from a packet of prawn cocktail flavoured crisps. 'So how is Marc?'

They were in a bar off Stricklandgate. At the next table, Greg Wharf was regaling Donna and Maggie with a lusty account of his part in the murderers' downfall. Everyone was in celebratory mood, except for Hannah, who was sipping lemonade. Half an hour earlier, she'd sat at Marc's bedside in Westmorland General.

He was a wreck, but the doctors reckoned he'd make it through without too many scars. At least, not physical scars. The last thing Hannah wanted right now was to spend the evening in company; the urge to run away and hide was overwhelming, but it was vital to make an effort. No choice, she must tough it out. Couldn't have everyone feeling sorry for her. Pity so easily tipped into scorn.

'He'll live.'

'And learn, I bet.'

Hannah shrugged. 'We'll see.'

Fern leaned towards her. 'Don't be too hard on him, kid. Men are all the same. She was a gorgeous woman, and she set out to snare him.'

'Didn't have to make it so easy for her, did he?'

'Give it time.' Fern hesitated. 'If you want to.'

'Meaning what?'

'You like Daniel Kind, don't you?'

On the way here, Hannah had called Daniel. It was only fair to tell him the news, before he heard it on television, and she'd thanked him for pointing her in the direction of Arlo Denstone. He sounded subdued and said Louise was showing signs of depression. The reality of discovering Stuart Wagg's remains was kicking in.

Hannah supposed his book about De Quincey and murder would become a best-seller after this, but he wouldn't find that much consolation. He and his sister had been through the mangle during the last few days. They needed time to come to terms with everything that had happened.

'Fern, don't go there, okay?'

'All right, all right. Keep your hair on. Last thing I want is to sour the mood. Not on a day like this, when we've solved three cases at a stroke. And claimed a special bonus by saving the courts the time and expense of putting on a double trial.'

The bodies of Cassie Weston and Arlo Denstone had been recovered. Their bloody corpses lay in a thicket yards away from the Serpent Pool. Greg's siren had disrupted the killer's plan, but Hannah was sure Arlo intended them both to die once they'd feasted on the spectacle of Marc's death—as, she guessed, he'd drooled over the sight of Cassie pushing Bethany Friend's head under water. The symmetry would have appealed to him. Two lovers, dying together at the scene of their first crime. An elegant example of murder and suicide as a fine art. Not even De Quincey could have made it up.

'Greg told me Denstone wasn't lying about the cancer, after all.'

Fern nodded. 'Yeah, he had skin cancer three years back in London and his GP gave him bad news a week before Christmas. Prostate cancer this time, and pretty aggressive.'

Across the room, laughter erupted at Greg's table. Donna was loudest, her merriment raucous and uninhibited. A young, pretty woman, out for a good time. Hannah felt a pang of envy, then reminded herself about the disease that had wrought havoc inside Arlo Denstone's body. As malignant and destructive as jealousy.

'Come on,' Fern said. 'Give us a smile. We did a great job, you and me.'

'You think so?'

'All right, then—you did.'

Hannah finished her lemonade. 'I'll be off.'

'See you in the morning. We're going to be busy.'

'Too right.'

Hannah didn't have much in common with Scarlett O'Hara, except for a name. But that line in *Gone With the Wind* summed it up.

Tomorrow would be another day.

To receive a free catalog of Poisoned Pen Press titles, please contact us in one of the following ways:

Phone: 1-800-421-3976
Facsimile: 1-480-949-1707
Email: info@poisonedpenpress.com
Website: www.poisonedpenpress.com

Poisoned Pen Press
6962 E. First Ave. Ste. 103
Scottsdale, AZ 85251